DRAMATISTS SOURCEBOOK

2001–2002 EDITION

DRAMATISTS SOURCEBOOK

2001-2002 EDITION

Complete opportunities for playwrights, translators, composers, lyricists and librettists

EDITED BY
Kathy Sova
Samantha R. Healy
Jennifer Sokolov

THEATRE COMMUNICATIONS GROUP NEW YORK

Published by Theatre Communications Group, Inc.
355 Lexington Ave., New York, NY 10017-6603.

This publication is made possible in part with public funds from the New York
State Council on the Arts, a State Agency.

TCG books are exclusively distributed to the book trade by Consortium Book Sales
and Distribution, 1045 Westgate Dr., St. Paul, MN 55114.

Manufactured in the United States of America

ISSN 0733-1606
ISBN 1-55936-203-0

CONTENTS

PREFACE

Published annually since 1981, this is the 21st edition of the *Dramatists Sourcebook*.

Every year the *Sourcebook* is fully revised. Every organization listed in this *Sourcebook* has been contacted directly, and the accuracy of their listing confirmed at press time.

It is important to always use the most recent edition of the *Sourcebook*, as most listings are revised in some way every year, and others are removed or added.

Changes. We no longer include those organizations to which playwrights cannot contact or submit work directly. For the most part, this has meant the removal of theatres that directly solicit playwrights or agents, and do not accept unsolicited requests of any kind.

We have changed the method of alphabetizing listings for this edition of the *Sourcebook* (see "Using the *Sourcebook*" below).

Using the *Sourcebook*. Study Tony Kushner's "A Simple Working Guide for Playwrights" (page xi, the Prologue). It's filled with great advice.

Select those listings your work is best suited for and follow the guidelines meticulously. The Special Interests Index is helpful in finding those listings that may be suited to your type of work. When instructed to write for guidelines, do so. This is a good idea in general, as sometimes dates and guidelines change after the *Sourcebook* is published. Most important is to ALWAYS ENCLOSE AN SASE with every mailed script, unless the entry specifies that scripts will not be returned. If a listing states that an organization accepts scripts, it should always be assumed that an SASE must be sent along; we do not restate this for every listing. Always assume the deadline dates in this book refer to the day materials should arrive, not the postmark date.

"Full-length play" means just that—a full-length, original work for adult audiences, without a score or libretto. One-acts, musicals, adaptations, translations, plays for young audiences, solo pieces, performance art and screenplays are listed separately. "Young audiences" refers to audiences age 18 or younger, "young playwrights" refers to playwrights age 18 or younger, "students" refers to students in college or in an affiliated writing program.

Entries are alphabetized by first word (excluding "the") even if they start with a person's name. So, for example, "Mark Taper Forum" is listed under "M." In the index, you will also find this theatre cross-listed under "T." Regardless of the way "theatre" is spelled in an organization's name, we alphabetize it as if it were spelled "re." This year we are using a letter-by-letter alphabetizing method, which differs greatly from our word-by-word method of years past. The current method alphabetizes terms based strictly on the order of letters of an entire phrase, regardless of spaces between words or punctuation; the previous method alphabetized phrases, word by word, each word (separated by a space) considered a complete unit. This year, for example, "Academy Theatre," comes before "A. D. Players," since "ac" comes before "ad." In prior editions, "Academy Theatre," followed "A. D." because by itself the complete word "A" preceded "Academy." We thought it important to note for previous readers that this change has been made.

The editorial process for producing the *Sourcebook* is labor-intensive, and dominates TCG staff for most of the year. There are many people whose contributions are invaluable to this project. Most thanks must be given to Samantha Healy, who expertly supervised the editorial phases, edited the listings and pulled the whole book together; thanks to Gretchen Van Lente, who maintained our database, contacted the listing organizations and prepared the galleys always with good humor and energy; heartfelt gratitude to Jennifer Sokolov for editing the Online chapter and lending her proofing and editing skills to us when we really needed a hand; thank you to Wendy Weiner and Ruth Hein Schmitt, meticulous editors and proofreaders; and much appreciation must go to Warren Nichols, Kitty Suen and Rochelle Krause, for all their hard work in creating this book.

We thank all the organizations listed here who worked hard to provide us with their updated information in a timely fashion, and spent their valuable time with us in preparing their listing.

Most importantly, we thank all the artists, who, year after year, purchase this book and put their faith in us. We admire you for your hard work, talent and determination. We hope that the more than 1000 listings here offer encouragement and proof that many many organizations around the country are hungry for new work. Our goal is to serve you well. Let us know how we can improve our work, we love to hear form you. We wish you success, good health and a fabulous year of writing plays.

Kathy Sova
Editorial Director/TCG Publications
July 2001

PROLOGUE

A Simple Working Guide for Playwrights
by Tony Kushner

A) Format: Most playwrights use a format in which character headings are placed centered above the line and capitalized:

LIONEL

I don't possess a mansion, a car, or a string of polo ponies...

Lines should be single-spaced. Stage directions should be indented and single-spaced. If a character's line is interrupted at the end of the page, its continuance on the following page should be marked as such:

LIONEL (CONT'D)

or a string of polo ponies...

There are denser, and thus more economical, formats; since Xeroxing is expensive, and heavy scripts cost more to ship, you may be tempted to use these, but a generously spaced format is much easier to read, and in these matters it doesn't pay to be parsimonious.

B) Typing and reproducing: Scripts should be typed neatly and reproduced clearly. Remember that everyone who reads your script will be reading many others additionally, and it will work to your serious disadvantage if the copy's sloppy, faded, or otherwise unappealing. If you use a computer printer, eschew old-fashioned dot-matrix and other robotic kinds of print. Also, I think it's best to avoid using incredibly fancy word-processing printing programs with eight different typefaces and decorative borders. Simple typescript, carefully done, is best. Check for typos. A playwright's punctuation may be idiosyncratic for purposes of expressiveness, but not too idiosyncratic, and spelling should be correct.

C) Sending the script:

1) The script should have a title page with the title, your name, address and phone number, or that of your agent or representative. Scripts are now automatically copyrighted at the moment of creation, but simply writing © and the date on the title page can serve as a kind of scarecrow for thievish magpies.

2) Never, never send an unbound script. Loose pages held together by a rubber band don't qualify as bound, nor do pages clamped together with a mega-paperclip. A heavy paper cover will protect the script as it passes from hand to hand.

3) Always, always enclose a self-addressed stamped envelope (SASE) or you will never see your script again. You may enclose a note telling the theatre to dispose of the copy instead of returning it; but you must have the ultimate fate of the script planned for in the eventuality of its not being selected for production. Don't leave this up to the theatre! If you want receipt of the script acknowledged, include a self-addressed, stamped postcard (SASP).

D) Letter of inquiry and synopsis: If a theatre states, in its entry in the *Sourcebook*, that it does not accept unsolicited scripts, believe it. Don't call and ask if there are exceptions; there aren't. A well-written and concise letter of inquiry, however, accompanied by a synopsis possessed of similar virtues can get you an invitation to submit your play. It's prudent, then, to spend time on both letter and synopsis. It is, admittedly, very hard for a writer to sum up his or her work in less than a page, but this kind of boiling-down can be of value beyond its necessity as a tool for marketing; use it to help clarify for yourself what's central and essential about your play. A good synopsis should briefly summarize the basic features of the plot without going into excessive detail; it should evoke both the style and the thematic substance of the play without recourse to clichéd description ("This play is about what happens when people lose their dreams..."); and it should convey essential information, such as cast size, gender breakdown, period, location, or anything else a literary manager deciding whether to send for the play might want to know. Make reference to other productions in your letter, but don't send thick packets of reviews and photos. And don't offer your opinion of the play's worth, which will be inferred as being positive from the fact that you are its parent.

E) Waiting: Theatres almost always take a long time to respond to playwrights about a specific play, frequently far in excess of the time given in their listings in the *Sourcebook*. This is due neither to spite nor indolence. Literary departments are usually understaffed and their workload is fearsome. Then, too, the process of selection invariably involves a host of people and considerations of all kinds. In my opinion you do yourself no good by repeatedly calling after the status of your script; you will become identified as a pest. It's terribly expensive to copy and mail scripts, but you must be prepared to shoulder the expense and keep making copies if they don't get returned. If, after a certain length of time past the deadline, you haven't heard from a theatre, send a letter inquiring politely about the play, reminding the appropriate people that you'd sent an SASE with the script; and then forget about it. In most cases, you will get a response and the script returned eventually.

One way to cut down on the expenses involved is to be selective about venues for submission. Reading *Sourcebook* entries and scrutinizing a copy of *Theatre Profiles* (see Useful Publications) will help you select the theatres most compatible with your work. If you've written a musical celebration of the life of Phyllis Schlafly, for example, you won't want to send it to theatres with an interest in radical feminist dramas. Or you won't necessarily want to send your play about the history of Western imperialism to a theatre that produces an annual season of musical comedy.

F) Produce yourself! In *Endgame*, Clov asks Hamm, "Do you believe in the life to come?" and Hamm responds, "Mine was always that." The condition of endless deferment is one that modern American playwrights share with Beckett's characters and other denizens of the postmodern world. Don't spend your life waiting. You may not be an actor, but that doesn't mean that action is forbidden you. Playwrights can, with very little expense, mount readings of their work; they can band together with other playwrights for readings and discussions; and they can, if they want to, produce their work themselves. Growth as a writer for the stage depends on seeing your work on stage, and if no one else will put it there, the job is up to you. At the very least, and above all else, while waiting, waiting, waiting for responses and offers, keep reading, thinking and writing.

Tony Kushner's plays include *Angels in America* (Parts One and Two), *A Bright Room Called Day* and *Slavs!* His current projects include *Homebody/Kabul*, *Henry Box Brown or The Mirror of Slavery*, *St. Cecilia or The Power of Music* and *Caroline or Change*. He is the recipient of numerous awards, including the Pulitzer Prize and two Tony Awards for *Angels in America*. He grew up in Lake Charles, Louisiana, and he lives in New York.

PART 1
SCRIPT
OPPORTUNITIES

Production

Prizes

Publication

Development

PRODUCTION

What theatres are included in this section?

The overwhelming majority of the not-for-profit professional theatres throughout the United States, which accept submissions, is represented here. Theatres to which playwrights cannot contact or submit work are no longer included. (Generally these are theatres that directly solicit playwrights or agents and do not accept any unsolicited requests). In order to be included, a theatre must meet professional standards of staffing, programming and budget; most have been operating for at least two years. Commercial and amateur producers are not included.

How should I go about deciding where to submit my play?

Don't send it out indiscriminately. Take time to study the listings and select those theatres most likely to be receptive to your material. Find out all you can about each of the theatres you select. Visit the theatre's website. Read *American Theatre* to see what plays the theatres are currently presenting and what their other activities are (see Useful Publications for more information). Whenever possible, go to see the theatre's work.

When I submit my play, what can I do to maximize its chances?

First, read carefully the Simple Working Guide for Playwrights in the Prologue of this *Sourcebook* for good advice on script submission. Then follow each theatre's guidelines meticulously. Pay particular attention to the

Special Interests section: If a theatre specifies "gay and lesbian themes only," do not send them your heterosexual romantic comedy, however witty and well written it is. Also, bear in mind the following points about the various submission procedures:

1) "Accepts unsolicited scripts": Don't waste the theatre's time and yours by writing to ask permission to submit your play—just send it. If you want an acknowledgment of receipt, say so and enclose a self-addressed stamped postcard (SASP) for this purpose. **Always enclose a self-addressed stamped envelope (SASE) for the return of a script.**

2) "Synopsis and letter of inquiry": Never send an unsolicited script to these theatres. Prepare a clear, cogent and *brief* synopsis of your play and send it along with any other materials requested in the listing. The letter of inquiry is a cover note asking for permission to submit the script; if there is something about your play or about yourself as a writer that you think may spark the theatre's interest, by all means mention it, but keep the letter brief. We've asked theatres requiring letters and synopses to give us two response times—one for letters and one for scripts should they ask to see one. All response times are approximate, and theatres may take longer to respond than stated. Always enclose an SASP for the theatre's response, unless the theatre specifies that it only responds if it wants to see the script.

3) "Professional recommendation": Send a script (not a letter of inquiry) accompanied by a letter of recommendation from a theatre professional. Wait until you have obtained such a letter before approaching these theatres.

4) "Agent submission": If you do not have an agent yet, do not submit to these theatres. Wait until you have had a production or two and have acquired a representative who can submit your script for you.

5) Do not email your submissions. Email and web addresses are included for the purpose of general inquiries and, when noted, to obtain guidelines or applications.

A *Sourcebook* reminder:

The listings for this edition are alphabetized by a different method than in years past (see Preface for a description).

ABOUT FACE THEATRE

(Founded 1995)
3212 North Broadway; Chicago, IL 60657; (773) 549–7943,
FAX 935–4483; email faceline1@aol.com;
website www.aboutfacetheatre.com
Literary Department

Submission procedure: no unsolicited scripts; synopsis, first 10 pages of script, cast list, resume and letter of inquiry. **Types of material:** full-length plays, one-acts, adaptations, musicals, performance art. **Special interests:** "queer" plays only; prefers lesbian plays; material that challenges moral expectations and ideas about gender and sexuality in historical or contemporary contexts; imaginative scripts of literary caliber that break traditional ideas about dramatic form, structure, presentation and characters. **Facilities:** About Face Theatre, 99 seats, flexible thrust stage. **Production considerations:** no fly space, limited backstage space. **Best submission time:** year-round. **Response time:** 3 months letter; 6 months script. **Special programs:** Face to Face Workshop Series: readings, rough stagings and audience response.

A CONTEMPORARY THEATRE

(Founded 1965)
The Eagles Building, 700 Union St; Seattle, WA 98101–4037;
(206) 292–7660, FAX 292–7670; website www.acttheatre.org
Gordon Edelstein, *Artistic Director*

Submission procedure: no unsolicited scripts; direct solicitation to playwright or agent; will accept synopsis, 10-page dialogue sample and letter of inquiry from Northwest playwrights only. **Types of material:** full-length plays, translations, adaptations, musicals, solo pieces. **Special interests:** current social, political and psychological issues; plays theatrical in imagination, and storytelling; multicultural themes; prefer no kitchen-sink realism or message plays. **Facilities:** The Allen, 387 seats, arena stage; The Falls, 381 seats, thrust stage; The Bullitt, 150 seats, cabaret. **Best submission time:** Sep-Apr. **Response time:** 4-6 months letter; 6-12 months script. **Special programs:** new play development workshops. FirstACT: play commissions and workshops. ACT/Hedgebrook Women Playwrights Festival (See listing in Development).

THE ACTING COMPANY

(Founded 1972)
Box 898, Times Square Station; New York, NY 10108;
    (212) 944-5517, FAX 944-5524;
    email mail@theactingcompany.org;
    website www.theactingcompany.org
Margot Harley, *Producing Director*
Richard Corley, *Associate Producing Director*

Submission procedure: no unsolicited scripts; professional recommendation. **Types of material:** full-length plays, one-acts, translations, adaptations, musicals. **Special interests:** mainly classical repertory but occasionally produces new works suited to acting ensemble of approximately 8 men, 3 women, age range 24-45; prefers works with poetic dimension and heightened language. **Facilities:** no permanent facility; touring company which plays in New York City for 1 or 2 weeks a year. **Production considerations:** productions tour in repertory; simple, transportable proscenium-stage set. **Best submission time:** Nov-Jan. **Response time:** 3 months.

ACTORS & PLAYWRIGHTS' INITIATIVE

(Founded 1989)
359 South Burdick St, Suite 205; The Epic Center;
    Kalamazoo, MI 49007; (616) 343-8310, FAX 343-8450
Robert C. Walker, *Artistic Director*

Submission procedure: no unsolicited scripts; professional recommendation. **Types of material:** full-length plays, one-acts, translations, adaptations, plays for young audiences, musicals, solo pieces. **Special interests:** aggressive and provocative social-political plays; plays that explore heterosexual, gay and bisexual relationships. **Facilities:** API Theatre at the Epic Center, 120 seats, black box. **Production considerations:** cast limit of 10, minimal set, costumes, props; minimal fly space. **Best submission time:** Oct-Feb. **Response time:** 6 months. **Special programs:** Firstage Script Development Reader's Theatre: developmental year-round reading series.

ACTOR'S EXPRESS

(Founded 1988)
King Plow Arts Center, J-107; 887 West Marietta St NW;
   Atlanta, GA 30318; (404) 875-1606, FAX 875-2791;
   email actorsexpress@mindspring.com
Literary Manager

Submission procedure: no unsolicited scripts; 10-page dialogue sample, character breakdown, professional recommendation and letter of inquiry. **Types of material:** full-length plays, translations, adaptations, musicals. **Special interests:** new musicals; socially relevant material; minority and gay themes; works with poetic dimension. **Facilities:** Actor's Express, 150 seats, black box. **Production considerations:** modest production demands; no fly space. **Best submission time:** Nov-Jan. **Response time:** 6 weeks letter; 4-6 months script.

ACTORS' GANG THEATER

(Founded 1981)
6201 Santa Monica Blvd; Hollywood, CA 90038; (323) 465-0566,
   FAX 467-1246; email actorsgng1@aol.com
Tim Robbins, *President/CEO*

Submission procedure: no unsolicited scripts; synopsis and letter of inquiry. **Types of material:** full-length plays, plays for young audiences. **Special interests:** highly theatrical political or avant-garde works. **Facilities:** Actors' Gang Theater, 99 seats, flexible stage; Actors' Gang El Centro, 40 seats, flexible stage. **Best submission time:** year-round. **Response time:** 2 months letter; 2 months script.

ACTORS' GUILD OF LEXINGTON

(Founded 1984)
139 West Short St; Lexington, KY 40507; (859) 233-7330,
   FAX 233-3773; email agl@lex.infi.net;
   website www.actorsguildoflexington.org
Deb Shoss, *Producing Director*

Submission procedure: no unsolicited scripts; synopsis and letter of inquiry; prefers email submission. **Types of material:** full-length plays, solo pieces. **Facilities:** Main Stage, 99-120 seats, proscenium/stadium stage. **Production considerations:** cast limit of 8; no wing or fly space; prefers single set. **Best submission time:** year-round. **Response time:** 1 month letter; 2-3 months script.

ACTORS' THEATRE

(Founded 1983)
Box 780; Talent, OR 97540; (541) 535-5250; email
alzado47@aol.com
Creighton Barnes, *Literary Department*

Submission procedure: no unsolicited scripts; synopsis, dialogue sample and letter of inquiry. **Types of material:** full-length plays, one-acts, translations, adaptations. **Facilities:** Actors' Theatre, 108 seats, thrust stage. **Best submission time:** year-round. **Response time:** 3 months letter; 4 months script.

ACTOR'S THEATRE OF CHARLOTTE

(Founded 1989)
Box 12325; Charlotte, NC 28220-2325; (704) 342-2251,
    FAX 342-1229; email actorstheatre@mindspring.com
Dan Shoemaker, *Executive Director*

Submission procedure: no unsolicited scripts; synopsis, character breakdown and letter of inquiry. **Types of material:** full-length plays, adaptations. **Facilities:** Spirit Square, 169 seats, proscenium stage. **Production considerations:** cast limit of 7, minimal or unit set. **Best submission time:** summer. **Response time:** 3 months letter; 3 months script.

ACTORS THEATRE OF LOUISVILLE

(Founded 1964)
316 West Main St; Louisville, KY 40202-4218; (502) 584-1265,
    FAX 561-3300; website www.actorstheatre.org
Tanya Palmer, *Literary Manager*
Amy Wegener, *Dramaturg/Director of New Play Development*

Submission procedure: direct solicitation to playwright or agent; for Humana Festival (see below): no unsolicited scripts; accepts synopsis and dialogue sample (but prefers professional recommendation or agent submission). **Types of material:** full-length plays, one-acts, translations, adaptations, solo pieces. **Special interests:** plays of ideas; language-oriented plays; plays with passion, humor and experimentation. **Facilities:** Pamela Brown Auditorium, 637 seats, thrust stage; Bingham Theatre, 320 seats, arena stage; Victor Jory Theatre, 159 seats, thrust stage. **Best submission time:** Apr-Oct. **Response time:** 6-9 months (most scripts returned in late fall). **Special programs:** National Ten-Minute Play Contest (see Prizes); Humana Festival of New

American Plays: annual presentation of new work in rotating rep; *deadline:* ongoing; *notification:* fall 2001; *dates:* Feb–Mar 2002.

ACTORS THEATRE OF PHOENIX

(Founded 1985)
Box 1924; Phoenix, AZ 85001–1924; (602) 253–6701,
    FAX 254–9577; email info@atphx.org;
    website www.actorstheatrePHX.org
Mathew Wiener, *Producing Artistic Director*

Submission procedure: no unsolicited scripts; professional recommendation. **Types of material:** full-length plays, translations, adaptations. **Special interests:** plays dealing with the Southwest. **Facilities:** Herberger Theater Center, Stage West, 300 seats, proscenium stage. **Production considerations:** cast limit of 8. **Best submission time:** year-round. **Response time:** 8-10 months.

ACT II PLAYHOUSE

(Founded 1998)
Box 555, 56 E Butler Ave; Ambler, PA 19002; (215) 654–0200,
    FAX 654–5001; email act2@libertynet.org; website www.act2.org
Steve Blumenthal, *Producing Artistic Director*

Submission procedure: accepts unsolicited scripts. **Types of material:** full-length plays, musicals, solo pieces. **Special interests:** no experimental plays; contemporary works. **Facilities:** Act II Playhouse, 130 seats, black box. **Production considerations:** cast limit of 6, 1 set; low ceiling, limited fly space, approximately 600 square feet. **Best submission time:** year-round. **Response time:** 1 month.

A. D. PLAYERS

(Founded 1967)
2710 West Alabama St; Houston, TX 77098; (713) 526–2721,
    FAX 439–0905; email adplayers@hern.org;
    website www.adplayers.org
Literary Manager

Submission procedure: accepts unsolicited scripts. **Types of material:** full-length plays, one-acts, adaptations, plays for young audiences, musicals. **Special interests:** plays for students pre-kindergarten–grade 6; "plays that uphold family values and support moral decisions that allow for growth of individuals with themselves, others and God"; children's plays which allow for audience participation and have strong role models; no plays about "witchcraft, demons or ghosts." **Facilities:** Grace Theater, 220 seats, proscenium stage; Rotunda Theater, 148 seats, arena stage. **Production considerations:** for Grace Theater: cast limit of 12, prefers less than 10, no more than 2 sets, maximum height 11' 6"; no fly space, minimal lighting. For Rotunda Theater: cast limit of 6, minimal scenery, shows no longer than one hour, prefers musicals; no wing space. **Best submission time:** year-round. **Response time:** 6-10 months. **Special programs:** Theater Arts Academy: includes playwriting classes.

ADOBE THEATRE COMPANY

(Founded 1991)
138 South Oxford St, #4C; Brooklyn, NY 11217; (718) 398-3698,
 FAX 398-3698; website www.adobe.org
Lisa Timmell, *Literary Manager*

Submission procedure: no unsolicited scripts; synopsis, dialogue sample and letter of inquiry. **Types of material:** full-length plays, one-acts, adaptations. **Special interests:** comedies that subvert conventional theatrical form and genre. **Facilities:** Ohio Theatre, 75 seats, flexible stage. **Production considerations:** prefers large cast and characters in their thirties. **Best submission time:** year-round. **Response time:** 2 months letter; 4 months script.

AFRICAN CONTINUUM THEATRE CO. (ACTCO)

(Founded 1996)
3523 12th St NE, 2nd floor; Washington, DC 20017;
 (202) 529-5763, FAX 529-5782; email actco@msn.com;
 website www.onwashington.com/groups-actco
Jennifer L. Nelson, *Producing Artistic Director*

Submission procedure: accepts unsolicited scripts. **Types of material:** full-length plays, translations, adaptations, musicals. **Special interests:** multicultural work, must be relevant to African-American community. **Facilities:** no permanent facility. **Production considerations:** small cast, single set. **Best submission time:** year-round. **Response time:** 6-12 months.

ALABAMA SHAKESPEARE FESTIVAL

(Founded 1972)
1 Festival Dr; Montgomery, AL 36117-4605; (334) 271-5300
Kent Thompson, *Artistic Director*
Gwen Orel, *Literary Manager*

Submission procedure: accepts unsolicited scripts with letter of inquiry for Southern Writers' Project only (see below); agent submission for all other plays. **Types of material:** full-length plays, adaptations, plays for young audiences. **Special interests:** new plays with southern or African-American themes. **Facilities:** Festival Stage, 750 seats, modified thrust stage; Octagon, 225 seats, flexible stage. **Best submission time:** year-round. **Response time:** 2 months letter; 12 months script. **Special programs:** Southern Writers' Project: project to commission and develop plays based on southern and/or African-American issues; address submissions to Southern Writers' Project.

ALLEY THEATRE

(Founded 1947)
615 Texas Ave; Houston, TX 77002; (713) 228-9341
Gregory Boyd, *Artistic Director*

Submission procedure: no unsolicited scripts; professional recommendation. **Types of material:** full-length plays, translations, adaptations, musicals. **Facilities:** Main Stage, 800 seats, thrust stage; Arena Stage, 300 seats, arena stage. **Best submission time:** year-round. **Response time:** 2-6 months.

ALLIANCE THEATRE COMPANY

(Founded 1968)
1280 Peachtree St NE; Atlanta, GA 30309; (404) 733-4650,
    FAX 733-4625; website www.alliancetheatre.org
Literary Department

Submission procedure: no unsolicited scripts; synopsis, maximum 10-page dialogue sample and letter of inquiry with SASE. **Types of material:** full-length plays, one-acts, plays for young audiences, musicals. **Special interests:** work that speaks to a culturally diverse community; plays with compelling stories and engaging characters, told in adventurous ways. **Facilities:** Alliance Theatre, 800 seats, proscenium stage; Studio Theatre, 200 seats, flexible stage. **Best submission time:** Mar-Sep. **Response time:** 1-2 months letter; 6 months script.

ALLIED THEATRE GROUP/STAGE WEST

(Founded 1979)
3055 South University Dr; Fort Worth, TX 76109–5608;
    (817) 924–9454, FAX 926–8650; email atg@slash.net;
    website www.stagewest.org
Jim Covault, *Artistic Director*

Submission procedure: no unsolicited scripts; synopsis and letter of inquiry. **Types of material:** full-length plays, translations, adaptations. **Special interests:** plays by Texas and Southwest playwrights; Hispanic plays; contemporary issues; Texas and Southwest themes. **Facilities:** Stage West, 190 seats, arena stage. **Production considerations:** prefers cast limit of 9. **Best submission time:** Jan-Mar. **Response time:** 1 month letter; 3 months script.

AMAS MUSICAL THEATRE, INC.

(Founded 1968)
450 West 42nd St, Suite 2J; New York, NY 10036; (212) 563–2565,
    FAX 268–5501; email amas@ amasmusical.org;
    website www.amasmusical.org
Donna Trinkoff, *Producing Director*

Submission procedure: accepts unsolicited scripts. **Types of material:** musicals, cabaret/revues. **Special interests:** multicultural casts and themes. **Facilities:** no permanent facility; company performs in various proscenium or black box venues with 74-99 seats. **Production considerations:** cast limit of 15. **Best submission time:** summer, winter. **Response time:** 3-6 months. **Special programs:** Amas Six O'Clock Musical Theatre Lab: a reading series for new musicals open to composers, lyricists and librettists; writer must supply cast and musical director; Amas provides theatre and publicity.

AMERICAN CABARET THEATRE

(Founded 1989)
401 East Michigan St; Indianapolis, IN 46204; (317) 631–0334,
    FAX 686–5443; email cabaret@americancabarettheatre.com;
    website americancabarettheatre.com
Claude McNeal, *Artistic Director/Founder*

Submission procedure: no unsolicited scripts; synopsis and letter of inquiry; prefers professional recommendation. **Types of material:** cabaret/revues. **Special interests:** cabaret/revues dealing with original American themes. **Facilities:** mainstage, 400 seats, proscenium stage; Second Stage, 150 seats, proscenium stage. **Production considerations:** cast limit of 6-12; limited fly, wing and storage space. **Best submission time:** Jul-Sep. **Response time:** 1-2 months letter; 2-3 months script.

AMERICAN CONSERVATORY THEATER

(Founded 1965)
30 Grant Ave, 6th Floor; San Francisco, CA 94108-5800;
    (415) 439-2445, FAX 834-3360
Paul Walsh, *Dramaturg*

Submission procedure: no unsolicited scripts; agents may send synopsis, maximum 10-page dialogue sample and letter of inquiry. **Types of material:** full-length plays, translations, adaptations. **Facilities:** Geary Theater, 1000 seats, proscenium stage. **Best submission time:** year-round. **Response time:** 6-12 months.

AMERICAN FOLKLORE THEATRE

(Founded 1999)
Box 273; Fish Creek, WI 54212; (920) 854-6117, FAX 854-9106;
    email aft@folkloretheatre.com; website www.folkloretheatre.com
M. Kaye Christman, *Managing Director*

Submission procedure: no unsolicited scripts; synopsis and letter of inquiry. **Types of material:** full-length plays, one-acts, adaptations, plays for young audiences, musicals. **Special interests:** musicals with a historical/cultural basis appropriate for families. **Facilities:** Peninsula State Park Theatre, 700 seats, modified proscenium stage; various town halls, 125-200 seats. **Production considerations:** cast limit of 6-10, summer show cast limit of 3-4, minimal set requirements. **Best submission time:** year-round. **Response time:** 1 month letter (with SASE); 2-4 months script. **Special programs:** workshops of new work.

AMERICAN MUSIC THEATER FESTIVAL/ PRINCE MUSIC THEATER

(Founded 1984)
100 South Broad St, Suite 650; Philadelphia, PA 19110;
    (215) 972-1000, FAX 972-1020; website www.amtf.org
Ben Levit, *Artistic Director*

Submission procedure: no unsolicited scripts; synopsis, cassette and letter of inquiry. **Types of material:** music-theatre works including musical comedy, music drama, opera, experimental works, solo pieces. **Facilities:**

Prince Music Theater, 450 seats, proscenium stage. **Best submission time:** year-round. **Response time:** 3 weeks letter; 6 months script.

AMERICAN RENEGADE THEATRE COMPANY

(Founded 1991)
11136 Magnolia Blvd; North Hollywood, CA 91601; (818) 763–4430
Barry Thompson, *Literary Manager*

Submission procedure: accepts unsolicited scripts. **Types of material:** full-length plays. **Special interests:** contemporary American plays. **Facilities:** Front Theatre, 99 seats, proscenium stage; Back Theatre, 45 seats, black box. **Best submission time:** year-round. **Response time:** 3-6 months. **Special Programs:** American Renegade Playwriting Contest (see Prizes).

AMERICAN REPERTORY THEATRE

(Founded 1979)
64 Brattle St; Cambridge, MA 02138; (617) 495–2668;
website www.amrep.org
Scott Zigler, *Artistic Coordinator, New Play Development*

Submission procedure: no unsolicited scripts; agent submission. **Types of material:** full-length plays, translations, adaptations, musicals, cabaret/revues. **Special interests:** prefers plays "which lend themselves to poetic use of the stage" and "heightened language." **Facilities:** Loeb Drama Center, 556 seats, flexible stage; Holyoke Street Theatre, 350 seats, proscenium stage; Church Street Theatre, 200 seats, black box. **Production considerations:** cast limit of 15. **Best submission time:** Sep-Jan. **Response time:** 1-3 months.

AMERICAN STAGE

(Founded 1977)
Box 1560; St. Petersburg, FL 33731; (727) 823–1600, FAX 821–2444
Kenneth Noel Mitchell, *Artistic Director*

Submission procedure: no unsolicited scripts; professional recommendation. **Types of material:** full-length plays, adaptations, plays for young audiences. **Facilities:** American Stage, 130 seats, thrust stage. **Production considerations:** cast limit of 8, 1 set. **Best submission time:** year-round. **Response time:** 12 months. **Special programs:** New Visions: new play festival.

AMERICAN STAGE COMPANY

(Founded 1986)
Box 336; Teaneck, NJ 07666
Matthew Parent, *Producing Artistic Director*

Submission procedure: no unsolicited scripts; synopsis, dialogue sample and letter of inquiry. **Types of material:** full-length plays, musicals. **Facilities:** Bergen Community College Theater, 300 seats, proscenium stage; American Stage in Residence at Fairleigh Dickinson University, 290 seats, proscenium stage. **Production considerations:** cast limit of 15, orchestra limit of 6. **Best submission time:** year-round. **Response time:** 1 month letter; 6 months script.

AMERICAN STAGE FESTIVAL

(Founded 1971)
14 Court St; Nashua, NH 03060; (603) 889–2330, FAX 889–2336
Attn: New Scripts, EARLY STAGES

Submission procedure: accepts unsolicited scripts with SASE for response; include cassette of 2–3 songs for musicals. **Types of material:** full-length plays, musicals. **Special interests:** comedies, musicals; material with strong emotional content that tells a compelling story, including ones that explore what used to be called "The American Dream." **Facilities:** Summer Stage, 492 seats, proscenium stage; Year-Round Stage, 277 seats, thrust stage. **Production considerations:** cast limit of 10 for plays, 15 plus 5 musicians for musicals. **Best submission time:** Sep-Dec. **Response time:** 2–3 months letter; 4–6 months script. **Special Programs:** EARLY STAGES: summer staged reading series with audience response.

AMERICAN THEATER COMPANY

(Founded 1985)
1909 West Byron St; Chicago, IL 60613; (773) 929–5009,
    FAX 929–5171; email atcdir@aol.com; website www.atcweb.org
Brian Russell, *Artistic Director*

Submission procedure: no unsolicited scripts; synopsis and letter of inquiry with SASP for response. **Types of material:** full-length plays, translations, adaptations, musicals. **Special interests:** language-oriented plays that utilize heightened theatrical reality; musicals; substantive comedies; social and political themes. **Facilities:** American Theater Company, 137 seats, modified thrust stage. **Production considerations:** prefers cast limit of 15; modest technical demands. **Best submission time:** year-round. **Response time:** 2–4 months letter; 6–12 months script.

AMERICAN THEATRE OF ACTORS, INC.

(Founded 1976)
314 West 54th St; New York, NY 10019; (212) 581–3044
James Jennings, *Artistic Director*

Submission procedure: accepts unsolicited scripts. **Types of material:** full-length plays, one-acts. **Special interests:** realistic plays dealing with contemporary social issues. **Facilities:** Chernuchin Theatre, 140 seats, proscenium stage; Sargent Theatre, 65 seats, proscenium stage; Beckmann Theatre, 35 seats, arena stage. **Production considerations:** cast limit of 8, minimal sets. **Best submission time:** year-round. **Response time:** 2 weeks.

A NOISE WITHIN

(Founded 1991)
3603 Seneca Ave; Los Angeles, CA 90039; (323) 953–7787,
    FAX 953–7794
Art Manke, *Artistic Co-Director*

Submission procedure: accepts unsolicited scripts. **Types of material:** translations, adaptations. **Special interests:** translations and adaptations of classical material only. **Facilities:** A Noise Within, 145 seats, thrust stage. **Best submission time:** fall. **Response time:** 6–8 months.

ARDEN THEATRE COMPANY

(Founded 1988)
40 North 2nd St; Philadelphia, PA 19106; (215) 922–8900,
    FAX 922–7011; website www.ardentheatre.org
Terrence J. Nolen, *Producing Artistic Director*

Submission procedure: no unsolicited scripts; synopsis and letter of inquiry. **Types of material:** full-length plays, translations, adaptations, musicals. **Special interests:** new adaptations of literary works. **Facilities:** Haas Stage/mainstage, 400 seats, flexible stage; Arcadia Stage/studio theatre, 175 seats, flexible stage. **Best submission time:** year-round. **Response time:** 3 months letter; 6 months script.

ARENA STAGE

(Founded 1950)
1101 6th St SW; Washington, DC 20024; (202) 554-9066,
FAX 488-4056
Literary Manager

Submission procedure: no unsolicited scripts; accepts letter of inquiry from DC, MD, VA writers only; other playwrights send synopsis, 10-page dialogue sample, bio and letter of inquiry. **Types of material:** full-length plays, translations, adaptations, solo pieces. **Special interests:** unproduced works; North and South American themes only; plays for a multicultural company; plays by women, writers of color, physically disabled writers and other "nonmainstream" artists. **Facilities:** Fichandler Stage, 827 seats, arena stage; The Kreeger Theater, 514 seats, modified thrust stage; The Old Vat Room, 110 seats, cabaret stage. **Best submission time:** year-round. **Response time:** 1 week letter; 6-12 months script. **Special programs:** Downstairs: new play development initiative; scripts selected through theatre's normal submission procedure. Student Playwright's Project Performance: staged reading for 4 writers, grades 3-12.

ARIZONA THEATRE COMPANY

(Founded 1966)
Box 1631; Tucson, AZ 85702-1631; (520) 884-8210
Samantha K. Wyer, *Associate Artistic Director*

Submission procedure: no unsolicited scripts; synopsis, 10-page dialogue sample, production history, resume and letter of inquiry. **Types of material:** full-length plays, translations, adaptations, musicals. **Facilities:** Herberger Theater Center (in Phoenix), 800 seats, proscenium stage; Temple of Music and Art (in Tucson), 600 seats, proscenium stage. **Best submission time:** spring-summer. **Response time:** 1 month letter; 4-6 months script. **Special programs:** New Play Reading Series: rehearsed readings followed by discussion with audience. National Latino Playwriting Award (see Prizes).

ARKANSAS ART CENTER CHILDREN'S THEATRE

(Founded 1979)
Box 2137; Little Rock, AR 72202; (501) 372-4000;
email banderson@arkarts.com; website www.arkarts.com
Bradley Anderson, *Artistic Director*

Submission procedure: no unsolicited scripts; professional recommendation. **Types of material:** full-length plays, one-acts, adaptations, plays for young audiences, musicals. **Facilities:** Arkansas Art Center, 348 seats, proscenium stage; studio, 150 seats, flexible stage. **Best submission time:** Nov–Dec. **Response time:** 2 months letter; 2 months script.

ARKANSAS REPERTORY THEATRE

(Founded 1976)
Box 110; Little Rock, AR 72203–0110; (501) 378–0445,
    FAX 378–0012
Brad Mooy, *Literary Manager*

Submission procedure: no unsolicited scripts; synopsis and letter of inquiry. **Types of material:** full-length plays, musicals, cabaret/revues, solo pieces. **Facilities:** Arkansas Repertory Theatre, 354 seats, proscenium stage; Second Stage, 99 seats, black box. **Production considerations:** prefers small cast. **Best submission time:** year-round. **Response time:** 3 months letter; 3–6 months script. **Special programs:** New Play Reading Series.

ARTISTS REPERTORY THEATRE

(Founded 1981)
1516 Southwest Alder St; Portland, OR 97205; (503) 241–9807,
    FAX 241–8268; email allen@artistsrep.org;
    website www.artistsrep.org
Allen Nause, *Artistic Director*

Submission procedure: no unsolicited scripts; synopsis and letter of inquiry. **Types of material:** full-length plays, adaptations. **Facilities:** Reiersgaard Theatre, 170 seats, flexible black box. **Production considerations:** cast limit of 13. **Best submission time:** year-round. **Response time:** 1 month letter; 6 months script. **Special programs:** Play Lab: staged reading series.

ARTS AT ST. ANN'S

(Founded 1979)
70 Washington St; Brooklyn, NY 11201; (718) 834–8794,
    FAX 522–2470
Susan Feldman, *Artistic Director*

Submission procedure: no unsolicited scripts; synopsis and letter of inquiry. **Types of material:** full-length plays, musicals. **Special interests:** musical-theatre works. **Facilities:** no permanent facility. **Best submission time:** Jan–Feb; Jul–Aug. **Response time:** 2 months letter; 3 months script.

ART STATION

(Founded 1986)
Box 1998; Stone Mountain, GA 30086; (770) 469-1105,
FAX 469-0355; email jon@artstation.org;
website www.artstation.org
Jon Goldstein, *Literary Manager*

Submission procedure: accepts unsolicited scripts. **Types of material:** full-length plays, adaptations, musicals, solo pieces. **Special interests:** works not produced professionally; plays by southern playwrights, or which describe the southern experience. **Facilities:** ART Station Theatre, 100 seats, proscenium/thrust stage. **Production considerations:** cast limit of 6, single set; no fly space. **Best submission time:** Jun-Dec. **Response time:** 4 months. **Special programs:** ART Station Playwrights Project: year-round playwrights group meets bimonthly to critique and develop new works; presents monthly staged readings.

ARVADA CENTER FOR THE ARTS & HUMANITIES

(Founded 1976)
6901 Wadsworth Blvd; Arvada, CO 80003; (303) 431-3080,
FAX 431-3083; www.arvadacenter.org
Kathy Kuehn, *Performing Arts Director*

Submission procedure: no unsolicited scripts; synopsis and letter of inquiry. **Types of material:** plays for young audiences only. **Special interests:** plays for preschool-grade 6. **Facilities:** Arvada Center Amphitheater, 1200 seats, proscenium stage; Arvada Center Main Stage, 498 seats, thrust stage. **Production considerations:** cast limit of 6-9, minimal set. **Best submission time:** Sep-Mar. **Response time:** 3-5 months letter; 5-8 months script.

ASIAN AMERICAN THEATER COMPANY

(Founded 1973)
1840 Sutter St, Suite 207; San Francisco, CA 94115; (415) 440-5545,
FAX 440-5597; email info@asianamericantheater.org;
website www.asianamericantheater.org
Pamela A. Wu, *Producing Director*

Submission procedure: accepts unsolicited scripts with synopsis, character breakdown, resume and letter of inquiry. **Types of material:** full-length plays, adaptations, plays for young audiences. **Special interests:** plays that explore diversity of the Asian-Pacific-American experience. **Facilities:** no permanent facility. **Best submission time:** year-round. **Response time:** 3-6 months.

ASOLO THEATRE COMPANY

(Founded 1960)
5555 North Tamiami Trail; Sarasota, FL 34243-2141;
   (941) 351-9010, FAX 351-5796;
   email bruce_rodgers@asolo.org; website www.asolo.org
Bruce E. Rodgers, *Associate Artistic Director*

Submission procedure: no unsolicited scripts; 1-page synopsis and letter of inquiry with SASE for response. **Types of material:** full-length plays, translations, adaptations, solo pieces. **Special interests:** adaptations of great literature. **Facilities:** The Mertz Theatre, 499 seats, proscenium stage; The Cook Theatre, 161 seats, proscenium stage. **Best submission time:** Jun-Aug. **Response time:** 2 months letter; 6 months script.

ATLANTIC THEATER COMPANY

(Founded 1984)
336 West 20th St, New York, NY 10011; (212) 645-8015,
   FAX 645-8755
Maggie Kiley, *Artistic Associate*

Submission procedure: no unsolicited scripts; agent submission. **Types of material:** full-length plays, one-acts, adaptations. **Facilities:** Atlantic Theater Mainstage, 160 seats, proscenium stage; Black Box, 70 seats, proscenium stage. **Best submission time:** year-round. **Response time:** 3-6 months. **Special programs:** Atlantic 453: year-round play readings, workshops and productions in Black Box.

ATTIC THEATRE CENTRE

(Founded 1987)
8663 Chalmers Dr; Los Angeles, CA 90035; (310) 659-3637;
   email AtticTheatre@aol.com; website www.AtticTheatre.org
James Carey, *Producing Artistic Director*

Submission procedure: no unsolicited scripts; synopsis, dialogue sample and letter of inquiry with SASE for response. **Types of material:** full-length plays, one-acts, solo pieces. **Facilities:** no permanent facility. **Production considerations:** simple sets; no fly or wing space. **Best submission time:** year-round. **Response time:** 1 month letter; 3-6 months script. **Special**

programs: play reading series; developmental workshops; Attic Theatre Ensemble's One-Act Marathon (see Prizes).

AURORA THEATRE COMPANY

(Founded 1992)
2315 Durant Ave; Berkeley, CA 94704; (510) 843–4822,
    FAX 843–4826; website auroratheatre.org
Literary Manager

Submission procedure: no unsolicited scripts; synopsis and letter of inquiry. **Types of material:** full-length plays, adaptations. **Special interests:** plays emphasizing language and ideas. **Facilities:** Aurora Theatre, 67 seats, arena stage. **Production considerations:** cast limit of 8; minimal production demands. **Best submission time:** year-round. **Response time:** 6 months letter; 6 months script.

AURORA THEATRE, INC.

(Founded 1998)
3087 B Main St; Duluth, GA 30096
Anthony Rodriguez, *Producing Artistic Director*

Submission procedure: accepts unsolicited scripts with bio; include cassette or CD with script containing at least 1 song for musicals. **Types of material:** full-length plays, musicals. **Special interests:** Hispanic plays; plays appealing to all ages. **Facilities:** mainstage, 200 seats, thrust stage. **Production consideration:** prefers small cast, simple set; no fly space. **Best submission time:** year-round. **Response time:** 1-3 months.

AXIS THEATRE

(Founded 1992)
3600 Clipper Mill Rd, #114; Baltimore, MD 21211; (410) 243–5237,
    FAX 243–1294; website www.axistheatre.org
Brian Klaas, *Artistic Director*

Submission procedure: accepts unsolicited scripts; include cassette or CD for musicals. **Types of material:** full-length plays, musicals. **Special interests:** nonrealistic plays. **Facilities:** Axis Theatre, 68 seats, proscenium stage. **Production considerations:** cast limit of 10; small space. **Best submission time:** Apr-Aug. **Response time:** 3-5 months script.

BAILIWICK REPERTORY

(Founded 1982)

Bailiwick Arts Center; 1229 West Belmont; Chicago, IL 60657–3205;
(773) 883–1090; email bailiwickr@aol.com;
website www.bailiwick.org

David Zak, *Artistic Director*

Submission procedure: submission guidelines available on web. **Types of material:** full-length plays, translations, adaptations, musicals, solo pieces. **Special interests:** translations and adaptations; theatrically inventive and/or politically intriguing works; work appropriate for Deaf Bailiwick Artists, especially work by deaf or hard-of-hearing writers. **Facilities:** mainstage, 150 seats, flexible/thrust stage; cabaret/studio, 100 seats, flexible stage. **Best submission time:** year-round. **Response time:** 8-12 months. **Special programs:** Pride Performance Series: year-round exploration of works of interest to the lesbian and gay communities, culminating in summer festival. Director's Festival: annual directors' showcase of 48 plays, 10-50 minutes long, staged in black-box setting. Studio Series: workshops and readings of plays, performance pieces and musicals. Submission guidelines for special programs available on web.

BAPA'S IMAGINATION STAGE

(Founded 1992)

7300 Whittier Blvd; Bethesda, MD 20817; (301) 881–9112,
FAX 881–9112; email janetstanford@hotmail.com;
website www.bapaarts.org

Janet Stanford, *Artistic Director*

Submission procedure: no unsolicited scripts; dialogue sample and letter of inquiry. **Types of material:** plays for young audiences, musicals. **Special interests:** 45-90 minute plays, "innovative treatment of children's classics," culturally diverse material. **Facilities:** Imagination Stage, 120 seats, black box/thrust. **Production considerations:** cast size 4-12, simple set; technically limited space. **Best submission time:** year-round. **Response time:** 3 weeks letter; 12 months script.

BARKSDALE THEATRE

(Founded 1953)
1601 Willow Lawn Dr, Suite 301E; Richmond, VA 23230;
   (804) 282-9440, FAX 288-6470; email barksdalev@aol.com;
   website www.barksdaletheatre.com
Richard St. Peter, *Associate Artistic Director*

Submission procedure: no unsolicited scripts; synopsis and letter of inquiry. **Types of material:** full-length plays, one-acts. **Facilities:** mainstage, 214 seats, arena stage. **Production considerations:** small cast, minimal production demands; no fly or wing space. **Best submission time:** summer. **Response time:** 6 months letter; 12 months script.

THE BARROW GROUP

(Founded 1986)
Box 5112; New York, NY 10185; (212) 253-2001, FAX 253-1909
Literary Manager

Submission procedure: no unsolicited scripts; professional recommendation. **Types of material:** full-length plays, translations, adaptations. **Facilities:** no permanent facility. **Production considerations:** cast limit of 12, minimal sets. **Best submission time:** year-round. **Response time:** 1-6 months.

BARTER THEATRE

(Founded 1933)
Box 867; Abingdon, VA 24212-0867; (540) 628-2281,
   FAX 628-4551; email barter@naxs.com;
   website www.bartertheatre.com
Richard Rose, *Producing Artistic Director*

Submission procedure: no unsolicited scripts; synopsis, dialogue sample and letter of inquiry; include cassette for musicals. **Types of material:** full-length plays, translations, adaptations, plays for young audiences, musicals. **Special interests:** social issues and current events; works that expand theatrical form; nonurban-oriented material. **Facilities:** Barter Theatre, 508 seats, proscenium stage; Barter's Stage II, 140 seats, flexible stage. **Production considerations:** cast limit of 4-10. **Best submission time:** Mar, Sep. **Response time:** 9 months letter; 12 months script. **Special programs:** Barter's Early Stages: script development program.

BAY STREET THEATRE

(Founded 1991)
Box 810; Sag Harbor, NY 11963; (631) 725-0818, FAX 725-0906;
   website www.baystreet.org
Mia Emlen Grosjean, *Literary Manager*

Submission procedure: no unsolicited scripts; agent submission. **Types of material:** full-length plays, musicals, solo pieces. **Special interests:** plays that challenge as well as entertain; plays that "address the heart of our community and champion the human spirit." **Facilities:** mainstage, 299 seats, thrust stage. **Production considerations:** cast limit of 8-9, prefers unit set, small-scale musicals only; no fly or wing space. **Best submission time:** year-round. **Response time:** 3-6 months. **Special programs:** reading series: readings of 3 new plays each fall and spring; playwright receives $50 honorarium and travel from New York City; scripts for special programs selected through theatre's normal submission procedure.

THE BELMONT PLAYHOUSE

(Founded 1991)
2385 Arthur Ave; Bronx, NY 10458; (718) 364-4700, FAX 563-5053;
   email thebelmont@hotmail.com
Dante Albertie, *Artistic Director*

Submission procedure: accepts unsolicited scripts. **Types of material:** full-length plays, translations, adaptations. **Special interests:** plays with Italian-American or urban themes. **Facilities:** Belmont Playhouse, 75 seats, black box; Performance Space, 25-100 seats, platform. **Production considerations:** cast limit of 6, one set; no fly space. **Best submission time:** year-round. **Response time:** 3-5 months.

BERKSHIRE THEATRE FESTIVAL

(Founded 1928)
Box 797; Stockbridge, MA 01262; (413) 298-5536, FAX 298-3368;
   email admin@berkshiretheatre.org;
   website www.berkshiretheatre.org
Kate Maguire, *Producing Director*

Submission procedure: no unsolicited scripts; agent submission. **Types of material:** full-length plays, musicals, solo pieces. **Facilities:** Playhouse, 450 seats, proscenium stage; Unicorn Theatre, 122 seats, thrust stage. **Production considerations:** cast limit of 8 for plays, small orchestra for musicals. **Best submission time:** Oct-Dec. **Response time:** 12 months.

BILINGUAL FOUNDATION OF THE ARTS

(Founded 1973)
421 North Ave 19; Los Angeles, CA 90031; (323) 225-4044,
FAX 225-1250
Agustin Coppola, *Dramaturg*

Submission procedure: accepts unsolicited scripts. **Types of material:** full-length plays, translations, adaptations, plays for young audiences. **Special interests:** plays by Hispanic playwrights or with Hispanic themes only. **Facilities:** BFA's Little Theatre, 99 seats, thrust stage; uses theatres at Los Angeles Center for the Arts for some mainstage productions. **Production considerations:** cast limit of 10, simple set. **Best submission time:** year-round. **Response time:** 3-6 months.

BIRMINGHAM CHILDREN'S THEATRE

(Founded 1947)
Box 1362; Birmingham, AL 35201; (205) 458-8181, FAX 458-8895;
website www.bct123.org
Burt Brosowsky, *Executive Director*

Submission procedure: accepts unsolicited scripts; prefers synopsis and letter of inquiry. **Types of material:** plays for young audiences. **Special interests:** interactive plays for preschool-grade 2; presentational plays for K-6. **Facilities:** Birmingham-Jefferson Civic Center Theatre, 1073 seats, thrust stage; Studio Theatre, up to 250 seats, lab space. **Production considerations:** prefers cast of 4-6. **Best submission time:** Sep-Dec. **Response time:** 2 weeks letter; 2-6 months script.

BLOOMSBURG THEATRE ENSEMBLE

(Founded 1978)
226 Center St; Bloomsburg, PA 17815; (570) 784-5530,
FAX 784-4912; website www.bte.org
Play Selection Chair

Submission procedure: no unsolicited scripts; synopsis, dialogue sample, professional recommendation and letter of inquiry. **Types of material:** full-length plays, translations, adaptations. **Special interests:** new translations of classics; rural themes; plays suitable for small acting ensemble. **Facilities:** Alvina Krause Theatre, 350 seats, proscenium stage. **Production considerations:** small to mid-sized cast, 1 set or unit set. **Best submission time:** summer. **Response time:** 3 months letter; 6 months script.

BOARSHEAD THEATER

(Founded 1966)
425 South Grand Ave; Lansing, MI 48933; (517) 484–7800,
FAX 484–2564
John Peakes, *Artistic Director*

Submission procedure: no unsolicited scripts; synopsis, character breakdown, 6-10-page dialogue sample and letter of inquiry with SASP for response. **Types of material:** full-length plays, plays for young audiences. **Special interests:** one-act plays for young audiences only; social issues; comedies; plays that make use of theatrical conventions or create new ones; no musicals. **Facilities:** Center for the Arts, 249 seats, thrust stage. **Production considerations:** cast limit of 4-6 for children's shows. **Best submission time:** year-round. **Response time:** 1 month letter; 3-6 months script. **Special programs:** staged readings of 5 new plays a year.

BORDERLANDS THEATER

(Founded 1986)
Box 2791; Tucson, AZ 85702; (520) 882–8607,
FAX 882–7406 (call first); email bltheater@aol.com

Submission procedure: no unsolicited scripts; synopsis and letter of inquiry. **Types of material:** full-length plays, translations, adaptations. **Special interests:** cultural diversity; race relations; "border" issues, including concerns of the geographical border region as well as the metaphorical borders of gender, class and race. **Facilities:** Pima Community College Center for the Arts: 1st theatre, 400 seats, proscenium stage; 2nd theatre, 160 seats, black box. **Production considerations:** cast limit of 12; minimal set. **Best submission time:** year-round. **Response time:** 1 month letter; 3-6 months script.

BRAT PRODUCTIONS

(Founded 1998)
340 North 12th St, Suite 417; Philadelphia, PA 19107;
(215) 413–0975, FAX 413–0976;
email Greg@bratproductions.org;
website www.bratproductions.org
Greg Gephart, *Producing Director*

Submission procedure: no unsolicited scripts; synopsis, dialogue sample and letter of inquiry. **Types of material:** full-length plays, translations, adaptations, musicals, solo pieces. **Special interests:** "Material that connects with audiences in new and unique ways." **Facilities:** no permanent facility. **Production considerations:** cast limit of 5, prefers unit set. **Best submission time:** summer. **Response time:** 1 month letter; 6 months script.

BRAVA! FOR WOMEN IN THE ARTS

(Founded 1986)
2781 24th St; San Francisco, CA 94110; (415) 641-7657,
    FAX 641-7684; email ellen@brava.org; website www.brava.org
Ellen Gavin, *Artistic/Executive Director*

Submission procedure: no unsolicited scripts; synopsis, dialogue sample and letter of inquiry. **Types of material:** full-length plays, one-acts, plays for young audiences. **Special interests:** premieres by women of color; lesbian playwrights. **Facilities:** Brava Theater Center, 375 seats, thrust stage; second theater, 100 seats, flexible black box. **Best submission time:** year-round. **Response time:** 6 months letter; 8 months script. **Special programs:** Teatro Armonia: year-round playwriting and performance classes for young artists. Adult playwriting workshops. S.F. Running Crew: technical theatre training program for youth.

BRISTOL RIVERSIDE THEATRE

(Founded 1986)
Box 1250; Bristol, PA 19007; (215) 785-6664, FAX 785-2762;
    email brtboss@aol.com; website www.brtstage.org
David J. Abers, *Assistant to Artistic Director*

Submission procedure: accepts unsolicited scripts. **Types of material:** full-length plays, one-acts, translations, adaptations, musicals, solo pieces. **Special interests:** cutting-edge works; plays that experiment with form; translations; musicals. **Facilities:** Bristol Riverside Theatre, 302 seats, flexible stage. **Production considerations:** cast limit of 10 for plays, 18 for musicals, 9 for orchestra, minimal production demands. **Best submission time:** spring. **Response time:** 12-18 months. **Special programs:** year-round reading series.

THE B STREET THEATRE

(Founded 1991)
2711 B St; Sacramento, CA 95816; (916) 443-5391, FAX 443-0874;
    email bstreetfac@aol.com
Buck Busfield, *Producing Director*

Submission procedure: no unsolicited scripts; agent submission. **Types of material:** full-length plays. **Special interests:** contemporary comedies and dramas. **Facilities:** The B Street Theatre, 150 seats, black box. **Production considerations:** cast limit of 6, modest production demands; no fly space. **Best submission time:** year-round. **Response time:** 3-6 months.

CALIFORNIA SHAKESPEARE FESTIVAL

(Founded 1973)
701 Heinz Ave; Berkeley, CA 94710; (510) 548-3422,
    FAX 843-9921; email letters@calshakes.org;
    website www.calshakes.org
Artistic Associate

Submission procedure: no unsolicited scripts; synopis and letter of inquiry. **Types of material:** translations, adaptations. **Special interests:** new translations and adaptations of classical plays suitable for large-scale, outdoor production only. **Facilities:** Bruns Amphitheatre, 521 seats, outdoor proscenium. **Best submission time:** fall. **Response time:** 6 months letter; 6 months script.

CALIFORNIA THEATRE CENTER

(Founded 1976)
Box 2007; Sunnyvale, CA 94087; (408) 245-2979, FAX 245-0235;
    email ctc@ctcinc.org
Will Huddleston, *Resident Director*

Submission procedure: accepts unsolicited scripts; prefers synopsis and letter of inquiry. **Types of material:** plays for young audiences. **Special interests:** classics adapted for young audiences; adaptations of literature, historical material. **Facilities:** company primarily tours to large proscenium-stage theatres; Sunnyvale Performing Arts Center (home theatre), 200 seats, proscenium stage. **Production considerations:** cast limit of 8 for professional touring productions, minimum cast of 15 for conservatory productions, modest production demands. **Best submission time:** year-round. **Response time:** 1 month letter; 4-6 months script.

CAPITAL REPERTORY COMPANY

(Founded 1981)
111 North Pearl St; Albany, NY 12207; (518) 462-4531, ext 219,
    FAX 465-0213
Margaret Mancinelli-Cahill, *Producing Artistic Director*

Submission procedure: no unsolicited scripts; synopsis and 10-page dialogue sample. **Types of material:** full-length plays, translations, adaptations, music-theatre works. **Facilities:** Capital Repertory Theatre, 299 seats, thrust stage. **Best submission time:** late spring. **Response time:** 6 months.

CARMEL PERFORMING ARTS FESTIVAL

(Founded 1996)
Box 221473; Carmel, CA 93922; (408) 644–8383, FAX 647–0758;
    email robinm1668@aol.com; website www.carmelfest.org
Robin McKee, *Producing Artistic Director*

Submission procedure: no unsolicited scripts; professional recommendation. **Types of material:** full-length plays, one-acts, translations, adaptations, plays for young audiences, solo pieces, performance art. **Special interests:** short full-length plays. **Facilities:** no permanent facility. **Production considerations:** prefers cast limit of 6. **Best submission time:** Jan. **Response time:** 3 months. **Special programs:** CPAF Reading Series: annual readings; submit synopsis and letter of inquiry to Readings Coordinator; *deadline*: 30 Jan 2002; *notification* Mar 2002; *dates*: Oct 2002.

CELEBRATION THEATRE

(Founded 1982)
7985 Santa Monica Blvd, Suite 109–1; West Hollywood, CA 90046;
    (323) 957–1884, FAX 957–1826;
    website www.celebrationtheatre.com
Tom Jacobson, *Literary Manager*

Submission procedure: accepts unsolicited scripts, prefers letter of inquiry. **Types of material:** full-length plays, one-acts, adaptations, musicals, cabaret/revues. **Special interests:** plays not previously produced on the West Coast with gay and lesbian themes. **Facilities:** Celebration Theatre, 65 seats, thrust stage. **Production considerations:** cast limit of 12, single set. **Best submission time:** year-round. **Response time:** 6 months.

CENTER STAGE

(Founded 1963)
700 North Calvert St; Baltimore, MD 21202–3686; (410) 685–3200,
    FAX 539–3912; email cstoudt@centerstage.org
Charlotte Stoudt, *Resident Dramaturg*

Submission procedure: no unsolicited scripts; synopsis, sample pages and letter of inquiry. **Types of material:** full-length plays, translations, adaptations, music-theatre works, solo pieces. **Special interests:** plays with no previous mainstage production; plays about the African-American experience. **Facilities:** Pearlstone Theater, 541 seats, modified thrust stage; Head Theater, 100-400 seats, flexible space. **Best submission time:** year-round. **Response time:** 5-7 weeks letter; 4-6 months script.

CENTRE STAGE-SOUTH CAROLINA!

(Founded 1983)
Box 8451; Greenville, SC 29604-8451; (864) 233-6733,
    FAX 233-3901; email cbla@infoave.net
Claude W. Blakely, *Administrative Director*

Submission procedure: accepts unsolicited scripts. **Types of material:** full-length plays, one-acts, plays for young audiences, musicals, cabaret/revues. **Special interests:** plays not previously produced; plays for young audiences; issues of interest to senior citizens and minorities; musical revues. **Facilities:** mainstage, 292 seats, thrust stage. **Production considerations:** 2 sets; no fly space, limited wing space. **Best submission time:** year-round. **Response time:** 2 months. **Special programs:** Sunday Evenings Readers Theatre: regularly scheduled rehearsed readings presented for public followed by audience discussion.

CHARLESTON STAGE

(Founded 1977)
Box 356; Charleston,SC 29402; (843) 577-5967, FAX 577-5422;
    email cstage@charlestonstage.com;
    website www.charlestonstage.com
Julian Wiles, *Producing Artistic Director*

Submission procedure: no unsolicited scripts; professional recommendation with SASE for response. **Types of material:** full-length plays. **Facilities:** The Historic Dock Street Theatre, 450 seats, proscenium stage. **Production considerations:** prefers small cast. **Best submission time:** year-round. **Response time:** 1-2 months.

CHARLOTTE REPERTORY THEATRE

(Founded 1976)
129 West Trade St; Charlotte, NC 28202; (704) 333-8587,
    FAX 333-0224
Claudia Carter Covington, *Literary Manager*

Submission procedure: no unsolicited scripts; letter of inquiry from playwright; professional recommendation; agent submission. **Types of material:** full-length plays. **Special interests:** work not produced professionally; no plays for young audiences. **Facilities:** Booth Theatre at North Carolina Blumenthal Performing Arts Center, 450 seats, flexible stage. **Best submission time:** year-round. **Response time:** 3-6 months. **Special programs:** Festival of New American Plays: annual festival of staged readings; stipend, transportation and housing provided.

CHERRY LANE ALTERNATIVE

(Founded 1997)
38 Commerce St; New York, NY 10014; (212) 989-2159,
 FAX 989-2867; email CherryLaneAlt40@aol.com;
 website www.cherrylanetheatre.com
Director of Development

Submission procedure: no unsolicited scripts; professional recommendation. **Types of material:** full-length plays, one-acts. **Facilities:** Cherry Lane Theatre, 178 seats, proscenium stage; Alternative theatre, 55 seats, black box. **Best submission time:** Mar–Jun. **Response time:** 15 Jun for one-acts; Oct for full-length plays. **Special programs:** Mentor Project: 5 writers work with a master playwright for a season, plays produced in 2-week run, no unsolicited scripts; professional recommendation only. Play Reading Series: 2 writers from mentor project chosen for Feb reading series. Alternation One-Act Play Festival: annual summer festival in late Jul or Aug; *deadline*: May 2002, no submissions before Mar 2002.

CHICAGO DRAMATISTS

See Membership and Service Organizations.

CHICAGO THEATRE COMPANY

(Founded 1984)
500 East 67th St; Chicago, IL 60637; (773) 493-0901,
 FAX 493-0360; email LutherGoins@aol.com;
 website www.chicagotheatrecompany.com
Luther Goins, *Managing Director*

Submission procedure: no unsolicited scripts; synopsis and letter of inquiry. **Types of material:** full-length plays, adaptations, plays for young audiences, musicals. **Special interests:** African-American issues and themes. **Facilities:** Chicago Theatre Company, 90 seats, thrust. **Production**

considerations: minimal set and technical requirements. **Best submission time:** year-round. **Response time:** 2 months letter; 4 months script.

THE CHILDREN'S THEATRE COMPANY

(Founded 1965)
2400 Third Ave S; Minneapolis, MN 55404–3597; (612) 874–0500,
   FAX 874–8119
Elissa Adams, *Director of New Play Development*

Submission procedure: no unsolicited scripts; synopsis, first 20 pages of script, resume and letter of inquiry. **Types of material:** full-length plays, one-acts, translations, adaptations, plays for young audiences, musicals. **Special interests:** adaptations or original plays for young audiences; work samples from writers with no previous experience writing for children's theatre. **Facilities:** Children's Theatre Company, 745 seats, proscenium stage. **Best submission time:** Jul-Feb. **Response time:** 1 month letter; 6 months script. **Special programs:** Threshold: 1-4 works for young audiences commissioned each year for developmental laboratory.

CHILDSPLAY

(Founded 1977)
Box 517; Tempe, AZ 85280; (402) 350–8101, FAX 350–8584
David Saar, *Artistic Director*

Submission procedure: accepts unsolicited scripts or synopsis, 10-page dialogue sample and letter of inquiry. **Types of material:** plays for young audiences including full-length plays, adaptations, musicals, performance art. **Special interests:** nontraditional plays; material that entertains and challenges both performers and audiences; 2nd and 3rd productions of unpublished work. **Facilities:** Herberger Theater Center Stage, 800 seats, proscenium stage; Scottsdale Center for the Arts, 800 seats, proscenium stage; Stage West, 350 seats, proscenium stage; Tempe Performing Arts Center, 175 seats, black box; also performs in Tucson (no permanent space). **Production considerations:** some van-sized touring productions. **Best submission time:** Jun-Oct. **Response time:** 1 month letter; 3 months script. **Special programs:** commissioning program.

CINCINNATI PLAYHOUSE IN THE PARK
(Founded 1960)
Box 6537; Cincinnati, OH 45206-0537; (513) 345-2242;
    website www.cincyplay.com
Edward Stern, *Producing Artistic Director*

Submission procedure: no unsolicited scripts; agent submission. **Types of material:** full-length plays, translations, adaptations, musicals. **Facilities:** Robert S. Marx Theatre, 626 seats, thrust stage; Thompson Shelterhouse, 225 seats, thrust stage. **Best submission time:** year-round. **Response time:** 6-8 months. **Special programs:** Lois and Richard Rosenthal New Play Prize (see Prizes).

CINCINNATI SHAKESPEARE FESTIVAL
(Founded 1993)
717-719 Race St; Cincinnati, OH 45202; (513) 381-2289,
    FAX 381-2298; email csfed@cincyshakes.com;
    website www.cincyshakes.com
Jasson Minadakis, *Artistic Director*

Submission procedure: no unsolicited scripts; synopsis, first 20 pages or dialogue and letter of inquiry. **Types of material:** full-length plays, translations, adaptations, solo pieces. **Special interests:** language plays, heightened text. **Facilities:** Cincinnati Shakespeare Festival Theater, 180 seats, thrust stage. **Production considerations:** minimal production demands. **Best submission time:** year-round. **Response time:** 2 months letter; 6 months script. **Special programs:** CSF Studio (see Development).

CITY GARAGE
(Founded 1987)
Box 2016; Santa Monica, CA 90406; (310) 319-9939,
    FAX 396-1040; email citygarage@earthlink.net;
    website www.citygarage.org
Paul Rubenstein, *Literary Manager*

Submission procedure: no unsolicited scripts; synopsis and letter of inquiry. **Types of material:** full-length plays, translations, adaptations. **Special interests:** only nonrealistic experimental work; no family dramas, personal or confessional plays, nothing naturalistic or conventional. **Facilities:** City Garage, 48 seats, thrust stage. **Production considerations:** single set. **Best submission time:** year-round. **Response time:** 2 weeks letter; 6 weeks script.

CITY THEATRE COMPANY

(Founded 1974)
57 South 13th St; Pittsburgh, PA 15203; (412) 431–4400,
    FAX 431–5535; email caquiline@citytheatre–pgh.org;
    website www.citytheatre–pgh.org
Carlyn Aquiline, *Literary Manager/Dramaturg*

Submission procedure: no unsolicited scripts; synopsis, 15-20-page dialogue sample, character breakdown, resume, development/production history and letter of inquiry with SASE for response; include cassette for musicals. **Types of material:** full-length plays, translations, adaptations, musicals, solo pieces. **Special interests:** "offbeat and innovative plays of substance and ideas"; unconventional form, content and/or use of language; plays by underrepresented voices (e.g., women writers of color, disabled writers). **Facilities:** mainstage, 272 seats, flexible stage; HamburgStudio, 99 seats, black box. **Production considerations:** prefers cast limit of 10. **Best submission time:** year-round. **Response time:** 2 months letter; 10 months script. **Special Programs:** New Works On Stage: play commissioning and development program; City Theatre Young Playwrights: contest with productions for 7th-12th graders in Western Pennsylvania (call for spring deadline).

CLARENCE BROWN THEATRE COMPANY

(Founded 1974)
206 McClung Tower; Knoxville, TN 37996; (865) 974–6011,
    FAX 974–4867; email cbt@utk.edu;
    website www.clarencebrowntheatre.com
Blake Robinson, *Producing Artistic Director*

Submission procedure: no unsolicited scripts; synopsis, character breakdown, 1-2 pages of dialogue and letter of inquiry. **Types of material:** full-length plays. **Special interests:** contemporary American plays. **Facilities:** Clarence Brown Theatre, 600 seats, proscenium stage; Carousel Theatre, 250 seats, arena stage. **Best submission time:** year-round. **Response time:** 1 month letter; 1 month script.

CLASSIC STAGE COMPANY

(Founded 1969)
136 East 13th St; New York, NY 10003; (212) 677–4210,
FAX 477–7504
Literary Associate

Submission procedure: no unsolicited scripts; synopsis, dialogue sample and letter of inquiry. **Types of material:** translations and adaptations of "classic literature and themes only." **Special interests:** translations and adaptations of classic plays; adaptations of major nondramatic classics; prefers highly theatrical work. **Facilities:** Classic Stage Company, 180 seats, flexible stage. **Best submission time:** year-round. **Response time:** 2 months letter; 3 months script.

THE CLEVELAND PLAY HOUSE

(Founded 1916)
8500 Euclid Ave; Cleveland, OH 44106–0189; (216) 795–7000,
FAX 795–7007
Seth Gordon, *Director of New Play Development*

Submission procedure: no unsolicited scripts; resume and letter of inquiry with SASE for response. **Types of material:** full-length plays, adaptations, musicals. **Facilities:** Kenyon C. Bolton Theatre, 548 seats, proscenium stage; Francis E. Drury Theatre, 504 seats, proscenium stage; Baxter Stage, 300 seats, thrust stage. **Best submission time:** year-round. **Response time:** 1-2 months letter; 1-3 months script. **Special programs:** The Next Stage Festival of New Plays (see Development).

CLEVELAND PUBLIC THEATRE

(Founded 1981)
6415 Detroit Ave; Cleveland, OH 44102–3011; (216) 631–2727,
FAX 631–2575; email cpt@en.com;
website www.clevelandartists.net/cpt
James A. Levin, *Artistic Director*

Submission procedure: no unsolicited scripts; synopsis, 5-page dialogue sample and letter of inquiry. **Types of material:** full-length plays, one-acts, solo pieces. **Special interests:** experimental, poetic, politically, intellectually and spiritually challenging works; voices not heard in the mainstream (people of color, women, gays and lesbians, seniors, youth under 18); no standard commercial fare or "anything you might see on TV." **Facilities:** Gordon Square Theatre, 550 seats, flexible thrust; Cleveland Public Theatre, 150-175 seats, flexible stage (arena/proscenium). **Production considerations:** cast limit of 10, simple set. **Best submission time:** year-round. **Response time:** 6 weeks letter;

9 months script. **Special programs:** New Plays Festival: 4-week developmental workshops of 8 plays culminating in stage readings; scripts selected through theatre's normal submission procedure; cash prize awarded for best new play in festival; *deadline:* 1 Aug 2001; *notification:* Dec 2001; *dates:* Jan–Mar 2002.

COCONUT GROVE PLAYHOUSE

(Founded 1954)
3500 Main Highway; Miami, FL 33133; (305) 442–2662,
    FAX 444–6437
Arnold Mittelman, *Producing Artistic Director*

Submission procedure: no unsolicited scripts; synopsis and letter of inquiry. **Types of material:** full-length plays, translations, musicals, cabaret/revues. **Special interests:** dramas, musicals. **Facilities:** mainstage, 1100 seats, proscenium stage; Encore Room, 150 seats, cabaret. **Best submission time:** year-round. **Response time:** 1 week letter; 2 months script.

THE COLONY THEATRE COMPANY

(Founded 1975)
555 North Third St; Burbank, CA 91502; (818) 558–7000,
    FAX 558–7110; email wayneliebman@colonytheatre.org;
    website www.colonytheatre.org
Wayne Liebman, *Literary Manager*

Submission procedure: no unsolicited scripts; agent submission; professional recommendation with 1-page synopsis, first 10 pages of play, cast breakdown, production history, resume and SASE for response. **Types of material:** full-length plays, adaptations. **Special interests:** comedies; dramas; well-crafted plays of theatrical imagination and emotional resonance which address universal themes; plays by women. **Facilities:** Burbank Center Stage, 276 seats, thrust stage. **Production considerations:** cast limit of 3–12; plays cast from resident company. **Best submission time:** Feb-Nov. **Response time:** 2 months letter; 1 year script

COLUMBUS CHILDREN'S THEATRE

(Founded 1963)
372 Dublin Ave; Columbus, OH 43215–2310; (614) 224–6672,
    FAX 224–8844; email BGShows@aol.com;
    website www.colschildrenstheatre.org
William Goldsmith, *Artistic Director*

Submission procedure: accepts unsolicited scripts. **Types of material:** one-acts, plays for young audiences. **Special interests:** social-issue one-acts suitable for touring to schools. **Facilities:** Columbus Children's Theatre, 170 seats, black box/thrust. **Production considerations:** prefer unit sets for mainstage season; cast limit of 4 for touring productions. **Best submission time:** Sep–Nov. **Response time:** 4 months.

COMMONWEAL THEATRE COMPANY

(Founded 1989)
Box 15; Lanesboro, MN 55949; (507) 467–2905, FAX 467–2468;
　　email cmmnweal@means.net
Hal Cropp, *Core Artist*

Submission procedure: no unsolicited scripts; professional recommendation. **Types of material:** full-length plays, translations, adaptations. **Facilities:** St. Mane Theatre, 126 seats, proscenium stage. **Production considerations:** prefers cast limit of 9, 1 set; no wing space. **Best submission time:** Oct–Dec. **Response time:** 1 month. **Special programs:** Commonweal New Play Workshop: annual 2-week developmental workshop for 1 script chosen from regular submissions; play receives rehearsals culminating in staged reading for invited audience; playwright receives housing during workshop.

COMPANY OF FOOLS

(Founded 1992)
Box 329; Hailey ID 83333; (208) 788–6520, FAX 788–1053;
　　email Denise@companyoffools.org;
　　website www.companyoffools.org
Denise Simone, *Associate Artistic Director*

Submission procedure: no unsolicited scripts; synopsis and letter of inquiry. **Types of material:** full-length plays, one-acts, translations, adaptations, plays for young audiences. **Special interests:** plays with focus on American themes; stories of "the human heart in conflict with itself." **Facilities:** Liberty, 240 seats, proscenium stage; Mint, 30–90 seats, flexible stage. **Production considerations:** cast limit of 13. **Best submission time:** year-round. **Response time:** 3 months letter; 4 months script.

CONTEMPORARY AMERICAN THEATRE COMPANY

(Founded 1985)
77 South High St; Columbus, OH 43215; (614) 461–1382,
FAX 461–4917; email tdilorenzo@catco.org;
website www.catco.org
Jonathan Putnam, *Resident Actor*

Submission procedure: accepts unsolicited scripts. **Types of material:** full-length plays, one-acts, adaptations, solo pieces. **Special interests:** 10-15 minute plays. **Facilities:** Studio One, 243 seats, proscenium stage; Studio Two, 147 seats, thrust stage. **Production considerations:** prefers cast limit of 8. **Best submission time:** year-round. **Response time:** 1 year. **Special programs:** The Shorts Festival: biennial festival of 10-15 minute plays with common setting; *deadline*: exact date tba; *notification*: exact date tba; *dates*: May 2002.

CONTEMPORARY AMERICAN THEATER FESTIVAL

(Founded 1991)
Box 429; Shepherdstown, WV 25443; (304) 876–3473,
FAX 876–0955; website www.catf.org
Ed Herendeen, *Producing Director*
Catherine Irwin, *Managing Director*

Submission procedure: no unsolicited scripts; synopsis and letter of inquiry. **Types of material:** full-length plays. **Special interests:** new American plays; contemporary issues. **Facilities:** Frank Center Stage, 350 seats, proscenium stage; Studio Theater, 99 seats, black box. **Best submission time:** fall. **Response time:** 1 month letter; 3-6 months script.

CORNERSTONE THEATER COMPANY

(Founded 1986)
708 Traction Ave; Los Angeles, CA 90013; (213) 613–1700,
FAX 613–1714; email tparran@cornerstonetheater.org
Teeko Parran, *Program Associate*

Submission procedure: no unsolicited scripts; letter of inquiry only. **Types of material:** full-length plays, adaptations, musicals. **Special interests:** company primarily interested in collaborating with playwrights to develop new works or contemporary adaptations of classics, focusing on specific communities. **Facilities:** no permanent facility. **Best submission time:** year-round. **Response time:** 2 months.

THE COTERIE THEATRE

(Founded 1979)
2450 Grand Ave; Kansas City, MO 64108-2520; (816) 474-6785,
 FAX 474-7112; email jefchurch@aol.com;
 website www.thecoterie.com
Jeff Church, *Producing Artistic Director*

Submission procedure: no unsolicited scripts; synopsis, resume and letter of inquiry with SASE for response. **Types of material:** works for young and family audiences only, including adaptations, musicals and solo pieces. **Special interests:** ground-breaking works only; plays with culturally diverse casts or themes; social issues; adaptations of classic or contemporary literature; musicals. **Facilities:** The Coterie Theatre, 240 seats, flexible stage. **Production considerations:** cast limit of 12, prefers 5-7; no fly or wing space. **Best submission time:** year-round. **Response time:** 6-8 months letter; 6-8 months script.

COURT THEATRE

(Founded 1955)
5535 South Ellis Ave; Chicago, IL 60637; (773) 702-7005,
 FAX 834-1897
Resident Dramaturg

Submission procedure: no unsolicited scripts; synopsis, dialogue sample and letter of inquiry with email address for response. **Types of material:** translations and adaptations of classic texts only. **Special interests:** infrequently produced or "undiscovered" material. **Facilities:** Abelson Auditorium, 253 seats, thrust stage. **Production considerations:** limited fly space. **Best submission time:** summer. **Response time:** 6 weeks letter; 1-6 months script.

CUMBERLAND COUNTY PLAYHOUSE

(Founded 1965)
Box 830; Crossville, TN 38557; (931) 484-4324, FAX 484-6299
Jim Crabtree, *Producing Director*

Submission procedure: no unsolicited scripts; synopsis and letter of inquiry. **Types of material:** full-length plays, adaptations, plays for young audiences, musicals. **Special interests:** works for family audiences; works with southern or rural background; works about Tennessee history or culture. **Facilities:** Cumberland County Playhouse, 490 seats, proscenium stage; Theater-in-the-Woods, 200 seats, outdoor arena; Adventure Theater, 180-220 seats, flexible black box. **Best submission time:** Aug–Dec. **Response time:** 2 weeks letter (if interested); 6–12 months script.

DAD'S GARAGE THEATRE CO.

(Founded 1995)
280 Elizabeth St, Suite C101; Atlanta, GA 30307; (404) 523–3141,
 FAX 688–6644; email sean@dadsgarage.com;
 website www.dadsgarage.com
Sean Daniels, *Artistic Director*

Submission procedure: accepts unsolicited scripts. **Types of material:** full-length plays, translations, adaptations, musicals, solo pieces. **Special interests:** non-traditional plays, comedy. **Facilities** Dad's Garage, 160 seats, proscenium stage; Top Shelf, 40 seats, flexible stage. **Best submission time:** year-round. **Response time:** 3 months letter; 3 months script.

DALLAS CHILDREN'S THEATER

(Founded 1984)
2215 Cedar Springs; Dallas, TX 75201; website www.dct.org
Artie Olaisen, *Administrative Artist*

Submission procedure: no unsolicited scripts; synopsis, character/set breakdown and letter of inquiry. **Types of material:** full-length plays, adaptations, plays for young audiences. **Special interests:** works for family audiences; adaptations of classics; historical plays; socially relevant works. **Facilities:** El Centro Theater, 500 seats, proscenium stage; Crescent Theater, 180 seats, flexible stage. **Best submission time:** year-round. **Response time:** 3 months letter; 6 months script.

DALLAS THEATER CENTER

(Founded 1959)
3636 Turtle Creek Blvd; Dallas, TX 75219–5598; (214) 526–8210,
 FAX 521–7666
Elizabeth Stevens, *Literary Office*

Submission procedure: no unsolicited scripts; professional recommendation. **Types of material:** full-length plays, adaptations, translations, solo pieces. **Special interests:** plays that explore language or form; material relating to the African-American or Hispanic experience. **Facilities:** Arts District Theater, 530 seats, flexible stage; Kalita Humphreys Theater, 466 seats, thrust stage. **Best submission time:** year-round. **Response time:** 9–12 months.

DELAWARE THEATRE COMPANY

(Founded 1978)
200 Water St; Wilmington, DE 19801-5030; (302) 594-1104,
    FAX 594-1107
Fontaine Syer, *Artistic Director*

Submission procedure: no unsolicited scripts; synopsis and letter of inquiry from DE, MD and PA playwrights only. **Types of material:** full-length plays, translations, adaptations. **Facilities:** Delaware Theatre Company, 390 seats, thrust stage. **Production considerations:** cast limit of 10. **Best submission time:** Feb-May. **Response time:** 1 month letter; 3 months script.

THE DELL'ARTE COMPANY

(Founded 1971)
Box 816; Blue Lake, CA 95525; (707) 668-5663, FAX 668-5665;
    email dellarte@aol.com; website www.dellarte.com
Michael Fields, *Managing Artistic Director*

Submission procedure: no unsolicited scripts; synopsis and letter of inquiry. **Types of material:** full-length plays, adaptations. **Special interests:** physical theatre; new adaptations of classics; physical plays for young audiences. **Facilities:** Dell'Arte Players, 100 seats, flexible stage; 400 seats, outdoor amphitheatre. **Production considerations:** company of 3-4 actors; production demands adaptable to touring. **Best submission time:** Jan-Mar. **Response time:** 3 weeks letter; 6 weeks script.

DENVER CENTER THEATRE COMPANY

(Founded 1979)
1050 13th St; Denver, CO 80204; website www.denvercenter.org
Bruce K. Sevy, *Associate Artistic Director/New Play Development*

Submission procedure: no unsolicited scripts; write for guidelines with SASE for response or download from web. **Types of material:** full-length plays. **Special interests:** work not produced professionally. **Facilities:** The Stage, 642 seats, thrust stage; The Space, 450 seats, arena stage; The Ricketson, 250 seats, proscenium stage; The Source, 200 seats, thrust stage. **Best submission time:** year-round. **Response time:** 4-6 weeks letter; 4-6 months script. **Special programs:** Denver Center Theatre Company TheatreFest (see Development); Francesca Primus Prize (see Prizes).

DETROIT REPERTORY THEATRE

(Founded 1957)
13103 Woodrow Wilson Ave; Detroit, MI 48238; (313) 868–1347,
    FAX 868–1705; email DetRepTh@aol.com
Barbara Busby, *Literary Manager*

Submission procedure: accepts unsolicited scripts. **Types of material:** full-length plays. **Special interests:** issue-oriented plays. **Facilities:** Detroit Repertory Theatre, 194 seats, proscenium stage. **Production considerations:** prefers cast limit of 5–7. **Best submission time:** Sep–Feb. **Response time:** 3–6 months.

DOBAMA THEATRE

(Founded 1960)
1846 Coventry Rd; Cleveland Heights, OH 44118; (216) 932–6838,
    FAX 932–3259

Submission procedure: accepts unsolicited scripts from OH playwrights only; others send synopsis, sample pages and letter of inquiry. **Types of material:** full-length plays, solo pieces. **Special interests:** plays with opportunities for ethnically diverse casting; plays that make a statement about contemporary life. **Facilities:** Dobama Theatre, 200 seats, thrust stage. **Production considerations:** prefers cast limit of 9, limited production demands; no fly space. **Best submission time:** year-round. **Response time:** 9 months letter; 9–12 months script. **Special programs:** one world premiere: production of 1 new play included in mainstage season each year; preference given to members of Cleveland Play House Playwrights' Unit; Owen Kelly Adopt-a-Playwright Program: 2 full-length plays by OH residents each given developmental work with director, dramaturg and cast, culminating in readings; playwright must be available to participate; to apply, submit script to the attention of the program; *deadline:* 1 Feb 2002; *notification:* 15 May 2002; *dates:* Jun 2002. Marilyn Bianchi Kids' Playwriting Festival: annual short-play competition open to students attending Cuyahoga County schools, grades 1-12; winners receive savings bonds, publication and/or full production; write for application starting Sep 2001; *deadline:* Feb 2002; exact date TBA.

DORSET THEATRE FESTIVAL

(Founded 1976)
Box 510; Dorset, VT 05251-0510; (802) 867-2223, FAX 867-0144;
　　email theatre@sover.net; website www.theatredirectories.com
Jill Charles, *Artistic Director*

Submission procedure: no unsolicited scripts; synopsis, 10-page dialogue sample, character/set breakdown and letter of inquiry with SASP for response; include production history of readings in New York City–New England area if available. **Types of material:** full-length plays. **Special interests:** plays with broad commercial appeal. **Facilities:** Dorset Playhouse, 295 seats, proscenium stage. **Production considerations:** cast limit of 8, prefers 1 set or unit set. **Best submission time:** Sep-Dec. **Response time:** 3 months letter; 6-12 months script. **Special programs:** Dorset Colony for Writers (see Colonies).

DOUBLE EDGE THEATRE

(Founded 1982)
948 Conway Rd, Ashfield, MA 01330; (413) 628-0277,
　　FAX 628-0026; email DETfarm@aol.com
Carlos Uriona, *Associate Director*

Submission procedure: no unsolicited scripts; accepts video of original performance only. **Types of material:** solo pieces, performance art. **Special interests:** artists who create their own work. **Facilities:** DET Performance Space, 100 seats, flexible stage; DET Pavillion, 75 seats, flexible stage. **Best submission time:** year-round. **Response time:** 6 months. **Special programs:** Artists-in-Residence: 1-3-month program in which artists create original performance work at DET, housing and rehearsal space provided. Residency program, 2 days-2 weeks long, in which artists conduct necessary research.

DUDLEY RIGGS INSTANT THEATRE COMPANY

(Founded 1954)
1586 Burton St; St. Paul, MN 55108; (651) 647-6748, FAX 647-5637
Dudley Riggs, *Producing Director*

Submission procedure: accepts unsolicited scripts with synopsis and letter of inquiry; include cassette for musicals. **Types of material:** capsule musicals/songs, cabaret/revues, solo pieces. **Special interests:** prefers work with no previous mainstage productions, comedies, satiric comedies about contemporary issues such as intergenerational relationships, aging, retirement, loss and recovery. **Facilities:** Dudley Riggs Theatre, 260 seats, modified thrust stage. **Production considerations:** cast limit of 3-7. **Best submission time:** year-round. **Response time:** 8 months.

EAST WEST PLAYERS

(Founded 1965)
244 South San Pedro St, Suite 301; Los Angeles, CA 90012;
    (213) 625-7000, FAX 625-7111;
    email info@eastwestplayers.org; website eastwestplayers.org
Ken Narasaki, *Literary Manager*

Submission procedure: accepts unsolicited scripts with SASE for response. **Types of material:** full-length plays, translations, adaptations, plays for young audiences, musicals. **Special interests:** plays by or about Asian-Pacific-Americans. **Facilities:** The David Henry Hwang Theatre at Union Center for the Arts, 265 seats, proscenium stage. **Production considerations:** minimal production demands. **Best submission time:** year-round. **Response time:** 3-8 months. (See David Henry Hwang Writers Institute in Development.)

ECCENTRIC THEATRE COMPANY

(Founded 1992)
413 D St; Anchorage, AK 99501; (907) 274-2599, FAX 277-4698;
    email cyrano@ak.net; website www.cyrano.org
Sandy Harper, *Producer*

Submission procedure: no unsolicited scripts; professional recommendation. **Types of material:** full-length plays, one-acts, adaptations, solo pieces. **Facilities:** Cyrano's Off Center Playhouse, 86 seats, black box. **Best submission time:** year-round. **Response time:** 8 months.

EDYVEAN REPERTORY THEATRE

(Founded 1967)
Box 47509; Indianapolis, IN 46227-7509; (317) 788-2075,
    FAX 788-2079; email ert@indy.net; website www.edyvean.org
Frederick Marshall, *Administrative Director*

Submission procedure: no unsolicited scripts; synopsis and letter of inquiry. **Types of material:** full-length plays, musicals. **Facilities:** mainstage, 750 seats, proscenium stage. **Best submission time:** summer. **Response time:** 6 months letter; 9 months script.

EL CENTRO SU TEATRO

(Founded 1971)
4725 High St; Denver, CO 80216; (303) 296-0219, FAX 296-4614;
     email elcentro@suteatro.org; website www.suteatro.org
Tony Garcia, *Artistic Director*
Phil Luna, *Cultural Arts Director*

Submission procedure: accepts unsolicited scripts. **Types of material:** full-length plays, one-acts, translations, adaptations, plays for young audiences. **Special interests:** bilingual and/or Spanish language plays; plays dealing with the Chicano/Latino cultural and political experience. **Facilities:** mainstage, 107 seats, black box. **Production considerations:** cast limit of 6-8; minimal production requirements. **Best submission time:** year-round. **Response time:** 4 months.

EL PORTAL CENTER FOR THE ARTS

(Founded 1971)
El Portal Center for the Arts; 5269 Lankershim Blvd;
     North Hollywood, CA 91601; (818) 508-4234, FAX 508-5113;
Jim Brochu, *Artistic Director*

Submission procedure: no unsolicited scripts; agent submission. **Types of material:** full-length plays, translations, adaptations, plays for young audiences. **Special interests:** works by southern CA-based writers. **Facilities:** Pavilion, 350 seats, proscenium/thrust stage; Circle Forum, 99 seats, flexible stage; Store Front Theatre, 42 seats, proscenium stage. **Production considerations:** small cast for Store Front. **Best submission time:** Nov. **Response time:** 12 months. **Special programs:** year-round reading series.

THE EMELIN THEATRE FOR THE PERFORMING ARTS

(Founded 1973)
Library Lane; Mamaroneck, NY 10543; (914) 698-3045,
     FAX 698-1404; email emelin98@aol.com;
     website www.emelin.org
John Raymond, *Managing Director*

Submission procedure: accepts unsolicited scripts with professional recommendation only; include video for solo pieces. **Types of material:** full-length plays, chamber musicals, cabaret/revues, solo pieces. **Facilities:** The Emelin Theatre, 280 seats, proscenium stage. **Production considerations:** small cast; no fly space. **Best submission time:** year-round. **Response time:** 2 months.

THE EMPTY SPACE THEATRE

(Founded 1970)
3509 Fremont Ave N; Seattle, WA 98103–8813; (206) 547–7633,
    FAX 547–7635; website emptyspace.org
Allison Narver, *Artistic Director*
Adam Greenfield, *Literary Manager*

Submission procedure: accepts unsolicited scripts with SASE for response from Puget Sound region playwrights only; others send synopsis, 10-page dialogue sample and letter of inquiry with SASP for response. **Types of material:** full-length plays, translations, adaptations, musicals, solo pieces. **Special interests:** "plays unique to the event of live theatre." **Facilities:** The Empty Space Theatre at the Fremont Palace, 150 seats, endstage. **Production considerations:** prefers small casts. **Best submission time:** year-round. **Response time:** 2-4 months. **Special programs:** Play Readings: reading series dedicated to unproduced work by Northwest writers. Plays selected through theatre's regular submission procedure.

ENSEMBLE STUDIO THEATRE

(Founded 1972)
549 West 52nd St; New York, NY 10019; (212) 247–4982,
    FAX 664–0041; website www.ensemblestudiotheatre.org
Jamie Richards, *Executive Producer*

Submission procedure: accepts unsolicited scripts. **Types of material:** full-length plays, one-acts. **Facilities:** Mainstage, 99 seats, black box; Studio, 60 seats, proscenium stage. **Best submission time:** year-round. **Response time:** 6 months. **Special programs:** summer reading series and playwriting workshops. First Look: reading series of full-length plays. Going to the River: annual festival and ongoing monthly reading series celebrating African-American women playwrights. First Light: festival of new works exploring the worlds of science and technology; write or call for guidelines; *deadline:* 19 Oct 2001; *dates:* Apr 2002. Annual Marathon of One-Act Plays: one-act play festival; *deadline:* 1 Dec 2001; *dates:* May-Jun 2002.

THE ENSEMBLE THEATRE

(Founded 1977)
3535 Main St; Houston, TX 77002–9529; (713) 520–0055,
    FAX 520–1269
Marsha Jackson Randolph, *Producing Artistic Director*

Submission procedure: accepts unsolicited scripts with professional recommendation and SASE for young audiences only; synopsis, dialogue sample, resume and letter of inquiry with SASE for all others; include cassette or CD for musicals. **Types of material:** full-length plays, adaptations, plays for young audiences, musicals. **Special interests:** plays portraying African or African-American experience; imaginative plays performed by and/or for young audiences; plays suitable for touring by small ensemble; contemporary plays or adaptations. **Facilities:** Performance Stage, 400 seats; Hawkins Stage, 199 seats, proscenium stage; Lawson Arena Stage, 80 seats, black box. **Production considerations:** cast limit of 7, no more than 2 sets; limited wing space. **Best submission time:** Jan. **Response time:** 5 months script. **Special programs:** George Hawkins Playwrighting Contest (see Prizes).

ENSEMBLE THEATRE COMPANY

(Founded 1979)
Box 2307; Santa Barbara, CA 93120; (805) 965–6252,
    FAX 965–5322; email production@ensembletheatre.com;
    website www.ensembletheatre.com
Shawn Wilson, *Assistant to Artistic Director*

Submission procedure: no unsolicited scripts; synopsis and letter of inquiry from playwright; professional recommendation and agent submission. **Types of material:** full-length plays, one-acts, translations, adaptations, plays for young audiences. **Facilities:** Alhecama Theatre, 140 seats, proscenium/thrust stage. **Production considerations:** cast limit of 2–8; unit set. **Best submission time:** Dec-Feb. **Response time:** 1 month letter; 6 weeks script. **Special programs:** Story Book Theatre: 2 plays for elementary school age audiences presented in fall and spring. Starting Point Series: New Plays given 1 week readings each spring.

ENSEMBLE THEATRE OF CINCINNATI

(Founded 1986)
1127 Vine St; Cincinnati, OH 45210–1926; (513) 421–3555,
   FAX 562–4104
D. Lynn Meyers, *Producing Artistic Director*

Submission procedure: no unsolicited scripts; synopsis, dialogue sample, resume and letter of inquiry. **Types of material:** full-length plays, adaptations, plays for young audiences. **Facilities:** Ensemble Theatre of Cincinnati, 202 seats, thrust stage. **Production considerations:** cast limit of 6, simple set. **Best submission time:** Sep. **Response time:** 1 month letter; 4 months script.

ESSENTIAL THEATRE

(Founded 1987)
995 Greenwood Ave, #6; Atlanta, GA 30306; (404) 876–8471
Peter Hardy, *Producing Artistic Director*

Submission procedure: accepts unsolicited scripts. **Types of material:** full-length plays. **Special interests:** work not produced professionally; will also consider second or third production. **Facilities:** no permanent facility. **Best submission time:** spring. **Response time:** 6 months.

EUREKA THEATRE COMPANY

(Founded 1972)
215 Jackson St; San Francisco, CA 94111; (415) 788–7469;
   website www.eurekatheatre.org
Dawson Moore, *Literary Manager*

Submission procedure: no unsolicited scripts; 5–10-page dialogue sample, character list and letter of inquiry. **Types of material:** full-length plays, translations, solo pieces. **Special interests:** dynamic contemporary plays; unconventional comedies. **Facilities:** mainstage, 200 seats, proscenium stage. **Best submission time:** year-round. **Response time:** 2 months letter; 6 months script. **Special programs:** Discovery Series: monthly readings of new plays presented for the public and followed by audience discussion.

EXPRESS CHILDREN'S THEATRE

(Founded 1991)
Box 980817; Houston, TX 77098; (713) 759-1314, FAX 802-9908;
    email expresstheatre@EVI.net; website www.expresstheatre.com
Marianne Pendino, *Artistic Director*

Submission procedure: no unsolicited scripts; synopsis and letter of inquiry. **Types of material:** plays for young audiences. **Special interests:** 40 minute plays; multicultural plays; bilingual plays. **Facilities:** no permanent facility; touring company. **Production considerations:** cast limit of 3-4, portable minimal set. **Best submission time:** year-round. **Response time:** 2 weeks letter; 4-8 weeks script. **Special programs:** commissioning program; after-school education program.

EYE OF THE STORM THEATRE

(Founded 1991)
3754 Pleasant Ave S, Suite 2; Minneapolis, MN 55409;
    (612) 728-5859, FAX 722-7315; email eyeotstorm@aol.com
Larissa Kokernot, *Artistic Associate*

Submission procedure: no unsolicited scripts; synopsis, dialogue sample, resume and letter of inquiry from playwright; professional recommendation and agent submission. **Types of material:** full-length plays, adaptations, musicals. **Special interests:** women writers, new plays (written in the past 10 years), social and political themes. **Facilities:** Minneapolis Theatre Garage, 140 seats, flexible stage. **Best submission time:** year-round. **Response time:** 2 months letter; 4-6 months script. **Special programs:** Seed the Storm Festival: annual festival of commissioned "starts" of new plays fully produced in Mar or Apr.

FAMOUS DOOR THEATRE

(Founded 1987)
Box 57029, Chicago, IL 60657; (773) 404-8283, FAX 404-8292;
    email theatre@famousdoortheatre.org;
    website www.famousdoortheatre.org
Karen Kessler, *Artistic Director*

Submission procedure: no unsolicited scripts; synopsis, 10-15 page dialogue sample, resume and letter of inquiry. **Types of material:** full-length plays, translations, adaptations. **Facilities:** Theatre Building North Theatre, 150 seats, thrust stage. **Best submission time:** Nov-Mar. **Response time:** 1

month letter; 3 months script. **Special programs:** 9th Annual Women at the Door Staged Reading Series (see Development).

FIRST STAGE CHILDREN'S THEATER

(Formerly First Stage Milwaukee)
(Founded 1987)
929 North Water St; Milwaukee, WI 53202; (414) 273-2314,
    FAX 273-5595; email goodman@firststage.org;
    website www.firststage.org
Rob Goodman, *Producer/Artistic Director*

Submission procedure: no unsolicited scripts; synopsis, resume and letter of inquiry. **Types of material:** works for young audiences, including translations, adaptations and musicals. **Facilities:** Marcus Center for the Performing Arts's Todd Wehr Theater, 500 seats, thrust stage. **Best submission time:** spring-summer. **Response time:** 1 month letter; 3 months script.

FLEETWOOD STAGE

(Founded 1993)
44 Wildcliff Dr; New Rochelle, NY 10805; (914) 654-8533,
    FAX 235-4459
Lewis Arlt, *Producing Director*

Submission procedure: accepts unsolicited scripts; prefers professional recommendation. **Types of material:** full-length plays. **Facilities:** Fleetwood Stage, 100 seats, flexible stage. **Production considerations:** cast limit of 8, prefers unit set. **Best submission time:** year-round. **Response time:** 6-9 months. **Special programs:** Platform Series: developmental workshop of works in progress for affiliated artists; staged readings.

FLORIDA STAGE

(Founded 1987)
262 South Ocean Blvd; Manalapan, FL 33462; (561) 585-3404,
    FAX 588-4708; email info@floridastage.org;
    website www.floridastage.org
Louis Tyrrell, *Producing Director*

Submission procedure: no unsolicited scripts; agent submission. **Types of material:** full-length plays, plays for young audiences. **Special interests:** contemporary issues and ideas. **Facilities:** Florida Stage, 250 seats, thrust stage. **Production considerations:** cast limit of 2-6, 1 set. **Best submission**

time: year-round. **Response time:** 3-4 months. **Special programs:** reading series.

FLORIDA STUDIO THEATRE

(Founded 1973)
1241 North Palm Ave; Sarasota, FL 34236; (941) 366-9017
James Ashford, *Casting & Literary Coordinator*

Submission procedure: no unsolicited scripts; synopsis and letter of inquiry with SASE for response. **Types of material:** full-length plays, translations, adaptations, musicals, cabaret/revues, solo pieces. **Facilities:** Florida Studio Theatre, 173 seats, semi-thrust stage; FST Cabaret Club, 100 seats, cabaret space. **Best submission time:** Aug-Apr. **Response time:** 1-2 weeks letter; 6 months script. **Special programs:** Sarasota Festival of New Plays: 4-tier festival includes Young Playwrights Festival: workshop productions of plays by playwrights grades 2-12; *deadline:* 1 Apr 2002; *dates:* May 2002. Burdick New Play Festival: workshop productions of 3 new plays; playwright receives stipend, travel, housing; scripts selected through theatre's normal submission procedure; *dates:* May 2002. New Play Summer Fest: workshop productions of 3 new plays; playwright receives stipend, travel, housing; scripts selected through theatre's normal submission procedure; *dates:* Jul-Aug 2002. Fall staged reading series. Florida Shorts Contest (see Prizes).

THE FOOTHILL THEATRE COMPANY

(Founded 1977)
Box 1812; Nevada City, CA 95959; (530) 265-9320, FAX 265-9325;
    email ftc@foothilltheatre.org
Gary Wright, *Literary Manager*

Submission procedure: accepts unsolicited scripts; letters of inquiry. **Types of material:** full-length plays, one-acts, translations, adaptations, plays for young audiences, solo pieces. **Facilities:** The Nevada Theatre, 246 seats, proscenium stage; also rents small spaces with 50-100 seats. **Production considerations:** very limited fly and wing space. **Best submission time:** year-round. **Response time:** 6-12 months. **Special programs:** New Voices of the Wild West: annual fall reading series of 4 plays dealing with issues pertaining to rural American West; *deadline:* 1 May 2002.

FORD'S THEATRE

(Founded 1968)
511 Tenth St NW; Washington, DC 20004; (202) 638-2941,
    FAX 737-3017
Brian J. Laczko, *Managing Director*

Submission procedure: no unsolicited scripts; synopsis, sample pages and letter of inquiry. **Types of material:** full-length plays, musicals. **Special interests:** small-scale musicals and works celebrating the African-American experience. **Facilities:** Ford's Theatre, 699 seats, proscenium/thrust stage. **Production considerations:** cast limit of 15. **Best submission time:** spring-summer. **Response time:** 3 months letter; 6-12 months script.

THE FOUNTAIN THEATRE

(Founded 1990)
5060 Fountain Ave; Los Angeles, CA 90029; (323) 663-2235,
    FAX 663-1629
Simon Levy, *Producing Director/Dramaturg*

Submission procedure: no unsolicited scripts; synopsis and letter of inquiry. **Types of material:** full-length plays, translations, adaptations. **Special interests:** lyrical dramas; contemporary comedies; works with dance; adaptations of American literature. **Facilities:** Fountain Theatre Mainstage, 78 seats, thrust stage. **Production considerations:** cast limit of 12, 1 set; no fly space, low ceiling. **Best submission time:** year-round. **Response time:** 3 months letter; 6 months script.

FREEDOM REPERTORY THEATRE

(Founded 1966)
1346 North Broad St; Philadelphia, PA 19121; (215) 765-2793,
    FAX 765-4191; website www.freedomtheatre.org
Barbara Silzle, *Director of Artistic Initiatives*

Submission procedure: no unsolicited scripts; synopsis, 5-10-page dialogue sample, character breakdown, resume and letter of inquiry. **Types of material:** full-length plays, musicals, cabaret/revues. **Special interests:** contemporary plays with African-American themes. **Facilities:** John E. Allen Theatre, 299 seats, proscenium stage; Freedom Cabaret Theatre, 120 seats, flexible stage. **Best submission time:** year-round. **Response time:** 6-12 weeks. **Special programs:** Freedom Fest: play reading series; resident playwright program; commissioning program; all programs are by invitation only.

FREE STREET PROGRAMS

(Founded 1969)
1419 West Blackhawk St; Chicago, IL 60622; (773) 772-7248,
    FAX 772-7248; email gogogo@freestreet.org
Ron Bieganski, *Artistic Director*
David Schein, *Executive Director*

Submission procedure: no unsolicited scripts; letter from writer with "a concept for the creation of a new performance with youth"; prefers email inquiries. **Types of material:** work developed by company. **Special interests:** "creating with youth to enhance literacy and experiment with play structure, content and shape." **Facilities:** national/international touring company of youth (Teen Street). **Production considerations:** limited technical support, youth production crew. **Best submission time:** year-round. **Response time:** 1 week. **Special programs:** PANG (Performing Arts for a New Generation): producing company of youth curates fringe, edgy performances; performers and music groups send letter of inquiry to PANG.

FREMONT CENTRE THEATRE

(Founded 1997)
1000 Fremont Ave; South Pasadena, CA 91030; (626) 441-5977,
    FAX 296-6921; email kathrynpaul@earthlink.net;
    website www.fremontcentretheatre.com
Paul Anderson, *Contest Manager*

Submission procedure: accepts unsolicited scripts. **Types of material:** full-length plays, plays for young audiences. **Special interests:** unpublished and unproduced American plays, 1- or 2-person plays based on historical events or people. **Facilities:** Fremont Centre Theatre, 99 seats, black box. **Production considerations:** cast limit of 10. **Best submission time:** year-round. **Response time:** 4 months. **Special programs:** Fremont Centre Theatre New-Playwright Contest (see Prizes).

FRONTERA @ HYDE PARK THEATRE

(Founded 1992)
511 West 43rd St; Austin, TX 78751; (512) 479-7530,
    FAX 479-7531
Vicky Boone, *Artistic Director*

Submission procedure: no unsolicited scripts; synopsis and letter of inquiry. **Types of material:** full-length plays, translations, adaptations, musicals, solo pieces. **Facilities:** Hyde Park Theatre, 90 seats, flexible. **Best submission time:** year-round. **Response time:** 3 months letter; 6 months script.

FULTON OPERA HOUSE/ACTOR'S COMPANY OF PENNSYLVANIA

(Founded 1963)
Box 1865; Lancaster, PA 17608-1865; (717) 394-7133,
    FAX 397-3780; email artdir@fultontheatre.org;
    website www.fultontheatre.org
Michael Mitchell, *Artistic Director*

Submission procedure: no unsolicited scripts; synopsis and letter of inquiry. **Types of material:** full-length plays, adaptations. **Special interests:** mainstream works on contemporary issues; plays that embrace diversity. **Facilities:** Fulton Opera House, 630 seats, proscenium stage; Studio Theatre, 100 seats, black box. **Production considerations:** cast limit of 10. **Best submission time:** fall. **Response time:** 3-6 months letter; 6 months script.

GALA HISPANIC THEATRE

(Founded 1976)
Box 43209; Washington, DC 20010; (202) 234-7174,
    FAX 332-1247; email galadc@aol.com; website www.galadc.org
Hugo J. Medrano, *Producing/Artistic Director*

Submission procedure: no unsolicited scripts; synopsis/description of play and letter of inquiry. **Types of material:** full-length plays, solo pieces. **Special interests:** plays by Spanish, Latino or Hispanic-American writers in Spanish or English only; prefers Spanish-language works with accompanying English translation; works that reflect sociocultural realities of Hispanics in Latin America, the Caribbean or Spain, as well as the Hispanic-American experience. **Facilities:** GALA Hispanic Theatre, 200 seats, proscenium stage. **Production considerations:** cast limit of 6-8. **Best submission time:** Apr-May. **Response time:** 1 month letter; 12 months script. **Special programs:** poetry onstage.

GEFFEN PLAYHOUSE

(Founded 1995)
10886 LeConte Ave; Los Angeles, CA 90024; (310) 208-6500,
    FAX 208-0341
Amy Levinson, *Literary Manager*

Submission procedure: no unsolicited scripts; synopsis, dialogue sample and letter of inquiry. **Types of material:** full-length plays, adaptations, musicals. **Facilities:** Geffen Playhouse, 498 seats, proscenium stage. **Best submission time:** year-round. **Response time:** 6 weeks letter; 6 months script.

GEORGE STREET PLAYHOUSE

(Founded 1974)
9 Livingston Ave; New Brunswick, NJ 08901–1903; (732) 846–2895,
    FAX 247–9151; website www.georgestplayhouse.org
George Ryan, *Literary Manager*

Submission procedure: no unsolicited scripts; synopsis, 10-page dialogue sample, character breakdown and letter of inquiry. **Types of material:** full-length plays, one-acts. **Special interests:** social issue one-acts suitable for touring to schools (not seeking any other kind of one-acts); comedies and dramas that present a fresh perspective on our society; "work that tells a compelling, personal, human story while entertaining, challenging and stretching the imagination." **Facilities:** mainstage, 367 seats, proscenium/thrust stage. **Production considerations:** prefers cast limit of 7. **Best submission time:** year-round. **Response time:** 8-10 months. **Special programs:** Next Stage Festival: workshops of 1-3 new plays. The Diva & Gentle Man Projects: presentation of new material written and performed by 8 solo artists.

GEORGIA REPERTORY THEATRE

(Founded 1990)
Department of Drama, University of Georgia;
    Athens, GA 30602–3154; (706) 542–2836, FAX 542–2080;
    email longman@arches.uga.edu
Stanley V. Longman, *Dramaturg*

Submission procedure: no unsolicited scripts; letter of inquiry. **Types of material:** full-length plays. **Special interests:** plays not produced professionally. **Facilities:** Fine Arts Theatre, 750 seats, proscenium stage; Cellar Theatre, 100 seats, proscenium stage; Seney Stovall Theatre, 250 seats, proscenium stage. **Production considerations:** cast limit of 10, minimal set. **Best submission time:** Aug-Mar only. **Response time:** 3-6 months.

GERMINAL STAGE DENVER

(Founded 1974)
2450 West 44th Ave; Denver, CO 80211; (303) 455-7108;
    email gsden@privatei.com; website www.germinalstage.com
Ed Baierlein, *Director/Manager*

Submission procedure: no unsolicited scripts; synopsis, 5-page dialogue sample and letter of inquiry with SASP for response. **Types of material:** full-length plays, translations, adaptations. **Special interests:** adaptations that use both dialogue and narration. **Facilities:** Germinal Stage Denver, 100 seats, thrust stage. **Production considerations:** cast limit of 10; minimal production requirements. **Best submission time:** year-round. **Response time:** 2 weeks letter; 6 months script.

GEVA THEATRE

(Founded 1972)
75 Woodbury Blvd; Rochester, NY 14607-1717; (716) 232-1366
Jean Ryon, *New Plays Coordinator*

Submission procedure: no unsolicited scripts; synopsis, dialogue sample, production history, resume and letter of inquiry. **Types of material:** full-length plays, translations, adaptations. **Facilities:** Elaine P. Wilson Theatre, 552 seats, modified thrust stage; Ronald and Donna Fielding Nextstage, 180 seats, modified proscenium. **Best submission time:** year-round. **Response time:** 1 month letter; 6 months script. **Special programs:** American Voices New Play Reading Series; Hibernatus Interruptus, A Winter Festival of New Plays: 2-week workshops of 3 plays; Regional Playwrights and Young Writers Festival.

THE GLINES

(Founded 1976)
240 West 44th St; New York, NY 10036; (212) 354-8899

Submission procedure: accepts unsolicited scripts with SASE for response. **Types of material:** full-length plays. **Special interests:** plays dealing with gay experience only; plays not previously produced in New York City. **Facilities:** no permanent facility. **Best submission time:** year-round. **Response time:** 2 months.

THE GLOBE THEATRES

(Founded 1935)
Box 2171; San Diego, CA92112-2171; (619) 231-1941
Raúl Moncada, *Literary Associate*

Submission procedure: no unsolicited scripts; synopsis and letter of inquiry with SASE for response. **Types of material:** full-length plays, translations, adaptations. **Special interests:** well-crafted, strongly theatrical material. **Facilities:** Lowell Davies Festival Stage, 620 seats, outdoor stage; Old Globe Theatre, 581 seats, modified thrust stage; Cassius Carter Centre Stage, 225 seats, arena stage. **Production considerations:** prefers cast limit of 8. **Best submission time:** year-round. **Response time:** 2-3 months letter; 6-10 months script.

GOODMAN THEATRE

(Founded 1925)
170 North Dearborn St; Chicago, IL 60601; (312) 443-3811,
    FAX 443-5579; email susanbooth@goodman-theatre.org
Susan V. Booth, *Director of New Play Development*

Submission procedure: no unsolicited scripts; synopsis, professional recommendation and letter of inquiry. **Types of material:** full-length plays, translations, musicals. **Special interests:** social or political themes. **Facilities:** Albert Ivar Goodman Theatre, 830 seats, proscenium stage; Owen Bruner Goodman Theatre, 200-400 seats, flexible stage. **Best submission time:** year-round. **Response time:** 2-3 months letter; 6-8 months script.

GOODSPEED MUSICALS

(Formerly Goodspeed Opera House)
(Founded 1963)
Box A; East Haddam, CT 06423; (860) 873-8664, FAX 873-2329;
    email info@goodspeed.org; website www.goodspeed.org
Lawrence Thelen

Submission procedure: no unsolicited scripts; synopsis, cassette or CD and letter of inquiry. **Types of material:** original musicals only. **Facilities:** Goodspeed Opera House, 400 seats, proscenium stage; The Norma Terris Theatre, 200 seats, proscenium stage. **Best submission time:** Jan-Feb. **Response time:** 6-8 months letter; 6-8 months script.

GORILLA THEATRE, THE

(Founded 1990)
4419 North Manhattan Ave; Tampa, FL 33614; (813) 354-0550,
FAX 354-9274; email info@gorillatheatre.com;
website www.gorilla-theatre.com
Steve Mountan, *Managing Director*

Submission procedure: accepts unsolicited scripts. **Types of material:** full-length plays, one-acts, translations, adaptations, plays for young audiences, musicals. **Special interests:** social themes; the environment; Florida. **Facilities:** Gorilla Theatre, 80 seats, thrust stage. **Production considerations:** cast limit of 10, single or unit set. **Best submission time:** year-round. **Response time:** 3 months.

GREAT LAKES THEATER FESTIVAL

(Founded 1961)
1501 Euclid Ave, Suite 423; Cleveland, OH 44115; (216) 241-5490,
FAX 241-6315; website www.greatlakestheater.org
James Bundy, *Artistic Director*

Submission procedure: no unsolicited scripts; professional recommendation or agent submission only. **Types of material:** full-length plays, translations, adaptations. **Special interests:** translations and adaptations of classic plays, new works with specific relevance to the classic repertoire. **Facilities:** Ohio Theatre, 1000 seats, proscenium stage. **Best submission time:** year-round. **Response time:** 3 months.

THE GUTHRIE THEATER

(Founded 1963)
725 Vineland Place; Minneapolis, MN 55403; (612) 347-1185,
FAX 347-1188; email joh@guthrietheater.org
Literary Department

Submission procedure: no unsolicited scripts; professional recommendation with SASE for response. **Types of material:** full-length plays, translations, adaptations. **Special interests:** well-crafted, highly theatrical works of depth and significance; richly poetic language dealing with universal themes in today's context; adaptations of classic literature; no sitcoms. **Facilities:** Guthrie Theater, 1309 seats, thrust stage; Guthrie Lab, 350 seats, flexible stage. **Best submission time:** year-round. **Response time:** 3-4 months.

HANGAR THEATRE

(Founded 1964)
Box 205; Ithaca, NY 14851; (607) 273-8588, FAX 273-4516;
    website www.hangartheatre.org
Jamie Grady, *Managing Director*

Submission procedure: no unsolicited scripts; synopsis, first 10 pages of dialogue; agent submission. **Types of material:** full-length plays, one-acts, musicals. **Facilities:** Mainstage, 377 seats, thrust stage. **Best submission time:** Sep-Dec. **Response time:** 3 months. **Special programs:** commissioning program for plays for young audiences and one-acts. Developmental readings and workshops. Annual New Play Festival in Jul.

THE HARBOR THEATRE

(Founded 1998)
160 West 71st St, PHA; New York, NY 10023; (212) 787-1945
Stuart Warmflash, *Artistic Director*

Submission procedure: no unsolicited scripts; synopsis and letter of inquiry. **Types of material:** full-length plays, musicals. **Facilities:** no permanent facility. **Production considerations:** all productions developed in the workshop (see below). **Best submission time:** year-round. **Response time:** 2 weeks letter; 3 months script. **Special programs:** The Harbor Theatre Workshop (see Membership and Service Organizations).

HEDGEROW THEATRE

(Founded 1923)
146 West Rose Valley Rd; Wallingford, PA 19086; (610) 565-4211;
    website www.hedgerowtheatre.org
Walt Vail, *Literary Manager*

Submission procedure: no unsolicited scripts; synopsis and letter of inquiry. **Types of material:** full-length plays. **Special interests:** new plays by DE, NJ and PA playwrights; mysteries; comedies. **Facilities:** mainstage, 144 seats, proscenium stage. **Production considerations:** minimal production demands; small stage. **Best submission time:** year-round. **Response time:** 2 months letter; 4 months script.

THE HENLOPEN THEATRE PROJECT

(Founded 1987)
Box 606; Rehoboth Beach, DE 19971; (302) 226-4103,
FAX 226-4104; email stars@ce.net;
website www.henlopentheatreproject.com
James FitzSimmons, *Executive Director*

Submission procedure: no unsolicited scripts; dialogue sample and letter of inquiry. **Types of material:** full-length plays, one-acts, adaptations, plays for young audiences, musicals, cabaret/revues, solo pieces. **Special interests:** Hispanic playwrights encouraged. **Facilities:** Little Theatre, 250 seats, proscenium stage. **Production considerations:** cast limit of 6, minimal technical demands. **Best submission time:** Sep. **Response time:** 2 months letter; 3 months script.

HIDDEN THEATRE

(Founded 1994)
2301 Franklin Ave E; Minneapolis, MN 55406; (612) 822-6060;
website www.hiddentheatre.org
David Pisa, *Audience Services Manager*

Submission procedure: no unsolicited scripts; synopsis, 10-page dialogue sample, bio and letter of inquiry. **Types of material:** full-length plays, translations, adaptations. **Special interests:** theatrically inventive new material that asks challenging questions suitable for core ensemble 20-30 years old. **Facilities:** no permanent facility. **Best submission time:** year-round. **Response time:** 6-10 weeks letter; 6-10 months script.

HIP POCKET THEATRE

(Founded 1977)
Box 136758; Fort Worth, TX 76136; (817) 246-9775,
FAX 246-5651; email mdmolemo@aol.com;
website hippocket.org
Johnny Simons, *Artistic Director*

Submission procedure: no unsolicited scripts; synopsis and dialogue sample; include cassette for musicals. **Types of material:** full-length plays, translations, adaptations, plays for young audiences, musicals, solo pieces, multimedia works. **Special interests:** well-crafted stories with poetic, mythic slant that incorporate ritual and ensemble; works utilizing masks, puppetry, music, dance, mime and strong visual elements. **Facilities:** Oak Acres Amphitheatre, 175 seats, outdoor amphitheatre. **Production**

considerations: simple sets. **Best submission time:** Oct-Feb. **Response time:** 6 weeks.

THE HIPPODROME STATE THEATRE

(Founded 1973)
25 Southeast Second Place; Gainesville, FL 32601-6596;
    (352) 373-5968, FAX 371-9130; website hipp.gator.net
Tamerin Dygert, *Dramaturg*

Submission procedure: no unsolicited scripts; professional recommendation. **Types of material:** full-length plays, one-acts. **Special interests:** multicultural plays. **Facilities:** Mainstage Theatre, 266 seats, thrust stage; Second Stage, 87 seats, flexible stage. **Production considerations:** cast limit of 6, unit set. **Best submission time:** May-Aug. **Response time:** 1-2 months letter; 3-5 months script. **Special programs:** informal play reading series: possibility of production on the second stage or in site-specific gallery and bar spaces; scripts selected through theatre's normal submission procedure.

HONOLULU THEATRE FOR YOUTH

(Founded 1955)
2846 Ualena St; Honolulu, HI 96819-1910; (808) 839-9885,
    FAX 839-7018; email mark@htyweb.org; website htyweb.org
Mark Lutwak, *Artistic Director*

Submission procedure: no unsolicited scripts; synopsis, resume and letter of inquiry. **Types of material:** plays for young audiences. **Special interests:** plays with contemporary themes for audiences from pre-school through high school; small-cast adaptations of classics; new works based on Pacific Rim cultures; plays with compelling language that are imaginative and socially relevant. **Facilities:** Richardson Theatre, 800 seats, proscenium stage; Leeward Community College Theatre, 650 seats, proscenium stage; McCoy Pavilion, 300 seats, flexible stage; Tenney Theatre, 300 seats, flexible stage; shows also tour to school theatres, gymnasiums and cafeterias. **Production considerations:** cast limit of 6. **Best submission time:** year-round. **Response time:** 1 month letter; 4-5 months script.

HORIZON THEATRE COMPANY

(Founded 1983)
Box 5376; Atlanta, GA 31107; (404) 523-1477, FAX 584-8815;
  email horizonco@mindspring.com;
  website www.horizontheatre.com.
Stephanie Harvey, *Literary Manager*

Submission procedure: no unsolicited scripts except for Festival (see below); synopsis, resume and letter of inquiry. **Types of material:** full-length plays, translations, adaptations, musicals. **Special interests:** contemporary issues; plays by women; southern urban themes; comedies. **Facilities:** Horizon Theatre, 170-200 seats, flexible stage. **Production considerations:** plays cast from ensemble of up to 12 actors. **Best submission time:** year-round. **Response time:** 6 months letter; 12 months script. **Special programs:** Teen Ensemble: one-acts about teen issues to be performed by teens. Senior Citizens Ensemble: one-acts about senior citizen issues to be performed by senior citizens. New South for the New Century Festival: annual festival of readings, workshops and full productions of plays by playwrights speaking from, for and about the South; *deadline:* 15 Mar 2002; *notification:* 1 May 2002; *dates:* Jun-Jul 2002.

HORSE CAVE THEATRE

(Founded 1977)
Box 215; Horse Cave, KY 42749; (270) 786-1200, FAX 786-5298;
  email hctstaff@scrtc.com; website www.horsecavetheatre.org
Warren Hammack, *Artistic Director*

Submission procedure: no unsolicited scripts; professional recommendation. **Types of material:** full-length plays. **Special interests:** KY-based plays by KY playwrights. **Facilities:** Horse Cave Theatre, 346 seats, thrust stage. **Production considerations:** cast limit of 10, 1 set. **Best submission time:** Oct-Apr. **Response time:** varies.

HUDSON THEATRE

(Founded 1991)
6539 Santa Monica Blvd; Hollywood, CA 90038; (323) 856-4252,
  FAX 856-4316
Elizabeth Reilly, *Artistic Director*

Submission procedure: no unsolicited scripts; synopsis and letter of inquiry. **Types of material:** full-length plays, one-acts, musicals, solo pieces. **Facilities:** mainstage, 99 seats, modified thrust stage; Avenue Theatre, 99 seats, runway; Guild Theatre, 43 seats, proscenium stage. **Best submission time:** year-round. **Response time:** 3-6 months letter; 1 year script.

THE HUMAN RACE THEATRE COMPANY

(Founded 1986)
126 North Main St, Suite 300; Dayton, OH 45402-1710;
  (937) 461-3823, FAX 461-7223; email hrtheatre@aol.com;
  website www.humanracetheatre.org
Tony Dallas, *Playwright in Residence*

Submission procedure: no unsolicited scripts; professional recommendation. **Types of material:** full-length plays, one-acts, adaptations, plays for young audiences. **Special interests:** OH playwrights; adaptations and original works for junior and senior high school audiences; contemporary issues. **Facilities:** The Loft, 219 seats, thrust stage. **Production considerations:** small cast, plays for young audiences tour to schools; no fly space. **Best submission time:** Dec-Feb. **Response time:** 6 months.

HUNTINGTON THEATRE COMPANY

(Founded 1981)
264 Huntington Ave; Boston MA 02115-4606; (617) 266-7900,
  FAX 353-8300; website www.huntingtontheatre.org
Christopher Wigle, *Associate Artistic Director*

Submission procedure: no unsolicited scripts; agent submission only. **Types of material:** full-length plays, translations, adaptations. **Facilities:** Huntington Theatre, 850 seats, proscenium stage. **Best submission time:** year-round. **Response time:** 6 months.

HYPOTHETICAL THEATRE CO., INC.

(Founded 1992)
344 East 14th St; New York, NY 10003; (212) 780-0800, ext 254,
  FAX 780-0859; email hypothetical@bigfoot.com
Literary Manager

Submission procedure: no unsolicited scripts; synopsis, 10-page dialogue sample, character breakdown with SASE for response. **Types of material:** full-length plays, one-acts. **Special interests:** contemporary, ground-breaking plays. **Facilities:** Hypothetical Theatre, 99 seats, proscenium stage. **Best submission time:** year-round. **Response time:** 2 months letter; 6

months script. **Special programs:** Hypothetically Speaking: annual festival for 10-30-minute plays; send complete script for festival.

ILLINOIS THEATRE CENTER

(Founded 1976)
Box 397; Park Forest, IL 60466; (708) 481-3510, FAX 481-3693;
    email ilthctr@bigplanet.com; website www.ilthctr.org
Etel Billig, *Producing Director*

Submission procedure: no unsolicited scripts; synopsis and letter of inquiry with SASE for response. **Types of material:** full-length plays, musicals. **Facilities:** Illinois Theatre Center, 180 seats, proscenium/thrust stage. **Production considerations:** cast limit of 9 for plays, 14 for musicals. **Best submission time:** year-round. **Response time:** 1 month letter; 2 months script.

ILLUSION THEATER

(Founded 1974)
528 Hennepin Ave, Suite 704; Minneapolis, MN 55403;
    (612) 339-4944, FAX 337-8042; email info@illusiontheatre.org
Michael Robins, *Executive Producing Director*

Submission procedure: no unsolicited scripts; professional recommendation. **Types of material:** full-length plays, one-acts, translations, adaptations, musicals, solo pieces. **Special interests:** writers to collaborate on new works with company. **Facilities:** Illusion Theater, 250 seats, semi-thrust stage. **Best submission time:** Jul-Nov. **Response time:** 6-12 months. **Special programs:** Fresh Ink Series: 5-6 plays each presented with minimal set and costumes for 1 weekend; post-performance discussion with audience, who are seated on stage; scripts selected through theatre's normal submission procedure.

INDIANA REPERTORY THEATRE

(Founded 1972)
140 West Washington St; Indianapolis, IN 46204-3465;
    (317) 635-5277, FAX 236-0767
Literary Manager

Submission procedure: no unsolicited scripts; synopsis and letter of inquiry with SASE for response. **Types of material:** full-length plays, translations, adaptations, solo pieces. **Special interests:** adaptations of classic literature; plays that explore cultural/ethnic issues "with a

Midwestern voice." **Facilities:** mainstage, 600 seats, modified proscenium stage; Upperstage, 300 seats, modified thrust stage. **Production considerations:** cast limit of 6-8. **Best submission time:** year-round (season chosen by Jan each year). **Response time:** 3-4 months letter; 6 months script. **Special programs:** Discovery Series: presentation of plays for family audiences with a focus on youth and culturally/ethnically diverse plays with an emphasis on history and literature; scripts selected through theatre's normal submission procedure.

INTAR Hispanic American Arts Center

(Founded 1966)
Box 756; New York, NY 10108; (212) 695-6134, ext 11,
    FAX 268-0102
Lorenzo Mans, *Artistic Associate*

Submission procedure: accepts unsolicited scripts. **Types of material:** full-length plays. **Special interests:** new plays by Hispanic-American writers and translations and adaptations of Hispanic works only. **Facilities:** INTAR 53, 74 seats, black box. **Production considerations:** small cast, modest production values. **Best submission time:** year-round (season chosen late summer–early fall). **Response time:** 3 months. **Special programs:** NewWorks Lab: workshop productions; reading series.

InterAct Theatre Company

(Founded 1988)
2030 Sansom St; Philadelphia, PA 19103; (215) 568-8077,
    FAX 568-8095; email interact@interacttheatre.org;
    website www.interacttheatre.org
Seth Rozin, *Producing Artistic Director*
Larry Loebell, *Literary Manager*

Submission procedure: no unsolicited scripts; synopsis, bio and letter of inquiry with SASE for response. **Types of material:** full-length plays. **Special interests:** contemporary plays that theatrically explore issues of cultural and social significance; no kitchen-sink family dramas, relationship plays or light romantic comedies. **Facilities:** The Adrienne, 106 seats, proscenium stage. **Production considerations:** cast limit of 10. **Best submission time:** year-round. **Response time:** 1-3 months letter; 3-6 months script. **Special programs:** Showcase of New Plays: developmental and fully staged readings by primarily (but not exclusively) local playwrights; send SASE for guidelines.

INTIMAN THEATRE

(Founded 1972)
Box 19760; Seattle, WA 98109; (206) 269-1901, FAX 269-1928;
    website www.intiman.org
Mame Hunt, *Artistic Associate*

Submission procedure: no unsolicited scripts; professional recommendation. **Types of material:** full-length plays, translations, adaptations. **Special interests:** plays of complex ideas; unique use of form; language-oriented plays; no domestic realism; no solo pieces. **Facilities:** Intiman Playhouse, 480 seats, modified thrust stage. **Best submission time:** Nov-Mar. **Response time:** 4 months.

INVISIBLE THEATRE

(Founded 1976)
1400 North 1st Ave; Tucson, AZ 85719; (520) 882-9721,
    FAX 884-5410

Submission procedure: no unsolicited scripts; professional recommendation only. **Types of material:** full-length plays, one-acts, musicals, solo pieces. **Special interests:** mainly but not exclusively works with contemporary settings; works with strong female roles; social and political issues. **Facilities:** Invisible Theatre, 78 seats, black box. **Production considerations:** cast limit of 10, simple set, minimal props, small-cast musicals only. **Best submission time:** Oct-Dec. **Response time:** 6-12 months.

IRISH CLASSICAL THEATRE COMPANY

(Founded 1990)
625 Main St; Buffalo, NY 14203; (716) 853-0592, FAX 853-0592;
    email iclassical@aol.com; website www.irishclassicaltheatre.com
Fortunato Pezzimenti, *Associate Artistic Director*

Submission procedure: no unsolicited scripts; professional recommendation. **Types of material:** full-length plays, one-acts, translations, adaptations, musicals, cabaret/revues, solo pieces. **Special interests:** plays by Irish or Irish-American writers, plays with Irish or Irish-American themes. **Facilities:** Andrews Theatre, 200 seats, arena stage. **Production considerations:** unit set, fluid set changes; limited storage space. **Best submission time:** May, June. **Response time:** 1 month letter; 3 months script.

IRONDALE ENSEMBLE PROJECT

(Founded 1983)
Box 150604; Brooklyn, NY 11215; (718) 488-9233, FAX 488-9185;
    email irondalert@aol.com; website www.irondale.org
Jim Niesen, *Artistic Director*

Submission procedure: no unsolicited scripts; letter of inquiry from playwright interested in developing work with ensemble through ongoing workshop process. **Types of material:** full-length plays, adaptations, plays with music. **Special interests:** works with political or social relevance. **Facilities:** no permanent facility. **Production considerations:** cast limit of 8-9. **Best submission time:** Apr-Sep. **Response time:** 10 weeks.

JEWISH ENSEMBLE THEATRE

(Founded 1989)
6600 West Maple Rd; West Bloomfield, MI 48322-3002;
    (248) 788-2900, FAX 788-5160; email jetplay@aol.com;
    website www.comnet.org/jet
Evelyn Orbach, *Artistic Director*

Submission procedure: accepts unsolicited scripts. **Types of material:** full-length plays, one-acts, plays for young audiences. **Special interests:** works on Jewish themes and/or by Jewish writers; work not produced professionally. **Facilities:** Aaron DeRoy Theatre, 193 seats, thrust stage. **Production considerations:** no fly space. **Best submission time:** late spring-early fall. **Response time:** 6 months. **Special programs:** Festival of New Plays in Staged Readings: 4 plays given readings, possibly leading to mainstage production; scripts selected through theatre's normal submission procedure.

THE J. HOWARD WOOD THEATRE

(Founded 1991)
220 Periwinkle Way; Sanibel Island, FL 33957; (941) 472-4109,
    FAX 472-0055; email info@thewoodtheatre.com
Robert Schelhammer, *Artistic Director*

Submission procedure: no unsolicited scripts; 10-page dialogue sample, character breakdown and letter of inquiry with SASP for response. **Types of material:** full-length plays. **Special interests:** comedies, dramas, mysteries. **Facilities:** J. Howard Wood Theatre, 170 seats, thrust stage. **Production considerations:** cast limit of 8. **Best submission time:** year-round. **Response time:** 1-5 months letter; 1-5 months script. **Special programs:** Congress Jewelers Play Reading and Playwrights Festival: annual winter festival for 5 plays; $100 honorarium, staged reading with post-show discussion, possible full production in following season; scripts selected through theatre's normal submission procedure; *dates:* 11 Jan–2 Feb 2002. Pirate Players: children's theatre company performing season of plays for young audiences as well as running a summer instructional program.

JOMANDI PRODUCTIONS, INC.
(Founded 1978)
City Hall East; 675 Ponce de Leon Ave, 8th Floor; Atlanta, GA 30308;
    (404) 876–6346, FAX 872–5764; email jomandi@bellsouth.net;
    website www.jomandi.com
Lisa L. Watson, *Production Manager*

Submission procedure: accepts unsolicited scripts with synopsis, dialogue sample, resume and letter of inquiry. **Types of material:** full-length plays, adaptations, plays for young audiences, musicals, solo pieces. **Special interests:** historical or contemporary portrayals of the African-American experience; adaptations of African-American literature. **Facilities:** 14th Street Playhouse, 370 seats, proscenium/thrust stage. **Production considerations:** prefers small cast, prefers unit set. **Best submission time:** spring–summer. **Response time:** 3 months letter; 6 months–1 year (if interested).

THE JOSEPH PAPP PUBLIC THEATER/NEW YORK SHAKESPEARE FESTIVAL
(Founded 1954)
The Joseph Papp Public Theater; 425 Lafayette St;
    New York, NY 10003; (212) 539–8530, FAX 539–8505
Rick Des Rochers, *Literary Manager*

Submission procedure: no unsolicited scripts; synopsis, 10-page sample scene and letter of inquiry; include cassette of 3–5 songs for musicals and operas. **Types of material:** full-length plays, translations, adaptations, musicals, operas, solo pieces. **Facilities:** Newman Theater, 299 seats, proscenium stage; Anspacher Theater, 275 seats, thrust stage; Martinson Hall, 200 seats, proscenium stage; LuEsther Hall, 150 seats, flexible stage; Shiva Theater, 100 seats, flexible stage. **Best submission time:** year-round. **Response time:** 1 month letter; 6 months script.

JUMP-START PERFORMANCE CO.

(Founded 1985)
108 Blue Star; San Antonio, TX 78204; (210) 227-5867,
    FAX 222-2231; email jumpman@dcci.com;
    website www.jump-start.org
Sterling Houston, *Administrative Director/Writer-in-Residence*

Submission procedure: no unsolicited scripts; company performs works by long-term writers-in-residence; playwrights interested in joining company may write for information. **Types of material:** full-length plays, one-acts, translations, adaptations, musicals. **Special interests:** voices not heard in mainstream theatre; social and political issues including civil and social rights. **Facilities:** Jump Start Theater, 100 seats, black box. **Production considerations:** small cast, minimal production demands.

JUNGLE THEATER

(Founded 1990)
2951 South Lyndale Ave; Minneapolis, MN 55408; (612) 822-4002,
    FAX 822-9408; email info@jungletheater.com
Bain Boehlke, *Artistic Director*

Submission procedure: no unsolicited scripts; synopsis, sample pages, resume and letter of inquiry. **Types of material:** full-length plays. **Facilities:** The Jungle Theater, 135 seats, proscenium stage. **Best submission time:** year-round. **Response time:** 1 month letter; 3 months script. **Special programs:** Emerging Playwrights Reading Series: sit-down and staged readings of new plays by early-career playwrights; scripts selected through theater's normal submission procedure and by professional recommendation; *dates:* Aug 2002.

THE KAVINOKY THEATRE

(Founded 1981)
320 Porter Ave; Buffalo, NY 14221; (716) 881-7652, FAX 881-7790;
    email TMZmail@aol.com; website www.kavinokytheatre.com
David Lamb, *Artistic Director*

Submission procedure: no unsolicited scripts; professional recommendation. **Types of material:** full-length plays, adaptations. **Special interests:** comedies. **Facilities:** Kavinoky Theatre, 260 seats, proscenium/thrust stage. **Production considerations:** prefers cast limit of 7; no fly and limited wing space. **Best submission time:** Jun-Aug. **Response time:** 1 month.

KITCHEN DOG THEATER COMPANY

(Founded 1990)
3120 McKinney Ave; Dallas, TX 75204; (214) 953-2258,
   FAX 953-1873; email admin@kitchendogtheater.org;
   website www.kitchendogtheater.org
Dan Day, *Artistic Director*

Submission procedure: accepts unsolicited scripts. **Types of material:** full-length plays, translations, adaptations, solo pieces. **Special interests:** plays by TX and Southwest playwrights. **Facilities:** The McKinney Avenue Contemporary, 100-150 seats, thrust stage; Second Space, 75-100 seats, black box. **Production considerations:** cast limit of 5, moderate production demands, moderate set. **Best submission time:** year-round. **Response time:** 6-8 months. **Special programs:** New Works Festival: annual presentation of new plays, including one full production, staged readings, mini workshops and artist residencies; submit script, $10 check or money order with SASP for response; *deadline:* 15 Mar 2002; *notification:* 15 Apr 2002; *dates:* Jun-Jul 2002.

KUMU KAHUA THEATRE

(Founded 1971)
46 Merchant St; Honolulu, HI 96813; (808) 536-4222,
   FAX 536-4226
Harry Wong III, *Artistic Director*

Submission procedure: accepts unsolicited scripts with SASE for response. **Types of material:** full-lenth plays, one-acts, adaptations. **Special interests:** plays set in Hawaii or dealing with the Hawaiian experience. **Facilities:** Kumu Kahua Theatre, 100 seats, black box. **Best submission time:** year-round. **Response time:** 3-4 months. **Special programs:** Kumu Kahua Theatre/UHM Theatre Department Playwriting Contest: includes the Hawai'i Prize, Pacific Rim Prize and Resident Prize (see Prizes).

LACC THEATRE COMPANY—ANNUAL SHORT PLAY FESTIVAL

(Founded 1929)
Los Angeles City College Theatre Academy; 855 North Vermont Ave;
　　Los Angeles, CA 90029; (323) 953–4336, FAX 953–4500;
　　email theatre@email2.lacc.cc.ca.us;
　　website theatre_academy.lacc.cc.ca.us
Fred Fate, *Chair*

Submission procedure: accepts unsolicited scripts. **Types of material:** one-acts. **Special interests:** 10-15 minute plays, plays not returned. **Facilities:** Caminito, 99 seats, black box. **Production considerations:** college-age characters, cast limit of 5, 1 set. **Best submission time:** year-round. **Response time:** 3 months (if interested).

LA JOLLA PLAYHOUSE

(Founded 1947)
Box 12039; La Jolla, CA 92039; (858) 550–1070, FAX 550–1075
Literary Manager

Submission procedure: no unsolicited scripts; synopsis, 10-page dialogue sample and letter of inquiry. **Types of material:** full-length plays, translations, musicals. **Special interests:** "material pertinent to the lives we are leading at the start of this new century"; innovative form and language. **Facilities:** Mandell Weiss Center for the Performing Arts, 500 seats, proscenium stage; Weiss Forum, 400 seats, thrust stage. **Best submission time:** Jun-Nov. **Response time:** 1 month letter; 10 months script.

LA MAMA EXPERIMENTAL THEATER CLUB

(Founded 1961)
74A East 4th St; New York, NY 10003; (212) 254–6468,
　　FAX 254–7597; email lamama@lamama.org;
　　website www.lamama.org
Ellen Stewart, *Artistic Director*
Beverly Petty, *Associate Director*

Submission procedure: no unsolicited scripts; accepts unsolicited videotapes of projects with synopsis; prefers professional recommendation. **Types of material:** full-length plays, one-acts, musicals, solo pieces, performance art. **Special interests:** culturally diverse works with music, movement and media **Facilities:** Annex Theater, 199 seats, flexible stage; The Club Theater, 99 seats, black box; First Floor Theater, 99 seats, black box. **Best submission time:** year-round. **Response time:** 2-6 months.

Special programs: Experiments 2001: a weekly concert play reading series curated by George Ferencz. Cross Cultural Institute of Theater Art Studies (C.C.I.T.A.S): theatrical workshops and premiere productions involving collaboration among artists of varying geographic and ethnic origins that promote intercultural understanding and artistic exchange. La MaMa Umbria: summer artist's residency program outside of Spoleto in Umbria, Italy; contact theatre for more information.

LAMB'S PLAYERS THEATRE
(Founded 1971)
Box 182229; Coronado, CA 92178; (619) 437-6050, FAX 437-6053
Jeffrey S. Miller, *Director of Outreach*

Submission procedure: no unsolicited scripts; synopsis, maximum 10-page dialogue sample and letter of inquiry; include cassette for musicals. **Types of material:** full-length plays, one-acts, plays for young audiences, musicals, cabaret/revues. **Facilities:** Harder Stage, 350 seats, thrust stage; Hahn, 250 seats, proscenium stage; Lyceum, 200 seats, flexible stage. **Best submission time:** year-round. **Response time:** 4-6 weeks letter; 4-6 months script.

L. A. THEATRE WORKS
(Founded 1974)
681 Venice Blvd; Venice, CA 90291; (310) 827-0808, FAX 827-4949;
    email latworks@aol.com
Susan Raab, *Associate Producer*

Submission procedure: no unsolicited scripts; agent submission. **Types of material:** full-length plays, one-acts, adaptations. **Special interests:** highly theatrical, nonrealistic new plays; contemporary adaptations of classic themes. **Facilities:** no permanent facility. **Best submission time:** year-round. **Response time:** 4-6 months.

LIFELINE THEATRE
(Founded 1982)
6912 North Glenwood Ave; Chicago, IL 60626; (773) 761-0667,
    FAX 761-4582; website www.lifelinetheatre.com
Dorothy Milne, *Artistic Director*

Submission procedure: no unsolicited scripts; synopsis and letter of inquiry. **Types of material:** adaptations only. **Facilities:** Lifeline Theatre, 100 seats, proscenium stage. **Best submission time:** year-round. **Response time:** 1 month letter; 6 months script.

LINCOLN CENTER THEATER

(Founded 1966)
150 West 65th St; New York, NY 10023; (212) 362-7600;
   website www.lct.org
Anne Cattaneo, *Dramaturg*

Submission procedure: no unsolicited scripts; agent submission. **Types of material:** full-length plays, one-acts, translations, adaptations, musicals. **Facilities:** Vivian Beaumont, 1000 seats, thrust stage; Mitzi E. Newhouse, 300 seats, thrust stage. **Best submission time:** year-round. **Response time:** 2–4 months.

LIVE BAIT THEATRICAL COMPANY

(Founded 1987)
3914 North Clark; Chicago, IL 60613; (773) 871-1212,
   FAX 871-3191; email info@livebaittheater.org;
   website www.livebaittheater.org
Lotti Pharriss, *Managing Director*

Submission procedure: no unsolicited scripts; synopsis and letter of inquiry from Chicago-area playwrights only; no other submissions accepted. **Types of material:** full-length plays, translations, adaptations, solo pieces. **Special interests:** nonrealistic plays; performance poetry; performance art; multimedia works; works that emphasize visual aspects of staging. **Facilities:** Live Bait Theater, 70 seats, black box. **Production considerations:** prefers cast limit of 9, 1 set; no fly or wing space. **Best submission time:** year-round. **Response time:** 6 weeks letter; 6 months script.

LONG BEACH PLAYHOUSE;

(Founded 1929)
5021 East Anaheim St; Long Beach, CA 90804; (562) 494-1014,
   FAX 961-8616; email lbphmandir@earthlink.net;
   website www.longbeachplayhouse.com
Robert Leigh, *Managing Director*

Submission procedure: accepts unsolicited scripts. **Types of material:** full-length plays, translations, adaptations, plays for young audiences. **Special interests:** plays not produced professionally; ethnically inclusive and diverse projects with strong social themes and/or unusual theatricality. **Facilities:** mainstage, 200 seats, thrust stage; Studio, 98 seats, proscenium stage. **Production considerations:** simple sets; no wing space. **Best**

submission time: year-round. **Response time:** 3-6 months. **Special programs:** New Works Festival: 4 plays chosen for annual staged reading attended by professional critics who provide written and oral feedback; playwright receives $100 honorarium and videotape of reading; plays must be submitted with submission form (available on website or by fax); *deadline:* 1 Nov 2001 *notification:* Feb 2002; *dates:* spring 2002.

LONG WHARF THEATRE

(Founded 1965)
222 Sargent Dr; New Haven, CT 06511; (203) 787–4284,
    FAX 776–2287
Kelly Miller, *Literary Associate*

Submission procedure: no unsolicited scripts; synopsis, 10-page dialogue sample, resume and letter of inquiry with SASE for response. **Types of material:** full-length plays, translations, adaptations. **Special interests:** dramatic plays and comedies about human relationships, social concerns, ethical and moral dilemmas. **Facilities:** Newton Schenck Stage, 484 seats, thrust stage; Stage II, 199 seats, proscenium stage. **Best submission time:** year-round. **Response time:** 2 months letter; 6-12 months script.

THE LYRIC STAGE COMPANY OF BOSTON

(Founded 1974)
140 Clarendon St; Boston, MA 02116; website www.lyricstage.com
Spiro Veloudos, *Artistic Director*

Submission procedure: no unsolicited scripts; dialogue sample (1 complete scene) and letter of inquiry; include cassette for musicals. **Types of material:** full-length plays, musicals. **Special interests:** Boston or MA writers; women and minority writers; small-cast comedies and musicals; Boston themes. **Facilities:** mainstage, 236 seats, thrust stage. **Production considerations:** cast limit of 6 for plays, 9 for musicals, limited backstage space; prefers unit set. **Best submission time:** Jun–Jul. **Response time:** 2 months letter; 4-6 months script. **Special programs:** reading series; commissioning program for MA writers.

MABOU MINES

(Founded 1970)
150 First Ave; New York, NY 10009; (212) 473-0559,
    FAX 473-2410; email office@maboumines.org;
    website www.maboumines.org
Karen Houppert, *Company Manager*

Submission procedure: no unsolicited scripts; professional recommendation. **Types of material:** full-length plays, one-acts, translations, adaptations. **Special interests:** contemporary works on contemporary issues. **Facilities:** The TOny, ROn, NAncy & DAvid-TORO NADA: NO BULL Theater at the 122 Community Center, 60 seats, flexible stage. **Best submission time:** year-round. **Response time:** 6 months.

MADISON REPERTORY THEATRE

(Founded 1969)
122 State St, Suite 201; Madison, WI 53703-2500; (608) 256-0029,
    FAX 256-7433; email postmaster@madisonrep.org;
    website www.madisonrep.org
D. Scott Glasser, Artistic Director

Submission procedure: no unsolicited scripts; synopsis and letter of inquiry. **Types of material:** full-length plays, translations, adaptations, musicals. **Facilities:** Isthmus Playhouse, 330 seats, thrust stage. **Production considerations:** cast limit of 15; no fly space. **Best submission time:** year-round. **Response time:** 4-6 months letter; 4-6 months script. **Special programs:** reading series for plays in development.

MAGIC THEATRE

(Founded 1967)
Fort Mason Center, Bldg D; San Francisco, CA 94123;
    (415) 441-8001, FAX 771-5505
Laura Hope Owen, *Literary Manager*

Submission procedure: no unsolicited scripts; synopsis, first 10 pages of play, resume and letter of inquiry. **Types of material:** full-length plays. **Special interests:** new plays that are innovative and/or nonlinear in form and content; political themes. **Facilities:** Magic Theatre Southside, 170 seats, proscenium stage; Magic Theatre Northside, 155 seats, thrust stage. **Production considerations:** prefers cast limit of 6. **Best submission time:** Sep-May. **Response time:** 6 weeks letter; 6-8 months script.

MAIN STREET ARTS

(Founded 1993)
94 Main St; Nyack, NY 10960; (845) 358-7701, FAX 358-7701;
    email msapaul@cs.com
Literary Manager

Submission procedure: no unsolicited scripts; synopsis, dialogue sample and letter of inquiry. **Types of material:** full-length plays, one-acts. **Facilities:** mainstage, 65 seats, black box. **Production considerations:** cast limit of 6 for full-length plays, cast limit of 4 for one-acts. **Best submission time:** year-round. **Response time:** 3 weeks letter; 6 weeks script. **Special programs:** Developmental Reading Series: monthly rehearsed reading of one new play with director and actors followed by audience question and answer period; local authors preferred. Midsummernights Shorts One Act Festival: festival of 6-9 one-acts; *deadline:* 1 Mar 2002; no submissions prior to 1 Nov 2001; *notification:* 31 Mar 2002; *dates:* Jul-Aug 2002. Flying Blind Festival: presentation of short one-acts with no set requirements; $5 reading fee; *deadline:* 30 Jun 2002; *notification:* 15 July 2002; *dates:* Sep-Oct 2002.

MAIN STREET THEATER

(Founded 1975)
2540 Times Blvd; Houston, TX 77005-3225; (713) 524-3622,
    FAX 524-3977; email Mnstthtr@aol.com;
    website www.mainstreettheater.com
Rebecca Greene Udden, *Artistic Director*

Submission procedure: no unsolicited scripts; synopsis and letter of inquiry. **Types of material:** full-length plays, one-acts, translations, adaptations, plays for young audiences, musicals. **Special interests:** plays by women, plays dealing with multicultural issues. **Facilities:** MST-Chelsea Market, 196 seats, thrust stage; MST-Times Blvd, 92 seats, thrust stage. **Production considerations:** cast limit of 8-12. **Best submission time:** year-round. **Response time:** 1 month letter; 6 months script.

MANHATTAN THEATRE CLUB

(Founded 1972)
311 West 43rd St, 8th Floor; New York, NY 10036; (212) 399-3000,
    FAX 399-4329; website www.manhattantheatreclub.com
Christian Parker, *Literary Manager*
Clifford Lee Johnson III, *Artistic Development*

Submission procedure: no unsolicited scripts; agent submission. **Types of**

material: full-length plays, musicals. **Facilities:** Stage I at City Center, 299 seats, proscenium stage; Stage II, 150 seats, thrust stage. **Production considerations:** prefers cast of 6-8, 1 set or unit set. **Best submission time:** year-round. **Response time:** 4 months. **Special programs:** readings and workshop productions of new musicals. 6@6: Discovering the Next Generation reading series: in-house readings of new plays or first drafts. Manhattan Theatre Club Playwriting Fellowships (see Fellowships and Grants).

MARIN SHAKESPEARE COMPANY

(Founded 1989)
Box 4053; San Rafael, CA 94913; (415) 499-1108, FAX 499-1492;
　website www.marinshakespeare.org
Robert Currier, *Artistic Director*

Submission procedure: no unsolicited scripts; synopsis, production history and letter of inquiry. **Types of material:** full-length plays, translations, adaptations. **Special interests:** classical, family-oriented or Shakespeare-related plays suitable for outdoor production. **Facilities:** Forest Meadows Amphitheatre, 600 seats, proscenium/thrust stage. **Best submission time:** year-round. **Response time:** 2 months letter; 2 months script.

MARIN THEATRE COMPANY

(Founded 1967)
397 Miller Ave; Mill Valley, CA 94941; (415) 388-5200,
　FAX 388-0768; email info@marintheatre.org;
　website www.marintheatre.org
Lee Sankowich, *Artistic Director*

Submission procedure: no unsolicited scripts; agent submission. **Types of material:** full-length plays, translations, adaptations, plays for young audiences. **Facilities:** Marin Theatre, 250 seats, proscenium stage; 2nd theatre, 109 seats, black box. **Best submission time:** Jun-Aug. **Response time:** 6 months.

MARK TAPER FORUM

(Founded 1967)
135 North Grand Ave; Los Angeles, CA 90012; (213) 972-8033
Pier Carlo Talenti, *Literary Manager*

Submission procedure: no unsolicited scripts; synopsis, 5-10 sample pages and letter of inquiry with SASE. **Types of material:** full-length plays, translations, adaptations, plays for young audiences, musicals, literary cabaret, solo pieces, performance art. **Facilities:** Mark Taper Forum, 742 seats, thrust stage. **Best submission time:** year-round. **Response time:** 8-10 weeks letter; 8-10 weeks script. **Special programs:** Performing for Los Angeles Youth: 55-minute plays that tour Southern CA schools; maximum 6 actors; suitable for grades K-8; scripts selected through theatre's normal submission procedure. Mark Taper Forum Developmental Programs (see Development).

McCarter Theatre Center
(Founded 1972)
91 University Place; Princeton, NJ 08540; (609) 683–9100,
    FAX 497–0369; email literary@mccarter.org;
    website www.mccarter.org
Charles McNulty, *Literary Manager*

Submission procedure: no unsolicited scripts; synopsis, 10-page dialogue sample and letter of inquiry. **Types of material:** full-length plays, musicals. **Facilities:** McCarter Theatre, 1077 seats, proscenium stage. **Best submission time:** Sep–May. **Response time:** 1 month letter; 3 months script.

MCC Theater
(Founded 1986)
120 West 28th St; New York, NY 10001; (212) 727–7722,
    FAX 727–7780
Stephen Willems, *Literary Manager*

Submission procedure: no unsolicited scripts; synopsis, 10-page dialogue sample and letter of inquiry with SASE or SASP for response. **Types of material:** full-length plays, one-acts, translations, adaptations, musicals. **Facilities:** MCC Theater, 99 seats, black box. **Production considerations:** cast limit of 10. **Best submission time:** year-round. **Response time:** 2 weeks letter; 2 months script.

Meadow Brook Theatre
(Founded 1967)
Oakland University; Wilson Hall; Rochester, MI 48309;
    (248) 370–3310, FAX 370–3108; email mbtheatre@oakland.edu
Debra L. Wicks, *Artistic Director*

Submission procedure: no unsolicited scripts; professional recommendation. **Types of material:** full-length plays, adaptations. **Special**

interests: plays with a Michigan location or subject matter. **Facilities:** Meadow Brook Theatre, 584 seats, proscenium stage. **Production considerations:** no fly space. **Best submission time:** Sep-May. **Response time:** 1-2 months (if interested).

MERRIMACK REPERTORY THEATRE

(Founded 1979)
50 East Merrimack St; Lowell, MA 01852; (978) 454-6324,
FAX 934-0166; website www.merrimackrep.org
Charles Towers, *Artistic Director*

Submission procedure: no unsolicited scripts; synopsis and letter of inquiry. **Types of material:** full-length plays, translations, adaptations, plays for young audiences, musicals. **Special interests:** well-crafted stories with a poetic and human focus; varied ethnic tapestries of American life and love. **Facilities:** Liberty Hall, 372 seats, thrust stage. **Production considerations:** moderate cast size, simple set. **Best submission time:** spring-summer. **Response time:** 1 month letter (if interested); 6 months script.

MERRY-GO-ROUND PLAYHOUSE

(Founded 1958)
Box 506; Auburn, NY 13021; (315) 255-1305, FAX 252-3815;
email mgrplays@dreamscape.com;
website www.merry-go-round.com
Kathy Hadley, *Literary Manager*

Submission procedure: accepts unsolicited scripts. **Types of material:** full-length plays, translations, adaptations, plays for young audiences, musicals. **Special interests:** participatory plays for young audiences with cast limit of 3-4, plays for grades K-12. **Facilities:** Merry-Go-Round Playhouse (adaptable), 364 seats, proscenium stage or 100 seats, thrust stage. **Production considerations:** cast limit of 6. **Best submission time:** Jan-Feb. **Response time:** 2 months.

METROSTAGE

(Founded 1984)
1201 North Royal St; Alexandria, VA 22314; (703) 548-9044,
FAX 548-9089
Carolyn Griffin, *Producing Artistic Director*

Submission procedure: no unsolicited scripts; synopsis, first 10 pages of dialogue, list of productions/readings and letter of inquiry. **Types of**

material: full-length plays. **Facilities:** MetroStage, 150 seats, thrust stage. **Production considerations:** cast limit of 8, prefers 4, prefers 1 set. **Best submission time:** year-round. **Response time:** 1 month letter; 1 month script. **Special programs:** First Stage: staged reading series Oct–May.

METRO THEATER COMPANY

(Founded 1973)
8308 Olive Blvd; St. Louis, MO 63132–2814; (314) 997–6777,
    FAX 997–1811; email bravomtc@aol.com
Carol North, *Artistic Director*

Submission procedure: no unsolicited scripts; professional recommendation. **Types of material:** plays for young audiences. **Special interests:** no works longer than 60 minutes; plays with music that are not dramatically limited by traditional concepts of "children's theatre." **Facilities:** no permanent facility; touring company. **Production considerations:** works cast from ensemble of 5, sets suitable for touring. **Best submission time:** year-round. **Response time:** 2–3 months. **Special programs:** new play readings, commissioning program; interested writers send letter of inquiry with recommendations from theatres who have produced writer's work.

MILL MOUNTAIN THEATRE

(Founded 1964)
1 Market Square SE; Roanoke, VA 24011–1437; (540) 342–5749,
    FAX 342–5745; email outreach@millmountain.org;
    website www.millmountain.org
Literary Coordinator

Submission procedure: accepts unsolicited one-acts only; synopsis, 10-page dialogue sample and letter of inquiry for all other submissions; include cassette for musicals. **Types of material:** full-length plays, one-acts, musicals, solo pieces. **Special interests:** plays with racially mixed casts. **Facilities:** Mill Mountain Theatre, 400 seats, flexible proscenium stage; Waldron Stage, 125 seats, flexible stage. **Production considerations:** cast limit of 15 for plays, 24 for musicals, prefers unit set. **Best submission time:** year-round. **Response time:** 6 weeks letter; 6–8 months script. **Special programs:** Centerpieces: monthly lunchtime staged readings of one-acts by emerging playwrights; unpublished one-acts 25–35 minutes long (no 10-minute plays). The Mill Mountain Theatre New Play Competition: The Norfolk Southern Festival of New Works (see Prizes).

MILWAUKEE CHAMBER THEATRE

(Founded 1975)
158 North Broadway; Milwaukee, WI 53202; (414) 276-8842,
    FAX 277-4477; email mail@chamber-theatre.com
Montgomery Davis, *Artistic Director*

Submission procedure: no unsolicited scripts; professional recommendation. **Types of material:** full-length plays, one-acts, translations, adaptations. **Special interests:** strong, well-crafted plays; plays about Shaw for annual Shaw Festival. **Facilities:** Broadway Theatre Center: Cabot Theatre, 358 seats, proscenium stage; studio, 96 seats, black box. **Production considerations:** 1 set or unit set. **Best submission time:** summer. **Response time:** 4 months.

MILWAUKEE REPERTORY THEATER

(Founded 1954)
108 East Wells St; Milwaukee, WI 53202; (414) 224-1761,
    FAX 224-9097; email pkosidowski@milwaukeerep.com
Paul Kosidowski, *Literary Manager*

Submission procedure: no unsolicited scripts; agent submission. **Types of material:** full-length plays, translations, adaptations, cabaret/revues. **Facilities:** Quadracci Powerhouse Theatre, 720 seats, thrust stage; Stiemke Theatre, 200 seats, flexible stage; Stackner Cabaret, 100 seats, cabaret stage. **Production considerations:** works for cabaret must not exceed 80 minutes in length. **Best submission time:** year-round. **Response time:** 2-3 months.

THE MIRACLE THEATRE GROUP

(Founded 1985)
425 Southeast Sixth Ave; Portland, OR 97214; (503) 236-7253,
    FAX 236-4174; email board@milagro.org;
    website www.milagro.org
Francisco Garcia, *Program Associate*

Submission procedure: no unsolicited scripts; synopsis and letter of inquiry. **Types of material:** full-length plays, translations, adaptations. **Special interests:** Hispanic playwrights, plays that deal with the Hispanic experience. **Facilities:** Miracle Theatre, 120 seats, thrust stage. **Production considerations:** cast limit of 10, unit set; no fly space. **Best submission time:** spring-summer. **Response time:** 3-5 months letter; 3-5 months script.

MISSOURI REPERTORY THEATRE

(Founded 1964)
4949 Cherry St; Kansas City, MO 64110-2263; (816) 235-2727,
    FAX 235-6562; email theatre@umkc.edu;
    website www.missourireptheatre.org
Peter Altman, *Producing Artistic Director*

Submission procedure: no unsolicited scripts; agent submission only.
Types of material: full-length plays, translations, adaptations. **Facilities:**
Spencer Theatre, 702 seats, modified thrust stage.

MIXED BLOOD THEATRE COMPANY

(Founded 1975)
1501 South Fourth St; Minneapolis, MN 55454; (612) 338-0937
David Kunz, *Script Czar*

Submission procedure: no unsolicited scripts; synopsis and letter of
inquiry. **Types of material:** full-length plays, musicals, cabaret/revues.
Special interests: comedies dealing with racial issues, politics or sports.
Facilities: Main Stage, 200 seats, flexible stage. **Best submission time:** Aug-
Jan. **Response time:** 2 months letter; 3-6 months script.

THE MONTANA REPERTORY THEATRE

(Founded 1968)
Department of Drama and Dance; The University of Montana;
    Missoula, MT 59812-8136; (406) 243-6809, FAX 243-5726;
    email mrt@selway.umt.edu
Greg Johnson, *Artistic Director*

Submission procedure: no unsolicited scripts; synopsis, resume and letter
of inquiry. **Types of material:** full-length plays, one-acts, musicals. **Special
interests:** plays by and about Native Americans. **Facilities:** no permanent
facility; touring company. **Best submission time:** summer. **Response time:** 3
months letter; 6 months script.

MOVING ARTS

(Founded 1992)
514 South Spring St; Los Angeles, CA 90013; (213) 622-8906,
    FAX 622-8946; email treynichols@movingarts.org;
    website www.movingarts.org
Trey Nichols, *Literary Director*

Submission procedure: no unsolicited scripts; synopsis, dialogue sample, resume and letter of inquiry with SASE. **Types of material:** full-length plays, translations, adaptations. **Special interests:** work not previously produced in Los Angeles area. **Facilities:** Los Angeles Theatre Center, 60 seats, black box. **Production considerations:** modest production demands; limited wing and fly space. **Best submission time:** year-round. **Response time:** 1-3 months letter; 6-9 months script. **Special Programs:** Premiere One-Act Festival: annual fall festival of one-acts chosen from one-act competition. (See Premiere One-Act Competition in Prizes.)

NATIONAL THEATRE OF THE DEAF

(Founded 1967)
55 Van Dyke Ave, Suite 312; Hartford, CT 06106;
   (860) 724-5179 (voice), (800) 300-5179 (TTY),
   FAX (860) 550-7974; email info@ntd.org; website www.ntd.org
Jerry Goehring, *Executive Director*

Submission procedure: no unsolicited scripts; synopsis, character breakdown, sample pages and letter of inquiry with SASE for response. **Types of material:** full-length plays, adaptations, plays for young audiences. **Special interests:** work not produced professionally; deaf issues; culturally diverse plays. **Facilities:** no permanent facility; touring company. **Production considerations:** cast limit of 10; production must tour. **Best submission time:** year-round. **Response time:** 1 month letter; 3-6 months script.

NEBRASKA THEATRE CARAVAN

(Founded 1976)
6915 Cass St; Omaha, NE 68132; (402) 553-4890, FAX 553-6288;
   email mlucca@omahaplayhouse.com
Marya Lucca-Thyberg, *Director of the Caravan*

Submission procedure: no unsolicited scripts; synopsis and letter of inquiry. **Types of material:** adaptations, plays for young audiences, musicals. **Special interests:** work suitable for elementary, intermediate and high school audiences only. **Facilities:** no permanent facility; touring company. **Production considerations:** cast limit of 6, cast limit of 5-7 for musicals, 1 set. **Best submission time:** Sep-Dec. **Response time:** 1 month letter; 3 months script.

NEVADA SHAKESPEARE FESTIVAL

(Founded 1989)
Box 871; Virginia City, NV 89440; (775) 324-4198;
email information@nevada-shakespeare.org;
website www.nevada-shakespeare.org
Martha Quarkziz, *Communications Director*

Submission procedure: no unsolicited scripts; synopsis, resume and letter of inquiry; prefers email scripts. **Types of material:** full-length plays, translations, adaptations, plays for young audiences, musicals, caberet/revues, solo pieces. **Special interests:** avant-garde, innovative treatments of imaginative literature. **Facilities:** Piper's Opera House, 350–500 seats, proscenium stage; NSF Studio, 100 seats, thrust stage. **Best submission time:** year-round. **Response time:** 1 month letter; 1 month script.

NEVADA THEATRE COMPANY

(Founded 1997)
2928 Lake East Dr; Las Vegas, NV 89117; (702) 873-0191,
FAX 877-6051; email nvtheatreco@aol.com
Deanna Duplechino, *Artistic Director*

Submission procedure: no unsolicited scripts; professional recommendation. **Types of material:** plays for young audiences. **Special interests:** irreverent, innovative storytelling low on production values and high on actor-driven theatricality. **Facilities:** no permanent facility, touring company. **Production considerations:** cast limit of 4. **Best submission time:** year-round. **Response time:** 2-4 months. **Special programs:** BOOKS ALIVE!: touring program performs original scripts based on books and/or history; 50-minute maximum, cast limit of 4.

NEW AMERICAN THEATER

(Founded 1972)
118 North Main St; Rockford, IL 61101; (815) 963-9454,
FAX 963-7215; website www.newamericantheater.com
Richard Raether, Artistic Director

Submission procedure: no unsolicited scripts; synopsis and SASE for response. **Types of material:** full-length plays. **Facilities:** David W. Knapp Stage, 280 seats, thrust stage; Amcore Cellar, 90 seats, flexible stage. **Production considerations:** small-to-medium cast size, modest production demands. **Best submission time:** fall. **Response time:** 3 months letter; 3 months script. **Special Programs:** New Voices in the Heartland: annual festival of staged readings of works not previously produced; send synopsis with SASE; *deadline*: Dec 2001; *dates*: Sep 2002.

THE NEW CONSERVATORY THEATRE CENTER

(Founded 1981)
25 Van Ness, Lower Lobby; San Francisco, CA 94102;
    (415) 861–4914, FAX 861–6988; email nctcsf@yahoo.com;
    website www.nctcsf.org
Ed Decker, *Artistic/Executive Director*

Submission procedure: no unsolicited scripts; synopsis and letter of inquiry. **Types of material:** plays for young audiences, musicals. **Special interests:** gay plays for adult audiences. **Facilities:** Decker Theatre, 132 seats, proscenium stage; Walker Theatre, 75 seats, black box; City Theatre, 55 seats, black box. **Best submission time:** year-round. **Response time:** 3 months letter; 6 months script.

NEW DRAMATISTS

See Membership and Service Organizations.

NEW FEDERAL THEATRE

(Founded 1970)
292 Henry St; New York, NY 10002; (212) 353–1176, FAX 353–1088;
    email newfederal@metrobase.com;
    website www.metrobase.com/newfederal
Woodie King, Jr., *Producing Director*

Submission procedure: no unsolicited scripts; professional recommendation. **Types of material:** full-length plays. **Special interests:** social and political issues; family and community themes related to minorities and women. **Facilities:** Henry Street Settlement: Harry Dejour Playhouse, 300 seats, proscenium stage; Experimental Theatre, 100 seats, black box; Recital Hall, 100 seats, thrust stage. **Production considerations:** small cast, no more than 2 sets. **Best submission time:** year-round. **Response time:** 5 months.

NEW GEORGES

(Founded 1992)
90 Hudson St, #2E; New York, NY 10013; (212) 620-0113,
 FAX (646) 336-8077; email newgeorges@aol.com;
 website www.newgeorges.org
Ellen Melaver, *Literary Manager*

Submission procedure: accepts unsolicited scripts. **Types of material:** full-length plays. **Special interests:** plays by women only; works with "vigorous use of language and heightened perspectives on reality." **Facilities:** no permanent facility. **Best submission time:** year-round. **Response time:** 2 months letter; 3-6 months script.

THE NEW GROUP

(Founded 1991)
154 Christopher St, Suite 2A-A; New York, NY 10014;
 email newgroup1@earthlink.net; website newgrouptheater.com
Ian Morgan, *Literary Manager*

Submission procedure: accepts unsolicited scripts with resume (only 1 submission per playwright per year). **Types of material:** full-length plays. **Special interests:** works not previously produced in New York City; "challenging, risk-taking plays that explore character and emotion in a contemporary context." **Facilities:** no permanent facility. **Best submission time:** year-round. **Response time:** 6-9 months. **Special programs:** New Group Associates Program: regular meetings and reading series for playwrights; writers admitted based on quality of submitted script.

NEW JERSEY REPERTORY COMPANY

(Founded 1997)
179 Broadway; Long Branch, NJ 07740; (732) 229-3166,
 FAX 229-3167; email info@njrep.org; website www.njrep.org
SuzAnne Barabas, *Artistic Director*

Submission procedure: accepts unsolicited scripts with synopsis and character breakdown. **Types of material:** full-length plays, one-acts, musicals. **Special interests:** work not produced professionally; social, humanistic themes. **Facilities:** Main Stage, 72 seats, black box; Second Stage, 50 seats, flexible stage. **Production considerations:** cast limit of 7, unit or simple set. **Best submission time:** year-round. **Response time:** 6-12 months. **Special programs:** Script-in-Hand: year-round reading series for more than 20 plays; of these, up to 6 selected for Main Stage production.

NEW REPERTORY THEATRE

(Founded 1985)
Box 610418; Newton Highlands, MA 02461; (617) 928-9831;
email adamnewrep@aol.com; website www.newrep.org
Rick Lombardo, *Producing Artistic Director*

Submission procedure: no unsolicited scripts; synopsis, dialogue sample and letter of inquiry. **Types of material:** full-length plays, translations, adaptations. **Special interests:** plays of ideas that center around pressing issues of our time; multicultural themes; intimate, interpersonal themes. **Facilities:** New Repertory Theatre, 160 seats, thrust stage. **Production considerations:** cast limit of 7. **Best submission time:** May-Aug. **Response time:** 2 months letter; 6 months script. **Special programs:** reading series.

NEW STAGE THEATRE

(Founded 1966)
1100 Carlisle; Jackson, MS 39202; (601) 948-0143, FAX 948-3538;
website www.newstagetheatre.com
John Maxwell, *Artistic Director*

Submission procedure: no unsolicited scripts; synopsis and letter of inquiry. **Types of material:** full-length plays, one-acts, solo pieces. **Facilities:** Meyer Crystal Auditorium, 364 seats, proscenium stage. **Production considerations:** cast limit of 3-8. **Best submission time:** summer-fall. **Response time:** 1 month letter; 3 months script. **Special programs:** Eudora Welty New Play Series; theatre produces one new play every season.

NEW THEATRE

(Founded 1986)
4120 Laguna St; Coral Gables, FL 33146; (305) 443-5373,
FAX 443-1642; email admin@new-theatre.com;
website www.new-theatre.com
Rafael De Acha, *Artistic Director*

Submission procedure: no unsolicited scripts; synopsis, resume and letter of inquiry. **Types of material:** full-length plays, translations, adaptations. **Special interests:** prefer language-driven plays, theatricality vs. realism. **Facilities:** New Theatre, 120 seats, end stage. **Production considerations:** cast limit of 7. **Best submission time:** year-round. **Response time:** 3 months letter; 6 months script.

NEW TUNERS THEATRE/THE THEATRE BUILDING

(Founded 1969)
1225 West Belmont; Chicago, IL 60657-3205;
    (773) 929-7367, ext 22, FAX 327-1404; email tbtuners@aol.com
John Sparks, *Artistic Director*

Submission procedure: no unsolicited scripts; synopsis, 1 scene, 3-song cassette, bio and letter of inquiry. **Types of material:** musicals. **Facilities:** 3 theatres, 150 seats each, black box. **Best submission time:** year-round. **Response time:** 4 months letter; 6 months script. **Special programs:** Annual STAGES Festival held every summer. New Tuners Workshop: musical developmental workshop. Monthly reading series.

NEW YORK STAGE AND FILM

(Founded 1984)
151 West 30th St, Suite 905; New York, NY 10001; (212) 239-2334,
    FAX 239-2996; email nysaf@aol.com
Johanna Pfaelzer, *Managing Producer*

Submission procedure: no unsolicited scripts; synopsis, resume and letter of inquiry. **Types of material:** full-length plays. **Facilities:** Powerhouse Theatre, 135 seats, proscenium stage; Coal Bin, 110 seats, black box. **Best submission time:** 1 Sep-31 Oct only. **Response time:** 2 months letter; 3 months script.

NEW YORK STATE THEATRE INSTITUTE

(Founded 1974)
37 First St; Troy, NY 12180; (518) 274-3200, FAX 274-3815;
    email nysti@capital.net; website www.nysti.org
Ed Lange *Associate Artistic Director*

Submission procedure: no unsolicited scripts; synopsis, cast/scene breakdown and letter of inquiry. **Types of material:** full-length plays, adaptations, musicals. **Special interests:** works for family audiences only. **Facilities:** Schacht Fine Arts Center, 800 seats, proscenium stage. **Best submission time:** Mar-Sep. **Response time:** 2 months letter; 6 months script. **Special programs:** new work developmental workshops; playwrights receive staged reading or workshop production, negotiable remuneration, travel and housing.

NEW YORK THEATRE WORKSHOP

(Founded 1979)
79 East 4th St; New York, NY 10003; (212) 780-9037
Kate Spencer, *Artistic Associate/Literary Department*

Submission procedure: no unsolicited scripts; synopsis, 10-page dialogue sample, resume and letter of inquiry. **Types of material:** full-length plays, one-acts, translations, music-theatre works, solo pieces, proposals only for performance art. **Special interests:** socially relevant and/or minority issues; innovative form and language. **Facilities:** 79 East 4th Street Theatre, 180 seats, proscenium stage. **Best submission time:** fall–spring. **Response time:** 1 month letter; 5 months script. **Special programs:** Mondays at Three: reading series, developmental workshops and symposia. Summer writing residency. New York Theatre Workshop Playwriting Fellowship for emerging writers of color based in New York (see Fellowships and Grants).

NEXT ACT THEATRE

(Founded 1990)
Box 394; Milwaukee, WI 53201; (414) 278-7780, FAX 278-5930
David Cecsarini, *Artistic Director/Producer*

Submission procedure: no unsolicited scripts; agent submission of synopsis, cast list, production requirements and letter of inquiry. **Types of material:** full-length plays, adaptations, solo pieces. **Facilities:** Studio Space, 99 seats, thrust stage. **Production considerations:** small cast size, minimal production demands. **Best submission time:** spring. **Response time:** 1 month letter; 6 months script.

NORTH COAST REPERTORY THEATRE

(Founded 1982)
987D Lomas Santa Fe Dr; Solana Beach, CA 92075; (858) 481-2155,
    FAX 481-1527; email NCRT@northcoastrep.org;
    website www. northcoastrep.org
Sean Murray, *Artistic Director*

Submission procedure: no unsolicited scripts; synopsis, bio and letter of inquiry. **Types of material:** full-length plays, one-acts, translations, adaptations, plays for young audiences, musicals, cabaret/revues, solo pieces. **Facilities:** NCRT, 194 seats, thrust stage. **Production considerations:** small cast size; limited space. **Best submission time:** year-round. **Response time:** 6 months letter; 6 months script.

The Northeast Theatre (TNT)

(Founded 1992)
Keystone College, One College Green; La Plume, PA 18440;
(570) 945–6976; email tnttheatre@excite.com;
website tnt.pa.webjump.com

Submission procedure: no unsolicited scripts; send SASE for guidelines. **Types of material:** full-length plays, solo pieces, spoken word/poetry performance. **Special interests:** writer-directors, contemporary themes, multicultural artists. **Facilities:** The Brooks Theatre, 99-150 seats, flexible stage. **Production considerations:** small cast (prefers 1-6); minimal production demands. **Best submission time:** May–Aug. **Response time:** 2 month letter; 2 month script. **Special programs:** staged reading series. Written and Directed By: annual series culminating in production for 1 writer-director.

Northern Stage

(Founded 1992)
Box 4287; White River Junction, VT 05001; (802) 291–9009,
FAX 291–9156; email northern.stage@valley.net;
website www.northernstage.org
Brooke Wetzel, *Artistic Director*

Submission procedure: accepts unsolicited scripts. **Types of material:** full-length plays, one-acts, musicals. **Special interests:** New England playwrights. **Facilities:** Briggs Opera House, 245 seats, thrust stage. **Production considerations:** minimal production requirements. **Best submission time:** year-round. **Response time:** 6-8 months.

Northlight Theatre

(Founded 1975)
9501 North Skokie Blvd; Skokie, IL 60076; (847) 679–9501,
FAX 679–1879; email gwitt@northlight.org
Gavin Witt, *Dramaturg/Literary Manager*

Submission procedure: no unsolicited scripts; synopsis, cast list and letter of inquiry. **Types of material:** full-length plays, translations, adaptations, musicals. **Special interests:** translations and adaptations of "lost" plays; the public world and public issues; plays of ideas; works that are passionate and/or hilarious. **Facilities:** Center East Theatre, 850 seats, proscenium stage; Northlight Theatre, 345 seats, thrust stage. **Production**

considerations: cast limit of 2-8, 1 unit or flexible set. **Best submission time:** year-round. **Response time:** 1 month letter; 4 months script.

NORTH SHORE MUSIC THEATRE

(Founded 1955)
62 Dunham Rd; Beverly, MA 01915; (978) 232-7203, FAX 921-0793;
    website www.nsmt.org
John LaRock, *Associate Producer*

Submission procedure: no unsolicited scripts; synopsis and letter of inquiry with SASE for response; include cassette for musicals. **Types of material:** musicals. **Special interests:** musicals only. **Facilities:** Main Stage, 1800 seats, arena stage; Workshop, 100 seats, flexible stage. **Production considerations:** prefers cast limit of 12 for workshop productions. **Best submission time:** year-round. **Response time:** 1 month letter; 3-6 months script. **Special programs:** New Works Development Program: spring and fall workshop productions of new works with authors in residence; theatre pays (rate varies) and houses writers; contact theatre for information.

NORTH STAR THEATRE

(Founded 1991)
347 Gerard St; Mandeville, LA 70448; (504) 624-5266,
    FAX 626-1692; website www.northstartheatre.com
Lori Bennett, *Producing Director*

Submission procedure: no unsolicited scripts; synopsis, first 10 pages of dialogue and letter of inquiry. **Types of material:** full-length plays, plays for young audiences. **Special interests:** social issue plays. **Facilities:** North Star Theatre, 150 seats, thrust stage. **Production considerations:** minimal production demands, simple sets. **Best submission time:** year-round. **Response time:** 3 months letter; 6 months script.

ODYSSEY THEATRE ENSEMBLE

(Founded 1969)
2055 South Sepulveda Blvd; Los Angeles, CA 90025; (310) 477-2055
Sally Essex-Lopresti, *Director of Literary Programs*

Submission procedure: no unsolicited scripts; synopsis, 8-10-page dialogue sample, play's production history (if any), resume and letter of inquiry with SASE for response; include cassette for musicals. **Types of material:** full-length plays, translations, adaptations, musicals. **Special interests:** culturally diverse works; works with innovative form or provocative subject matter; works exploring the enduring questions of human existence and the possibilities of the live theatre experience; works with political or sociological impact. **Facilities:** Odyssey 1, 99 seats, flexible stage; Odyssey 2, 99 seats, thrust stage; Odyssey 3, 99 seats, endstage. **Production considerations:** plays must be 90 minutes or longer. **Best submission time:** year-round. **Response time:** 2–4 weeks letter; 6 months script.

OLDCASTLE THEATRE COMPANY
(Founded 1972)
Box 1555; Bennington, VT 05201–1555; (802) 447–1267,
    FAX 442–3704
Eric Peterson, *Producing Artistic Director*

Submission procedure: accepts unsolicited scripts. **Types of material:** full-length plays, musicals. **Facilities:** Bennington Center for the Arts, 300 seats, modified proscenium stage. **Best submission time:** winter. **Response time:** 4–6 months.

OLNEY THEATRE CENTER FOR THE ARTS
(Founded 1937)
2001 Olney–Sandy Spring Rd; Olney, MD 20832; (301) 924–4485,
    FAX 924–2654
David Jackson, *Literary Manager*

Submission procedure: no unsolicited scripts; professional recommendation. **Types of material:** full-length plays, translations, adaptations, solo pieces. **Facilities:** mainstage, 500 seats, proscenium stage; The Lab Theatre, 200 seats, flexible stage. **Production considerations:** cast limit of 8. **Best submission time:** year-round. **Response time:** 6 months.

OMAHA THEATER COMPANY FOR YOUNG PEOPLE
(Founded 1949)
2001 Farnam St; Omaha, NE 68102; (402) 345–4852, FAX 344–7255
James Larson, *Artistic Director*

Submission procedure: no unsolicited scripts; professional recommendation. **Types of material:** one-acts. **Special interests:** plays for family audiences only; plays based on children's literature and contemporary issues; multicultural themes. **Facilities:** Omaha Theater Company, 932 seats, proscenium stage; second stage, 175 seats, black box. **Production considerations:** cast limit of 10; prefers unit set. **Best submission time:** year-round. **Response time:** 6 months.

OPEN CIRCLE THEATER

(Founded 1992)
429 Boren Ave N; Seattle, WA 98109; (206) 382-4250;
   website www.opencircletheater.org
Melanie White, *Artistic Director*

Submission procedure: no unsolicited scripts; synopsis, 10-page dialogue sample, resume and letter of inquiry; local professional recommendation. **Types of material:** full-length plays, adaptations, musicals. **Special interests:** plays suitable for site-specific staging; plays incorporating new music and dance or movement; language-oriented plays; no naturalism. **Facilities:** Open Circle Theater, 70 seats, flexible stage. **Best submission time:** year-round. **Response time:** 2-3 months letter; 6 months script.

THE OPEN EYE THEATER

(Founded 1972)
Box 959; Margaretville, NY 12455; (914) 586-1660, FAX 586-1660;
   email openeye@catskill.net; website www.theopeneye.org
Amie Brockway, *Producing Artistic Director*

Submission procedure: no unsolicited scripts; synopsis and letter of inquiry with self-addressed envelope (no postage) for response. **Types of material:** full-length plays, one-acts, translations, adaptations, plays for young audiences. **Special interests:** plays for young and multigenerational audiences; culturally diverse themes; plays with music; ensemble plays; plays of any length (10 minutes or more); Catskill Mountain-area writers. **Facilities:** no permanent facility. **Production considerations:** minimal set. **Best submission time:** Oct-Apr. **Response time:** 1 week letter (if interested); 3-6 months script. **Special programs:** New Play Works: new-play developmental program of readings and workshop productions.

OREGON SHAKESPEARE FESTIVAL

(Founded 1935)
Box 158; Ashland, OR 97520; (541) 482-2111, FAX 482-0446
Stephany Smith-Pearson, *Literary Assistant*

Submission procedure: no unsolicited scripts; synopsis and dialogue sample; agent submission. **Types of material:** full-length plays. **Special interests:** plays of ideas; language-oriented plays; women and minority writers encouraged. **Facilities:** Elizabethan Theatre, 1194 seats, outdoor Elizabethan stage; Angus Bowmer Theatre, 600 seats, thrust stage; Black

Swan, 140 seats, black box. **Best submission time:** fall. **Response time:** 6 months. **Special programs:** reading series; commissioning programs.

PAN ASIAN REPERTORY THEATRE

(Founded 1977)
47 Great Jones St; New York, NY 10012; (212) 505–5655,
FAX 505–6014; email panasian@aol.com;
website www.panasianrep.org
Tisa Chang, *Artistic/Producing Director*

Submission procedure: no unsolicited scripts; synopsis and letter of inquiry. **Types of material:** full-length plays, translations, adaptations, musicals. **Special interests:** Asian or Asian-American themes only. **Facilities:** West End Theatre (in the church of St. Paul and St. Andrew), 99 seats, proscenium stage. **Production considerations:** prefers cast limit of 7. **Best submission time:** summer. **Response time:** 9 months letter; 9 months script. **Special programs:** staged readings and workshops.

PANGEA WORLD THEATER

(Founded 1995)
2509 Dupont Ave S, #209; Minneapolis, MN 55405; (612) 377–1728,
FAX 377–1728; email quest@pangeaworldtheater.org;
website www.pangeaworldtheater.org
Meena Natarajan, *Executive & Literary Director*

Submission procedure: no unsolicited scripts; letter of inquiry. **Types of material:** full-length plays, translations, adaptations, solo pieces. **Special interests:** adaptations of international literature; multiethnic works. **Facilities:** no permanent facility. **Best submission time:** year-round. **Response time:** 3-6 months.

THE PASADENA PLAYHOUSE

(Founded 1917)
80 South Lake Ave, Suite 500; Pasadena, CA 91101; (626) 792–8672,
FAX 792–7343; email patroninfo@pasadenaplayhouse.org;
website www.pasadenaplayhouse.org
David A. Tucker II, *Literary Manager*

Submission procedure: no unsolicited scripts; agent submission. **Types of material:** full-length plays, musicals. **Facilities:** The Pasadena Playhouse, 686 seats, proscenium stage. **Production considerations:** cast limit of 2-7, 1 set or unit set, modest musical requirements. **Best submission time:** year-round. **Response time:** 6-12 months.

PEGASUS PLAYERS

(Founded 1978)
1145 West Wilson; Chicago, IL 60640; (773) 878-9761,
    FAX 271-8057; email pegasusp@megsinet.net
Alex Levy, *Literary Manager*

Submission procedure: no unsolicited scripts; synopsis and letter of inquiry. **Types of material:** full-length plays, translations, adaptations, musicals, solo pieces. **Facilities:** The O'Rourke Center for the Performing Arts, 250 seats, proscenium stage. **Best submission time:** year-round. **Response time:** 1 month letter; 4-6 months script. **Special programs:** Chicago Young Playwrights Festival: annual Jan festival of plays by Chicago-area high school students; write for information.

PEGASUS THEATRE

(Founded 1985)
3916 Main St; Dallas, TX 75226-1228; (214) 821-6005,
    FAX 826-1671; website www.pegasustheatre.com
Steve Erwin, *Literary Manager*

Submission procedure: no unsolicited scripts; synopsis, 10-page dialogue sample, character breakdown and letter of inquiry. **Types of material:** full-length plays. **Special interests:** comedies only, especially contemporary satire; no mysteries. **Facilities:** mainstage, 141 seats, proscenium stage. **Production considerations:** cast limit of 10, single set; limited fly space. **Best submission time:** Mar-Jun. **Response time:** 1 month letter; 6 months script.

PENDRAGON THEATRE

(Founded 1980)
148 River St; Saranac Lake, NY 12983-2031; (518) 891-1854,
    FAX 891-7012; email pdragon@northnet.org;
    website www.northnet.org/pendragon
Bob Pettee, *Managing Director*

Submission procedure: no unsolicited scripts; synopsis, dialogue sample and letter of inquiry with SASP for response. **Types of material:** full-length plays, plays for young audiences. **Special interests:** plays suitable for performance by adolescents ages 11-16. **Facilities:** Pendragon Theatre, 132 seats, black box. **Production considerations:** cast limit of 8; simple set. **Best submission time:** year-round. **Response time:** 3–4 weeks letter; 3 months script.

PENGUIN REPERTORY COMPANY

(Founded 1977)
Box 91; Stony Point, NY 10980; (845) 786–2873, FAX 786–3638
Joe Brancato, *Artistic Director*

Submission procedure: no unsolicited scripts; agent submission only. **Types of material:** full-length plays, adaptations. **Facilities:** Barn Playhouse, 108 seats, proscenium stage. **Production considerations:** cast limit of 5; simple set. **Best submission time:** Sep–Jan. **Response time:** 3 months.

THE PENUMBRA THEATRE COMPANY

(Founded 1976)
The Martin Luther King Bldg; 270 North Kent St;
    St. Paul, MN 55102–1794; (651) 224–4601, FAX 224–7074
Lou Bellamy, *Artistic Director*

Submission procedure: accepts unsolicited scripts with resume. **Types of material:** full-length plays, one-acts, translations, adaptations, plays for young audiences, musicals. **Special interests:** works that address the African-American experience and the African diaspora. **Facilities:** Hallie Q. Brown Theatre, 260 seats, proscenium/thrust stage. **Best submission time:** year-round. **Response time:** 6–9 months. **Special programs:** Cornerstone Dramaturgy and Development Project (see Development).

THE PEOPLE'S LIGHT AND THEATRE COMPANY

(Founded 1974)
39 Conestoga Rd; Malvern, PA 19355–1798; (215) 647–1900
Alda Cortese, *Literary Manager*

Submission procedure: no unsolicited scripts; synopsis, cast list, 10-page dialogue sample and letter of inquiry. **Types of material:** full-length plays, translations, adaptations. **Special interests:** intelligent, original scripts for a family audience. **Facilities:** People's Light and Theatre, 350 seats, flexible stage; Steinbright Stage, 99–150 seats, flexible stage. **Production considerations:** 1 set or unit set. **Best submission time:** year-round. **Response time:** 2 weeks letter; 8–10 months script.

PERFORMANCE NETWORK OF ANN ARBOR

(Founded 1981)
120 East Huron; Ann Arbor, MI 48104; (734) 663-0696,
   FAX 663-7367; email pnetwork@bizserve.com;
   website www.performancenetwork.org
Daniel C. Walker, *Artistic Director*

Submission procedure: accepts unsolicited scripts. **Types of material:** full-length plays, musicals. **Special interests:** plays not produced professionally. **Facilities:** Performance Network, 139 seats, black box/thrust. **Production considerations:** prefers cast limit of 10; no fly space. **Best submission time:** year-round. **Response time:** 2-3 months.

PERFORMANCE RIVERSIDE

(Founded 1983)
4800 Magnolia Ave; Riverside, CA 92506; (909) 222-8399,
   FAX 222-8940
Steven A. Glaudini, *Executive Director*

Submission procedure: no unsolicited scripts; synopsis and letter of inquiry. **Types of material:** musicals only. **Facilities:** Landis Auditorium, 850 seats, proscenium stage. **Production considerations:** cast limit of 25, inclusive of chorus; limited backstage and wing space. **Best submission time:** year-round. **Response time:** 1 month letter; 3 months script.

PERSEVERANCE THEATRE

(Founded 1979)
914 3rd St; Douglas, AK 99824; (907) 364-2421, FAX 364-2603;
   email info@perseverancetheatre.org;
   website www.perseverancetheatre.org
Peter DuBois, *Artistic Director*

Submission procedure: no unsolicited scripts; synopsis, dialogue sample and letter of inquiry from AK playwrights only. **Types of material:** full-length plays, one-acts, solo pieces, musicals. **Special interests:** AK playwrights; gay/lesbian playwrights and themes; women playwrights; Native American playwrights and themes; political/social issues; musicals. **Facilities:** mainstage, 150 seats, thrust stage; Phoenix, 50-75 seats, flexible stage. **Best submission time:** year-round. **Response time:** 1 month letter; 3 months script. **Special programs:** Voices from the Edge Playreading Festival: annual spring presentation of diverse new work from across AK and the country; Native Playreading and Performance Festival: annual Nov presentation of Native American work.

PHILADELPHIA THEATRE COMPANY
(Founded 1974)
230 South 15th St, 4th Floor; Philadelphia, PA 19102;
    (215) 985-1400, FAX 985-5800
Michele Volansky, *Dramaturg*

Submission procedure: no unsolicited scripts; agent submission. **Types of material:** full-length plays, small-scale musicals. **Special interests:** new American plays; social/humanistic themes; no mysteries or plays for young audiences. **Facilities:** Plays and Players Theater, 324 seats, proscenium stage. **Best submission time:** year-round. **Response time:** 3-6 months. **Special programs:** STAGES: program of staged readings, possibly leading to mainstage production; scripts selected through theatre's normal submission procedure.

PHOENIX THEATRE
(Founded 1920)
100 East McDowell Rd; Phoenix, AZ 85004; (602) 258-1974,
    FAX 253-3626; website www.phoenixtheatre.net
Michael Barnard, *Artistic Director*

Submission procedure: no unsolicited scripts; synopsis, production history (if any) and letter of inquiry with SASE for response. **Types of material:** plays for young audiences, musicals, cabaret/revues. **Special interests:** plays with strong narratives suitable for a general audience. **Facilities:** mainstage, 373 seats, proscenium stage; Cookie Company, 150 seats, arena stage. **Best submission time:** year-round. **Response time:** 6 months letter; 6 months script.

THE PHOENIX THEATRE
(Founded 1983)
749 North Park Ave; Indianapolis, IN 46202; (317) 635-7529,
    FAX 635-0010; email phoenixt@oaktree.net;
    website www.phoenixtheatre.org
Bryan Fonseca, *Producing Director*

Submission procedure: no unsolicited scripts; agent submission. **Types of material:** full-length plays, one-acts. **Facilities:** mainstage, 150 seats, proscenium stage; Underground, 75 seats, black box. **Best submission time:**

Jan-Feb. **Response time:** 1 week letter; 3 months script. **Special programs:** The Festival of Emerging American Theatre (FEAT) Competition (direct solicitation to playwright only).

PILLSBURY HOUSE THEATRE
(Founded 1992)
3501 Chicago Ave S; Minneapolis, MN 55407; (612) 825-0459
Brian Goranson, *Literary Manager*

Submission procedure: no unsolicited scripts; synopsis and letter of inquiry. **Types of material:** full-length plays, one-acts, translations, adaptations. **Facilities:** Pillsbury House Theatre, 100 seats, proscenium stage. **Best submission time:** year-round. **Response time:** 5 months letter; 6 months script.

PIONEER THEATRE COMPANY
(Founded 1962)
University of Utah, 300 South, 1400 East, Room 205;
    Salt Lake City, UT 84112-0660; (801) 581-6356, FAX 581-5472
Charles Morey, *Artistic Director*

Submission procedure: no unsolicited scripts; synopsis and letter of inquiry. **Types of material:** full-length plays, translations, adaptations, musicals. **Facilities:** Simmons Pioneer Memorial Theatre, 912 seats, proscenium stage. **Best submission time:** fall. **Response time:** 1 month letter; 6 months script.

PITTSBURGH IRISH & CLASSICAL THEATRE, INC.
(Founded 1997)
Box 23607; Pittsburgh, PA 15222; (412) 396-6426, FAX 396-4792;
    email pict@duq.edu; website trfn.clpgh.org/pict
Andrew S. Paul, *Artistic Director*

Submission procedure: accepts unsolicited scripts. **Types of material:** full-length plays, translations, adaptations. **Special interests:** Irish plays, adaptations and translations of classic European plays. **Facilities:** City Theatre, 268 seats, proscenium/thrust stage. **Production considerations:** prefers cast limit of 4-10; no fly space. **Best submission time:** fall. **Response time:** 3 months. **Special programs:** Readings and workshops of new work.

PITTSBURGH PUBLIC THEATER

(Founded 1975)
621 Penn Ave; Pittsburgh, PA 15222–3204; (412) 316–8200,
    FAX 316–8216; email rrickard@ppt.org; website www.ppt.org
Becky Rickard, *Assistant to the Artistic Director*

Submission procedure: no unsolicited scripts; synopsis, dialogue sample and letter of inquiry with SASE for response. **Types of material:** full-length plays, translations, adaptations, musicals. **Facilities:** O'Reilly Theater, 650 seats, thrust stage. **Best submission time:** Feb-Apr. **Response time:** 2 months letter; 6 months script.

PLAYHOUSE ON THE SQUARE

(Founded 1968)
51 South Cooper St; Memphis, TN 38104; (901) 725–0776,
    FAX 272–7530
Jackie Nichols, *Executive Producer*

Submission procedure: accepts unsolicited scripts. **Types of material:** full-length plays, musicals. **Facilities:** Playhouse on the Square, 250 seats, proscenium stage; Circuit Playhouse, 136 seats, proscenium stage. **Best submission time:** year-round. **Response time:** 3-5 months. **Special programs:** Playhouse on the Square New Play Competition (see Prizes).

PLAYMAKERS REPERTORY COMPANY

(Founded 1976)
CB# 3235 Center for Dramatic Art; Country Club Rd;
    Chapel Hill, NC 27599–3235; (919) 962–2484, FAX 962–4069
David Hammond *Artistic Director*

Submission procedure: no unsolicited scripts; agent submission. **Types of material:** full-length plays, translations, adaptations. **Facilities:** Paul Green Theatre, 498 seats, thrust stage. **Best submission time:** Aug-May. **Response time:** 6 months.

THE PLAYWRIGHTS' CENTER

See Membership and Service Organizations.

PLAYWRIGHTS HORIZONS

(Founded 1971)
416 West 42nd St; New York, NY 10036–6896; (212) 564–1235,
    FAX 594–0296; website www.playwrightshorizons.org
Sonya Sobieski, *Literary Manager*

Submission procedure: accepts unsolicited scripts with resume and cover letter; if necessary, will accept synopsis, dialogue sample and letter of inquiry; for musicals, send script and cassette or CD (no synopses) to musical theatre department. **Types of material:** full-length plays, musicals. **Special interests:** works by American writers only; works with strong sense of language that take theatrical risks; no adaptations, translations, solo pieces or one-acts. **Facilities:** mainstage, 145 seats, proscenium stage; Studio Theater, 72 seats, black box. **Best submission time:** year-round. **Response time:** 1 month letter; 6-8 months script.

PLAYWRIGHTS PROJECT

(Founded 1985)
450 B St, Suite 1020; San Diego, CA 92101–8093; (619) 239–8222,
    FAX 239–8225; email write@playwrightsproject.com;
    website www.playwrightsproject.com
Deborah Salzer, *Executive Director*

Submission procedure: accepts unsolicited scripts. **Types of material:** one-acts. **Special Interests:** CA playwrights under 19 only. **Facilities:** Old Globe Theatre/Cassius Carter Center Stage, 225 seats, arena stage. **Best submission time:** Jan-Apr. **Response time:** 3-4 months.

PORTLAND CENTER STAGE

(Founded 1988)
1111 Southwest Broadway; Portland, OR 97205; (503) 248–6309,
    FAX 796–6509; website www.pcs.org
Chris Coleman, *Artistic Director*

Submission procedure: no unsolicited scripts; synopsis and letter of inquiry. **Types of material:** full-length plays, translations, adaptations. **Facilities:** Newmark Theatre, Portland Center for the Performing Arts, 860 seats, proscenium stage. **Production considerations:** prefers cast limit of 8-12. **Best submission time:** year-round. **Response time:** 1-2 months letter; 2-3 months script. **Special programs:** playwriting festival and readings (write for submission guidelines).

PORTLAND STAGE COMPANY

(Founded 1970)

Box 1458; Portland, ME 04104; (207) 774-1043, FAX 774-0576;
email portstage@aol.com; website www.portlandstage.com

Lisa DiFranza, *Literary and Education Director*

Submission procedure: no unsolicited scripts; synopsis, 10-page dialogue sample and letter of inquiry. **Types of material:** full-length plays, translations, adaptations. **Facilities:** Performing Arts Center Theatre, 290 seats, proscenium stage; PSC Rehearsal Hall, 90 seats, flexible stage (readings only). **Best submission time:** May-Jan. **Response time:** 3 months letter; 6 months script. **Special programs:** The Little Festival of the Unexpected: annual spring festival of new work; scripts chosen through theatre's normal submission process.

PRIMARY STAGES

(Founded 1983)

131 West 45th St; New York, NY 10036; (212) 840-9705,
FAX 840-9725; website nytheatre.com/primary.htm

Casey Childs, *Artistic Director*

Submission procedure: no unsolicited scripts; synopsis, 10-page dialogue sample, description of play style, resume and letter of inquiry with SASE for response; include cassette for musicals. **Types of material:** full-length plays, musicals. **Special interests:** plays not previously produced in New York City only; highly theatrical works by American playwrights for American or New York City premiere; plays by women and minorities; no strict realism or standard film and television fare. **Facilities:** Primary Stages Theatre, 99 seats, proscenium stage; Phil Bosakowski Theatre, 65 seats, proscenium stage. **Production considerations:** cast limit of 2-8; unit set or simple set changes; no fly or wing space. **Best submission time:** Sep-Jun. **Response time:** 2-4 months letter; 6 months-1 year script.

PULSE ENSEMBLE THEATRE

(Founded 1989)

432 West 42nd St; New York, NY 10036; (212) 695-1596,
FAX 736-1255; email brian@pulseensembletheatre.org;
website www.pulseensembletheatre.org

Brian Richardson, *Company Manager*

Submission procedure: no unsolicited scripts; synopsis, dialogue sample, character breakdown, resume and letter of inquiry; include cassette or CD for musicals. **Types of material:** full-length plays, one-acts, musicals, solo pieces. **Special interests:** plays with science themes or social relevance. **Facilities:** mainstage, 55 seats, black box; studio, 40 seats, flexible stage. **Production considerations:** no fly space. **Best submission time:** year-round. **Response time:** 6 months letter; 6 months script.

THE PURPLE ROSE THEATRE COMPANY

(Founded 1991)
Box 220; Chelsea, MI 48118; (734) 433–PRTC, FAX 475–0802;
    email purplerose@earthlink.net;
    website www.purplerosetheatre.org
Anthony Caselli, *Literary Manager*

Submission procedure: accepts unsolicited scripts; prefers synopsis, dialogue sample and letter of inquiry. **Types of material:** full-length plays. **Special interests:** plays that speak to a middle-American audience. **Facilities:** Garage Theatre, 168 seats, thrust stage. **Production considerations:** cast limit of 10; no fly or wing space. **Best submission time:** year-round. **Response time:** 2 months letter; 6–9 months script.

RED BARN THEATRE

(Founded 1981)
Box 707; Key West, FL 33040; (305) 293–3035, FAX 293–3035;
    email mmcdon3444@aol.com
Mimi McDonald, *Managing Director*

Submission procedure: no unsolicited scripts; synopsis and letter of inquiry with professional recommendation. **Types of material:** full-length plays, musicals, cabaret/revues. **Facilities:** Red Barn Theatre, 88 seats, proscenium stage. **Production considerations:** cast limit of 8, small band for musicals; no fly space, limited wing space. **Best submission time:** Mar–Jul. **Response time:** 6 months letter (if interested); 6 months script.

REPERTORIO ESPAÑOL

(Founded 1968)
138 East 27th St; New York, NY 10016;
    email repertorio@mindspring.com; website www.repertorio.org
Robert Weber Federico, *Artistic Associate Producer*

Submission procedure: no unsolicited scripts; synopsis and letter of inquiry. **Types of material:** full-length plays, adaptations, plays for young audiences, musicals, operas. **Special interests:** plays dealing with Hispanic themes. **Facilities:** Gramercy Arts Theatre, 130 seats, proscenium stage. **Production considerations:** small cast. **Best submission time:** summer. **Response time:** 2-3 months letter; 8-10 months script. **Special programs:** Metropolitan Life Foundation Nuestras Voces: playwriting competition; download guidelines from web. (See listing in Prizes.)

THE REPERTORY THEATRE OF ST. LOUIS

(Founded 1966)
130 Edgar Rd; Box 191730; St. Louis, MO 63119; (314) 968-7340;
    email sgregg@repstl.org
Susan Gregg, *Associate Artistic Director*

Submission procedure: no unsolicited scripts; synopsis, character breakdown, technical requirements and letter of inquiry. **Types of material:** full-length plays. **Special interests:** nonnaturalistic plays; contemporary social and political issues. **Facilities:** Main Stage, 750 seats, thrust stage; Studio Theatre, 130 seats, black box. **Production considerations:** small cast; modest production demands. **Best submission time:** year-round. **Response time:** 1 month letter; 2 years script.

RIVERLIGHT AND COMPANY

(Founded 1981)
75 Wendell St; Battle Creek, MI 49017-3821; (616) 962-2453,
    FAX 441-2707; email jkline_hobbs@glfn.org
J. Kline Hobbs, *Project Director*

Submission procedure: no unsolicited scripts; letter of inquiry; agent submission. **Types of material:** full-length plays, adaptations, plays for young audiences, musicals, cabaret/revues, solo pieces. **Special interests:** American history, literature and social issues. **Facilities:** Binda Theatre, 375 seats, proscenium stage; Discovery Theatre, 175 seats, thrust stage. **Production considerations:** cast limit of 1-8, variable space. **Best submission time:** year-round. **Response time:** 2 weeks letter; 1 month script.

RIVERSIDE THEATRE

(Founded 1985)
3250 Riverside Park Dr; Vero Beach, FL 32963; (561) 231-5860;
email backstage@riversidetheatre.com;
website www.riversidetheatre.com
New Play Department

Submission procedure: no unsolicited scripts; synopsis and letter of inquiry. **Types of material:** full-length plays, translations, adaptations, plays for young audiences, musicals. **Facilities:** Riverside Theatre, 615 seats, proscenium stage; Ann Morton Theatre, 300 seats, flexible stage. **Production considerations:** cast limit of 10. **Best submission time:** spring. **Response time:** 3 months letter; 3-5 months script.

RIVERSIDE THEATRE

(Founded 1981)
213 North Gilbert St; Iowa City, IA 52245; (319) 338-7672,
FAX 887-1362; email artistic@riversidetheatre.org;
website www.riversidetheatre.org
Ron Clark and Jody Hovland, *Artistic Directors*

Submission procedure: no unsolicited scripts; synopsis and letter of inquiry. **Types of material:** full-length plays, translations, adaptations, cabaret/revues, solo pieces. **Facilities:** Riverside Theatre, 118 seats, flexible stage. **Production considerations:** small cast, simple set. **Best submission time:** year-round. **Response time:** 1 month letter (if interested); 3-5 months script.

RM 120 THEATRE

(Founded 2000)
Box 300165; Austin, TX 78703; (512) 481-8366, FAX 481-8366;
email rm120theatre@aol.com
Greg Romero, *Dramaturg*

Submission procedure: accepts unsolicited scripts. **Types of material:** full-length plays, one-acts, adaptations, musicals, solo pieces. **Special interests:** provocative, imaginative new works with limited or no production history. **Facilities:** no permanent facility. **Production considerations:** cast limit of 8. **Best submission time:** year-round. **Response time:** 2 months. **Special programs:** Workshop Series: up to 4 month-long developmental workshops resulting in public reading and moderated discussion, some works later selected for production. Writers are compensated $150 and out-of-town writers are compensated for travel expenses (contingent on funding). Reading Night: up to 8 casual readings and discussions of new works by dramaturgy staff and acting company. Some works later selected for production. Writers are compensated $30 (contingent on funding).

ROADSIDE THEATER

(Founded 1975)
91 Madison Ave; Whitesburg, KY 41858; (606) 633-0108,
    FAX 633-1009; email roadside@appalshop.org;
    website www.appalshop.org/rst
Dudley Cocke, *Director*

Submission procedure: no unsolicited scripts; synopsis, dialogue sample and letter of inquiry. **Types of material:** full-length plays. **Special interests:** plays about the Appalachian region only. **Facilities:** Appalshop Theater, 150 seats, thrust stage. **Production considerations:** small cast, simple sets suitable for touring. **Best submission time:** year-round. **Response time:** 3 weeks letter; 2 months script. **Special programs:** reading and workshop series. Playwright residencies initiated by theatre; playwright may not apply.

ROADWORKS PRODUCTIONS

(Founded 1992)
1144 West Fulton Market, Suite 105; Chicago, IL 60607;
    (312) 492-7150, FAX 492-7155; email info@roadworks.org;
    website www.roadworks.org
Shade Murray, *Artistic Director*

Submission procedure: no unsolicited scripts; professional recommendation. **Types of material:** full-length plays. **Special interests:** scripts suitable for ensemble aged 20-30; "explosive, high-energy" plays. **Facilities:** no permanent facility. **Best submission time:** Sep-Nov. **Response time:** 2 months.

THE ROCKY MOUNTAIN PLAYWRIGHTING FESTIVAL

(Founded 1991)
The Rocky Mountain Student Theater Project; Box 1626;
    Telluride, CO 81435; (719) 685-5167; email PlayFest@aol.com;
    website members.aol.com/PlayFest/RMSTP.html
Owen Perkins, *Executive Director*

Submission procedure: accepts unsolicited scripts. **Types of material:** full-length plays, one-acts, adaptations, solo pieces. **Facilities:** The Nugget Theatre, 220 seats, proscenium stage. **Production considerations:** prefers small casts; simple sets. **Best submission time:** year-round. **Response time:** 3 months. **Special programs:** The Playwrighting Academy: 1-6 week workshops held on school campuses and in communities nationwide on all aspects of theatre including playwrighting. The Roy Barker Playwrighting Prize (see Prizes). Additional summer playwrighting academy held prior to announcement of Roy Barker prize winners; write or visit web for guidelines.

ROUND HOUSE THEATRE

(Founded 1978)
12210 Bushey Dr, Suite 101; Silver Spring, MD 20902;
(301) 933-9530, FAX 933-2321; website www.Round-House.org
Production Department

Submission procedure: no unsolicited scripts; synopsis, 10-page dialogue sample, cast breakdown, technical requirements, resume and SASE for response. **Types of material:** full-length plays, translations, adaptations, plays for young audiences, musicals, solo pieces. **Special interests:** contemporary issues; new translations of lesser-known classics; experimental works; humorous plays. **Facilities:** Round House Theatre, 218 seats, modified thrust stage. **Production considerations:** cast limit of 8, prefers 1 set. **Best submission time:** year-round. **Response time:** 2 months letter; minimum 1 year script. **Special programs**: Round the Edges Series: reading series showcasing smaller more experimental pieces; solo work preferred; scripts selected through theatre's regular submission procedure. New Voices Play Reading Series: Monday night reading series of new, unproduced plays and musicals by regional (DC, MD, VA) playwrights; submit full-length plays, one-acts, musicals and ten-minute plays to Nick Olcott, Associate Artistic Director/New Voices Coordinator; *deadline:* spring 2002; *dates:* Jun 2002.

THE SALT LAKE ACTING COMPANY

(Founded 1970)
168 West 500 N; Salt Lake City, UT 84103; (801) 363-0526,
FAX 532-8513
David Mong, *Literary Manager*

Submission procedure: no unsolicited scripts; synopsis, 5-10-page dialogue sample, resume and letter of inquiry with SASE for response. **Types of material:** full-length plays, translations, adaptations, musicals. **Special interests:** western American writers "who understand the unique synergistic effect that playwright, actor and audience enjoy when a work is produced for the stage." **Facilities:** Upstairs, 150 seats, thrust stage; Chapel Theatre,

99 seats, thrust stage. **Best submission time:** year-round. **Response time:** 4 months letter; 8 months script. **Special programs:** reading series four times annually.

SAN DIEGO REPERTORY THEATRE

(Founded 1976)
79 Horton Plaza; San Diego, CA 92101; (619) 231–3586,
    FAX 235–0939
Artistic Department

Submission procedure: no unsolicited scripts; synopsis and letter of inquiry. **Types of material:** full-length plays, translations, adaptations, musicals, literary cabaret, mixed media events. **Special interests:** multiethnic and intercultural work; hard-hitting social and political work; offbeat hip musicals; dramatic work with unusual incorporation of music; women's issues; sharp-edged comedy; poetic visions. **Facilities:** Lyceum Stage, 570 seats, modified thrust stage; Lyceum Space, 270 seats, flexible stage. **Production considerations:** no fly space in Lyceum Space. **Best submission time:** year-round. **Response time:** 3 months letter; 12 months script. **Special programs:** readings and workshop productions.

SAN JOSE REPERTORY THEATRE

(Founded 1980)
101 Paseo de San Antonio; San Jose, CA 95113; (408) 367–7266,
    FAX 367–7237; website www.sjrep.com
Nakissa Etemad, *Literary Manager/Dramaturg*

Submission procedure: no unsolicited scripts; agent submission. **Types of material:** full-length plays, translations, adaptations, musicals, solo pieces. **Special interests:** small-cast musicals. **Facilities:** San Jose Repertory Theatre, 525 seats, proscenium stage. **Best submission time:** Sep–Nov. **Response time:** 3-6 months.

SANTA FE STAGES

(Founded 1995)
100 North Guadalupe St; Santa Fe, New Mexico 87501;
    (505) 982–6690; email sfstages@ix.netcom.com;
    website www.santafestages.org
Craig Strong, *Producing Director*

Submission procedure: no unsolicited scripts; agent submission. **Types of material:** full-length plays, translations, adaptations. **Special interests:**

translations and adaptations of classics not in the standard repertoire; cutting-edge works. **Facilities:** Lensic Performing Arts Center, 835 seats, proscenium stage; Firestone Plaza Theater, 200 seats, proscenium stage. **Best submission time:** Sep-Apr. **Response time:** 3 months letter; 6 months script.

SANTA MONICA PLAYHOUSE

(Founded 1962)
1211 4th St; Santa Monica, CA 90401-1391; (310) 394-9779,
FAX 393-5573; website www.santamonicaplayhouse.com
Chris DeCarlo and Evelyn Rudie, *Co-Artistic Directors*

Submission procedure: no unsolicited scripts; synopsis and letter of inquiry. **Types of material:** full-length plays, one-acts, translations, adaptations, plays for young audiences, musicals. **Facilities:** The Main Stage, 88 seats, arena/thrust stage; The Other Space, 70 seats, black box. **Production considerations:** cast limit of 8, simple production demands. **Best submission time:** year-round. **Response time:** 3 months letter; 6 months script.

SEACOAST REPERTORY THEATRE

(Founded 1986)
125 Bow St; Portsmouth, NH 03801; (603) 433-4793,
FAX 431-7818; email info@seacoastrep.org;
website www.seacoastrep.org
Roy M. Rogosin, *Producing Artistic Director*
Jean Benda, *Assistant to Producer*

Submission procedure: no unsolicited scripts; agent submission (1-page synopsis only; include cassette for musicals). **Types of material:** full-length plays, plays for young audiences, musicals. **Special interests:** new American plays; small-scale musicals; plays for young audiences. **Facilities:** Seacoast Repertory Theatre, 230 seats, thrust stage. **Best submission time:** year-round. **Response time:** 3-6 months.

SEASIDE MUSIC THEATER

(Founded 1977)
Box 2835; Daytona Beach, FL 32120; (904) 252-3394,
FAX 252-8991; website www.seasidemusictheater.org
Lester Malizia, *General Manager*

Submission procedure: no unsolicited scripts; synopsis, cassette or CD of music and letter of inquiry. **Types of material:** musicals for young and adult audiences, cabaret/revues. **Facilities:** Winter Theater, 576 seats, proscenium stage; Summer Theater, 500 seats, proscenium stage; Theater for Children, 576 seats, proscenium stage. **Production considerations:** cast limit of 20 for Winter Theater, 30 for Summer Theater, 10 for Theater for Children; small musical combo for Theater for Children and Winter Theater, 25-member orchestra for Summer Theater; no wing or orchestra space in Winter Theater, no fly space except in Summer Theater. **Best submission time:** Sep-Nov. **Response time:** 1-3 months letter; 3-6 months script.

SEATTLE CHILDREN'S THEATRE

(Founded 1975)
201 Thomas St; Seattle, WA 98109; (206) 443-0807;
    website www.sct.org
Literary Manager

Submission procedure: accepts unsolicited scripts for Drama School Summerstages only; professional recommendation for mainstage. **Types of material:** full-length plays for family audiences, translations, adaptations, musicals, solo pieces. **Special interests:** sophisticated works for young audiences that also appeal to adults. **Facilities:** Charlotte Martin Theatre, 485 seats, proscenium stage; Eve Alvord Theatre, 280 seats, modified proscenium. **Best submission time:** year-round. **Response time:** 8 months. **Special programs:** Drama School Summerstages: one-act plays, 30-60 minutes long for student performance, must have roles for 12-18 actors, ages 8-19; submit script with SASE for response to Don Fleming; Program Director; *deadline:* 1 Dec 2001.

SECOND STAGE THEATRE

(Founded 1979)
Box 1807, Ansonia Station; New York, NY 10023; (212) 787-8302,
    FAX 877-9886; email CBURNEY@secondstagetheatre.com
Christopher Burney, *Associate Artistic Director*

Submission procedure: no unsolicited scripts; synopsis, 5-10-page dialogue sample, resume, production history and letter of inquiry. **Types of material:** full-length plays, adaptations, musicals. **Special interests:** new and previously produced American plays; "heightened" realism; sociopolitical issues; plays by women and minority writers. **Facilities:** Midtown Theatre, 296 seats, proscenium stage; McGinn/Cazale Theatre, 108 seats, endstage. **Best submission time:** year-round. **Response time:** 1 month letter; 5-6 months script. **Special programs:** annual series of 4-6 readings of new and previously produced plays. Constance Klinsky Award for Excellence in the Composition of Musical Theatre: 3-4 awards of $1000 given to composers and lyricists; write for guidelines.

SEVEN ANGELS THEATRE

(Founded 1991)
Box 3358; Waterbury, CT 06705; (203) 591–8223, FAX 591–8223
Semina De Laurentis, *Artistic Director*

Submission procedure: no unsolicited scripts; professional recommendation. **Types of material:** full-length plays, musicals. **Facilities:** Seven Angels Theatre, 350 seats, proscenium stage. **Production considerations:** cast limit of 10; prefers unit set; no fly space. **Best submission time:** year-round. **Response time:** 1 year script, only if interested.

SHADOWLIGHT PRODUCTIONS

(Founded 1994)
22 Chattanooga St; San Francisco, CA 19114; (415) 648–4461,
   FAX 641–9734; email info@shadowlight.com;
   website www.shadowlight.com
Kate Sheehan, *Managing Director*

Submission procedure: no unsolicited scripts; synopsis and letter of inquiry with SASE for response. **Types of material:** full-length plays, one-acts, translations, adaptations, plays for young audiences, musicals, solo pieces, cabaret/revues. **Special interests:** plays suitable for shadow theatre only, utilizing puppets as well as live actors; scripts dealing with mythological or historical figures; adaptations of stories or novels. **Facilities:** no permanent facility. **Production considerations:** cast limit of 15. **Best submission time:** year-round. **Response time:** 1 month letter; 1 month script.

SHAKESPEARE & COMPANY

(Founded 1978)
The Mount; 70 Kemble St; Lenox, MA 01240; (413) 637–1199,
   FAX 637–4274; email hammond@shakespeare.org;
   website www.shakespeare.org
Michael Hammond, *Artistic Associate for Submissions*

Submission procedure: no unsolicited scripts; synopsis, 4-page dialogue sample and letter of inquiry. **Types of material:** full-length plays and one-acts. **Special interests:** plays based on or adapted from works by Edith Wharton and other women authors, Henry James, Herman Melville, Nathaniel Hawthorne or other writers with connections to the Berkshires. **Facilities:** Mainstage Theatre, 600 seats, outdoor amphitheatre; Founders' Theatre, 428 seats, Elizabethan stage; Stables Theatre, 108 seats, thrust stage; Spring Lawn Theatre, 100 seats, salon. **Production considerations:** small casts, minimal set pieces. **Best submission time:** winter, spring. **Response time:** 6 months letter (if interested); 6 months script.

THE SHAKESPEARE THEATRE

(Founded 1986)
516 8th St; Washington, DC 20003-2834; (202) 547-3230,
    FAX 547-0226; email smazzola@shakespearedc.org;
    website www.shakespearedc.org
Steven Scott Mazzola, *Assistant to the Artistic Director*

Submission procedure: no unsolicited scripts; professional recommendation. **Types of material:** translations, adaptations. **Special interests:** translations and adaptations of classics only. **Facilities:** The Shakespeare Theatre, 449 seats, proscenium stage. **Best submission time:** summer. **Response time:** 3-4 months.

SIGNATURE THEATRE

(Founded 1990)
3806 South Four Mile Run Dr; Arlington, VA 22206; (703) 820-9771
Marcia Gardner, *Literary Manager*

Submission procedure: accepts unsolicited scripts from DC playwrights only; agent submission for all other plays. **Types of material:** full-length plays, adaptations, musicals. **Special interests:** work not produced professionally only; social issues; comedies. **Facilities:** Signature Theatre, 126 seats, black box. **Production considerations:** prefers cast limit of 10; no fly space. **Best submission time:** Sep-May. **Response time:** 6 months. **Special programs:** Stages: staged readings of new plays-in-process; scripts selected through theatre's normal submission procedure; On the Edge Series: full production of 1 new play a year.

SKYLIGHT OPERA THEATRE
(Founded 1959)
158 North Broadway; Milwaukee, WI 53202; (414) 291-7811,
  FAX 291-7815; email dianac@skylightopera.org;
  website www.skylightopera.com
Diana Carl, *Artistic Administrator*

Submission procedure: no unsolicited scripts; synopsis and letter of inquiry; include cassette for musicals. **Types of material:** musicals, cabaret/revues. **Special interests:** small-scaled musicals and operas. **Facilities:** Cabot Theatre, 375 seats, proscenium stage. **Production considerations:** cast limit of 22, orchestra limit 18; prefer smaller casts. **Best submission time:** year-round. **Response time:** 2 months letter; 12 months script.

SOHO REPERTORY THEATRE
(Founded 1975)
46 Walker St; New York, NY 10013; (212) 941-8632, FAX 941-7148
Daniel Aukin, *Artistic Director*
Alexandra Conley, *Executive Director*

Submission procedure: accepts unsolicited scripts for Summer Camp only (see below); direct solicitation to playwright or agent for all other plays. **Types of material:** full-length plays, one-acts, solo pieces. **Facilities:** Soho Rep, 70 seats, black box. **Special programs**: Summer Camp: annual Jul festival of unproduced full-length plays, one-acts, solo pieces; *deadline:* 1 Feb 2001; *notification:* May 2001.

SOUTH COAST REPERTORY
(Founded 1964)
Box 2197; Costa Mesa, CA 92628-2197; (714) 708-5500
Jerry Patch, *Dramaturg*
Jennifer Kiger, *Literary Manager*

Submission procedure: no unsolicited scripts; synopsis, dialogue sample and letter of inquiry. **Types of material:** full-length plays, translations, adaptations, musicals. **Facilities:** mainstage, 507 seats, modified thrust stage; Second Stage, 161 seats, thrust stage. **Best submission time:** year-round. **Response time:** 1-3 weeks letter; 2-4 months script. **Special programs:** COLAB (Collaboration Laboratory) New Play Program: developmental program culminating in readings, staged readings, workshop productions and full productions; playwright receives grant, commission and/or royalties depending on nature of project. Pacific Playwrights

Festival: annual 3-week developmental program for playwrights writing in English culminating in staged readings, workshop productions and full productions performed for the public and theatre colleagues; plays are chosen through theatre's normal submission procedure and by invitation; not-for-profit theatres are also welcome to submit work; *dates:* Apr 2002.

SOUTHWEST REPERTORY THEATER

(Founded 1999)
Box 27409; Albuquerque, NM 87125; (505) 244–3634,
    FAX 244–3666; email info@southwestrep.com;
    website www.southwestrep.com
Laurie Thomas, *Literary Manager*

Submission procedure: accepts unsolicited scripts. **Types of material:** full-length plays, one-acts, musicals. **Special interests:** Native American and Hispanic subject matter and themes. **Facilities:** mainstage, 200 seats, thrust stage; multi-purpose space, 100 seats, flexible stage. **Production considerations:** cast limit of 12, prefers unit set; no fly space. **Best submission time:** year-round. **Response time:** 3 months. **Special programs:** workshop series; scripts selected through theatre's normal submission process.

SPOKANE INTERPLAYERS ENSEMBLE

(Founded 1981)
Box 1961; Spokane, WA 99210; (509) 455–7529, FAX 624–9348;
    email interplayers@interplayers.com;
    website www.interplayers.com
Robert A. Welch, *Managing Director*

Submission procedure: no unsolicited scripts; synopsis, dialogue sample, cast list, set requirements, production history, reviews (if any) and letter of inquiry. **Types of material:** full-length plays. **Facilities:** Spokane Interplayers Ensemble, 253 seats, thrust stage. **Production considerations:** prefers cast limit of 8, 1 set. **Best submission time:** year-round. **Response time:** 3 months letter (if interested); 3–6 months script.

SPRINGER OPERA HOUSE

(Founded 1871)
103 10th St; Columbus, GA 31901; (706) 324-5714,
 FAX 324-4681; email p_pierce@springeroperahouse.org;
 website www.springeroperahouse.org
Paul Pierce, *Producing Artistic Director*

Submission procedure: accepts unsolicited scripts. **Types of material:** full-length plays, plays for young audiences, musicals, cabaret/revues. **Special interests:** musicals; comedies. **Facilities:** mainstage, 700 seats, proscenium stage; studio II, 170 seats, flexible stage. **Production considerations:** small cast, unit set. **Best submission time:** Nov-Feb. **Response time:** 2 months letter; 6 months script.

STAGE ONE: THE LOUISVILLE CHILDREN'S THEATRE

(Founded 1946)
501 West Main; Louisville, KY 40202-2957; (502) 589-5946,
 FAX 588-5910; email stageone@stageone.org;
 website www.stageone.org
Moses Goldberg, *Producing Director*

Submission procedure: accepts unsolicited scripts. **Types of material:** plays for young audiences. **Special interests:** plays about young people in the real world; good, honest treatments of familiar titles. **Facilities:** Moritz von Bomard Theater, 610 seats, thrust stage; Louisville Gardens, 300 seats, arena stage. **Production considerations:** prefers cast limit of 12; some productions tour. **Best submission time:** Oct-Dec. **Response time:** 3 months. **Special programs:** Tomorrow's Playwrights: annual one-act competition open to high school students throughout KY region; 3 finalists receive staged readings and prepare rewrite to determine placement; cash awards for winners and sponsoring schools; submit play through school; *deadline:* 1 Mar 2001.

STAGES REPERTORY THEATRE

(Founded 1978)
3201 Allen Prkwy, #101; Houston, TX 77019-1897; (713) 527-0220,
 FAX 527-8669
Rob Bundy, *Artistic Director*

Submission procedure: accepts unsolicited scripts. **Types of material:** full-length plays, plays for young audiences. **Special interests:** nonrealistic, edgy works. **Facilities:** Stages Repertory Theatre, 235 seats, arena stage; Stages Repertory Theatre, 180 seats, thrust stage. **Production considerations:** cast limit of 6; maximum 1 hour running time for children's shows. **Best submission time:** year-round. **Response time:** 9 months. **Special programs:** Southwest Festival for New Plays (see Development).

STAGES THEATRE CENTER

(Founded 1982)
1540 North McCadden Place; Hollywood, CA 90028;
   (323) 463-5356, FAX 463-3904;
   email ask@stageshollywood.com;
   website www.stageshollywood.com
Don Boughton, *Literary Manager*

Submission procedure: accepts unsolicited scripts. **Types of material:** full-length plays, one-acts, translations, adaptations, plays for young audiences. **Special interests:** plays by foreign writers both in original language and in translation; theatre regularly produces plays in Spanish, French and English but can also find actors fluent in other languages; challenging, experimental work; non-text, movement-based work. **Facilities:** Ampitheatre, 99 seats, outdoor flexible stage; mainstage, 49 seats, proscenium stage; Lab, 25 seats, classroom. **Best submission time:** year-round. **Response time:** 6 months-1 year.

STAGEWORKS

(Founded 1993)
133 Warren St; Hudson, NY 12534-3118; (518) 828-7843;
   FAX 828-4026; email stagewrk@mhonline.net;
   website www.mhonline.net/~stagewrk
Laura Margolis, *Producing Artistic Director*

Submission procedure: no unsolicted scripts; synopsis and letter of inquiry. **Types of material:** full-length plays, translations, adaptations, musicals, solo pieces. **Facilities:** North Pointe, 90 seats, proscenium/thrust stage. **Production considerations:** cast limit of 10, 1 set or unit set; no fly space. **Best submission time:** year-round. **Response time:** 4-6 months letter; 6-8 months script. **Special programs:** Ten by Ten: annual festival of new short plays; participation by invitation only.

STAMFORD THEATRE WORKS

(Founded 1988)
95 Atlantic St; Stamford, CT 06901; (203) 359-4414, FAX 356-1846
Steve Karp, *Producing Director*

Submission procedure: no unsolicited scripts; agent submission;

professional recommendation. **Types of material:** full-length plays, translations, adaptations, musicals. **Special interests:** plays that are contemporary, innovative and thought-provoking; socially and culturally relevant; challenging and entertaining. **Facilities:** Center Stage, 150 seats, modified thrust stage. **Production considerations:** prefers small cast, unit set. **Best submission time:** year-round. **Response time:** 2 months letter; 6 months script. **Special programs:** Windows on the Work: developmental workshop for 3 new plays; each play receives rehearsals, staged readings and audience discussions; scripts selected through theatre's normal submission procedure; plays not produced professionally only; *dates:* Feb-Mar.

STATE THEATER COMPANY

(Founded 1982)
719 Congress Ave; Austin, TX 78701; (512) 692-0509,
 FAX 472-7199; email mpolgar@austintheatrealliance.org;
 website www.statetheatercompany.com
Michelle Polgar, *Dramaturg*

Submission procedure: accepts unsolicited scripts from TX playwrights only; accepts agent submission; others send synopsis, 15-page dialogue sample and letter of inquiry. **Types of material:** full-length plays, adaptations, solo pieces. **Special interests:** work not produced professionally; TX plays; comedies. **Facilities:** State Theater, 350 seats, flexible stage; Horton Foote Theatre, 90 seats, proscenium stage. **Best submission time:** 1 Jan-1 May. **Response time:** 3-6 weeks letter; 6-9 months script (most scripts returned in the fall). **Special programs:** Harvest Festival of New American Plays (see Development).

STEPPENWOLF THEATRE COMPANY

(Founded 1976)
758 West North Ave; 4th floor; Chicago, IL 60610; (312) 335-1888,
 FAX 335-0808; email theatre@steppenwolf.org;
 website www.steppenwolf.org
Edward Sobel, *Literary Manager*

Submission procedure: no unsolicited scripts; synopsis, 10-page dialogue sample, short bio or resume and letter of inquiry. **Types of material:** full-length plays. **Special interests:** ensemble pieces with dynamic acting roles. **Facilities:** mainstage, 510 seats, proscenium stage; Studio, 50-300 seats, flexible stage. Garage, 60 seats, flexible stage. **Best submission time:** year-round. **Response time:** 1-3 months letter, 6-9 months script.

St. Louis Black Repertory Company

(Founded 1976)
634 North Grand Blvd, Suite 10-F; St. Louis, MO 63103;
   (314) 534-3807, FAX 534-8456;
   email ronhimes@stlouisblackrep.com
Ronald J. Himes, *Producing Director*

Submission procedure: no unsolicited scripts; synopsis, 3-5-page dialogue sample, resume and letter of inquiry. **Types of material:** full-length plays, plays for young audiences, musicals. **Special interests:** works by African-American and Third World playwrights. **Facilities:** Grandel Theatre, 470 seats, thrust stage. **Best submission time:** Jun-Aug. **Response time:** 2 months letter; 2 months script. **Special programs:** touring company presenting works for young audiences.

Stratford Festival Theater

(Founded 1996)
1850 Elm St; Stratford, CT 06615; (203) 378-1200, FAX 378-9777
J. Wishnia, *Dramaturg*

Submission procedure: no unsolicited scripts; synopsis and letter of inquiry with SASE for response. **Types of material:** full-length plays, plays for young audiences, musicals, cabaret/revues. **Facilities:** Festival Stage, 1500 seats, proscenium stage. **Best submission time:** year-round. **Response time:** 2 months letter; 6 months script. **Special programs:** staged readings.

Studio Arena Theatre

(Founded 1965)
710 Main St; Buffalo, NY 14202-1990; website www.studioarena.org
Gavin Cameron, *Artistic Director*
Ken Nenfeld, *Executive Director*

Submission procedure: no unsolicited scripts; agent submission. **Types of material:** full-length plays, translations, adaptations. **Special interests:** plays of local interest; plays of a theatrical nature; American history and culture; ethnic cultures, including plays about minorities. **Facilities:** Studio Arena Theatre, 637 seats, thrust stage. **Production considerations:** cast limit of 6; no fly system and limited wing space. **Best submission time:** year-round. **Response time:** 6 months.

SYRACUSE STAGE

(Founded 1973)

820 East Genesee St; Syracuse, NY 13210-1508; (315) 443-4008,
	FAX 443-9846; website www.syracusestage.org

Richard Keller, *Director of Dramaturgy and Education*

Submission procedure: no unsolicited scripts; agent submission or synopsis, 10 page dialogue sample, character description and letter of inquiry with SASE for response. **Types of material:** full-length plays. **Special interests:** no one-acts, translations, adaptations or musicals. **Facilities:** John D. Archbold Theatre, 499 seats, proscenium stage. **Production considerations:** prefers small cast. **Best submission time:** year-round. **Response time:** 6 months.

TADA!

(Founded 1984)

120 West 28th St, 2nd Floor; New York, NY 10001; (212) 627-1732,
	FAX 243-6736; email tada@tadatheater.com;
	website www.tadatheater.com

Janine Nina Trevens, *Artistic Director*

Submission procedure: accepts unsolicited scripts. **Types of material:** one-acts, plays for young audiences, musicals. **Special interests:** work to be performed by children and teenagers. **Facilities:** mainstage, 98 seats, black box. **Production considerations:** modest production demands. **Best submission time:** year-round. **Response time:** 6 months.

TAMPA BAY PERFORMING ARTS CENTER

(Founded 1987)

1010 North W. C. MacInnes Place; Tampa, FL 33602;
	(813) 222-1000; FAX 222-1057; website www.tbpac.org

Karla Hartley, *Artistic Associate*

Submission procedure: accepts unsolicited scripts. **Types of material:** full-length plays. **Special interests:** plays by women writers. **Facilities:** Carol Morsani Hall, 2500 seats, proscenium stage; Ferguson Hall, 1000 seats, proscenium stage; Jaeb, 300 seats, proscenium stage; Shimberg Playhouse, 150 seats, black box. **Production considerations:** small cast, 1 set. **Best submission time:** summer. **Response time:** 2 months.

THALIA SPANISH THEATRE

(Founded 1977)
41–17 Greenpoint Ave; Sunnyside, NY 11104; (718) 729–3880,
  FAX 729–3388; email thaliatheatre@aol.com;
  website www.thaliatheatre.org
Angel Gil Orrios, *Artistic/Executive Director*

Submission procedure: accepts unsolicited scripts. **Types of material:** full-length plays, translations, adaptations. **Special interests:** plays with Hispanic themes. **Facilities:** Thalia Spanish Theatre, 74 seats, proscenium stage. **Best submission time:** year-round. **Response time:** 3 months.

THE THEATER AT MONMOUTH

(Founded 1970)
Box 385; Monmouth, ME 04259–0385; (207) 933–2952,
  FAX 933–2952; email tamoffice@theateratmonmouth.org;
  website www.theateratmonmouth.org
David Greenham, *Managing Director*

Submission procedure: no unsolicited scripts; synopsis and letter of inquiry. **Types of material:** adaptations, plays for young audiences. **Special interests:** large-cast adaptations of classic literature, plays for young audiences. **Facilities:** Cumston Hall, 275 seats, thrust stage. **Production considerations:** simple set. **Best submission time:** Sep. **Response time:** 4–6 weeks letter; 4–6 months script.

THEATER BY THE BLIND

(Founded 1979)
306 West 18th St; New York, NY 10011; (212) 243–4337,
  FAX 243–4337; email ashiotis@panix.com;
  website www.tbtb.org
Ike Schambelan, *Artistic Director*

Submission procedure: accepts unsolicited scripts. **Types of material:** full-length plays, one-acts, musicals. **Special interests:** work by and about the blind. **Facilities:** no permanent facility; company performs in various 99-seat venues. **Best submission time:** year-round. **Response time:** 2 months.

THEATRE DE LA JEUNE LUNE

(Founded 1979)
105 First St N; Minneapolis, MN 55401; (612) 332–3968,
    FAX 332–0048
Barbara Berlovitz, *Co–Artistic Director*

Submission procedure: no unsolicited scripts; synopsis and letter of inquiry. **Types of material:** full-length plays, translations, adaptations, musicals, cabaret/revues. **Special interests:** large-cast plays dealing with universal themes. **Facilities:** Theatre de la Jeune Lune, 500 seats, flexible stage. **Best submission time:** year-round. **Response time:** 8-10 weeks letter; 4 months script.

THE THEATRE DISTRICT AT THE CAST

(Formerly the Cast Theatre)
(Founded 1976)
804 North El Centro Ave; Hollywood, CA 90038; (323) 957–2343
Christi Sweeney, *Literary Manager*

Submission procedure: accepts unsolicited scripts. **Types of material:** full-length plays. **Special interests:** previously unproduced works. **Facilities:** Cast at the Circle, 99 seats, proscenium stage; Cast, 65 seats, proscenium stage. **Best submission time:** year-round. **Response time:** 6 months.

THEATER EMORY

(Founded 1985)
Rich Building, Room 230; Emory University; Atlanta, GA 30322;
    (404) 727–3465, FAX 727–6253; email vmurphy@emory.edu;
    website www.emory.edu/arts/
Vincent Murphy, *Artistic Director*

Submission procedure: accepts unsolicited scripts through members of Southeast Playwrights Project, Atlanta, GA only; professional recommendation from artistic director for all others. **Types of material:** full-length plays, one-acts, translations, adaptations. **Special interests:** adaptations and translations of literary and classic works. **Facilities:** MGM-I, 200 seats, thrust stage; MGM-II, 70 seats, flexible stage; Annex Studio, 60 seats, flexible stage. **Production considerations:** cast limit of 20; no fly or wing space. **Best submission time:** year-round. **Response time:** 2 months letter; 4 months script. **Special programs:** Brave New Works: biennial staged reading marathon of new plays in conjunction with the Southeast Playwrights Project; scripts chosen through regular submission procedure;

deadline: fall 2001; *dates:* spring 2002. The Playwriting Center of Theater Emory: biennial 5-13 week residency of major playwright to develop new work and teach playwriting workshop; *remuneration:* $25,000; residency during 2001-02 academic year.

THEATER FOR THE NEW CITY

(Founded 1970)
155-57 First Ave; New York, NY 10003-2906; (212) 254-1109,
    FAX 979-6570; email tnctheater@aol.com;
    website www.theaterforthenewcity.com
Crystal Field, *Executive Artistic Director*

Submission procedure: accepts unsolicited scripts with SASE for response. **Types of material:** full-length plays. **Special interests:** plays with no previous mainstage production; experimental American works; plays with poetry, music and dance; social issues. **Facilities:** Joyce and Seward Johnson Theater, 200 seats, flexible stage; 2nd theatre, 75 seats, flexible stage; 3rd theatre, 100 seats, flexible stage. **Best submission time:** summer. **Response time:** 9-12 months.

THEATRE IV

(Founded 1975)
114 West Broad St; Richmond, VA 23220; (804) 783-1688,
    FAX 775-2325; email bmiller@theatreiv.org;
    website www.theatreiv.org
Bruce Miller, *Artistic Director*

Submission procedure: no unsolicited scripts; synopsis and letter of inquiry. **Types of material:** plays for young audiences only, including full-length plays, translations and adaptations. **Special interests:** scripts adaptable for touring with cast of 3-5. **Facilities:** Empire Theatre, 604 seats, proscenium stage; Little Theatre, 84 seats, flexible space. **Best submission time:** year-round. **Response time:** 2 months letter; 2 years script.

THEATRE GAEL

(Founded 1984)
Box 77156; Atlanta, GA 30357; (404) 876-1131, FAX 876-1141;
  email theatregael@mindspring.com;
  website www.theatregael.com
John Stephens, *Artistic Director*
Ann Ritter, *Managing Director*

Submission procedure: no unsolicited scripts; synopsis, and letter of inquiry. **Types of material:** full-length plays, translations, adaptations, plays for young audiences, solo pieces. **Special interests:** plays depicting life in Ireland, Scotland, Wales; plays about Americans of Celtic heritage; plays that compare different cultural backgrounds, e.g., the African-American versus Irish-American experiences. **Facilities:** 14th Street Playhouse, 100-200 seats, flexible stage; company tours to 80-330-seat flexible-stage theatres. **Production considerations:** productions tour to local schools, festivals and churches. **Best submission time:** year-round. **Response time:** 1 month letter; 3 months script. **Special programs:** Worldsong Children's Theatre: company tours to local schools, recreational areas and libraries.

THEATRE IN THE SQUARE

(Founded 1982)
11 Whitlock Ave; Marietta, GA 30064; (770) 422-8369,
  FAX 424-2637
Literary Manager

Submission procedure: no unsolicited scripts; synopsis and letter of inquiry. **Types of material:** full-length plays, translations, plays for young audiences, musicals. **Special interests:** world and southeastern premieres. **Facilities:** mainstage, 225 seats, proscenium stage; Alley Stage, up to 120 seats, flexible stage. **Production considerations:** cast limit of 9, unit set; no fly space. **Best submission time:** Jun-Dec. **Response time:** 1 month letter (if interested); 6 months script.

THEATER J

(Founded 1991)
1529 16th St NW; Washington, DC 20036; (202) 777-3229,
  FAX 518-9421; email theaterj@dcjcc.org;
  website www.dcjcc.org/theaterj.htm
Ari Roth, *Artistic Director*

Submission procedure: accepts unsolicited scripts with synopsis and SASE for response. **Types of material:** full-length plays, one-acts, translations, adaptations, musicals, solo pieces. **Special interests:** Jewish themes. **Facilities:** Cecile Goldman Theater, 238 seats, proscenium stage. **Best submission time:** spring. **Response time:** 6 months.

THEATER MU

(Founded 1992)
711 West Lake St, Suite 212; Minneapolis, MN 55408;
   (612) 824–4804, FAX 824–3396; email info@theatermu.org;
   website www.theatermu.org
Rick Shiomi, *Artistic Director*

Submission procedure: accepts unsolicited scripts or synopsis, sample pages and letter of inquiry. **Types of material:** full-length plays, one-acts, adaptations, plays for young audiences. **Special interests:** plays combining traditional Asian performance with western theatre styles; short plays suitable for touring to schools. **Facilities:** no permanent facility; company performs in various proscenium venues with approximately 150 seats. **Production considerations:** cast limit of 10, simple sets. **Best submission time:** year-round. **Response time:** 2 months letter; 3 months script. **Special programs:** annual weekend staged reading series; touring and outreach programs.

THEATER OF THE FIRST AMENDMENT

(Founded 1990)
MS 3E6; George Mason University; Fairfax, VA 22030–4444;
   (703) 993–2195, FAX 993–2191; email rdavi4@gmu.edu
Rick Davis, *Artistic Director*

Submission procedure: no unsolicited scripts; synopsis, sample pages, resume and letter of inquiry. **Types of material:** full-length plays, one-acts, translations, adaptations, plays for young audiences. **Special interests:** sophisticated plays for younger audiences; "cultural history made dramatic as opposed to history dramatized; large battles joined; hard questions asked; word and image stretched." **Facilities:** TheaterSpace, 150-200 seats, flexible space. **Production considerations:** roles for younger actors welcome as TFA works with training program. **Best submission time:** Aug-Jan. **Response time:** 2 weeks letter; 6 months script. **Special programs:** readings, workshops and other development activities tailored to work that is under serious consideration for production.

THEATRE ON THE SQUARE

(Founded 1982)
450 Post St; San Francisco, CA 94102; (415) 433-6461,
 FAX 433-2910; email hreinis@aol.com;
 website theatreonthesquare.com
Jonathan Reinis, *Owner*

Submission procedure: no unsolicited scripts; synopsis and letter of inquiry. **Types of material:** full-length plays, musicals. **Facilities:** Theatre on the Square, 750 seats, proscenium/thrust stage. **Production considerations:** no fly space. **Best submission time:** year-round. **Response time:** 6 months letter; 1 year script.

THE THEATRE OUTLET

(Founded 1988)
29 North 9th St; Allentown, PA 18101-1102; (610) 820-9270,
 FAX 820-9130; email theatero@aol.com;
 website www.theatreoutlet.org
George Miller, *Artistic Director*

Submission procedure: no unsolicited scripts; synopsis, and letter of inquiry. **Types of material:** full-length plays, one-acts, translations, adaptations, solo pieces. **Special interests:** historical material relevant to eastern Pennsylvania; plays dealing with the Irish/Scotch/Welsh experience; topical work; work exploring cultural diversity. **Facilities:** mainstage, 100 seats, black box. **Production considerations:** limited fly and wing space. **Best submission time:** summer. **Response time:** 1 month letter; 2 months script. **Special programs:** The Counter-Culture Monday Café Series: 3 10-week reading series of new plays and performance art.

THEATRE PREVIEWS AT DUKE

(Founded 1986)
Box 90680; 209 Bivins Building; Durham, NC 27708-0680;
 (919) 660-3347, FAX 684-8906; email zannie@duke.edu
Zannie Giraud Voss, *Managing Director*

Submission procedure: no unsolicited scripts; synopsis and letter of inquiry. **Types of material:** full-length plays, translations, adaptations, musicals. **Facilities:** Reynolds Theatre, 600 seats, proscenium stage; Sheafer Theatre, 110 seats, black box. **Best submission time:** spring. **Response time:** 3 months letter; 2-6 months script.

THEATRE RHINOCEROS

(Founded 1977)
2926 16th St; San Francisco, CA 94103; (415) 552–4100,
    FAX 558–9044; website www.therhino.org
Doug Holsclaw, *Artistic Director*.

Submission procedure: accepts unsolicited scripts with SASE only. **Types of material:** full-length plays, one-acts, solo pieces. **Special interests:** gay and lesbian works only. **Facilities:** Theatre Rhinoceros, 112 seats, proscenium stage; The Studio at Theatre Rhinoceros, 60 seats, studio. **Best submission time:** year-round. **Response time:** 4-6 months.

THEATRE THREE

(Founded 1969)
Box 512; Port Jefferson, NY 11777–0512; (631) 928–9202,
    FAX 928–9120
Jeffrey Sanzel, *Artistic Director*

Submission procedure: no unsolicited scripts; send SASE for guidelines. **Types of material:** one-acts. **Special interests:** previously unproduced works only. **Facilities:** Second Stage, 80-100 seats, black box. **Production considerations:** prefers cast limit of 2-6, 1 set, minimal production demands. **Best submission time:** year-round. **Response time:** 1 month letter; 6 months script (if requested). **Special programs:** Annual Festival of One-Act Plays: fully staged productions; send SASE to theatre for guidelines; *deadline:* 30 Sep 2001; *notification:* 30 Dec 2001; *dates:* Feb-Mar 2002.

THEATRE THREE, INC.

(Founded 1961)
2800 Routh St; Dallas, TX 75201; (214) 871–2933, FAX 871–3139;
    email theatre3@airmail.net
Jac Alder, *Executive Producer–Director*

Submission procedure: no unsolicited scripts; agent submission only. **Types of material:** full-length plays, musicals. **Facilities:** Theatre Three, 242 seats, arena stage; Theatre Too, 60 seats, black box. **Best submission time:** year-round; prefers Sep-Dec. **Response time:** 3 months.

THEATREVIRGINIA

(Founded 1955)
2800 Grove Ave; Richmond, VA 23221-2466; (804) 353-6100
George Black, *Producing Artistic Director*

Submission procedure: no unsolicited scripts; agent submission. **Types of material:** full-length plays, musicals. **Facilities:** Main Stage, 500 seats, proscenium stage. **Best submission time:** year-round. **Response time:** 3-8 months. **Special programs:** New Voices for the Theatre: playwriting competition open to VA students grades 5-12; winners grades 9-12 attend 3-week summer residency program and receive dramaturgical assistance and professional staged reading; contact Education and Outreach Department for more information; *deadline*: 1 Feb 2002.

THEATERWORKS

(Founded 1985)
1 Gold St; Hartford, CT 06103; (860) 727-4027, FAX 525-0758
Mark Englehart, *General Manager*

Submission procedure: no unsolicited scripts; synopsis, dialogue sample and letter of inquiry. **Types of material:** full-length plays, solo pieces. **Facilities:** Hutensky Theater, 200 seats, thrust stage. **Production considerations:** cast limit of 6, simple set. **Best submission time:** year-round. **Response time:** 2 months letter; 3 months script.

THEATREWORKS

(Founded 1969)
1100 Hamilton Ct; Menlo Park, CA 94025; (650) 463-7126,
 FAX 463-1963; email jeannie@theatreworks.org;
 website www.theatreworks.org
Jeannie Barroga, *Literary Manager*

Submission procedure: accepts unsolicited full-length plays and musicals; for translations and adaptations, send letter of inquiry with SASP for response. **Types of material:** full-length plays, translations, adaptations, musicals. **Special interests:** works offering opportunities for multiethnic casting. **Facilities:** Mountain View Center, 625 seats, proscenium stage; Stage II, 117 seats, thrust stage. **Best submission time:** Jul-Nov. **Response time:** 1 month letter; 4 months script. **Special programs:** New Works Forum: developmental reading series for plays, musicals and music-theatre pieces.

THEATREWORKS/USA

(Founded 1961)
151 West 26th St, 7th Floor; New York, NY 10001; (212) 647-1100,
 FAX 924-5377; email info@theatreworksusa.org;
 website www.theatreworksusa.org
Barbara Pasternack, *Artistic Director*

Submission procedure: accepts unsolicited scripts; prefers synopsis, sample scene(s) and songs (include cassette or CD and lyric sheet) and letter of inquiry. **Types of material:** plays and musicals for young audiences grades Kindergarten-12th. **Special interests:** literary adaptations; historical/biographical themes; fairy tales; contemporary issues. **Facilities:** Auditorium at the Equitable Tower, 487 seats, proscenium stage; also tours. **Production considerations:** cast limit of 5-6 (can play multiple roles), sets suitable for touring. **Best submission time:** summer. **Response time:** 1 month letter; 6 months script. **Special programs:** Theatreworks/USA Commissioning Program (see Development).

THEATRE X

(Founded 1969)
158 North Broadway; Milwaukee, WI 53202; (414) 278-0555
David Ravel, *Producing Director*

Submission procedure: no unsolicited scripts; synopsis with SASE for response. **Types of material:** full-length plays. **Special interests:** contemporary plays; "pseudo-naturalism and self-conscious theatricality involving the ongoing fruits of interdisciplinary collaboration." **Facilities:** Black Box, 99 seats, flexible stage. **Production considerations:** theatre uses core acting company of 3 women and 2 men, late forties, early fifties. **Best submission time:** year-round. **Response time:** 6 months.

THEATRICAL OUTFIT

(Founded 1976)
Box 1555; Atlanta, GA 30301; (404) 577-5257, FAX 577-5259;
 email kate.warner@theatricaloutfit.org;
 website www.theatricaloutfit.org
Kate Warner, *Managing Director/Artistic Associate*

Submission procedure: no unsolicited scripts; 1-page synopsis and letter of inquiry with SASP for response. **Types of material:** full-length plays, adaptations, solo pieces. **Facilities:** Theatrical Outfit, 800 seats, proscenium stage. **Best submission time:** Apr-Jun. **Response time:** 2 months letter; 2 months script.

3 LEGGED RACE: NEW THEATRE & PERFORMANCE
(Founded 1996)
420 North 5th St, Room 540; Minneapolis, MN 55401
Gillian Martin, *Communications Associate*

Submission procedure: no unsolicited scripts; synopsis, up to 20 pages of script, visual sample (prefers videotape; copies of slides or audio tapes are acceptable); write for guidelines. **Types of material:** multimedia, performance-art. **Special interests:** performance-based collaborations incorporating new dance, circus arts, puppetry or object theatre; "unconventional and eclectic works which question, challenge and expand expectations about theatre and performance"; pieces running 10-90 minutes. **Facilities:** no permanent facility. **Production considerations:** cast limit of 4, set suitable for touring. **Best submission time:** fall. **Response time:** 1-4 months letter; 9 months script. **Special programs:** Summer Blizzard: annual festival of new shorts-in-progress in circus arts, dance, language-based performance and other experimental performance; write for dates and guidelines.

TOTEM POLE PLAYHOUSE
(Founded 1950)
Box 603; Fayetteville, PA 17222; (717) 352-2164, FAX 352-8870
Carl Schurr, *Producing Artistic Director*

Submission procedure: no unsolicited scripts; synopsis, sample pages and letter of inquiry. **Types of material:** full-length plays, one-acts, musicals. **Special interests:** light comedies and musicals that appeal to a general audience. **Facilities:** mainstage, 453 seats, proscenium stage. **Best submission time:** year-round. **Response time:** 1-2 months letter; 6 months script.

TOUCHSTONE THEATRE
(Founded 1981)
321 East 4th St; Bethlehem, PA 18015; (610) 867-1689,
    FAX 867-0561; email touchstone@nni.com;
    website www.touchstone.org
Mark McKenna, *Artistic Director*

Submission procedure: no unsolicited scripts; letter of inquiry. **Types of**

material: proposals for works to be created in collaboration with company's ensemble only. **Facilities:** Touchstone Theatre, 74 seats, black box. **Production considerations:** 18' x 21' playing area. **Best submission time:** year-round. **Response time:** 6-8 months.

TOVA, INC.

(Founded 1991)
126 East Baltimore Pike; Media, PA 19063; (484) 444-0418,
    FAX 444-0421; email tova@voicenet.com;
    website www.libertynet.org/tova
Paula Sepinuck, Artistic Director

Submission procedure: no unsolicited scripts; company performs works created collaboratively; playwrights and composers interested in joining company may write for information. **Types of material:** full-length plays. **Special interests:** "theatre of witness writing model"; voices not heard in society; social issues including homelessness, substance abuse, domestic violence, racial/sexual/class identity, aging and healing; video documentaries based on performers' lives. **Facilities:** no permanent facility; touring company. **Production considerations:** small cast, minimal production demands.

TRIANGLE PRODUCTIONS!

(Founded 1989)
3430 Southeast Belmont; Portland, OR 97214; (503) 230-9404,
    FAX 230-9303; email trianglepro@juno.com;
    website www.tripro.org
Donald L. Horn, *Artistic/Managing Director*

Submission procedure: no unsolicited scripts; letter of inquiry with email address for response. **Types of material:** full-length plays, plays for young audiences, musicals, solo pieces. **Special interests:** comedies, gay and lesbian themes. **Facilities:** World Trade Center, 223 seats, thrust stage; Arena Stage, 120 seats, arena stage; Black Box, 90 seats, thrust stage. **Production considerations:** cast limit of 4, set suitable for touring. **Best submission time:** fall. **Response time:** 1 month letter; 3-7 months script.

TRINITY REPERTORY COMPANY

(Founded 1964)
201 Washington St; Providence, RI 02903; (401) 521-1100,
   FAX 521-0447; website www.trinityrep.com
Craig Watson, *Literary Manager*

Submission procedure: no unsolicited scripts; synopsis, dialogue sample and letter of inquiry. **Types of material:** full-length plays, translations, adaptations, musicals, solo pieces. **Facilities:** Upstairs Theatre, 500 seats, thrust stage; Downstairs Theatre, 297 seats, thrust stage. **Best submission time:** Sep–May. **Response time:** 2 months letter; 4 months script.

TRUSTUS THEATRE

(Founded 1985)
Box 11721; Columbia, SC 29211-1721; (803) 254-9732,
   FAX 771-9153; email trustus88@aol.com;
   website www.trustus.org
Jon Tuttle, *Literary Manager*

Submission procedure: accepts unsolicited scripts. **Types of material:** one-acts. **Special interests:** experimental, hard-hitting, off-the-wall one-act comedies or "dramadies" for open-minded Late-Night series, no topic taboo; full-length plays accepted only for Trustus Playwrights' Festival (see below); no musicals or plays for young audiences. **Facilities:** mainstage, 100 seats, flexible proscenium stage. **Production considerations:** small cast, moderate production demands. **Best submission time:** Aug–Dec. **Response time:** 2-4 months. **Special programs:** Trustus Playwrights' Festival (see Prizes).

TWO RIVER THEATRE COMPANY

(Founded 1994)
Box 8035; Red Bank, NJ 07702; (732) 345-1400, FAX 345-1414;
   email info@tworivertheatre.org
Jonathan Fox, *Artistic Director*

Submission procedure: no unsolicited scripts; agent submissions only with SASE. **Types of material:** full-length plays, adaptations. **Facilities:** Algonquin Arts Theatre, 500 seats, proscenium stage. **Production considerations:** cast limit of 10. **Best submission time:** year-round. **Response time:** 8-10 months script.

UNDERMAIN THEATRE

(Founded 1984)
Box 141166; Dallas, TX 75214; (214) 747-1424, FAX 747-1863;
30-48 32nd St; Astoria, NY 11102; (646) 526-6246;
    email undermain@aol.com; website www.undermain.com
Katherine Owens, *Artistic Director*

Submission procedure: no unsolicited scripts; professional recommendation. **Types of material:** full-length plays, one-acts, translations, adaptations, solo pieces. **Facilities:** Ohio Theatre (New York), 99 seats, flexible stage; Undermain (Dallas), 89 seats, black box. **Best submission time:** year-round. **Response time:** 3-6 months.

UNICORN THEATRE

(Founded 1974)
3828 Main St; Kansas City, MO 64111; (816) 531-7529, ext 18,
    FAX 531-0421; website www.unicorntheatre.org
Herman Wilson, *Literary Assistant*

Submission procedure: accepts unsolicited scripts with synopsis, character breakdown, bio or resume and cover letter with SASE for response. **Types of material:** full-length plays. **Special interests:** contemporary social issues. **Facilities:** Unicorn Theatre, 180 seats, thrust stage. **Best submission time:** Sep-Apr. **Response time:** 4-8 months. **Special programs:** Unicorn Theatre New Play Development (see Prizes).

URBAN STAGES

(Founded 1985)
17 East 47th St; New York, NY 10017; .(212) 421-1380;
    email urbanstage@aol.com; website www.urbanstages.org
Frances Hill, *Artistic Director*
T. L. Reilly, *Producing Director*

Submission procedure: accepts unsolicited scripts; include production history and bio with SASE for response. **Types of material:** full-length plays. **Facilities:** mainstage, 70 seats, proscenium stage. **Best submission time:** Jun-Aug. **Response time:** 4-6 months. **Special programs:** Urban Stages Emerging Playwright Award: outreach program that tours throughout New York City library systems. (See listing in Prizes.)

UTAH SHAKESPEAREAN FESTIVAL

(Founded 1961)
351 West Center St; Cedar City, UT 84720-2498; (435) 586-7880,
    FAX 865-8003; email phillips@suu.edu; website www.bard.org
Douglas N. Cook, *Producing Artistic Director*
George Judy, *Director of New Plays Series*

Submission procedure: no unsolicited scripts; synopsis, professional recommendation and letter of inquiry. **Types of material:** full-length plays. **Special interests:** plays with no previous mainstage production only; plays by writers from western United States or plays with western themes; plays with classical themes; plays about minorities or the underserved. **Facilities:** Downtown Cinema Theatre, 150 seats, proscenium stage. **Production considerations:** cast limit of 10-12, no sets, minimal props and costumes; 5-rehearsal limit, 2 staged readings only; no full productions. **Best submission time:** May-Dec; plays received after Dec will not be considered. **Response time:** 15 Mar of the year following submission.

VICTORY GARDENS THEATER

(Founded 1974)
2257 North Lincoln Ave; Chicago, IL 60614; (773) 549-5788,
    FAX 549-2779
Sandy Shinner, *Associate Artistic Director*

Submission procedure: accepts unsolicited scripts from Chicago-area writers only; others send synopsis, 10-page dialogue sample and letter of inquiry with SASE for response. **Types of material:** full-length plays, adaptations, musicals. **Special interests:** Chicago and Midwest playwrights; plays by women and writers of color. **Facilities:** Mainstage Two, 200 seats, thrust stage; Mainstage One, 195 seats, modified thrust stage; 2 studio theatres, 70 seats each, black box. **Production considerations:** prefers cast limit of 10, simple set; small-cast musicals only. **Best submission time:** Mar-Jun. **Response time:** 2 months letter; 9 months script. **Special programs:** Victory Gardens Playwrights Ensemble: core group of twelve resident writers. Readers Theater: staged readings of works-in-progress by area writers twice a month. Artist Development Workshop: playwriting class offered throughout the year that brings people with and without disabilities together in a creative environment.

THE VICTORY THEATRE

(Founded 1979)
3326 West Victory Blvd; Burbank, CA 91505; (818) 841–4404,
FAX 841–6328; email thevictory@mindspring.com
website www.thevictorytheatres.com
Tom Ormeny, *Artistic Director*

Submission procedure: no unsolicited scripts; synopsis, first 15 pages of script, resume and letter of inquiry. **Types of material:** full-length plays, adaptations. **Special interests:** plays involving social and political issues; "well-made, but cutting-edge" plays. **Facilities:** The Victory Theatre, 91 seats, arena stage; The Little Victory, 48 seats, arena stage. **Production considerations:** prefers cast limit of 12, maximum 2 simple sets; no fly space. **Best submission time:** year-round. **Response time:** 2 months letter; 3 months script.

VINEYARD THEATRE

(Founded 1981)
108 East 15th St; New York, NY 10003–9689; (212) 353–3366,
FAX 353–3803
Douglas Aibel, *Artistic Director*

Submission procedure: no unsolicited scripts; synopsis or project description, 10-page dialogue sample and letter of inquiry; include cassette for musicals. **Types of material:** full-length plays, musicals. **Special interests:** plays that incorporate music in a unique way; musicals with strong narrative; "nervy, eccentric theatrical forms." **Facilities:** Vineyard Dimson Theatre, 129 seats, flexible stage. **Best submission time:** year-round. **Response time:** 6-12 months letter; 6 months script. **Special programs:** New Works at the Vineyard: developmental lab productions for new plays and musicals.

VIRGINIA STAGE COMPANY

(Founded 1979)
Box 3770; Norfolk, VA 23514; (757) 627–6988, FAX 628–5958;
website www.vastage.com
Patricia Darden, *Assistant to the Directors*

Submission procedure: no unsolicited scripts; synopsis and letter of inquiry. **Types of material:** full-length plays, musicals. **Special interests:** plays by VA writers; world premieres; works about "twenty-somethings" and youth culture; poetic drama and comedy; hard-hitting, issue-oriented plays. **Facilities:**

mainstage, 700 seats, proscenium stage; laboratory theatre, 99 seats, flexible stage. **Best submission time:** year-round. **Response time:** 1 month letter; 6 months script.

VOICE & VISION

(Founded 1990)
161 Avenue of the Americas, 14th Floor; New York, NY 10013;
(212) 633-9903, FAX 255-2053; email vandv@mindspring.com
Marya Mazor and Jean Wagner, *Artistic Directors*

Submission procedure: no unsolicited scripts; professional recommendation or agent submission. **Types of material:** full-length plays, one-acts, translations, adaptations, plays for young audiences, musicals, performance art, dance-theatre. **Facilities:** no permanent facility. **Best submission time:** year-round. **Response time:** 12 months. **Special programs:** Dramatic Action: educational program for young women. Enulsion Retreat and Laboratory for Women Theatre Artists.

THE WALNUT STREET THEATRE COMPANY

(Founded 1809)
825 Walnut St; Philadelphia, PA 19107-5107; (215) 574-3550,
FAX 574-3598
Beverly Elliott, *Literary Manager*

Submission procedure: no unsolicited scripts; synopsis, cast list, 10-20-page dialogue sample and letter of inquiry with SASE for response from Dramatist Guild members only; include professional-quality cassette for musicals. **Types of material:** full-length plays, musicals. **Special interests:** original, socially relevant musicals with uplifting themes; commercially viable works for Main Stage; meaningful comedies and dramas with some broad social relevance for Studio 3. **Facilities:** Main Stage, 1078 seats, proscenium stage; Studio 3, 79-99 seats, flexible stage. **Production considerations:** cast limit of 4 for Studio 3. **Response time:** 3 months letter; 6 months script.

WATERTOWER THEATRE, INC.

(Founded 1976)
15650 Addison Rd; Addison, TX 75001; (972) 450-6220,
FAX 450-6244; website www.watertowertheatre.org
Terry Martin, *Artistic Director*

Submission procedure: no unsolicited scripts; synopsis, dialogue sample, resume and letter of inquiry with SASE for response. **Types of material:** full-length plays, musicals, solo pieces. **Special interests:** comedies; plays that make creative use of flexible space. **Facilities:** Addison Conference & Theatre Centre, 100–300 seats, flexible stage. **Response time:** 3 months letter; 6 months script. **Special programs:** Stone Cottage New Works Festival: readings of previously unproduced full-length plays; submit synopsis, character breakdown and SASE for response; *deadline:* 15 Feb 2002; *notification:* 30 May 2002; *dates:* Jul 2002.

WEISSBERGER THEATER GROUP

(Founded 1992)
110 East 59th St; 29th Floor; New York, NY 10022; (212) 644–3335, FAX 644–3343
Jay Harris, *Producer*

Submission procedure: no unsolicited scripts; synopsis and letter of inquiry. **Types of material:** full-length plays. **Special interests:** topical issue-oriented plays. **Facilities:** no permanent facility. **Production considerations:** cast limit of 7. **Best submission time:** year-round. **Response time:** 1 month letter; 2 months script.

WESTBETH THEATRE CENTER

(Founded 1977)
151 Bank St; New York, NY 10014; (212) 691–2272, FAX 924–7185; email wbesthzach@aol.com; website www.westbeththeatre.com
Arnold Engelman, *Producing Director*

Submission procedure: no unsolicited scripts; 1-page synopsis, character breakdown, resume and letter of inquiry with SASE for response. **Types of material:** full-length plays, musicals, solo pieces. **Special interests:** comedies; non-traditional work; plays which combine multiple performance disciplines; prefer "sharp, urban contemporary" projects; no period pieces or plays set in specific rural or regional locales. **Facilities:** Music Hall, 100–250 seats, proscenium stage; Big Room, 99 seats, black box; Studio Theatre, 99 seats, black box; Café Theatre, 50–70 seats, cabaret. **Production considerations:** cast limit of 8, modest technical demands. **Best submission time:** year-round. **Response time:** 2 months letter; 4 months script. **Special programs:** Westbeth New Works Program (see Development).

WEST COAST ENSEMBLE

(Founded 1982)
Box 38728; Los Angeles, CA 90038; (323) 876-9337, FAX 876-8916
Les Hanson, *Artistic Director*

Submission procedure: accepts unsolicited scripts. **Types of material:** full-length plays, one-acts, translations, adaptations, musicals. **Special interests:** plays not produced in Southern CA only; musicals; short plays. **Facilities:** mainstage, 85 seats, proscenium stage. **Production considerations:** simple set; no fly space. **Best submission time:** Jun-Dec. **Response time:** 6 months. **Special programs:** staged readings of new plays. West Coast Ensemble Contests (see Prizes).

THE WESTERN STAGE

(Founded 1974)
156 Homestead Ave; Salinas, CA 93901; (831) 755-6990,
    FAX 755-6954
Jeffrey Heyer, *Literary Manager*

Submission procedure: no unsolicited scripts; synopsis and letter of inquiry; include cassette for musicals; for adaptations of work not in public domain, enclose copy of letter granting rights. **Types of material:** full-length plays, adaptations, plays for young audiences, musicals, cabaret/revues. **Special interests:** adaptations of works of literary significance; large-cast plays and ensemble pieces; plays for young performers; diverse casts; plays featuring strong roles for women. **Facilities:** mainstage, 500 seats, proscenium stage; Cabaret, 250 seats, proscenium stage; Studio, 100 seats, thrust stage. **Best submission time:** year-round. **Response time:** 4-6 weeks letter; 3 months script.

WILL GEER THEATRICUM BOTANICUM

(Founded 1973)
Box 1222; Topanga, CA 90290; (310) 455-2322, FAX 455-3724;
    email theatricum@earthlink.net
Ellen Geer, *Artistic Director*

Submission procedure: no unsolicited scripts; synopsis, dialogue sample and letter of inquiry; include cassette for musicals. **Types of material:** full-length plays, musicals. **Special interests:** work suitable for large outdoor playing space. **Facilities:** Will Geer Theatricum Botanicum, 300 seats, outdoor amphitheatre. **Production considerations:** cast limit of 4-10;

simple sets. **Best submission time:** Sep. **Response time:** 1 month letter; 6 months script.

WILLIAMSTOWN THEATRE FESTIVAL

(Founded 1955)
Sep–May: 229 West 42nd St; Suite 801; New York, NY 10036;
    (212) 395-9090, FAX 395-9099; website www.wtfestival.org
Jun–Aug: Box 517; Williamstown, MA 01267-0517; (413) 458-3200,
    FAX 458-3147
Michael Ritchie, *Producer*

Submission procedure: no unsolicited scripts; agent submission only. **Types of material:** full-length plays, adaptations, musicals, solo pieces. **Facilities:** Main Stage, 521 seats, proscenium stage; 2nd stage, 96 seats, thrust stage. **Best submission time:** 1 Oct–15 Feb. **Response time:** 6-12 months. **Special programs:** New Play Staged Readings Series.

WILLOWS THEATRE COMPANY

(Founded 1977)
1975 Diamond Blvd, Suite B–230; Concord, CA 94520;
    (925) 798-1300, FAX 676-5726; email rich@willowstheatre.org;
    website www.willowstheatre.org
 Richard H. Elliott, *Artistic Director*

Submission procedure: no unsolicited scripts; synopsis, character breakdown and letter of inquiry. **Types of material:** full-length plays, adaptations, musicals. **Special interests:** musicals and plays based on figures and events drawn from American history, especially CA history; contemporary comedies. **Facilities:** Willows Theatre, 210 seats, proscenium stage. **Production considerations:** cast limit of 35. **Best submission time:** 1 Jan–1 Apr. **Response time:** 3 months letter; 6-12 months script. **Special programs:** staged readings and workshop development productions.

THE WILMA THEATER

(Founded 1972)
265 South Broad St; Philadelphia, PA 19107; (215) 893-9456,
    FAX 893-0895; email info@wilmatheater.org;
    website www.wilmatheater.org
Literary Manager/Dramaturg

Submission procedure: no unsolicited scripts; professional recommendation. **Types of material:** full-length plays, translations, adaptations, musicals. **Special interests:** new translations and adaptations from the international repertoire with emphasis on innovative, bold staging; world premieres; ensemble works; works with poetic dimension; plays with music; multimedia works; social issues. **Facilities:** Wilma Theater, 300 seats, flexible/proscenium stage. **Production considerations:** prefers cast limit of 12; stage 44' x 46'. **Best submission time:** year-round. **Response time:** 9–12 months.

WINGS THEATRE COMPANY, INC.
(Founded 1986)
154 Christopher St; New York, NY 10014; (212) 627–2960,
FAX 462–0024; email jeffreycorrick@yahoo.com;
website www.brainlink.com/~cjeffer/
Tricia Gilbert, *Literary Manager*

Submission procedure: accepts unsolicited scripts. **Types of material:** full-length plays, musicals. **Special interests:** new musicals and gay-themed plays only. **Facilities:** Wings Theatre, 74 seats, proscenium stage. **Best submission time:** year-round. **Response time:** plays received by 1 May receive response in Sep of that year; plays received after 1 May receive response Sep of following year.

WOMEN'S PROJECT & PRODUCTIONS
(Founded 1978)
55 West End Ave; New York, NY 10023; (212) 765–1706,
FAX 765–2024; email wpp@earthlink.net;
website www.womensproject.org
Karen Keagle, *Literary Manager*

Submission procedure: no unsolicited scripts; synopsis, 10-page dialogue sample and letter of inquiry with SASE for response. **Types of material:** full-length plays. **Special interests:** plays by women only. **Facilities:** Theatre Four, 199 seats, proscenium stage. **Best submission time:** year-round. **Response time:** 2 months letter; 8 months script. **Special programs:** Playwrights Lab and Directors Forum: developmental program including play readings and work-in-progress presentations; participation by invitation only.

WOOLLY MAMMOTH THEATRE COMPANY

(Founded 1981)
917 M St NW; Washington, DC 20001; (202) 289–2443;
   email Woollymamm@aol.com; website www.woollymammoth.net
Mary Resing, *Literary Manager*

Submission procedure: no unsolicited scripts; professional recommendation. **Types of material:** full-length plays, translations, adaptations, solo pieces. **Special interests:** theatrical and provocative plays which combine elevated language with edgy situations and complex characters. **Facilities:** no permanent facility. **Production considerations:** prefers cast limit of 6. **Best submission time:** Jun. **Response time:** 12 months. **Special programs:** Foreplay: reading series of 5-6 plays each year under consideration for MainStage production.

WORCESTER FOOTHILLS THEATRE COMPANY

(Founded 1974)
100 Front St, Suite 137; Worcester, MA 01608; (508) 754–3314,
   FAX 767–0676
Michael Walker, *Executive Producer/Artistic Director*

Submission procedure: no unsolicited scripts; synopsis and letter of inquiry. **Types of material:** full-length plays, translations, adaptations. **Special interests:** plays suited to multigenerational audiences. **Facilities:** Worcester Foothills Theatre, 349 seats, proscenium stage. **Production considerations:** prefers cast limit of 10, simple set. **Best submission time:** Sep. **Response time:** 3 months letter; 4 months script.

WRITERS' THEATRE CHICAGO

(Founded 1992)
c/o Books on Vernon; 664 Vernon Ave; Glencoe, IL 60022;
   (847) 835–7366, FAX 835–5332; email writerstheatre@aol.com
Marilyn Campbell, *Literary Manager*

Submission procedure: accepts unsolicited scripts with professional recommendation if possible. **Types of material:** full-length plays, translations, adaptations. **Special interests:** highly literary plays by or about great writers and writing. **Facilities:** Nicholas Pennell Theatre, 50 seats, thrust stage. **Production considerations:** small cast; small space; minimal production demands. **Best submission time:** year-round. **Response time:** 3 months.

YALE REPERTORY THEATRE

(Founded 1965)
Box 208244, Yale Station; New Haven, CT 06520-8244;
   (203) 432-1560, FAX 432-1070;
   email catherine.sheehy@yale.edu
Catherine Sheehy, *Resident Dramaturg*

Submission procedure: no unsolicited scripts; synopsis and letter of inquiry. **Types of material:** full-length plays, translations, adaptations, solo pieces. **Special interests:** new work; new translations of classics; contemporary foreign plays. **Facilities:** University Theatre, 654 seats, proscenium stage; Yale Repertory Theatre, 487 seats, modified thrust stage. **Best submission time:** year-round. **Response time:** 2 months letter; 3 months script.

THE YORK THEATRE COMPANY

(Founded 1968)
The Theatre at St Peter's Church; Citicorp Center; 619 Lexington Ave;
   New York, NY 10022-4610; (212) 935-5824, FAX 832-0037
Literary Department

Submission procedure: no unsolicited scripts; synopsis and letter of inquiry with SASE for response. **Types of material:** musicals, revues. **Special interests:** small-cast musicals. **Facilities:** The Theatre at Saint Peter's Church, 177 seats, flexible stage. **Best submission time:** year-round. **Response time:** 1-2 months letter; 6-8 months script.

YOUNG PLAYWRIGHTS INC.

See Young Playwrights Festival in Prizes and Young Playwrights Inc. in Organizations.

PRIZES

What competitions are included here?

All the playwriting contests we know of that offer prizes of at least $200 or, in the case of awards to playwrights 19 or under, the equivalent in production or publication. Most awards for which the playwright cannot apply—the Joseph Kesselring Award, the Pulitzer Prize—are not listed. Exceptions are made when, as with The Susan Smith Blackburn Prize, the nominating process allows playwrights to encourage nomination of their work by theatre professionals.

How can I give myself the best chance of winning?

Send your script in well before the deadline, when the readers are fresh and enthusiastic rather than buried by an avalanche of submissions. Assume the deadline is the date your script must be received (not the postmark date unless otherwise stated). Make sure you don't mistake a notification date for the submission deadline. If a listing specifies "write for guidelines," be sure to follow this instruction. It usually means that we don't have space in our brief listing to give you all the information you need; also contests may change their rules or their deadlines after this book has been published. Always send an SASE with your submission, if you expect your materials to be returned.

Should I enter contests that charge entry fees?

It's true that a number of listings require a fee. Many contest sponsors are unable to secure sufficient funding to cover their costs, which are considerable. We have not included those listings with unusually high fees. Some playwrights will not pay fees as a matter of principle, others consider it part of doing business. It's up to you.

How can I find out about new prizes and updates throughout the year?

Write for guidelines to ensure that you have the most recent rules. Also refer to the Membership and Service Organizations, Useful Publications and Online Resources sections in this book for those groups that list current contest news.

A couple of *Sourcebook* reminders:

"Full-length play" means a full-length, original work without a score or libretto. One-acts, musicals, adaptations, translations, plays for young audiences and solo pieces are listed separately.

Sourcebook entries are alphabetized by first word (excluding "the") even if the title starts with a proper name. So, for instance, you'll find the "Harold Morton Landon Translation Award" under H. In the index, you will also find this prize cross-listed under L. The listings for this edition are alphabetized by a different method than in years past (see Preface for a description). We've included listings of biennial prizes with deadlines after the dates of this *Sourcebook* (September 2001–August 2002), so please read the deadlines carefully—don't mistake a March 2003 deadline for 2002.

AMERICAN RENEGADE PLAYWRITING CONTEST

American Renegade Theatre; 11136 Magnolia Blvd;
   North Hollywood, CA 91601; (818) 763–4430
David A. Cox, *Artistic Director*

Types of material: full-length plays. **Frequency:** annual. **Remuneration:** $500, full production, 5% of box office gross. **Guidelines:** unpublished work not produced professionally. **Submission procedure:** script and $20 fee (checks payable to ARTC). **Deadline:** 15 Nov 2001. **Notification:** 1 Dec 2001. (See American Renegade Theatre in Production.)

AMERICAN TRANSLATORS ASSOCIATION AWARDS

225 Reinekers Ln, Suite 590; Alexandria, VA 22314;
   FAX (703) 683–6122; email ata@atanet.org
JoAnne Engelbert, *Chair, ATA Honors and Awards*

GERMAN LITERARY TRANSLATION PRIZE

Types of material: translations of full-length plays and one-acts. **Frequency:** biennial. **Remuneration:** $1000, up to $500 expenses to attend ATA annual conference. **Guidelines:** translation from German published in U.S. by American publisher during 2 years before deadline as single volume or in collection. **Submission procedure:** no submission by translator; publisher nominates translation and submits 2 copies of book plus 10 consecutive pages of German original, extra jacket and any advertising copy, vita of translator. **Deadline:** 15 May 2003. **Notification:** fall 2003.

LEWIS GALANTIERE LITERARY TRANSLATION PRIZE

Types of material: translations of full-length plays and one-acts. **Frequency:** biennial. **Remuneration:** $1000, up to $500 expenses to attend ATA annual conference. **Guidelines:** translation from any language except German published in U.S. by American publisher during 2 years before deadline as single volume or in collection. **Submission procedure:** no submission by translator; publisher nominates translation and submits 2 copies of book plus 10 consecutive pages of original, extra jacket and any advertising copy, vita of translator. **Deadline:** 30 Mar 2002. **Notification:** fall 2002.

ANNA ZORNIO MEMORIAL CHILDREN'S THEATRE PLAYWRITING AWARD

Department of Theatre and Dance; University of New Hampshire;
  Paul Creative Arts Center; 30 College Rd;
  Durham, NH 03824-3538; (603) 862-3044, FAX 862-0298
Kay Megurden-Staten, *Educational Program Coordinator*

Types of material: plays and musicals for young audiences. **Frequency:** every 4 years. **Remuneration:** $1000, production by UNH Theatre in Education Program in May 2002. **Guidelines:** U.S. or Canadian resident; unpublished work not produced professionally and not more than 1 hour long; 2 submission limit; prefers single or unit set. **Submission procedure:** script with brief synopsis, character breakdown and statement of design/technical considerations; SASP for acknowledgment of receipt; include cassette for musical; write for guidelines. **Deadline:** 1 Sep 2001. **Notification:** May 2002; exact date TBA.

THE ANNUAL BLANK THEATRE COMPANY YOUNG PLAYWRIGHTS FESTIVAL

1301 Lucile Ave; Los Angeles, CA 90026-1519; (323) 662-7734;
  email info@theblank.com; websites www.theblank.com,
  www.youngplaywrights.com
Christopher Steele, *Producer*

Types of material: full-length plays, one-acts, plays for young audiences, musicals, operas, solo pieces. **Frequency:** annual. **Remuneration:** workshop production for approximately 9 playwrights; some scripts receive full production. **Guidelines:** playwright 19 years of age or younger as of deadline date; original play of any length on any subject; send SASE in late Jan 2002 for guidelines. **Submission procedure:** script with cover sheet containing name, date of birth, home address, phone number and name of school (if any). **Deadline:** 1 Apr 2002. **Notification:** May 2002.

THE ARTS & LETTERS PRIZE IN DRAMA

Georgia College & State University; Campus Box 89;
  Milledgeville, GA 31061-0490; (478) 445-1289;
  email al@mail.gcsu.edu; website al.gcsu.edu
David Muschell, *Drama Editor*

Types of material: one-acts. **Frequency:** annual. **Remuneration:** $1000, production, publication in *Arts & Letters* journal. **Guidelines:** unpublished one-act. **Submission procedure:** script with separate title page containing name and address of playwright and $15 fee. **Deadline:** 30 Apr 2002. **Notification:** Aug 2002.

ASF TRANSLATION PRIZE

The American–Scandinavian Foundation; 58 Park Ave;
New York, NY 10016; (212) 879–9779, FAX 249–3444;
email agyongy@amscan.org
Publishing Office

Types of material: translations. **Frequency:** annual. **Remuneration:** $2000, publication of excerpt in *Scandinavian Review*; $500 for runner-up. **Guidelines:** unpublished translation from a Scandinavian language into English of work written by a Scandinavian author after 1800; manuscript must be at least 50 pages long if prose drama, 25 pages if verse drama, and must be conceived as part of a book. **Submission procedure:** 4 copies of translation, 1 of original, permission letter from copyright holder; write for guidelines. **Deadline:** 1 Jun 2002. **Notification:** fall 2002.

ATTIC THEATRE ENSEMBLE'S ONE-ACT MARATHON

Attic Theatre Centre; 8663 Chalmas Dr; Los Angeles, CA 90035;
(310) 659–3637, FAX 659–3637; website www.attictheatre.org
James Carey, *Producing Artistic Director*

Types of material: one-acts. **Frequency:** annual. **Remuneration:** $500 1st prize; 6 finalists receive productions. **Guidelines:** unproduced one-act no longer than 45 minutes; no adaptations. **Submission procedure:** send SASE for guidelines and application or download from web. **Deadline:** 30 Sep 2001. **Notification:** Jan 2002. **Dates:** Jun 2002. (See Attic Theatre Ensemble in Production.)

AURAND HARRIS MEMORIAL PLAYWRITING AWARD

New England Theatre Conference; Northeastern University;
306 Huntington Ave; Boston, MA 02115; (617) 424–9275,
FAX 424–1057; email info@netconline.org;
website www.netconline.org

Types of material: plays for young audiences. **Frequency:** annual. **Remuneration:** $1000 1st prize; $500 2nd prize. **Guidelines:** resident of CT, MA, ME, NH, RI, VT or member of the New England Theatre Conference (NETC) (see Membership and Service Organizations); unpublished work not produced professionally; 1 submission limit. **Submission procedure:** bound script, synopsis, character breakdown and statement that play has not been published or professionally produced and is not under consideration for publication or production prior to 1 Sep 2001, $20 fee (fee is waived for NETC members); send SASP for acknowledgment of receipt; script will not be returned; send SASE for guidelines. **Deadline:** 1 May 2002 **Notification:** Sep 2002 (winners only).

AURICLE AWARD

Plays on Tape; Box 0152; Powell Butte, OR 97753; (541) 447-7033,
FAX 617-9104; email theatre@playsontape.com;
website www.playsontape.com
Beverly Friesen, *General Manager*

Types of material: full-length plays, long one-acts. **Frequency:** annual. **Remuneration:** $500 and 10 audio copies if play is produced as audio recording; $100 prize to winner if cost of producing audio recording is prohibitively expensive, i.e., too large a cast, complicated sound effects, etc. **Guidelines:** any play that has not been audio-produced, running time approximately 74 minutes; prefers 2-5 character play; special interest in plays by women and minorities. **Submission procedure:** script, synopis and $3 fee per script with SASE; write for guidelines. **Deadline:** 28 Feb 2002. **Notification:** 1 Jun 2002. (See Plays on Tape in Publication.)

BAKER'S PLAYS HIGH SCHOOL PLAYWRITING CONTEST

Baker's Plays; Box 699222; Quincy, MA 02269-9222;
(617) 745-0805, FAX 745-9891; email staff@bakersplays.com;
website www.bakersplays.com

Types of material: full-length plays, one-acts, plays for young audiences, musicals. **Frequency:** annual. **Remuneration:** $500 1st prize, publication; $250 2nd prize; $100 3rd prize. **Guidelines:** high school student sponsored by high school drama or English teacher; prefers play that has been produced or given public reading. **Submission procedure:** script with signature of sponsoring teacher; write for guidelines. **Deadline:** 31 Jan 2002. **Notification:** May 2002. (See Baker's Plays in Publication.)

BEVERLY HILLS THEATRE GUILD PLAYWRITING AWARDS

2815 North Beachwood Dr; Los Angeles, CA 90068-1923;
 (323) 465-2703
Dick Dotterer, *Competition Coordinator*

JULIE HARRIS PLAYWRITING AWARD

Types of material: full-length plays. **Frequency:** annual. **Remuneration:** $5000 1st prize; $2500 2nd prize; $1500 3rd prize; possible staged reading for all winners. **Guidelines:** U.S. citizen or legal resident; plays must be written in English; 1 submission, not previously submitted, published, produced, optioned or winner of any other major competition; no adaptations or musicals. **Submission guidelines:** signed entry form and bound script; script will not be returned; send SASE for guidelines and entry form. **Deadline:** 1 Nov 2001. **Notification:** Jun 2002.

THE MARILYN HALL AWARD

Types of material: adaptations, translations, plays for young audiences, plays with songs (no musicals). **Frequency:** annual. **Remuneration:** category 1: $750, possible staged reading; category 2: $250, possible staged reading. **Guidelines:** U.S. citizen or legal resident; category 1: plays suitable for grades 6-8, approximately 60 minutes or less; category 2: plays suitable for grades 3-5, approximately 30 minutes or less; plays must be written in English; not previously submitted, published, under professional option, or winner of any other major competition; plays may have had one non-professional or educational theatre production; authors may submit 1 script in each category. **Submission procedure:** signed entry form and bound script; scripts will not be returned; send SASE for guidelines and entry form. **Deadline:** 28 Feb 2002; no submission postmarked before 15 Jan 2002. **Notification:** Jun 2002.

BIENNIAL PROMISING PLAYWRIGHT AWARD

Colonial Players, Inc.; Box 2167; Annapolis, MD 21404
Frances Marchand, *Contest Coordinator*

Types of material: full-length plays, adaptations. **Frequency:** biennial. **Remuneration:** $750, production. **Guidelines:** resident of CT, DC, DE, GA, MA, MD, NC, NH, NJ, NY, PA, RI, SC, VA or WV; playwright must be available to attend rehearsals; play not produced professionally, suitable for arena stage, between 90-120 minutes; 2-set limit, cast limit of 10; only adaptation of material in public domain. **Submission procedure:** script and SASP for acknowledgment of receipt; send SASE for guidelines. **Deadline:** 31 Dec 2002; no submission before 1 Sep 2002. **Notification:** Jun 2003.

CALIFORNIA YOUNG PLAYWRIGHTS CONTEST

Playwrights Project; 450 B St, Suite 1020;
    San Diego, CA 92101–8002; (619) 239–8222, FAX 239–8225;
    email write@playwrightsproject.com;
    website www.playwrightsproject.com
Deborah Salzer, *Director*

Types of material: full-length plays, one-acts, musicals, solo pieces. **Frequency:** annual. **Remuneration:** $100, professional production, travel and housing to attend rehearsals to each of several winners (4 in 2000); all entrants receive written evaluation of work. **Guidelines:** CA writer or collaborating writers under 19 years of age as of deadline date; work at least 10 pages long; previous submissions ineligible. **Submission procedure:** 2 copies of script, brief bio and cover letter; script will not be returned; write for guidelines. **Deadline:** 1 Apr 2002. **Notification:** summer 2002.

CHICANO/LATINO LITERARY PRIZE

Department of Spanish & Portuguese; University of California-Irvine;
    322 Humanities Hall; Irvine, CA 92697–5275; (949) 824–5443;
    email cllp@uci.edu;
    website www.hnet.uci.edu/spanishandportuguese/contest.html
Barbara Caldwell, *Prize Coordinator*

Types of material: full-length plays. **Frequency:** every 4 years. **Remuneration:** $1000 1st prize, publication by Arte Público Press, travel to attend award ceremony; $500 2nd prize; $250 3rd prize. **Guidelines:** U.S. citizen or resident; unpublished play written in Spanish or English; 1 submission limit. **Submission procedure:** 3 copies of bound script, minimum 110 typed, double-spaced pages. **Deadline:** 1 Jun 2002. **Notification:** Oct 2002.

CIVIC THEATRE HOLIDAY COMPETITION

Kalamazoo Civic Auditorium; 329 South Park St;
    Kalamazoo, MI 49007; (616) 343–2280, FAX 343–0532;
    website www.kzoocivic.com
Duwain Hunt, *Executive Director*

Types of material: full-length plays. **Frequency:** annual. **Remuneration:**

$500, production. **Guidelines:** play not produced in MI and not scheduled for upcoming production; plays with holiday themes for family audiences; drama, comedy or musical; "not interested in adaptations of *A Christmas Carol.*" **Submission procedure:** script and bio with SASE. **Deadline:** 1 Nov 2001. **Notification:** 1 Feb 2002.

COE COLLEGE NEW WORKS FOR THE STAGE COMPETITION

Department of Theatre Arts; 1220 First Ave NE;
    Cedar Rapids, IA 52402; (319) 399–8624, FAX 399–8557;
    email swolvert@coe.edu
Susan Wolverton, *Chair, Playwriting Festival*

Types of material: full-length plays, plays for young audiences. **Frequency:** biennial, contingent on funding. **Remuneration:** $325, staged reading, travel, room and board for 1-week residency during Jan term. **Guidelines:** unpublished, unproduced play dealing with the theme of Playwriting Festival and Symposia (theme TBA); festival includes workshops and public discussions; no translations, adaptations or musicals; send SASE for guidelines. **Submission procedure:** script only. **Deadline:** 1 Jun 2002. **Notification:** 1 Sep 2002. **Dates:** Jan 2003.

THE CUNNINGHAM PRIZE FOR PLAYWRITING

The Theatre School; DePaul University; 2135 North Kenmore;
    Chicago, IL 60614–4111; (773) 325–7938, FAX 325–7920;
    email lgoetsch@wppost.depaul.edu;
    website theatreschool.depaul.edu/programs/prize.htm
Lara Goetsch, *Director of Marketing and Public Relations*

Types of material: full-length plays, plays for young audiences, musicals, solo pieces. **Frequency:** annual. **Remuneration:** $5000. **Guidelines:** Chicago-area playwright; play which "affirms the centrality of religion, broadly defined, and the human quest for meaning, truth and community." **Submission procedure:** script and brief statement which connects work to purpose of prize; write for guidelines. **Deadline:** 1 Dec 2001. **Notification:** 1 Mar 2002.

DAYTON PLAYHOUSE FUTUREFEST

1301 East Siebenthaler Ave; Dayton, OH 45414; (937) 333–7469,
    FAX 277–9539; website www.daytonplayhouse.com
Fran Pesch, *Theatre Manager*

Types of material: full-length plays. **Frequency:** annual. **Remuneration:**

$1000 1st prize, Speert Publishing Award and publication by Speert Publishing (see listing in Publication); 5 $100 runners-up; 3 plays receive full productions, 3 plays receive reading at Jul 2002 FutureFest weekend; travel and housing to attend weekend. **Guidelines:** unproduced, unpublished play. **Submission procedure:** bound script and resume; send SASE, fax number or visit website for guidelines. **Deadline:** postmarked by 30 Oct 2001. **Notification:** May 2002.

DOROTHY SILVER PLAYWRITING COMPETITION

Jewish Community Center of Cleveland; 3505 Mayfield Rd;
 Cleveland Heights, OH 44118; (216) 382-4000, ext 274,
 FAX 382-5401; email halletheatre@clevejcc.org
Amy Kenerup, *Administrative Director*

Types of material: full-length plays. **Frequency:** annual. **Remuneration:** $1000 (including $500 to cover residency expenses), staged reading, possible production. **Guidelines:** unproduced play that provides "fresh and significant" perspective on the range of the Jewish experience. **Submission procedure:** script only. **Deadline:** 1 Apr 2002 **Notification:** Aug 2002.

DRAMARAMA

The Playwrights' Center of San Francisco; Box 460466;
 San Francisco, CA 94146-0466; (415) 626-4603,
 FAX 863-0901; email playctrsf@aol.com;
 website www.playwrights.org
Sheppard Kominars, *Chairman*

LONG PLAY CONTEST

Types of material: full-length plays, solo pieces. **Frequency:** annual. **Remuneration:** $500; up to 4 scripts given 4-5 rehearsals and staged readings at fall festival. **Guidelines:** unproduced play minimum 60 minutes long. **Submission procedure:** application and $25 fee; send SASE for guidelines and application. **Deadline:** 15 Mar 2002. **Notification:** 15 Aug 2002. **Dates:** Oct 2002.

SHORT PLAY CONTEST

Types of material: one-acts, solo pieces. **Frequency:** annual. **Remuneration:** $500; up to 4 scripts given 4-5 rehearsals and staged readings at fall festival. **Guidelines:** unproduced play maximum 60 minutes long. **Submission procedure:** application and $25 fee; send SASE for guidelines and application. **Deadline:** 15 Mar 2002. **Notification:** 15 Aug 2002. **Dates:** Oct 2002.

DRURY UNIVERSITY ONE-ACT PLAY COMPETITION

Drury University; 900 North Benton Ave; Springfield, MO 65802;
  (417) 873-7430; email sasher@lib.drury.edu;
  website www.drury.edu/Academics/PLAYATT.html
Sandy Asher, *Writer-in-Residence*

Types of material: one-acts **Frequency:** biennial. **Remuneration:** $300 1st prize, possible production; winners recommended to The Open Eye Theater (see Production); 2 runners-up receive $150. **Guidelines:** unproduced, unpublished play 20-45 minutes long; prefers small cast, 1 set; 1 submission limit. **Submission procedure:** script only; send SASE for guidelines. **Deadline:** 1 Dec 2002. **Notification:** 1 Apr 2003.

DUBUQUE FINE ARTS PLAYERS NATIONAL ONE-ACT PLAYWRITING CONTEST

330 Clarke Dr; Dubuque, IA 52001-4427; (319) 588-0646;
  email snakelady@mwci.net;
  website community.iowa.com/ic/OneActPlayContest
Jennie G. Stabenow, *Coordinator*

Types of material: one-acts, one-act adaptations. **Frequency:** annual. **Remuneration:** $600 1st prize; $300 2nd prize; $200 3rd prize; possible production for all 3 plays. **Guidelines:** unproduced, unpublished play maximum 35 pages and 40 minutes long; prefers cast limit of 5, 1 set; no submission limit; only adaptations of material in public domain. **Submission procedure:** entry form, 2 copies of script, 1 paragraph synopsis and $10 fee per submission; optional SASE for critique and optional SASP for acknowledgment of receipt; send SASE for guidelines. **Deadline:** 31 Jan 2002; no submission before 1 Nov 2001. **Notification:** 30 Jun 2002.

EMERGING PLAYWRIGHT AWARD

Urban Stages; 17 East 47th St; New York, NY 10017;
  (212) 421-1380, FAX 421-1387; email urbanstage@aol.com;
  website www.urbanstages.org
T. L. Reilly, *Producing Director*

Types of material: full-length plays. **Frequency:** annual. **Remuneration:** $500, production, multiple staged readings, $25 per reading. **Guidelines:** play unproduced in New York; multicultural, multiethnic plays dealing with social issues in nondidactic manner. **Submission procedure:** script, production history (if any), bio and $5 fee. **Deadline:** ongoing; best submission time Jul-Aug. (See Urban Stages in Production.)

ESSENTIAL THEATRE PLAYWRITING AWARD

(Formerly Festival of New American Theatre)
Essential Theatre; 995 Greenwood Ave, #6; Atlanta, GA 30306;
(404) 876-8471
Peter Hardy, *Producing Artistic Director*

Types of material: full-length plays. **Frequency:** annual. **Remuneration:** $300, production in Festival of New American Theatre; runners-up given staged readings during festival. **Guidelines:** resident of GA; unproduced play. **Submission procedure:** script with SASE for response. **Deadline:** 15 May 2002. **Notification:** 1 Oct 2002. **Dates:** Jan-Feb 2003. (See Essential Theatre in Production.)

FESTIVAL OF FIRSTS PLAYWRITING COMPETITION

Sunset Center; Box 1950; Carmel, CA 93921; (831) 624-3996
Director

Types of material: full-length plays. **Frequency:** annual. **Remuneration:** up to $1000, possible production. **Guidelines:** unproduced play. **Submission procedure:** entry form, script, character breakdown, synopsis and $15 entry fee; send SASE for guidelines. **Deadline:** 31 Aug 2002; no submission before 15 Jun 2002. **Notification:** Sep 2002.

FLORIDA SHORTS CONTEST

Florida Studio Theatre; 1241 North Palm Ave; Sarasota, FL 34236

Types of material: comedy and cabaret sketches. **Frequency:** annual. **Remuneration:** $500, production for winning script and up to 12 others as part of evening of short works. **Guidelines:** resident of FL; sketch of 5 pages or less on specified theme TBA; prefers comedy. **Submission procedure:** script only; write for guidelines. **Deadline:** 30 Mar 2002. (See Florida Studio Theatre in Production.)

THE FRANCESCA PRIMUS PRIZE

Denver Center Theatre Company; 1050 13th St; Denver, CO 80204;
website www.denvercenter.org
Bruce K. Sevy, *Associate Artistic Director/New Play Development*

Types of material: full-length plays. **Frequency:** annual. **Remuneration:** $5000, workshop, reading as part of Denver Center Theatre Company TheatreFest (see Development), travel and housing to attend rehearsals, possible full production. **Guidelines:** plays by women only. **Submission procedure:** send SASE for guidelines or download from web. **Deadline:** 1 Sep

2001. **Notification:** Mar–Apr 2002. (See Denver Center Theatre Company in Production.)

FREMONT CENTRE THEATRE NEW PLAYWRIGHT CONTEST

California Performing Arts Centre (CPAC); 1000 Fremont Ave;
    South Pasadena, CA 91030; (626) 441–5977, FAX 296–6921;
    email kathynpaul@earthlink.net;
    website www.fremontcentretheatre.com
Paul Anderson, *Contest Manager*

Types of material: full-length plays, plays for young audiences, 1 or 2 person shows based on historical events. **Frequency:** annual. **Remuneration:** $350 1st prize; $250 2nd prize; $100 3rd prize; staged reading for 1st, 2nd and 3rd place scripts. **Guidelines:** unpublished plays not produced professionally. **Submission procedure:** script, resume and $15 fee. **Deadline:** 1 Mar 2002. **Notification:** 1 Jun 2002.

GEORGE HAWKINS PLAYWRITING CONTEST

The Ensemble Theatre; 3535 Main St; Houston, TX; (713) 520–0055,
    FAX 520–1269
Marsha Jackson Randolph, *Producing Artistic Director*

Types of material: one-acts, musicals for young audiences. **Frequency:** annual. **Remuneration:** $500 1st prize; staged reading for 1st, 2nd and 3rd place scripts; royalty paid for plays selected as part of Tour Education repertoire. **Guidelines:** original work, not professionally produced, that illuminates the African or African-American experience for ages 6-18; prefers works 45-60 minutes long, with cast limit of 7 with portable set and props. **Submission procedure:** script, synopsis, resume and SASE for response. **Deadline:** Jan–Feb 2002. **Notification:** May 2002. (See The Ensemble Theatre in Production.)

GEORGE R. KERNODLE PLAYWRITING CONTEST

Department of Drama; 619 Kimpel Hall; University of Arkansas;
    Fayetteville, AR 72701; (501) 575–2953, FAX 575–7602
Director

Types of material: one-acts. **Frequency:** annual. **Remuneration:** $300 1st prize; $200 2nd prize; $100 3rd prize; possible staged reading or production. **Guidelines:** U.S. or Canadian playwright; unproduced, unpublished play, maximum 1 hour long; cast limit of 8; 3 submission limit. **Submission procedure:** script with statement that play has not received full production, $3 fee per submission and optional SASE or SASP for acknowledgment of receipt; write for guidelines. **Deadline:** 1 Jun 2002; no submission before 1 Jan 2002. **Notification:** 1 Nov 2002.

GILMAN AND GONZALEZ-FALLA THEATRE FOUNDATION MUSICAL THEATRE AWARD

109 East 64th St; New York, NY 10021; (212) 734-8011,
    FAX 734-9606; email soncel@aol.com
Mandi Lee, *Coordinator*

Types of material: musicals. **Frequency:** annual. **Remuneration:** $25,000. **Guidelines:** writer(s) must have had a musical produced by commercial or not-for-profit theatre. **Submission procedure:** write for guidelines. **Deadline:** 31 Dec 2001.

GOSHEN COLLEGE PEACE PLAYWRITING CONTEST

Goshen College; 1700 South Main St; Goshen, IN 46526;
    (219) 535-7393, FAX 535-7660; email douglc@goshen.edu
Douglas Caskey, *Director of Theatre*

Types of material: one-acts. **Frequency:** biennial. **Remuneration:** $500 1st prize; $100 2nd prize; production, room and board to attend rehearsals and/or production. **Guidelines:** 1 unproduced submission, 20-30 minutes long, exploring a contemporary peace or justice theme "broadly defined." **Submission procedure:** script, 1 paragraph synopsis and resume. **Deadline:** 31 Dec 2001. **Notification:** 1 May 2002.

GREAT PLAINS PLAY CONTEST

University Theatre; 317 Murphy Hall; University of Kansas;
    Lawrence, KS 66045; (785) 864-3381, FAX 864-5251
Delbert Unruh, *Director*

Types of material: full-length plays, musicals, operas, plays/musicals for young audiences. **Frequency:** annual. **Remuneration:** $2000 1st prize, production, $500 to cover travel and housing; $500 2nd prize. **Guidelines:** play not produced professionally dealing with any historical or contemporary aspect of the Great Plains; 2nd prize gives theatre option to produce work. **Submission procedure:** script only. **Deadline:** 1 Sep 2001. **Notification:** 15 Jan 2002.

GREAT PLATTE RIVER PLAYWRIGHTS' FESTIVAL

University of Nebraska–Kearney Theatre; Kearney, NE 68849–5260;
(308) 865–8406, FAX 865–8806; email garrisonj@unk.edu
Jack Garrison, *Artistic Director*

Types of material: full-length plays, one-acts, plays for young audiences, musicals. **Frequency:** annual. **Remuneration** at least 3 prizes of $200–500; 1st prize includes production, travel and housing to attend rehearsals. **Guidelines:** unproduced, unpublished original work; submission of works-in-progress for possible development encouraged. **Submission procedure:** script, resume and cover letter; include cassette for musical. **Deadline:** 1 Apr 2002. **Notification:** 31 Jul 2002.

HAROLD MORTON LANDON TRANSLATION AWARD

The Academy of American Poets; 584 Broadway, Suite 1208;
New York, NY 10012; (212) 274–0343, FAX 274–9427;
email academy@poets.org; website www.poets.org
Michael Tyrell, *Awards Director*

Types of material: translations. **Frequency:** annual. **Remuneration:** $1000. **Guidelines:** U.S. citizen; published translation of verse, including verse drama, from any language into English verse, book must have been published in 2001. **Submission procedure:** 3 copies of book (no manuscripts). **Deadline:** 31 Dec 2001.

HENRICO THEATRE COMPANY ONE-ACT PLAYWRITING COMPETITION

The County of Henrico; Division of Recreation and Parks; Box 27032;
Richmond, VA 23273–7032; (804) 501–5138, FAX 501–5284;
email per22@co.henrico.va.us
Amy A. Perdue, *Cultural Arts Coordinator*

Types of material: one-acts, musicals, solo pieces. **Frequency:** annual. **Remuneration:** $300 1st prize, production; $200 2nd prize, possible production and video. **Guidelines:** unproduced, unpublished work; no controversial themes or "excessive language"; prefers small cast, simple set. **Submission procedure:** 2 copies of script; write for guidelines. **Deadline:** 1 Jul 2002. **Notification:** 31 Dec 2002.

HRC's ANNUAL PLAYWRITING CONTEST

Hudson River Classics, Inc; Box 940; Hudson, NY 12534;
(518) 828-0175
Jan M. Grice, *President*

Types of material: full-length plays. **Frequency:** annual. **Remuneration:** $500, staged reading. **Guidelines:** Northeast playwright; 60-90-minute unpublished play. **Submission procedure:** script, bio and $5 fee. **Deadline:** 1 May 2002; no submission before 1 Feb 2002. **Notification:** Sep 2002.

IHT/SRT INTERNATIONAL PLAYWRIGHTING COMPETITION

Singapore Repertory Theatre; 20 Merbau Rd; Robertson Quay;
Singapore 239035; 65-221-5585, FAX 65-221-1936;
email singrep@cyberway.com.sg; website www.singrep.com
Charlotte Nors, *Venue & Marketing Manager*

Types of material: full-length plays. **Frequency:** annual. **Remuneration:** $15,000 (U.S. dollars), full production, transportation, lodging and per diem to attend rehearsals and performances. **Guidelines:** playwright of any nationality or ethnicity; English-language play not produced professionally dealing with some aspect of modern Asian identity; 1 submission limit. **Submission procedure:** script only; script will not be returned. **Deadline:** 31 Mar 2002. **Notification:** May 2002.

JACKIE WHITE MEMORIAL NATIONAL CHILDREN'S PLAYWRITING CONTEST

309 Parkade Blvd; Columbia, MO 65202; (573) 874-5628
Betsy Phillips, *Director*

Types of material: plays and musicals to be performed by young actors. **Frequency:** annual. **Remuneration:** $250, optional production by Columbia Entertainment Company Children's Theatre School, room, board and travel to attend performance; all entrants receive written evaluation. **Guidelines:** unpublished original work, 60-90 minutes in length, with 20-30 speaking characters of all ages, at least 10 developed in some detail, to be played by students ages 10-15. **Submission procedure:** entry form, script, character breakdown, act/scene synopsis, resume and $10 fee; include cassette and score for musical; send SASE for guidelines. **Deadline:** 1 Jun 2002. **Notification:** 30 Aug 2002.

JAMES D. PHELAN AWARD IN LITERATURE

Intersection for the Arts/The San Francisco Foundation;
446 Valencia St; San Francisco, CA 94103; (415) 626–2787,
FAX 626–1636; email info@theintersection.org
Awards Coordinator

Types of material: full-length plays, one-acts, plays for young audiences. **Frequency:** annual. **Remuneration:** $2000. **Guidelines:** CA-born author 20–35 years of age as of 31 Jan 2002; unpublished play-in-progress. **Submission procedure:** application and script; send SASE for guidelines and application. **Deadline:** 31 Jan 2002; no submission before 15 Nov 2001. **Notification:** 15 Jun 2002.

JANE CHAMBERS PLAYWRITING AWARD

c/o Division of Theatre; Southern Methodist University; Box 750356;
Dallas, TX 75275–0356; email gesmith@mail.smu.edu
Gretchen E. Smith, *Administrator*

Types of material: full-length plays, one-acts, solo pieces, performance-art pieces. **Frequency:** annual. **Remuneration:** $1000, free registration and rehearsed reading at the Women and Theatre Conference in late Jul; student submissions eligible for $250 Student Award. **Guidelines:** work by a woman that reflects a feminist perspective and contains a majority of roles for women; special interest in works by and about women from a diversity of positions in respect to race, class, sexual preference, physical ability, age and geographical region; experimentation with dramatic form encouraged; 1 submission limit; award administered by the Association for Theatre in Higher Education (see Membership and Service Organizations). **Submission procedure:** application, 3 copies of script, synopsis and resume; if possible, professional recommendation; optional SASP for acknowledgment of receipt; send SASE for guidelines and application. **Deadline:** 1 Feb 2002. **Notification:** 30 Jun 2002.

JEWEL BOX THEATRE PLAYWRIGHTING AWARD

3700 North Walker; Oklahoma City, OK 73118–7099;
(405) 521–1786, FAX 525–6562
Charles Tweed, *Production Director*

Types of material: full-length plays. **Frequency:** annual. **Remuneration:** $500, possible production. **Guidelines:** unproduced ensemble play with emphasis on character rather than spectacle. **Submission procedure:** entry form, 2 copies of script, playwright's agreement and $10 fee; send SASE in

Oct for guidelines and forms. **Deadline:** 15 Jan 2002. **Notification:** Apr 2002.

JOHN GASSNER MEMORIAL PLAYWRITING AWARD

New England Theatre Conference; Northeastern University;
306 Huntington Ave; Boston, MA 02115; (617) 424–9275,
FAX 424–1057; email info@netconline.org;
website www.netconline.org

Types of material: full-length plays. **Frequency:** annual. **Remuneration:** $1000 1st prize; $500 2nd prize; staged reading, possible publication. **Guidelines:** New England resident or NETC member (see Membership and Service Organizations); unpublished play that has not had professional full production and is not under consideration for publication or professional production; 1 submission limit. **Submission procedure:** script with cover page, character breakdown, brief synopsis and statement that play has not been published or professionally produced and is not under consideration; $10 fee, except for NETC members; SASP for acknowledgment of receipt; script will not be returned; send SASE for guidelines. **Deadline:** 15 Apr 2002. **Notification:** 1 Sep 2002 (winners only).

THE KAUFMAN AND HART PRIZE FOR NEW AMERICAN COMEDY

Arkansas Repertory Theatre; Box 110; Little Rock, AR 72203–0110;
(501) 378–0445
Brad Mooy, *Literary Manager*

Types of material: full-length plays. **Frequency:** biennial. **Remuneration:** $10,000, staged reading and transportation; additional finalists receive $1000 and staged reading. **Guidelines:** U.S. citizens; comedies not previously published or produced; minimum 65 pages, cast limit of 12; no musicals or plays for young audiences, 1 submission limit. **Submission procedure:** script with recommendation from agent or theatre professional only. **Deadline:** 31 Dec 2001. **Notification:** Mar 2002. (See Arkansas Repertory Theatre in Production.)

KENNEDY CENTER AMERICAN COLLEGE THEATER FESTIVAL: MICHAEL KANIN PLAYWRITING AWARDS PROGRAM

The John F. Kennedy Center for the Performing Arts;
    Washington, DC 20566-0001; (202) 416-8857, FAX 416-8802;
    website www.kennedy-center.org/education/actf
Susan Shaffer, *Co-Manager for Administration*
Gregg Henry, Co-Manager/Artistic Director

ANCHORAGE PRESS THEATER FOR YOUTH PLAYWRITING AWARD

Types of material: full-length plays, adaptations, musicals. **Frequency:** annual. **Remuneration:** $1000, $1250 fellowship to attend either the New Visions/New Voices Festival (see Development) or the National Youth Theatre Symposium (see Waldo M. and Grace C. Bonderman IUPUI Playwriting Event for Young Audiences at the Indiana Repertory Theatre in this section), possible publication by Anchorage Press with royalties. **Guidelines:** writer enrolled as full-time student at college or university during year of production or during either of the 2 years preceding the production; play on theme appealing to young people from kindergarten-12th grade produced by an ACTF-participating college or university; download guidelines from web. **Submission procedure:** college or university which has entered production of work in ACTF registers work for awards program. **Deadline:** 1 Dec 2001. **Dates:** 15-23 Apr 2002.

THE DAVID MARK COHEN PLAYWRITING AWARD

Types of material: full-length plays, bills of related one-acts. **Frequency:** annual. **Remuneration:** $1000, up to $500 for travel, script-in-hand reading at annual Aug meeting of Association for Theatre in Higher Education (ATHE) (see Membership and Service Organization), Dramatic Publishing Company (see Publication) contract offer to publish, license and market play. **Guidelines:** unpublished play or bill of related one-acts not produced professionally, produced by a ACTF-participating college or university theatre program; download guidelines from web. **Submission procedure:** college or university which has entered production of play in ACTF registers work for awards program. **Deadline:** 1 Dec 2001. **Dates:** 15-23 Apr 2002.

THE JEAN KENNEDY SMITH PLAYWRITING AWARD

Types of material: full-length plays, adaptations, musicals. **Frequency:** annual. **Remuneration:** $2500 plus Dramatists Guild (see Membership and Service Organizations) membership and fellowship to attend prestigious playwriting program. **Guidelines:** writer enrolled as full-time student at college or university during year of production; play that explores the human experience of living with disabilities produced by an ACTF-participating college or university; download guidelines from web. **Submission procedure:** college or university which has entered production of work in ACTF registers work for awards program. **Deadline:** 1 Dec 2001. **Dates:** 15–23 Apr 2002.

THE JOHN CAUBLE SHORT PLAY AWARDS PROGRAM

Types of material: one-acts, one-act adaptations. **Frequency:** annual. **Remuneration:** $1000 for 3 or fewer playwrights, publication by Samuel French (see Publication), Dramatists Guild (see Membership and Service Organizations) membership. **Guidelines:** writer enrolled as full-time student at college or university during year of production or during either of the 2 years preceding the production; one-act must be produced by an ACTF-participating college or university; simple production demands (minimal setup and strike time); download guidelines from web. **Submission procedure:** college or university which has entered production of work in ACTF registers work for awards program. **Deadline:** 1 Dec 2001. **Dates:** 15–23 Apr 2002.

THE KC/ACTF MUSICAL THEATER AWARD

Types of material: musicals. **Frequency:** annual. **Remuneration:** $1000 for lyrics; $1000 for music; $1000 for book to producing college or university. **Guidelines:** at least 50% of writing team must be enrolled as full-time student(s) at college or university during year of production or during either of the 2 years preceding the production; original and copyrighted work produced by an ACTF-participating college or university; download guidelines from web. **Submission procedure:** college or university which has entered production of work in ACTF registers work for awards program. **Deadline:** 1 Dec 2001. **Dates:** 15–23 Apr 2002.

THE KENNEDY CENTER ACTF TEN-MINUTE PLAY FESTIVAL

Types of material: 10-minute plays. **Frequency:** annual. **Remuneration:** $1000 1st prize, best play in each of 8 regions published by Dramatic Publishing Company (see Publication), development work with director, dramaturg and actors, staged reading followed by response session at KC/ACTF annual Apr conference. **Guidelines:** Each region determines own submission criteria; download guidelines from web. **Submission procedure:** college or university which has entered production of work in ACTF registers work for awards program; regional submissions from schools with no other entries will pay $20 fee per submission. **Deadline:** Nov 2001. **Notification:** Dec 2001. **Dates:** Jan and Feb 2002 regional festival; Apr 2002 national festival.

THE LORRAINE HANSBERRY PLAYWRITING AWARD

Types of material: full-length plays. **Frequency:** annual. **Remuneration:** $2500 1st prize for playwright, internship at the O'Neill Playwrights Conference (see Development), publication of play by The Dramatic Publishing Company (see Publication), $750 to producing college or university; $1000 2nd prize to playwright, $500 to producing college or university. **Guidelines:** writer enrolled as full-time student at college or university during year of production or during either of the 2 years preceding the production; play dealing with the black experience produced by an ACTF-participating college or university; download guidelines from web. **Submission procedure:** college or university which has entered production of work in ACTF registers work for awards program. **Deadline:** 1 Dec 2001. **Dates:** 15–23 Apr 2002.

THE NATIONAL STUDENT PLAYWRITING AWARD

Types of material: full-length plays, adaptations, musicals. **Frequency:** annual. **Remuneration:** $2500 for playwright, production at Kennedy Center during festival, publication by Samuel French (see Publication) with royalties, fellowship to attend Sundance Theatre Laboratory (see Development), Dramatists Guild (see Membership and Service Organizations) membership, $1000 to producing college or university. **Guidelines:** writer enrolled as full-time student at college or university during year of production or during either of the 2 years preceding the production; work produced by an ACTF-participating college or university; download guidelines from web. **Submission procedure:** college or university which has entered production of work in ACTF registers work for awards program. **Deadline:** 1 Dec 2001. **Dates:** 15–23 Apr 2002.

Sí TV PLAYWRITING AWARD

Types of material: full-length plays, one-acts. **Frequency:** annual. **Remuneration:** $2500 and an internship at a playwriting retreat (summer 2000, the O'Neill Playwrights Conference); Dramatic Publishing Company (see Publication) contract offer to publish, license and market play, $500 grant to college or university theatre department producing play. **Guidelines:** produced Latino/Latina writer enrolled as full-time student at college or university during the year of production or during either of the 2 years preceding production; work produced by an ACTF-participating college or university; download guidelines from web. **Submission procedure:** college or university which has entered production of work in ACTF registers work for awards program. **Deadline:** 1 Dec 2001. **Dates:** 15–23 Apr 2002.

KUMU KAHUA THEATRE/UHM DEPARTMENT OF THEATRE & DANCE PLAYWRITING CONTEST

Kumu Kahua Theatre; 46 Merchant St; Honolulu, HI 96813;
(808) 536-4222, FAX 536-4226
Harry Wong III, *Artistic Director, Kumu Kahua Theatre*

HAWAI'I PRIZE

Types of material: full-length plays. **Frequency:** annual. **Remuneration:** $500. **Guidelines:** play set in HI or dealing with some aspect of HI experience; unproduced play; previous entries ineligible. **Submission procedure:** write for entry brochure. **Deadline:** 4 Jan 2002. **Notification:** 1 May 2002.

PACIFIC RIM PRIZE

Types of material: full-length plays. **Frequency:** annual. **Remuneration:** $400. **Guidelines:** play set in or dealing with Pacific Islands, Pacific Rim or Pacific Asian-American experience; unproduced play; previous entries ineligible. **Submission procedure:** write for entry brochure. **Deadline:** 4 Jan 2002. **Notification:** 1 May 2002.

RESIDENT PRIZE

Types of material: full-length plays, one-acts. **Frequency:** annual. **Remuneration:** $200. **Guidelines:** resident of HI at time of submission; previous entries ineligible. **Submission procedure:** write for entry brochure. **Deadline:** 4 Jan 2002. **Notification:** May 2002.

LAMIA INK! INTERNATIONAL ONE-PAGE PLAY COMPETITION

Box 202; Prince St Station; New York, NY 10012
(Ms.) Cortland Jessup, *Artistic Director*

Types of material: 1 page plays. **Frequency:** annual. **Remuneration:** $200, reading in New York City and publication in magazine (see Lamia Ink! in Publication) for winner and 11 other best plays; at least $50 2nd prize; $25 3rd prize. **Guidelines:** 3 submission limit. **Submission procedure:** script, SASE for response and $2 fee per submission or $5 for 3 submissions; send SASE for guidelines. **Deadline:** 15 Mar 2002. **Notification:** 15 May 2002.

THE LITTLE THEATRE OF ALEXANDRIA NATIONAL ONE-ACT PLAYWRITING COMPETITION

Little Theatre of Alexandria; 600 Wolfe St; Alexandria, VA 22314;
  (703) 683-5778, FAX 683-1378; email ltlthtre@erols.com
Chairman, One-Act Playwriting Competition

Types of material: one-acts. **Frequency:** annual. **Remuneration:** $350 1st prize; $250 2nd prize; $150 3rd prize; possible production. **Guidelines:** unpublished, unproduced work; prefers plays with running times of 20-60 minutes, few scenes and 1 set; 2 submission limit. **Submission procedure:** script, synopsis, character breakdown and $20 fee; send SASE for guidelines. **Deadline:** 30 Apr 2002; no submission before 1 Dec 2001. **Notification:** Sep 2002.

LOIS AND RICHARD ROSENTHAL NEW PLAY PRIZE

Cincinnati Playhouse in the Park; Box 6537;
  Cincinnati, OH 45206-0537; (513) 345-2242;
  website www.cincyplay.com
Literary Associate

Types of material: full-length plays, musicals. **Frequency:** annual. **Remuneration:** $10,000, production, travel and housing to attend rehearsals. **Guidelines:** unpublished work not produced professionally; no translations or adaptations; 1 submission limit. **Submission procedure:** 5-page dialogue sample, 2-page maximum abstract including synopsis, character breakdown and bio; include cassette for musicals. **Deadline:** 31 Dec 2001; no submission before 1 Jul 2001. **Notification:** 6-8 months.

LOS ANGELES DESIGNERS' THEATRE COMMISSIONS

Box 1883; Studio City, CA 91614-0883; (323) 650-9600,
  654-2700 (TDD), FAX 654-3260; email ladesigners@juno.com
Richard Niederberg, *Artistic Director*

Types of material: full-length plays, bills of related one-acts, translations, adaptations, plays for young audiences, musicals, solo pieces, operas. **Frequency:** ongoing. **Remuneration:** negotiable commissioning fee, possible travel to attend rehearsals if developmental work is needed. **Guidelines:** commissioning program for work with commercial potential which has not received professional full production, is not under option and is free of commitment to specific director, actors or other personnel; large casts and multiple sets welcome; prefers controversial material. **Submission procedure:** proposal or synopsis and resume; include cassette for musical;

materials will not be returned. **Deadline:** ongoing. **Notification:** at least 4 months.

LOVE CREEK ANNUAL SHORT PLAY FESTIVAL

Love Creek Productions; c/o 162 Nesbit St;
    Weehawken, NJ 07087-6817
Cynthia Granville-Callahan, *Festival Literary Manager/Chair, Reading Committee*

Types of material: one-acts. **Frequency:** annual. **Remuneration:** minimum of 60 finalists receive mini-showcase production in New York City during festival; $300 prize for best play of festival, may be shared by multiple winners. **Guidelines:** unpublished play not produced in NYC area within past year, maximum length of 40 minutes, cast of 2 or more, simple sets and costumes; 2 submission limit; strongly prefers women in major roles and predominantly female cast; mini-festivals centered around specific themes; upcoming themes include "Fear of God," gay and lesbian themes, political plays. **Submission procedure:** script with letter giving theatre permission to produce play if chosen and specifying whether Equity showcase is acceptable; send SASE for themes and deadlines. **Deadline:** ongoing. **Dates:** year-round.

THE MARC A. KLEIN PLAYWRITING AWARD

Department of Theater Arts; Case Western Reserve University;
    10900 Euclid Ave; Cleveland, OH 44106-7077; (216) 368-4868,
    FAX 368-5184; email ksg@po.cwru.edu
Ron Wilson, *Chair, Reading Committee*

Types of material: full-length plays, bills of related one-acts. **Frequency:** annual. **Remuneration:** $1000 ($500 used to cover residency expenses), production. **Guidelines:** student currently enrolled at U.S. college or university; work endorsed by faculty member of university theatre department that has not received professional full production or trade-book publication. **Submission procedure:** completed entry form and script. **Deadline:** 15 May 2002. **Notification:** 1 Aug 2002.

MAXIM MAZUMDAR NEW PLAY COMPETITION

Alleyway Theatre; 1 Curtain Up Alley; Buffalo, NY 14202-1911;
    (716) 852-2600, FAX 852-2266; email email@alleyway.com
Literary Manager

Types of material: full-length plays, one-acts, musicals. **Frequency:** annual.

Remuneration: $400, production with royalty, travel and housing to attend rehearsals for full-length play or musical; $100 and production for one-act play or musical. **Guidelines:** unproduced full-length work minimum 90 minutes long with cast limit of 10 and unit set or simple set, or unproduced one-act less than 40 minutes long with cast limit of 6 and simple set; prefers work with unconventional setting that explores the boundaries of theatricality; 1 submission limit in each category. **Submission procedure:** script, character breakdown and resume; include cassette of complete score for musicals; $5 fee per playwright. **Deadline:** 1 Jul 2002. **Notification:** 1 Oct 2002 for finalists; 1 Nov 2002 for winners.

McLaren Memorial Comedy Playwriting Competition

Midland Community Theatre; 2000 West Wadley Ave;
   Midland, TX 79705; (915) 682–2544, FAX 682–6136;
   website www.mct-cole.org
Coordinator

Types of material: full-length plays, one-acts, plays for young audiences. **Frequency:** annual. **Remuneration:** $300 for full-length play; $100 for one-act; 3 finalists receive staged reading. **Guidelines:** plays not produced professionally; comedies only. **Submission procedure:** script and $10 fee per play. **Deadline:** 31 Jan 2002; no submission before 1 Dec 2001. **Notification:** Jun 2002.

Metropolitan Life Foundation Nuestras Voces

Repertorio Español; 138 East 27th St; New York, NY 10016;
   (212) 889–2850, FAX 686–3732;
   email a.astorvargas@repertorio.org; website www.repertorio.org
Allison Astor–Vargas, *Special Projects Manager*

Types of material: full-length plays. **Frequency:** annual. **Remuneration:** $3000 1st prize, production, royalties depending on finances; $2000 2nd prize; $1000 3rd prize; 2 runners-up receive $500; 2nd and 3rd prizes and runners-up receive staged reading. **Guidelines:** unpublished work not produced professionally; Hispanic themes, characters and subjects; written in Spanish or English. **Submission procedure:** entry form and 2 copies of script. **Deadline:** exact date TBA (15 Feb in 2001). (See Repertorio Español in Production.)

MILDRED AND ALBERT PANOWSKI PLAYWRITING AWARD

Forest A. Roberts Theatre; Northern Michigan University;
  Marquette, MI 49855; (906) 227-2553, FAX 227-2567
James A. Panowski, *Director*

Types of material: full-length plays, adaptations, solo pieces. **Frequency:** annual. **Remuneration:** $2000; production; travel, room and board for 1-week residency. **Guidelines:** 1 unpublished, unproduced submission; rewrites of previous entries ineligible. **Submission procedure:** entry form and script; write for guidelines. **Deadline:** 22 Nov 2001. **Notification:** Apr 2002.

THE MILL MOUNTAIN THEATRE NEW PLAY COMPETITION: THE NORFOLK SOUTHERN FESTIVAL OF NEW WORKS

1 Market Square SE, 2nd Floor; Roanoke, VA 24011-1437;
  (540) 342-5749, FAX 342-5745;
  email outreach@millmountain.org;
  website www.millmountain.org
New Play Competition Coordinator

Types of material: full-length plays, musicals, solo pieces. **Frequency:** annual. **Remuneration:** $1000, staged reading and possible full production, travel stipend and housing for limited residency. **Guidelines:** U.S. resident; 1 unproduced, unpublished submission; no 10-minute plays. **Submission procedure:** agent submission or script with professional recommendation by director, literary manager or dramaturg; include cassette for musical; send SASE for guidelines or download from web. **Deadline:** postmarked by 1 Jan 2002; no submission before 1 Oct 2001. **Notification:** Aug 2002.

MORTON R. SARETT NATIONAL PLAYWRITING COMPETITION

Department of Theatre; University of Nevada, Las Vegas;
  4505 Maryland Pkwy, Box 455036; Las Vegas, NV 89154-5036;
  (702) 895-3666;
  website www.unlv.edu/colleges/Fine_Arts/Theatre/
Corrine A. Bonate, *Coordinator*

Types of material: full-length plays, musicals. **Frequency:** biennial. **Remuneration:** $3000, production, travel and housing to attend rehearsals and opening performance. **Guidelines:** unpublished, unproduced play or musical; no adaptations. **Submission procedure:** application, 2 firmly bound copies of script and 50-word synopsis; include score (prefer piano) or cassette for musicals; send SASE for guidelines and applications or download from web. **Deadline:** postmarked by 15 Dec 2001; no submission before 1 Sep 2001. **Notification:** Jul 2002.

MOVING ARTS PREMIERE ONE-ACT COMPETITION

514 South Spring St; Los Angeles, CA 90013; (213) 622–8906,
FAX 622–8946; email treynichols@movingarts.org;
website www.movingarts.org
Trey Nichols, *Literary Director*

Types of material: one-acts. **Frequency:** annual. **Remuneration:** $200, production in annual fall one-act festival. **Guidelines:** play not previously produced in L.A. area; single set, modest technical requirements. **Submission procedure:** script without author's name or address, cover letter, $10 fee per script payable to Moving Arts and SASE for response. **Deadline:** 28 Feb 2002. **Notification:** Jul 2002. (See Moving Arts in Production.)

NANTUCKET SHORT PLAY FESTIVAL AND COMPETITION

Nantucket Theatrical Productions; Box 2177; Nantucket, MA 02584;
(508) 228–5002
Jim Patrick, *Artistic Director*

Types of material: one-acts. **Frequency:** annual. **Remuneration:** $200; 1 or more staged readings for winning play and selected additional plays as part of summer festival. **Guidelines:** unpublished play which has not received Equity production, maximum length of 40 pages, simple production demands. **Submission procedure:** script and $8 fee; send SASE for guidelines. **Deadline:** 1 Jan 2002. **Notification:** ongoing. **Dates:** Jul 2002.

NATF SCRIPT COMPETITION.

The National Audio Theatre Festivals; 115 Dikeman St;
Hempstead, NY 11550; (516) 483–8321, FAX 538–7583;
website www.natf.org
Sue Zizza, *Executive Director*

Types of material: radio plays. **Frequency:** annual. **Remuneration:** $800 split between 2-4 winners, workshop production, published in *NATF Scriptbook.* **Guidelines:** radio plays only, 25 minutes or less, "dialogue that demonstrates how sound can color content," strong female roles and multicultural viewpoints; 1 submission limit. **Submission procedure:** 3 copies of script in radio format, cover letter stating authorship and $20 fee; download guidelines from web. **Deadline:** 15 Nov 2001. **Notification:** Apr

2002. (See The National Audio Theatre Festivals in Membership and Service Organizations.)

NATIONAL CHILDREN'S THEATRE FESTIVAL

Actors' Playhouse at the Miracle Theatre; 280 Miracle Mile;
    Coral Gables, FL 33134; (305) 444-9293, ext 615,
    FAX 444-4181; website www.actorsplayhouse.org
Earl Maulding, *Director of Theatre for Young Audiences*

Types of material: musicals for young audiences. **Frequency:** annual. **Remuneration:** $500 prize, production, travel and housing to attend festival. **Guidelines:** unpublished musical for young people ages 5-12, 45-60 minutes long, with cast limit of 8 (may play multiple roles) and minimal sets suitable for touring; translations and adaptations eligible only if writer owns copyright to material; special interest in works dealing with social issues including multiculturalism in today's society. **Submission procedure:** entry form, script and $10 fee; include score and cassette for musical; write for guidelines. **Deadline:** 1 Aug 2002. **Notification:** Nov 2002. **Dates:** Jan 2003.

NATIONAL LATINO PLAYWRITING AWARD

(Formerly National Hispanic Playwrighting Award)
Arizona Theatre Company; 40 East 14th St; Tucson, AZ 85701;
    (520) 884-8210, ext 5510, FAX 628-9129
Elaine Romero, *Playwright-in-Residence*

Types of material: full-length plays, adaptations. **Frequency:** annual. **Remuneration:** $1000. **Guidelines:** playwright of Latino heritage residing in U.S., U.S. territories or Mexico; 1 unproduced, unpublished submission written in English, Spanish or both languages, minimum 50 pages. **Submission procedure:** script (with English translation if original in Spanish), 1 page cover letter including development history, and bio. **Deadline:** 30 Nov 2001. **Notification:** summer 2002.

NATIONAL NEW PLAY AWARD

Department of Theatre Arts; Humboldt State University;
    Arcata, CA 95521; (707) 826-4606, FAX 826-5494;
    email mtk3@axe.humboldt.edu;
    website www.humboldt.edu/~mtk3
Margaret Thomas Kelso, *Assistant Professor of Theatre Arts*

Types of material: full-length plays. **Frequency:** triennial. **Remuneration:**

2 awards of $1000, full production, 2-week residency. **Guidelines:** unproduced, unpublished play. **Submission procedure:** script only; 2 submission limit. **Deadline:** 30 Jan 2002; no submission before 1 Nov 2001. **Notification:** spring 2002.

NATIONAL PLAY AWARD

Box 286; Hollywood, CA 90078; (323) 465-9517, FAX 417-4722;
   email nrtf@nrtf.org; website www.nrtf.org
C. Raul Espinoza, *Chair, National Repertory Theatre Foundation*

Types of material: full-length plays. **Frequency:** annual. **Remuneration:** $5000 1st prize; $500 each for 4 runners-up; all finalists receive staged reading in fall festival. **Guidelines:** unpublished play not produced with paid Equity cast, which has not won major award; previous entries ineligible. **Submission procedure:** script and $25 fee (check payable to NRTF); download guidelines from web. **Deadline:** postmarked by 31 Mar 2002; no submission before 1 Jan 2002. **Notification:** 1 Aug 2002 for finalists; 31 Dec 2002 for winner.

NATIONAL TEN-MINUTE PLAY CONTEST

Actors Theatre of Louisville; 316 West Main St;
   Louisville, KY 40202-4218; (502) 584-1265, FAX 584-1265;
   website www.actorstheatre.org
Tanya Palmer, *Literary Manager*
Amy Wegener, *Dramaturg/Director of New Play Development*

Types of material: 10-minute plays. **Frequency:** annual. **Remuneration:** $1000 Heideman Award; possible production with royalty. **Guidelines:** U.S. citizen or resident; play 10 pages long or less which has not had Equity production; 1 submission limit, previous entries ineligible. **Submission procedure:** script only; script will not be returned; write for guidelines. **Deadline:** postmarked before 1 Dec 2001. **Notification:** fall 2002.

NATIONAL TRANSLATION AWARD

American Literary Translators Association; University of Texas at
   Dallas; MC35; Box 830688; Richardson, TX 75083-0688;
   (972) 883-2093, FAX 883-6303; email ert@utdallas.edu;
   website www.utdallas.edu/research/ets/alta.htm
Eileen Tollett, *Executive Director*

Types of material: translations. **Frequency:** annual. **Remuneration:** $2000. **Guidelines:** translation from any language published in U.S. by American publisher. **Submission procedure:** no submission by translator; publisher nominates translation and submits 4 copies of book with cover letter. **Deadline:** 31 Mar 2002. **Notification:** 10 Sep 2002.

NEW AMERICAN COMEDY (NAC) WORKSHOP

Ukiah Players Theatre; 1041 Low Gap Rd; Ukiah, CA 95482;
    (707) 462–1210, FAX 462–1790; email players@pacific.net
Michael Ducharme, *Executive Director*

Types of material: full-length plays. **Frequency:** biennial. **Remuneration:** $50 per performance for play selected for full production (6 to 8 performances); $25 each per performance for 2 plays chosen as staged readings; up to $500 travel and $25 per diem to attend 1-week workshop. **Guidelines:** playwright must be available to participate in 1-week developmental workshop; unproduced, unpublished comedy; prefers small cast, simple set. **Submission procedure:** application, script with 1-page plot summary, scenic requirements, character breakdown, estimated running time and resume; write for guidelines. **Deadline:** 30 Nov 2001. **Notification:** Feb 2002. **Dates:** May–Jun 2002.

NEW PROFESSIONAL THEATRE WRITERS FESTIVAL

Box 799; New York, NY 10108; email newprof@aol.com
    website www.newprofessionaltheatre.com
Literary Manager

Types of material: full-length plays, musicals. **Frequency:** annual. **Remuneration:** $2000, 2-week residency with dramaturg, staged reading, business seminar, possible production. **Guidelines:** African-American writer. **Submission procedure:** script, resume and SASP for acknowledgment of receipt; include cassette for musical. **Deadline:** 1 Jun 2002. **Notification:** Sep 2002.

NEW YORK CITY 15 MINUTE PLAY FESTIVAL

Turnip Theatre Company; c/o Falzer; 6 South Brookwood Dr;
    Montclair, NJ 07042; (973) 744–4651, FAX 744–1745;
    email falzer@bellatlantic.net or turniptheatreco@aol.com
Gloria Falzer, *Managing Director*

Types of material: one-acts. **Frequency:** annual. **Remuneration:** $100–300 for festival winner, full production by Turnip Theatre Company. **Guidelines:** one-acts maximum 15 pages; work not produced in New York City; 1

submission limit. **Submission procedure:** write, call or email for guidelines. **Deadline:** 1 Dec 2001. **Notification:** 1 Feb 2002.

NEW YORK CITY PUBLIC SCHOOL PLAYWRITING CONTEST

(Formerly New York City High School Playwriting Contest)
Young Playwrights Inc; 321 West 44th St, Suite 906;
New York, NY 10036; (212) 307–1140, FAX 307–1454;
email writeaplay@aol.com; website youngplaywrights.org
Sheri M. Goldhirsch, *Artistic Director*

Types of material: full-length plays, one-acts. **Frequency:** annual. **Remuneration:** varies. **Guidelines:** New York City public school student; writers 18 years of age or younger automatically entered in Young Playwrights Festival National Playwriting Contest (see listing this section). **Submission procedure:** script with playwright's name, date of birth, home address, phone number, school and grade on title page; write for guidelines. **Deadline:** 1 Apr 2002. **Notification:** 1 Jun 2002.

THE NOMAD THEATRE'S PLAYWRITING COMPETITION

Nomad Theatre; 1410 Quince Ave; Boulder, CO 80304;
(303) 443–7510, ext 3, FAX 245–8777; email magilian@aol.com;
website www.nomadtheatre.net
Jennifer Berry, *Chair & Literary Coordinator*

Types of material: one-acts for young audiences. **Frequency:** annual. **Remuneration:** $300, workshop production in Jul by Nomad Theatre. **Guidelines:** unproduced one-act plays for teenage actors and audience; no longer than 60 minutes. **Submission procedure:** bound script, synopsis, character breakdown, resume, letter of inquiry with SASE and $20 fee. **Deadline:** Apr 2002; no submission before Jan 2002. **Notification:** Jun 2002.

OGLEBAY INSTITUTE TOWNGATE THEATRE CONTESTS

Oglebay Institute; Stifel Fine Arts Center; 1330 National Rd;
Wheeling, WV 26003; (304) 242–7700, FAX 242–7767
Performing Arts Department

PLAYWRITING CONTEST

Types of material: full-length plays. **Frequency:** annual. **Remuneration:** $300, production, partial travel to attend performances. **Guidelines:** unpublished, unproduced play, simple set. **Submission procedure:** script and resume. **Deadline:** 30 Dec 2001. **Notification:** 1 May 2002.

PLAYWRITING CONTEST FOR COLLEGE STUDENTS

Types of material: full-length plays. **Frequency:** annual. **Remuneration:** $100, production. **Guidelines:** unpublished, unproduced play, simple set. **Submission procedure:** script only. **Deadline:** 15 Mar 2002. **Notification:** 1 Jun 2002.

PEN-BOOK-OF-THE-MONTH CLUB TRANSLATION PRIZE

PEN American Center; 568 Broadway; New York, NY 10012;
(212) 334–1660, FAX 334–2181; email jm@pen.org
John Morrone, *Literary Awards Manager*

Types of material: translations. **Frequency:** annual. **Remuneration:** $3000. **Guidelines:** book-length translation from any language into English published in U.S. during current calendar year. **Submission procedure:** 3 copies of book. **Deadline:** 15 Dec 2001. **Notification:** spring 2002.

PEN CENTER USA WEST LITERARY AWARDS

672 South Lafayette Park Pl, Suite 41; Los Angeles, CA 90057;
(213) 365–8500, FAX 365–9616; email pen@pen–usa–west.org;
website www.pen–usa–west.org

Types of material: full-length plays, screenplays, teleplays. **Frequency:** annual. **Remuneration:** $1000 award in each of several categories, including drama, screenwriting and television writing. **Guidelines:** writer residing west of Mississippi River; only full-length (original or adapted) screenplays and teleplays, script first produced during 2001 calendar year. **Submission procedure:** 4 copies of script, playbill or press materials verifying eligibility and cover letter giving title of work, author's name and state of residence, name of producer and production dates and $20 fee. **Deadline:** 31 Jan 2002.

PEN/LAURA PELS FOUNDATION AWARD FOR DRAMA

PEN American Center; 568 Broadway; New York, NY 10012–3225;
(212) 334–1660, FAX 334–2181; email jm@pen.org
John Morrone, *Literary Awards Manager*

Types of material: full-length plays. **Frequency:** annual. **Remuneration:** $5000. **Guidelines:** mid-career American playwright who has had at least 2 full-length plays professionally produced in theatres 299 seats or larger. **Submission procedure:** playwright must be nominated by professional colleague through letter of support accompanied by list of candidate's produced work. **Deadline:** 3 Jan 2002. **Notification:** spring 2002.

PERISHABLE THEATRE WOMEN'S PLAYWRITING FESTIVAL

Box 23132; Providence, RI 02903; (401) 331-2695, FAX 331-7811;
     email info@perishable.org; website www.perishable.org
Vanessa Gilbert, *Festival Director*

Types of material: one-acts. **Frequency:** annual. **Remuneration:** 3 awards of $500, production, publication in anthology. **Guidelines:** woman playwright; unproduced one-act, no more than 40 minutes in length; 2 submission limit. **Submission procedure:** script, resume and $5 fee. **Deadline:** 15 Dec 2001. **Notification:** 31 Mar 2002.

PETERSON EMERGING PLAYWRIGHT COMPETITION

Theatre Arts Department, Catawba College; 2300 West Innes St;
     Salisbury, NC 28144-2488; (704) 637-4771, FAX 637-4207;
     email jepperso@catawba.edu
James R. Epperson, Chair, Theatre Arts Department

Types of material: full-length plays, musicals. **Frequency:** annual. **Remuneration:** $2000, full production, transportation, room and board to attend rehearsals and performances. **Guidelines:** unpublished, unproduced full-length work by emerging playwright; 2 one-acts with common theme accepted. **Submission procedure:** script and bio; send SASP for acknowledgment of receipt. **Deadline:** 15 Feb 2002. **Notification:** 1 May 2002.

PLAYHOUSE ON THE SQUARE NEW PLAY COMPETITION

Playhouse on the Square; 51 South Cooper St; Memphis, TN 38104;
     (901) 725-0776, 726-4498
Jackie Nichols, *Executive Director*

Types of material: full-length plays, musicals. **Frequency:** annual. **Remuneration:** $500, production. **Guidelines:** unproduced play, small cast; full arrangement for piano for musical; prefers southern playwrights. **Submission procedure:** script only. **Deadline:** 1 Apr 2002.

PLAYS FOR THE 21ST CENTURY

The Playwrights Theater; Box 803305; Dallas, TX 75380;
     (214) 754-9906, FAX 754-9907; email jackmarsh@earthlink.net;
     website www.playwrighttheatertexas.org
Jack Marshall, *Artistic Director*

Types of material: full-length plays. **Frequency:** annual. **Remuneration:** $1500 1st prize; 4 finalists receive full production in month-long festival.

Guidelines: play not produced professionally. **Submission procedure:** application, script, character breakdown, set requirements and $15 fee. **Deadline:** 31 Jan 2002. **Notification:** 30 Jun 2002. **Dates:** fall 2002.

PLAYWRIGHTS FIRST AWARD

c/o The National Arts Club; 15 Gramercy Park S;
New York, NY 10003; (212) 249-6299

Types of material: full-length plays. **Frequency:** annual. **Remuneration:** $1000 for best play; reading for selected plays; introductions to theatre professionals. **Guidelines:** 1 unproduced play written within last 2 years (no translations, adaptations or musicals). **Submission procedure:** script and resume; script will not be returned. **Deadline:** 15 Oct 2001. **Notification:** May 2002.

PREMIERE PERFORMANCES

Pennsylvania Playhouse; Box 20122; Lehigh Valley, PA 18002-0122;
(610) 865-6665, FAX 861-7337; website www.paplayhouse.org
Rob Adams, *One-Act Competition Chair*

Types of material: one-acts. **Frequency:** annual. **Remuneration:** $200 1st prize; $100 2nd prize; $50 3rd prize; $50 for audience favorite; 1st 2nd and 3rd prize receive staged reading. **Guidelines:** unproduced play, not longer than 40 minutes, cast limit 2-6, simple set; download guidelines from the web. **Submission procedure:** application, 4 copies of script and $10 fee. **Deadline:** 31 Oct 2001. **Notification:** Feb 2002.

REVA SHINER FULL-LENGTH PLAY CONTEST

Bloomington Playwrights Project; 308 South Washington St;
Bloomington, IN 47401; (812) 334-1188;
email bppwrite@bluemarble.net; website www.newplays.org
Richard Ford, *Artistic Director*
Eric R. Pfeffinger, *Literary Manager*

Types of material: full-length plays, musicals. **Frequency:** annual. **Remuneration:** $500, staged reading, production. **Guidelines:** unpublished, unproduced work 75-150 minutes long, suitable for production in small 65-seat theatre; welcomes innovative works, small-scale musicals, simple set; write for guidelines or download from web. **Submission procedure:** script, cover letter and $5 fee; include cassette for musical. **Deadline:** 15 Jan 2002. **Notification:** Apr 2002.

ROBERT J. PICKERING AWARD FOR PLAYWRITING EXCELLENCE

Coldwater Community Theater; 89 Division St; Coldwater, MI 49036;
(517) 278-2389, FAX 279-8095
J. Richard Colbeck, *Award Chairman*

Types of material: full-length plays, one-acts, adaptations, plays for young audiences, musicals. **Frequency:** annual. **Remuneration:** $200, full production, room and board. **Guidelines:** unproduced play. **Submission procedure:** application and script. **Deadline:** 31 Dec 2001. **Notification:** 15 Jan 2002.

THE ROY BARKER PLAYWRIGHTING PRIZE

The Rocky Mountain Student Theater Project; Box 1626;
Telluride, CO 81435; (719) 685-5167; email PlayFest@aol.com;
website members.aol.com/PlayFest/RMSTP.html
Owen Perkins, *Executive Director*

Types of material: full-length plays, one-acts, translations, adaptations, plays for young audiences, musicals, solo pieces. **Frequency:** annual. **Remuneration:** $500 1st prize, full production, travel and housing; $250 2nd prize, full production; $100 3rd prize, full production. **Guidelines:** plays by high school students only; prefers one-act plays 30-40 minutes long; write for guidelines or download from web. **Submission procedure:** script without author's name and address, cover letter and $5 fee. **Deadline:** 1 May 2002. **Notification:** 1 Jun 2002. (See The Rocky Mountain Playwriting Festival in Production.)

THE RUBY LLOYD APSEY AWARD

University of Alabama at Birmingham Theatre Department;
101 Bell Building; 700 13th St; Birmingham, AL 35294-3340;
(205) 934-3236, FAX 934-8076; email mpowers@uab.edu;
website uabtheatre.bham.net
Marc Powers, *Department Chair*

Types of material: full-length plays, bills of related one-acts, translations. **Frequency:** biannual. **Remuneration:** $1000, staged reading, possible full production; travel and housing if play is produced. **Guidelines:** plays by non-Americans living anywhere; work written in English or translated into English. **Submission procedure:** script and character/scene breakdown. **Deadline:** 1 Dec 2001. **Notification:** 1 Apr 2002.

THE SCHOLASTIC WRITING AWARDS

555 Broadway; New York, NY 10012; (212) 343-6892,
FAX 343-4885; website www.scholastic.com/artandwriting
Marc Powers, *Department Chair*

Types of material: one-acts. **Frequency:** annual. **Remuneration:** $5000 scholarship toward college tuition for author of each of 5 best senior portfolios; cash prizes totaling $175,000 awarded to several top students in each category, including dramatic writing. **Guidelines:** 2 categories: for high school seniors only, portfolios of 3-8 pieces (fiction, poetry, drama, etc.); for students grades 7-12, individual pieces in various categories, including drama (stage, film, television and radio scripts), unpublished script not more than 30 minutes long; write for further information after 1 Sep 2001. **Submission procedure:** application and script. **Deadline:** varies from state to state; many in mid-Jan 2002; exact date TBA. **Notification:** May 2002.

SHORT GRAIN CONTEST

Grain Magazine; Box 1154; Regina, SK S4P 3B4; Canada;
(306) 244-2828, FAX 244-0255;
email grain.mag@sk.sympatico.ca; website www.skwriter.com
Jennifer Still, *Business Manager*

Types of material: monologues. **Frequency:** annual. **Remuneration:** 3 prizes of $500. **Guidelines:** unpublished, unproduced monologue not submitted elsewhere; 500-word maximum. **Submission procedure:** U.S. and international entries: entry form and $22 fee plus $4 U.S. postage for subscription mailing cost; Canadian entries: entry form and $22 fee for first 2 entries ($5 fee for each additional entry); fee includes 1-year subscription; write or email for guidelines. **Deadline:** 31 Jan 2002. **Notification:** 30 Apr 2002.

SHUBERT FENDRICH MEMORIAL PLAYWRITING CONTEST

Pioneer Drama Service; Box 4267; Englewood, CO 80155-4267;
(303) 779-4035, FAX 779-4315;
email editors@pioneerdrama.com;
website www.pioneerdrama.com
Beth Somers, *Editor*

Types of material: full-length plays, one-acts, translations, adaptations, plays for young audiences, musicals. **Frequency:** annual. **Remuneration:** publication with $1000 advance on royalties (10% book royalty, 50% performance royalty); all entries considered for publication. **Guidelines:**

produced, unpublished work not more than 90 minutes long, subject matter and language appropriate for schools and community theatres; prefers works with a preponderance of female roles, minimal set requirements. **Submission procedure:** script with proof of production (e.g., program, reviews); include score or cassette for musical; send SASE for guidelines. **Deadline:** 1 Mar 2002 (scripts received after deadline will be considered for 2003 contest). **Notification:** 1 Jun 2002.

SIENA COLLEGE INTERNATIONAL PLAYWRIGHTS COMPETITION

Department of Creative Arts; Siena College; 515 Loudon Rd; Loudonville, NY 12211-1462; (518) 783-2381, FAX 783-4293; email maciag@siena.edu; website www.siena.edu/theatre
Gary Maciag, *Director of Theatre*

Types of material: full-length plays. **Frequency:** biennial. **Remuneration:** $2000, production, maximum $1000 to cover residency expenses. **Guidelines:** playwright available for 6-week residency in Jan/Feb 2003; play that has not had previous workshop or full production; prefers play suitable for college audience and featuring characters suitable for college-age performers; prefers small cast and unit set or minimal set change. **Submission procedure:** application and script; send SASE for application and guidelines after 1 Nov 2001. **Deadline:** 30 Jun 2002; no submission before 1 Feb 2002. **Notification:** 30 Sep 2002.

SOURCE THEATRE COMPANY 2002 LITERARY PRIZE

1835 14th St NW; Washington, DC 20009; (202) 462-1073
Keith Parker, *Literary Manager*

Types of material: full-length plays, one-acts, musicals, solo pieces. **Frequency:** annual. **Remuneration:** $250, staged reading, possible production in 22nd Annual Washington Theatre Festival (11 Jul-11 Aug 2002). **Guidelines:** work not produced professionally. **Submission procedure:** script, synopsis, resume and $10 fee; 1 submission limit; send SASE for response; materials will not be returned. **Deadline:** postmarked by 15 Jan 2002. **Notification:** 15 May 2002.

Southeastern Theatre Conference New Play Project

Box 9868; Greensboro, NC 27429-0868; (731) 424-3520, ext 438;
   email ssharp@jscc.cc.tn.us
Susan Sharp, *Coordinator*

Types of material: full-length plays, collections of related one-acts.
Frequency: annual. **Remuneration:** $1000, staged reading at SETC Annual
Convention, travel, room and board to attend convention. **Guidelines:**
resident of state in SETC region (AL, FL, GA, KY, MS, NC, SC, TN, VA, WV);
unproduced work; collection of one-acts bound in 1 cover; limit of 1 full-
length submission or collection of one-acts. **Submission procedure:**
application and script. **Deadline:** 1 Jun 2002. **Notification:** Nov 2002.

Southern Playwrights Competition

228 Stone Center; Jacksonville State University;
   Jacksonville, AL 36265; (256) 782-5411, FAX 782-5441;
   email swhitton@jsucc.jsu.edu;
   website www.jsu.edu/depart/english/southpla.htm
Steven J. Whitton, *Coordinator*

Types of material: full-length plays, solo pieces. **Frequency:** annual.
Remuneration: $1000, production, housing to attend rehearsals. **Guidelines:**
native or resident of AL, AR, FL, GA, KY, LA, MS, NC, SC, TN, TX, VA or WV; 1
unpublished, original submission that deals with the southern experience
and has not received Equity production. **Submission procedure:** entry form,
script and synopsis; write for guidelines after Sep 2001. **Deadline:** 15 Feb
2002. **Notification:** 1 May 2002.

The Stanley Drama Award

Wagner College Theatre; 1 Campus Rd; Staten Island, NY 10301;
   (718) 390-3157, FAX 390-3323
Kevin Kane, *Administrator*

Types of material: full-length plays, one-acts, plays for young audiences,
musicals. **Frequency:** annual. **Remuneration:** $2000. **Guidelines:**
unpublished, unproduced play or collection of one-acts; 1 submission limit.
Submission procedure: application, script, cassette for musicals; send SASE
for guidelines and application. **Deadline:** 1 Oct 2001. **Notification:** Apr
2002.

SUMMERFIELD G. ROBERTS AWARD

The Sons of the Republic of Texas; 1717 8th St; Bay City, TX 77414;
(979) 245-6644, FAX 244-3819; email srttexas@srttexas.org;
website www.srttexas.org
Melinda Williams

Types of material: full-length plays. **Frequency:** annual. **Remuneration:** $2500 given to work from 1 of several genres, including playwriting. **Guidelines:** play about living in the Republic of Texas, completed during calendar year preceding deadline. **Submission procedure:** 5 copies of script; scripts will not be returned. **Deadline:** 15 Jan 2002. **Notification:** early Apr 2002.

THE SUSAN SMITH BLACKBURN PRIZE

3239 Avalon Pl; Houston, TX 77019; (713) 308-2842,
FAX 654-8184
Emilie S. Kilgore, *Board of Directors*

Types of material: full-length plays. **Frequency:** annual. **Remuneration:** $10,000 1st prize plus signed Willem de Kooning print, made especially for Blackburn Prize; $500 to each of 8-11 other finalists. **Guidelines:** woman playwright of any nationality writing in English; unproduced play or play produced within one year of deadline; previous winners are not eligible. **Submission procedure:** no submission by playwright; professional artistic directors of specified theatres are invited to nominate play and submit 2 copies of script; playwright may bring script to attention of eligible nominator; send 55¢-postage SASE for guidelines, brochure and list of theatres eligible to nominate. **Deadline:** 20 Sep 2001. **Notification:** Jan 2002 for finalists; Feb 2002 for winner.

SWTA NATIONAL NEW PLAY CONTEST

Southwest Theatre Association, Inc;
c/o University of Texas at Arlington; Theatre Arts Program;
700 West 2nd St; Box 19103; Arlington, TX 76019-0103;
(817) 272-3141, -5708
Andrew Gaupp and Dennis Maher, *New Plays Committee Co-Chairs*

Types of material: full-length plays, one-acts. **Frequency:** annual. **Remuneration:** $200, reading at annual SWTA conference in Nov, possible excerpt publication in SWTA journal, *Theatre Southwest*, 1-year membership in SWTA. **Guidelines:** U.S. resident; unproduced, unpublished play; no plays for young audiences; 1 submission limit. **Submission procedure:** bound script, 1-page synopsis, 1-page bio and $10 fee (check payable to SWTA). **Deadline:** 15 Mar 2002. **Notification:** Sep 2002. **Dates:** Nov 2002.

TENNESSEE WILLIAMS/NEW ORLEANS LITERARY FESTIVAL ONE-ACT PLAY COMPETITION

c/o Creative Writing Workshop; University of New Orleans;
New Orleans, LA 70148; (504) 581–1144, FAX 529–2430;
email info@tennesseewilliams.net;
website www.tennesseewilliams.net

Types of material: one-acts. **Frequency:** annual. **Remuneration:** $1000, staged reading in spring 2002 festival, production in spring 2003 festival. **Guidelines:** unpublished play, not more than 1 hour long and not produced professionally. **Submission procedure:** script and $15 fee (check payable to Tennessee Williams Festival); script will not be returned; write for guidelines before submitting work. **Deadline:** 1 Dec 2001; no submission before 1 Sep 2001. **Dates:** 20–24 Mar 2002.

THEATRE CONSPIRACY ANNUAL NEW PLAY CONTEST

Theatre Conspiracy, Inc; 10091 McGregor Blvd; Ft. Myers, FL 33919;
(941) 936–3239
Bill Taylor, *Artistic Director*

Types of material: full-length plays. **Frequency:** annual. **Remuneration:** $500, production. **Guidelines:** play not previously produced, cast limit of 8, simple production demands. **Submission procedure:** script, 1-page synopsis, character breakdown, technical requirements, bio and $5 fee. **Deadline:** 31 Nov 2001. **Notification:** Mar 2002. **Dates:** late May–early Jun 2002.

THEATREFEST REGIONAL PLAYWRITING CONTEST

Montclair State University; Upper Montclair, NJ 07043;
(973) 655–7071, FAX 655–5335; website www.montclair.edu
John Wooten, *Artistic Director*

Types of material: full-length plays. **Frequency:** annual. **Remuneration:** $1500 John Golden Prize, full production, housing; $500 to 2 runners-up. **Guidelines:** resident of CT, NJ or NY; unproduced, unpublished work exploring contemporary issues, cast limit of 8. **Submission procedure:** 1–5 page synopsis, 5-page dialogue sample and SASE for response; write for guidelines. **Deadline:** 1 Jan 2002. **Notification:** 15 Feb 2002.

THEODORE WARD PRIZE FOR AFRICAN-AMERICAN PLAYWRIGHTS

Columbia College Chicago Theater/Music Center; 72 East 11th St; Chicago, IL 60605; (312) 344-6136, FAX 344-8077; email chigochuck@aol.com
Chuck Smith, *Facilitator*

Types of material: full-length plays, translations, adaptations, solo pieces. **Frequency:** annual. **Remuneration:** $2000 1st prize, production, travel and housing to attend rehearsals; $500 2nd prize, staged reading; 3rd prize, staged reading at Goodman Theatre (see Production). **Guidelines:** African-American U.S. resident; 1 full-length submission not produced professionally; translations and adaptations of material in public domain only. **Submission procedure:** script, short synopsis, production history and brief resume; write for guidelines. **Deadline:** 1 Jul 2002; no submission before 1 Apr 2002. **Notification:** Nov 2002.

TOWSON UNIVERSITY PRIZE FOR LITERATURE

Towson University; Towson, MD 21252; (410) 704-2128
Dean, College of Liberal Arts

Types of material: book or book-length manuscript; all literary genres eligible, including plays. **Frequency:** annual. **Remuneration:** $2000. **Guidelines:** author no more than 40 years of age, MD resident for 3 years and at time prize awarded; work published within 3 years prior to submission or scheduled for publication within the year. **Submission procedure:** publisher or playwright submits application and 5 copies of work; write for guidelines. **Deadline:** 15 Jun 2002. **Notification:** 1 Dec 2002.

TRUSTUS PLAYWRIGHTS' FESTIVAL

Trustus Theatre; Box 11721; Columbia, SC 29211-1721; (803) 254-9732, FAX 771-9153; email Trustus88@aol.com; website www.trustus.org
Jon Tuttle, *Literary Manager*

Types of material: full-length plays. **Frequency:** annual. **Remuneration:** $250, staged reading, 1-year development period followed by additional $500 and full production with travel and housing to attend opening. **Guidelines:** work not produced professionally, cast limit of 8; prefers challenging, innovative dramas and comedies; no musicals or plays for young audiences. **Submission procedure:** application, synopsis and resume;

send SASE for guidelines and application. **Deadline:** 1 Mar 2002; no submission before 1 Jan 2002. **Notification:** 1 Jun 2002.

UNICORN THEATRE NEW PLAY DEVELOPMENT

3828 Main St; Kansas City, MO 64111; (816) 531–7529, ext 18,
    FAX 531–0421
Herman Wilson, *Literary Assistant*

Types of material: full-length plays. **Frequency:** no set dates. **Remuneration:** $1000, production, possible travel and residency. **Guidelines:** unpublished play not produced professionally; contemporary (post-1950) themes and settings only; special interest in social issues; cast limit of 10; no musicals; 2 submission limit. **Submission procedure:** synopsis, at least 10 pages of dialogue, character breakdown, resume, cover letter and SASE for response; no scripts. **Deadline:** ongoing. **Notification:** 4 weeks; 4-8 months if script is requested.

UNIVERSITY OF LOUISVILLE GRAWEMEYER AWARD FOR MUSIC COMPOSITION

Grawemeyer Music Award Committee; School of Music;
    University of Louisville; Louisville, KY 40292; (502) 852–6907,
    FAX 852–0520; website www.louisville.edu/ur/onpi/grawemeyer
Paul Brink, *Chair*

Types of material: music-theatre works, operas. **Frequency:** annual. **Remuneration:** $200,000 (paid in 5 annual installments of $40,000). **Guidelines:** work premiered between 1997-2001; entry must be sponsored by professional music organization or individual. **Submission procedure:** application, score, cassette, supporting materials and $40 fee submitted jointly by composer and sponsor; write for guidelines. **Deadline:** 28 Jan 2002. **Notification:** TBA. **Dates:** spring 2003 for presentation of award.

VERMONT PLAYWRIGHTS AWARD

The Valley Players; Box 441; Waitsfield, VT 05673-0441;
    (802) 496–3751; website www.valleyplayers.com
Jennifer Howard, *Coordinator*

Types of material: full-length plays. **Frequency:** annual. **Remuneration:** $1000, probable production. **Guidelines:** resident of ME, NH or VT; unproduced, unpublished play, suitable for community group, that has not won playwriting competition, moderate production demands. **Submission**

procedure: entry form and 2 copies of script; send SASE for guidelines. **Deadline:** 1 Feb 2002.

VSA ARTS PLAYWRIGHT DISCOVERY AWARD

1300 Connecticut Ave NW, Suite 700; Washington, DC 20036;
  (800) 933-8721, (202) 737-0645 (TTY), FAX 737-0725;
  email playwright@vsarts.org; website www.vsarts.org

Types of material: one-acts. **Frequency:** annual. **Remuneration:** $750 1st prize; $500 2nd prize; $200 3rd and 4th prizes; travel, room and board to attend staged reading or production at John F. Kennedy Center for the Performing Arts in Washington, DC. **Guidelines:** U.S. citizen in grades 6-12; unproduced, unpublished play for family audience that deals with experience of living with a disability, less that 40 pages in length; previous submission ineligible; 1 submission limit. **Submission procedure:** application, 2 copies of script; scripts will not be returned; write for guidelines and application or download from web. **Deadline:** 15 May 2002.

WALDO M. AND GRACE C. BONDERMAN IUPUI PLAYWRITING EVENT FOR YOUNG AUDIENCES
AT THE INDIANA REPERTORY THEATRE

IUPUI University Theatre; 425 University Blvd, Suite 309;
  Indianapolis, IN 46202; (317) 274-2095, FAX 278-1025;
  email dwebb@iupui.edu;
  website iupui.edu/~comstudy/playsym/symhome.html
Dorothy Webb, *Artistic Director*

Types of material: plays for young audiences. **Frequency:** biennial. **Remuneration:** 4-5 prizes of $1000, 1 week of developmental work culminating in showcase reading at National Youth Theatre Playwriting Symposium, travel from within continental U.S. and housing during residency. **Guidelines:** writer must be available for week-long developmental residency; unpublished play at least 45 minutes long, appropriate for grades 3-12 with strong storyline, compelling characters and careful attention to language; not under current commission and not previously produced by Equity company. **Submission procedure:** send SASE for entry form and guidelines or download from web. **Deadline:** 8 Sep 2002. **Notification:** Dec 2002. **Dates:** Apr-May 2003 for residency; TBA for Showcase/Symposium.

WEST COAST ENSEMBLE CONTESTS

Box 38728; Los Angeles, CA 90038; (323) 876-9337, FAX 876-8916
Les Hanson, *Artistic Director*

WEST COAST ENSEMBLE FULL-LENGTH PLAY COMPETITION

Types of material: full-length plays. **Frequency:** annual. **Remuneration:** $500, production, royalty on any performances beyond 8-week run. **Guidelines:** 1 submission not produced in southern CA; cast limit of 12. **Submission procedure:** script with SASE or SASP for acknowledgment of receipt. **Deadline:** 31 Dec 2001. **Notification:** Jul 2002.

WEST COAST ENSEMBLE MUSICAL STAIRS

Types of material: music-theatre works. **Frequency:** annual. **Remuneration:** $500, production, royalty on any performances beyond 8-week run. **Guidelines:** 1 unpublished musical submission not produced in southern CA; all genres and styles eligible, including pop, rock, country and western, etc., cast limit of 12. **Submission procedure:** script, cassette or CD of music (include score and lead sheets if available). **Deadline:** 30 Jun 2002. **Notification:** Jan 2003.

WHITE BIRD PLAYWRITING CONTEST

White Bird Productions, Inc; 138 South Oxford St, #2-B;
 Brooklyn, NY 11217; (718) 369-3308, 398-3658, FAX 398-3658
Kathryn Dickinson, *Artistic Director*
John Istel, *Literary Manager*

Types of material: full-length plays. **Frequency:** annual. **Remuneration:** $200, staged reading, possible travel to attend rehearsals. **Guidelines:** play with theme, plot and/or central idea that deals in general or specific way with the environment; 2 submission limit. **Submission procedure:** script and resume. **Deadline:** 15 Feb 2002. **Notification:** Oct 2002.

WICHITA STATE UNIVERSITY PLAYWRITING CONTEST

University Theatre; Wichita State University; 1845 Fairmount;
 Wichita, KS 67260-0153; (316) 978-3368, FAX 978-3202
Bela Kiralyfalvi, *Contest Director*

Types of material: full-length plays, bills of related one-acts. **Frequency:** annual. **Remuneration:** production, expenses for playwright to attend production. **Guidelines:** unpublished, unproduced work at least 90 minutes long by student currently enrolled at U.S. college or university; no musicals or plays for young audiences. **Submission procedure:** bound script with unbound cover sheet containing author's name, address and phone number (no author's name on script); send SASP for acknowlegment of receipt; write for guidelines. **Deadline:** 15 Feb 2002. **Notification:** 15 Apr 2002.

WRITER'S DIGEST WRITING COMPETITION

1507 Dana Ave; Cincinnati, OH 45207-1005;
(513) 531-2690, ext 328, FAX 531-1843;
email competitions@fwpubs.com
Competition Coordinator

Types of material: full-length plays, screenplays, teleplays. **Frequency:** annual. **Remuneration:** $1500 Grand Prize, travel expenses paid to New York City to meet with editors and agents or to 2002 Maui Writer's Conference; $750 1st prize, $350 2nd prize, $250 3rd prize, each with $100 worth of Writer's Digest books; $100 4th prize plus current edition of *Writer's Market* and 1-year subscription to *Writer's Digest* magazine; $25 5th prize plus current edition of *Writer's Market* and 1-year subscription to *Writer's Digest* magazine. **Guidelines:** unpublished, unproduced work, not accepted by publisher or producer at time of submission; previous entries ineligible. **Submission procedure:** entry form, 1-page synopsis, first 15 pages of script, indication of projected market for work and $10 fee; send SASE for guidelines. **Deadline:** 15 May 2002. **Notification:** fall 2002.

YEAR-END-SERIES (Y.E.S.) NEW PLAY FESTIVAL

Department of Theatre; Northern Kentucky University;
Highland Heights, KY 41099; (859) 572-6303, FAX 572-6057;
email forman@nku.edu
Sandra Forman, *Project Director*

Types of material: full-length plays, adaptations, musicals. **Frequency:** biennial. **Remuneration:** 3 awards of $500, production, travel and expenses to attend late rehearsals and performance. **Guidelines:** unproduced work in which majority of roles can be handled by students; small orchestra for musicals; 1 submission limit. **Submission procedure:** application and script. **Deadline:** 31 Oct 2002. **Notification:** Jan 2003. **Dates:** 17-27 Apr 2003.

YOUNG CONNECTICUT PLAYWRIGHTS FESTIVAL

Maxwell Anderson Playwrights Series; Box 671;
West Redding, CT 06896; (203) 938-2770
Bruce Post, *Dramaturg*

Types of material: full-length plays, one-acts, musicals, translations, adaptations, plays for young audiences, solo pieces. **Frequency:** annual. **Remuneration:** staged reading in May festival, certificate. **Guidelines:** CT resident ages 12-19 only; script maximum 60 pages in length. **Submission procedure:** bound script with playwright's name, date of birth, home address, phone number and name of school on title page; send SASE for guidelines. **Deadline:** 27 Mar 2002. **Notification:** May 2002. **Dates:** May 2002.

YOUNG PLAYWRIGHTS FESTIVAL NATIONAL PLAYWRITING CONTEST

Young Playwrights Inc; 321 West 44th St, Suite 906;
New York, NY 10036; (212) 307-1140;
email writeaplay@aol.com; website youngplaywrights.org
Sheri M. Goldhirsch, *Artistic Director*

Types of material: full-length plays, one-acts. **Frequency:** annual. **Remuneration:** staged reading or production with royalty, travel and residency, 1-year Dramatists Guild membership (see Membership and Service Organizations). **Guidelines:** playwright 18 years of age or younger as of 1 Dec 2001; submissions from playwrights of all backgrounds encouraged. **Submission procedure:** script with playwright's name, date of birth, home address and phone number on title page; write for guidelines. **Deadline:** 1 Dec 2001.

YUKON PACIFIC NEW PLAY AWARD

Last Frontier Theatre Conference;
Prince William Sound Community College; Box 97;
Valdez, AK 99686; (907) 834-1612, FAX 834-1611;
email vntc@uaa.alaska.edu; website www.uaa.alaska.edu/pwscc
JoAnn C. McDowell, *President*

Types of material: full-length plays, one-acts. **Frequency:** annual. **Remuneration:** $1000, 5 scripts given staged reading at Last Frontier Theatre Conference. **Guidelines:** unproduced work; no musicals or plays for young audiences. **Submission procedure:** 3 copies of script, cast list, character descriptions, bio and photo. **Deadline:** 1 Mar 2002.

PUBLICATION

What is listed in this section?

Those who are primarily or exclusively play publishers, and literary magazines and small presses, all who accept work of unpublished writers. For online publication and production opportunities, see the Online Resources chapter.

How can I determine the best places to submit my play?

Think of these publishers as highly individual people looking for very particular kinds of material, which means you should find out as much as possible about their operations before submitting scripts. One of the best sources is the Council of Literary Magazines and Presses (154 Christopher St, Suite 3C; New York, NY 10014-9110; 212-741-9110; email info@clmp.org; website www.clmp.org), and their *Directory of Literary Magazines* (2002 edition due out in Jan 2002; $17.00 paper), a descriptive listing of hundreds of magazines, including many which publish plays. Other leads may be found in the *The International Directory of Little Magazines and Small Presses: 2000–2001* (Dustbooks; Box 100; Paradise, CA 95967; (530) 877-6110, orders (800) 477-6110; email dustbooks@dcsi.net; website www.dustbooks.com; $34.95 paper, $55.00 cloth, plus $7.00 shipping and handling regular mail, $9.00 priority). You should also write to individual publishers listed here and ask for style sheets, catalogs, sample copies, etc. Don't forget that when publishers say they accept unsolicited scripts, they *always* require you to enclose an SASE for return of the manuscript.

ALASKA QUARTERLY REVIEW

University of Alaska, Anchorage; 3211 Providence Dr;
 Anchorage, AK 99508; (907) 786–6916, FAX 786–6916;
 email ayaqr@uaa.alaska.edu; website www.uaa.alaska.edu/aqr
Ronald Spatz, *Editor*

Types of material: full-length plays, one-acts, translations. **Remuneration:** 1 complimentary copy; 1 year subscription; payment when grant money is available. **Guidelines:** semiannual literary magazine publishing up to 2 short plays a year in addition to fiction, poetry and nonfiction; interested in new voices; traditional and experimental work. **Submission procedure:** accepts unsolicited scripts. **Response time:** 1-4 weeks.

AMELIA MAGAZINE

329 "E" St; Bakersfield, CA 93304; (661) 323–4064, FAX 323–5326;
 email amelia@lightspeed.net
Frederick A. Raborg, Jr., *Editor*

Types of material: one-acts, including translations and solo pieces. **Remuneration:** $150 prize; 10 complimentary copies. **Guidelines:** winner of annual Frank McClure One-Act Play Award published in magazine; unpublished play maximum 45 minutes long. **Submission procedure:** accepts unsolicited scripts with list of any productions and $15 fee; sample copy $10.95. **Deadline:** 15 May 2002. **Notification:** 15 Sep 2002.

AMERICAN WRITING: A MAGAZINE

4343 Manayunk Ave; Philadelphia, PA 19128
Alexandra Grilikhes, *Editor*

Types of material: translations, solo pieces, short experimental theatre pieces, performance pieces, performance artists' in-progress notes and diaries. **Remuneration:** 3 complimentary copies. **Guidelines:** biannual literary/arts journal publishing 1 or 2 theatrical works a year; seeks new writing that takes risks and explores new forms; special interest in works exploring themes of androgyny, "the voice of the loner," "artist as shaman," "myth in urban life"; 4000-word maximum. **Submission procedure:** accepts unsolicited scripts. **Response time:** 3-6 months.

ANCHORAGE PRESS PLAYS

Box 2901; Louisville, KY 40201; (502) 583-2288, FAX 583-2281;
  email applays@bellsouth.net; website www.applays.com
Marilee Hebert Miller, *Publisher*

Types of material: works for young audiences, including full-length plays, one-acts, translations, adaptations and musicals. **Remuneration:** negotiated royalty. **Guidelines:** specialty house publishing quality works for young audiences only; only works produced a minimum of 3 times considered. **Submission procedure:** accepts unsolicited scripts with proof of production. **Response time:** 2-3 months.

ARTE PÚBLICO PRESS

University of Houston; Houston, TX 77204-2174; (713) 743-2841,
  FAX 743-2847; email artrer@jetson.uh.edu;
  website www.arte.uh.edu
Nicolás Kanellos, *Publisher*

Types of material: full-length plays, one-acts, adaptations, plays for young audiences, musicals. **Remuneration:** negotiated royalty; complimentary copies. **Guidelines:** unpublished works in English or Spanish by Hispanic writers only. **Submission procedure:** accepts unsolicited scripts. **Response time:** 6 months.

ASIAN PACIFIC AMERICAN JOURNAL

16 West 32nd St, Suite 10A; New York, NY 10001; (212) 494-0061,
  FAX 494-0062; email desk@aaww.org; website www.aaww.org
Hanya Yanagihara, *Editor*

Types of material: one-acts. **Remuneration:** 2 complimentary copies. **Guidelines:** semiannual literary journal publishing work by and/or of interest to Asian-Americans; plays maximum 4000 words. **Submission procedure:** accepts unsolicited scripts; send 4 copies of script. **Response time:** 3 months.

AUDREY SKIRBALL-KENIS PLAY COLLECTION

630 West 5th St; Los Angeles, CA 90071; (213) 228-7327,
  FAX 228-7339; website www.askplay.org
Tom Harris, *Project Director*

Types of material: full-length plays, one-acts, translations, adaptations, plays for young audiences, musicals, solo pieces, performance-art texts. **Remuneration:** descriptive listing of work in *Southern California*

Unpublished Plays Collection, catalog of plays housed in Central Library in downtown Los Angeles. **Guidelines:** unpublished plays professionally produced in Southern California only. **Submission procedure:** accepts unsolicited scripts.

BAKER'S PLAYS

Box 699222; Quincy, MA 02269-9222; (617) 745-0805,
    FAX 745-9891; email staff@bakersplays.com;
    website www.bakersplays.com
Editor

Types of material: full-length plays, one-acts, plays for young audiences, musicals, chancel dramas. **Remuneration:** negotiated book and production royalty. **Guidelines:** prefers produced plays; prefers plays suitable for high school, community and regional theatres; "Plays from Young Authors" division features plays by high school playwrights. **Submission procedure:** accepts unsolicited scripts with resume; include press clippings if play has been produced. **Response time:** 2-6 months. **Special programs:** Baker's Plays High School Playwriting Contest (see Prizes).

BROADWAY PLAY PUBLISHING, INC.

56 East 81st St; New York, NY 10028-0202; (212) 772-8334,
    FAX 772-8358; email BroadwayPl@aol.com;
    website www.broadwayplaypubl.com

Types of material: full-length plays. **Remuneration:** 10% book royalty, 80% amateur royalty, 90% stock royalty; 10 complimentary copies. **Guidelines:** major interest is in original, innovative work by American playwrights; no historical or autobiographical plays. **Submission procedure:** no unsolicited scripts; letter of inquiry. **Response time:** 2 months letter; 4 months script.

CALLALOO

322 Bryan Hall; Department of English; University of Virginia;
    Box 400121; Charlottesville, VA 22904-4121; (804) 924-6637,
    FAX 924-6472; email callaloo@virginia.edu;
    website www.people.virginia.edu/~callaloo
Charles H. Rowell, *Editor*

Types of material: one-acts (including translations), excerpts of full-length plays. **Remuneration:** complimentary copies and offprints. **Guidelines:** quarterly journal of African-American and African arts and letters published by Johns Hopkins University Press. **Submission procedure:**

accepts unsolicited scripts; send 3 copies of script with SASE for response. **Response time:** 6 months.

CONFRONTATION

English Department; C.W. Post College of Long Island University; Greenvale, NY 11548; (516) 299-2720, FAX 299-2735; email mtucker@liu.edu
Martin Tucker, *Editor*

Types of material: one-acts. **Remuneration:** $15-75; 1 complimentary copy. **Guidelines:** general magazine for "literate" audience; unpublished plays. **Submission procedure:** accepts unsolicited scripts. **Response time:** 8-10 weeks.

CONTEMPORARY DRAMA SERVICE

Meriwether Publishing, Ltd; 885 Elkton Dr; Colorado Springs, CO 80907; (719) 594-4422, FAX 594-9916
Arthur Zapel, *Executive Editor*

Types of material: one-acts, adaptations, plays for young audiences, musicals, readers' theatre, solo pieces. **Remuneration:** book royalties or payment for amateur and professional performance rights. **Guidelines:** publishes works suitable for teenage, high school and college market, as well as collections of scenes and practical books on theatre arts; prefers comedies. **Submission procedure:** no unsolicited scripts; send letter of inquiry and $2 for sample catalog and guidelines. **Response time:** 2 months.

THE DRAMATIC PUBLISHING COMPANY

311 Washington St; Box 129; Woodstock, IL 60098; (815) 338-7170, FAX 338-8981; email plays@dramaticpublishing.com; website www.dramaticpublishing.com
Linda Habjan, *Editor*

Types of material: full-length plays, one-acts, translations, adaptations, plays for young audiences, musicals. **Remuneration:** standard royalty; 10 complimentary copies (33% discount on additional copies). **Guidelines:** works for professional, stock and amateur markets; prefers produced plays. **Submission procedure:** accepts unsolicited scripts. **Response time:** 4-8 months.

DRAMATICS MAGAZINE

Educational Theatre Association; 2343 Auburn Ave;
   Cincinnati, OH 45219-2819; (513) 421-3900, FAX 421-7077;
   email dcorathers@etassoc.org
Don Corathers, *Editor*

Types of material: full-length plays, one-acts and solo pieces for young performers. **Remuneration:** payment for 1-time serial rights; complimentary copies. **Guidelines:** educational theatre magazine; plays suitable for high school production; prefers produced plays. **Submission procedure:** accepts unsolicited scripts. **Response time:** 2-3 months. (See Educational Theatre Association in Membership and Service Organizations.)

DRAMATISTS PLAY SERVICE, INC.

440 Park Avenue South; New York, NY 10016; (212) 683-8960,
   FAX 213-1539; email postmaster@dramatists.com;
   website www.dramatists.com
Stephen Sultan, *President*

Types of material: full-length plays, musicals. **Remuneration:** possible advance against royalties; 10% book royalty, 80% amateur royalty, 90% stock royalty; 10 complimentary copies (40% discount on additional copies). **Guidelines:** works for stock and amateur market; prefers works produced in New York City. **Submission procedure:** no unsolicited scripts; 1-page synopsis and letter of inquiry. **Response time:** 4-6 months letter; 4-6 months script.

EARTH'S DAUGHTERS

Box 41, Central Park Station; Buffalo, NY 14215;
   website www.earthsdaughters.org

Types of material: full-length plays, one-acts, translations, adaptations, plays for young audiences, solo pieces. **Remuneration:** 2 complimentary copies. **Guidelines:** triannual feminist literary and art periodical with focus on experience and creative expression of women; publishes play excerpts with occasional issue devoted to complete text of play. **Submission procedure:** accepts unsolicited scripts. **Response time:** 2 months.

ELDRIDGE PUBLISHING COMPANY

Box 1595; Venice, FL 34284–1595; (800) HI–STAGE;
email info@histage.com; website www.histage.com
Nancy S. Vorhis, *Editor*

Types of material: full-length plays, one-acts, musicals. **Remuneration:** outright purchase of religious material only; all other works, 10% book royalty, 50% amateur and educational royalty; complimentary copies (50% discount on additional copies). **Guidelines:** publishes 50-75 plays and musicals a year for school, church and community theatre; comedies, mysteries or serious drama. **Submission procedure:** accepts unsolicited scripts; if possible, include cassette for musicals. **Response time:** 2 months.

ENCORE PERFORMANCE PUBLISHING

Box 692; Orem, UT 84059; (801) 376–6199
Michael C. Perry, *President*

Types of material: full-length plays, one-acts, translations, adaptations, plays for young audiences, musicals, solo pieces. **Remuneration:** 10% book royalty, 50% performance royalty; 10 complimentary copies (discount on additional copies). **Guidelines:** publishes 10-30 plays and musicals a year; works must have had a minimum of 2 amateur or professional productions; special interest in works with strong family or Judeo-Christian message and in Christmas, Halloween and other holiday plays. **Submission procedure:** no unsolicited scripts; synopsis, production information and letter of inquiry; best submission time May-Aug. **Response time:** 2-4 weeks letter; 2-3 months script.

FREELANCE PRESS

Box 548; Dover, MA 02030; (508) 785–8250, FAX 785–8291
Narcissa Campion, *Managing Editor*

Types of material: musicals. **Remuneration:** 10% book royalty, 70% performance royalty; 1 complimentary copy. **Guidelines:** unpublished issue-oriented musicals and musical adaptations of classics; approximately 1 hour long; suitable for performing by young people only. **Submission procedure:** accepts unsolicited scripts. **Response time:** 3 months.

GREEN INTEGER

6026 Wilshire Blvd; Los Angeles, CA 90036; (323) 857-1115;
djmess@sunmoon.com; website www.greeninteger.com
Douglas Messerli, *Publisher*

Types of material: full-length plays, translations. **Remuneration:** royalty; 10 complimentary copies. **Guidelines:** press publishing average of 10 single-play volumes a year; unpublished plays; special interest in translations. **Submission procedure:** no unsolicited scripts; send letter of inquiry. **Response time:** 2 weeks-1 month.

HEUER PUBLISHING COMPANY

Box 248; Cedar Rapids, IA 52406; (319) 364-6311, FAX 364-1771;
email editor@hitplays.com; website www.hitplays.com
C. Emmett McMullen, *Editor and Publisher*

Types of material: works for young audiences, including full-length plays, one-acts and musicals. **Remuneration:** outright purchase or performance royalty; complimentary copies. **Guidelines:** dramatic works suitable for middle school or high school students; plays appropriate for family audiences. **Submission procedure:** accepts unsolicited scripts. **Response time:** 1-2 months.

I. E. CLARK PUBLICATIONS

Box 246; Schulenburg, TX 78956-0246; (979) 743-3232,
FAX 743-4765; email ieclark@cvtv.net; website www.ieclark.com
Donna Cozzaglio, *Editorial Department*

Types of material: full-length plays, one-acts, translations, adaptations, plays for young audiences, musicals. **Remuneration:** book and performance royalties. **Guidelines:** publishes for worldwide professional, amateur and educational markets; prefers produced works. **Submission procedure:** accepts unsolicited scripts; cassette or videotape must accompany musical; include proof of production with reviews and photos for produced works; send $3 for catalog; send SASE for submission guidelines. **Response time:** 2-6 months.

INTERNATIONAL READERS' THEATRE (IRT) PUBLISH-ON-DEMAND SCRIPT SERVICE

Blizzard Publishing; 73 Furby St; Winnipeg; Canada MB R3C 2A2
(204) 775-2923, FAX (204) 775-2947; email irt@blizzard.mb.ca;
website www.blizzard.mb.ca/catalog/IRT.html
David Fuller, *Production Manager*

Types of material: full-length plays, one-acts, plays for young audiences, solo pieces. **Remuneration:** 10% book royalty. **Guidelines:** publishes more than 30 plays a year in chapbook format; submissions also considered for Blizzard Publishing trade paperback publishing program; previously produced work only. **Submission procedure:** accepts unsolicited scripts with submission forms and SASE for response; write for submission guidelines and forms. **Response time:** 4-6 months.

KALLIOPE, A JOURNAL OF WOMEN'S LITERATURE & ART

Florida Community College; 3939 Roosevelt Blvd;
Jacksonville, FL 32205; website www.fccj.org/kalliope
Mary Sue Koeppel, *Editor*

Types of material: one-acts, including solo pieces. **Remuneration:** 2 complimentary copies or free 1-year subscription. **Guidelines:** biannual journal of women's literature and art publishing short fiction, poetry, artwork, photography, interviews, reviews and an average of 1 play a year; unpublished plays, less than 20 pages long, by women only; "no trite themes or erotica." **Submission procedure:** accepts unsolicited scripts. **Response time:** 3-6 months.

THE KENYON REVIEW

Kenyon College; Gambier, OH 43022-9623; (740) 427-5208,
FAX 427-5417; email kenyonreview@kenyon.edu;
website www.kenyonreview.org
David H. Lynn, *Editor*

Types of material: one-acts, solo pieces, excerpts from full-length plays. **Remuneration:** cash payment; 2 complimentary copies. **Guidelines:** literary journal publishing an average of 2 plays a year; unproduced, unpublished works maximum 30 pages long. **Submission procedure:** accepts unsolicited scripts with letter of inquiry. **Response time:** 3-4 months.

LAMIA INK!

Box 202; Prince St Station; New York, NY 10012
(Ms.) Cortland Jessup, *Artistic Director*

Types of material: very short monologues and performance pieces, 1-page plays for contest (see below). **Remuneration:** 4 complimentary copies. **Guidelines:** biannual "art rag" magazine; experimental theatre pieces maximum 5 pages long, prefers 2-3 pages; special interest in Japanese, Pacific Rim and Native American writers, and poets' theatre, performance poems, theatre manifestos and essays. **Submission procedure:** accepts unsolicited scripts with SASE for response. **Response time:** 2-3 weeks minimum. Special programs: Lamia Ink! International One-Page Play Competition (see Prizes).

LILLENAS DRAMA RESOURCES

Lillenas Publishing Company; Box 419527; Kansas City, MO 64141;
(816) 931-1900, (800) 877-0700, FAX (816) 412-8390;
email drama@lillenas.com; website www.lillenas.com/drama
Kimberly R. Messer, *Manager/Editor*

Types of material: full-length plays, one-acts, collections of sketches, playlets, children's recitations. **Remuneration:** outright purchase or royalty. **Guidelines:** unpublished "creatively conceived and practically producible scripts and outlines that provide church and school with an opportunity to glorify God and his creation in drama." **Submission procedure:** accepts unsolicited scripts; send SASE for guidelines and current need letter. **Response time:** 3 months.

NEW PLAYS

Box 5074; Charlottesville, VA 22905; (804) 979-2777,
FAX 984-2230; email patwhitton@aol.com;
website www.newplaysforchildren.com
Patricia Whitton Forrest, *Publisher*

Types of material: plays for young audiences. **Remuneration:** 10% book royalty, 50% performance royalty. **Guidelines:** innovative material not duplicated by other sources of plays for young audiences; produced plays, directed by someone other than author. **Submission procedure:** accepts unsolicited scripts. **Response time:** 1-2 months minimum.

PACIFIC REVIEW

English Department; California State University;
    5500 University Pkwy; San Bernardino, CA 92407-2397;
    (909) 880-5026
Jacqueline Rhodes, *Editor*

Types of material: one-acts, including solo pieces. **Remuneration:** 2 complimentary copies. **Guidelines:** annual literary journal; plays maximum 25 pages long. **Submission procedure:** accepts unsolicited scripts; 2 submission limit; submit 1 Sep-1 Feb only. **Response time:** 3 months.

PAJ: A JOURNAL OF PERFORMANCE AND ART

(Formerly Performing Arts Journal)
Box 260; Village Station; New York, NY 10014-0260;
    (212) 243-3885, FAX 243-3885; email pajpub@aol.com;
    website www.jhu.edu/journals/paj
Bonnie Marranca and Gautam Dasgupta, *Co-Publishers and Editors*

Types of material: short full-length plays, one-acts, translations, solo pieces. **Remuneration:** fee. **Guidelines:** publishes plays and critical essays on international performance, drama, video, music, film and photography; special interest in translations; plays less than 40 pages long. **Submission procedure:** no unsolicited scripts; synopsis and letter of inquiry. **Response time:** 1-2 months letter; 1-2 months script.

PIONEER DRAMA SERVICE

Box 4267; Englewood, CO 80155-4267; (303) 779-4035,
    FAX 779-4315; email editors@pioneerdrama.com;
    website www.pioneerdrama.com

Types of material: full-length plays, one-acts, plays for young audiences, musicals. **Remuneration:** royalty. **Guidelines:** produced work suitable for educational theatre, including melodramas and Christmas plays. **Submission procedure:** accepts unsolicited scripts; prefers synopsis and letter of inquiry. **Response time:** 2 weeks letter; 3-4 months script. **Special programs:** Shubert Fendrich Memorial Playwriting Contest (see Prizes).

PLAYERS PRESS

Box 1132; Studio City, CA 91614-0132; (818) 789-4980
Robert W. Gordon, *Senior Editor*

Types of material: full-length plays, one-acts, translations, adaptations, plays for young audiences, musicals, solo pieces, monologues, scenes, teleplays, screenplays. **Remuneration:** cash option and/or outright purchase or royalty; complimentary copies (20% discount on additional copies). **Guidelines:** theatre press publishing technical and reference books and scripts; produced works for professional, amateur and educational markets. **Submission procedure:** accepts unsolicited scripts with proof of production, resume and 2 business-size SASEs; prefers synopsis, proof of production, resume and letter of inquiry with SASE for response. **Response time:** 1-6 weeks letter; 1-6 months script.

PLAYSCRIPTS.COM
Box 380996; Cambridge, MA 02238-0996;
email questions@playscripts.com; website www.playscripts.com

Types of material: full-length plays, one-acts. **Remuneration:** negotiated royalties from performances and book sales. **Guidelines:** unpublished plays; full text of selected plays will appear online in a protected format; Playscripts.com prints acting editions on demand and secures performance rights. **Submission procedure:** emailed submissions preferred; for guidelines and application visit www.playscripts.com/submissions.shtml; to submit by post, send 3 copies of script, 2 stamped envelopes and 1 SASE to address above. **Response time:** 8 months. (See Playscripts.com listing in Online Resources.)

PLAYS ON TAPE
Box 0152; Powell Butte, OR 97753; (541) 447-7033, FAX 617-9104;
email theatre@playsontape.com; website www.playsontape.com
Beverly Friesen, *General Manager*

Types of material: full-length plays, one-acts. **Remuneration:** negotiable fee and royalty; 10 complimentary copies of audiotape or CD. **Guidelines:** audiobook company marketing primarily to theatre gift bookstores and libraries; "works that do not diminish in quality due to restrictions of audiotape" only; special interest in works by women and minorities; maximum 74 minutes. **Submission procedure:** accepts unsolicited scripts; prefers synopsis, letter of inquiry and up to 10 pages of dialogue with SASE or email address for response; accepts scripts and synopses via email or floppy disk; send SASE for guidelines. **Response time:** 3 months letter; 5-6 months script.

PLAYS, THE DRAMA MAGAZINE FOR YOUNG PEOPLE

Box 600160; Newton, MA 02460; (262) 796-8776;
website www.writermag.com
Elizabeth Preston, *Editor*

Types of material: one-act plays for young audiences, including adaptations of material in the public domain. **Remuneration:** $75-175 depending on length of play. **Guidelines:** publishes 70 plays a year; prefers work 20-30 minutes long for junior and senior high school, 15-20 minutes for middle grades, 8-15 minutes for lower grades; no religious plays; magazine acquires all rights. **Submission procedure:** accepts unsolicited original scripts; letter of inquiry for adaptations; prefers format used in magazine (send SASE for style sheet). **Response time:** 1 week letter; 2-3 weeks script.

POEMS & PLAYS

English Department; Middle Tennessee State University;
Murfreesboro, TN 37132; (615) 898-2712, FAX 898-5098;
website www.mtsu.edu/~english/poemplay.html
Gaylord Brewer, *Editor*

Types of material: one-acts and short plays. **Remuneration:** 1 complimentary copy. **Guidelines:** annual magazine of poetry and short plays published Apr, includes an average of 2-3 plays in each issue; unpublished works; prefers produced works not more than 10-15 pages long. **Submission procedure:** accepts unsolicited scripts 1 Oct-15 Jan only; sample issue $6. **Response time:** 1-2 months. **Special programs:** Tennessee Chapbook Prize: annual award for either a one-act play or collection of short plays or poetry, maximum manuscript length 24-30 pages; winning script published as interior chapbook in magazine; playwright receives 50 complimentary copies; submit script and $10 for reading fee and copy of next issue; *deadline:* 15 Jan 2002; no submissions before 1 Oct 2001.

PRISM INTERNATIONAL

Creative Writing Program; University of British Columbia;
Buch E462-1866 Main Mall; Vancouver, BC; Canada V6T 1Z1;
(604) 822-2514, FAX 822-3616;
email prism@interchange.ubc.ca; website www.arts.ubc.ca/prism
Chris LaBonte and Andrea MacPherson, *Co-Editors*

Types of material: one-acts (including translations and solo pieces), excerpts from full-length plays. **Remuneration:** $20-30 per printed page; 1-year subscription. **Guidelines:** quarterly literary magazine; unpublished plays, maximum 40 pages long; send SASE for guidelines. **Submission procedure:** accepts unsolicited scripts, include copy of original with translations. **Response time:** 3-6 months. **Special programs:** UBC's Creative Writing Residency Prize in Stageplay: a 1-month residency at UBC and $25,000 (Canadian) prize (about $16,500 U.S.); call or visit website for guidelines.

RESOURCE PUBLICATIONS, INC.

160 East Virginia St, #290; San Jose, CA 95112-5876;
(408) 286-8505, FAX 287-8748; email Ken@rpinet.com;
website www.rpinet.com
Ken Guentert, *Editor*

Types of material: plays 7-15 minutes long. **Remuneration:** royalty. **Guidelines:** collection of skits suitable for middle school or high school students; no one-acts. **Submission procedure:** accepts unsolicited scripts. **Response time:** 2 months.

ROCKFORD REVIEW

Box 858; Rockford, IL 61105; email dragonldy@prodigy.net;
website members.tripod.com/~rwguild
Max Dodson, *Prose Editor*

Types of material: one-acts, including solo pieces. **Remuneration:** 1 complimentary copy; one-acts selected for publication eligible for triquarterly "Editor's Choice" prize of $25 (winner invited to reading and reception as guest of honor in Jun). **Guidelines:** triquarterly journal publishing poetry, fiction, satire, artwork and an average of 4-5 plays a year; one-acts not more than 1300 words; interested in work that provides new insight into the human dilemma. **Submission procedure:** accepts unsolicited scripts with SASE; sample copy $5. **Response time:** 1-2 months.

SAMUEL FRENCH, INC.

45 West 25th St; New York, NY 10010-2751; (212) 206-8990,
FAX 206-1429; email samuelfrench@earthlink.net;
website www.samuelfrench.com
Lawrence Harbison, *Senior Editor*

Types of material: full-length plays, one-acts, plays for young audiences, musicals. **Remuneration:** 10% book royalty; 10 complimentary copies (40% discount on additional copies); pays production royalties, agency commissions vary. **Guidelines:** "Many of our publications have never been produced in New York; these are generally comprised of light comedies, mysteries, mystery-comedies, a handful of one-acts and plays for young audiences, and plays with a preponderance of female roles; however, do not hesitate to send in your future Pulitzer Prize Winner." **Submission procedure:** accepts unsolicited scripts in standard manuscript format; call or email for *Publication Guidelines.* **Response time:** 2 months minimum.

SHADES OF DECEMBER

Box 244; Seldon, NY 11784; email plays@shadesofdecember.com; website www.shadesofdecember.com
Alexander Danner, *Editor*

Types of material: short plays, 1-minute plays. **Remuneration:** 2 complimentary copies. **Guidelines:** quarterly literary journal publishing eclectic work including poetry, fiction and 2-4 plays a year; maximum 10 pages. **Submission procedure:** accepts unsolicited scripts. **Response time:** 1-2 months.

SINISTER WISDOM

Box 3252; Berkeley, CA 94703; email sinister@sirius.com; website www.sinisterwisdom.org

Types of material: one-acts, excerpts from full-length plays. **Remuneration:** 2 complimentary copies. **Guidelines:** lesbian quarterly of art and literature; works by lesbians reflecting the diversity of lesbians; no heterosexual themes; excerpts maximum 3000 words; send SASE for current themes. **Submission procedure:** accepts unsolicited scripts. **Response time:** 2-9 months.

SMITH AND KRAUS

Box 127; Lyme, NH 03768; (603) 643-6431, FAX 643-1831; email sandk@sover.net
Marisa Smith, *President*

Types of material: full-length plays, one-acts, translations, adaptations, plays for young audiences, solo pieces, monologues. **Remuneration:** usually fee or royalty; at least 10 complimentary copies. **Guidelines:** theatre press publishing works of interest to theatrical community, especially to actors, including collections of monologues and an average of 50 full-length plays a year. **Submission procedure:** no unsolicited scripts; synopsis and letter of inquiry. **Response time:** 2-3 weeks letter; 2-4 months script.

SPEERT PUBLISHING

Box 2281; New York, NY 10009; (212) 979-7656;
   email espeert@speertpublishing.com;
   website www.speertpublishing.com
Eleanore Speert, *President*

Types of material: full-length plays, one-acts, translations, adaptations, plays for young audiences, solo pieces. **Remuneration:** writer chooses number of books to be printed and keeps all copies. **Guidelines:** self-publishing company producing industry-standard acting editions for stock, regional theatre, nonprofessional and professional markets; no musicals. **Submission procedure:** call, email or write for information. **Response time:** 1 week. **Special programs:** supports the Dayton Playhouse FutureFest (see listing in Prizes), winning play is published free of charge.

SUN & MOON PRESS

6026 Wilshire Blvd; Los Angeles, CA 90036; (323) 857-1115;
   email djmess@sunmoon.com; website www.sunmoon.com
American Theater and Literature Program (ATL)

Types of material: full-length plays, one-acts, translations. **Remuneration:** royalty; 10 complimentary copies. **Guidelines:** press publishing average of 3 single-play volumes a year; unpublished plays. **Submission procedure:** accepts unsolicited scripts. **Response time:** 2-6 months.

THEATREFORUM

Theatre & Dance Department 0344;
   University of California–San Diego; 9500 Gilman Dr;
   La Jolla, CA 92093-0344; (858) 534-6598, FAX 534-1080;
   email TheatreForum@ucsd.edu; website www.theatreforum.org
Jim Carmody, Adele Edling Shank and Theodore Shank, *Editors*

Types of material: full-length plays, translations, adaptations. **Remuneration:** $200; 10 complimentary copies; discount for additional copies. **Guidelines:** biannual international journal focusing on innovative work, publishing 2 scripts in each issue, plus articles, interviews and photographs; professionally produced, unpublished plays. **Submission procedure:** no unsolicited scripts; professional recommendation. **Response time:** 3 months.

THEATER MAGAZINE

Yale School of Drama, Box 208244; New Haven, CT 06520-8244;
(203) 432-1568, FAX 432-8336;
email theater.magazine@yale.edu;
website www.yale.edu/drama/publications/theater
Erika Munk, *Editor*

Types of material: full-length plays, translations, adaptations, solo pieces. **Remuneration:** maximum fee of $150; complimentary copies. **Guidelines:** triquarterly theatre journal publishing an average of 2 plays in each volume, plus articles and essays; special interest in experimental, innovative work; "no standard psychological realism or TV-script clones." **Submission procedure:** accepts unsolicited scripts with resume and letter of inquiry. **Response time:** 3-6 months.

DEVELOPMENT

What's in this section?

Conferences, festivals, workshops and programs whose primary purpose is to develop plays and playwrights. Also listed are some playwright groups and membership organizations whose main activity is play development. Developmental organizations such as New Dramatists whose many programs cannot be adequately described in the brief format used in this section are listed in Membership and Service Organizations. Some programs listed in Prizes also include a developmental element. Note: Some programs provide writers with stipends or living situations, etc. Others require a small fee. Read the "financial arrangement" section carefully.

How can I get into these programs?

Keep applying to those for which you are convinced your work is suited. If you're turned down one year, you may be accepted the next on the strength of your latest piece. If you're required to submit a script with your application, don't forget your SASE!

ABINGDON THEATRE COMPANY

432 West 42nd St, 4th Floor; New York, NY 10036; (212) 736-6604,
    FAX 736-6608; email atcnyc@aol.com;
    website www.abingdon-nyc.org
Pamela Paul, *Co-Artistic Director*

Open to: playwrights. **Description:** biweekly in-house readings; 10 plays receive 12 hours of rehearsal and staged readings; of those, 3-4 plays selected for workshop production; of those, 2 plays selected for mainstage production. **Financial arrangement:** stipend for workshops and mainstage production. **Guidelines:** play unproduced in New York. **Application procedure:** script only. **Deadline:** ongoing. **Notification:** 6 months. **Dates:** year-round.

ACT/HEDGEBROOK WOMEN PLAYWRIGHTS FESTIVAL

A Contemporary Theatre; The Eagles Building, 700 Union St;
    Seattle, WA 98101-4037; (206) 292-7660, FAX 292-7670;
    website www.acttheatre.org
Gordon Edelstein, *Artistic Director*

Open to: playwrights. **Description:** 4 playwrights chosen for reading of play with audience feedback; playwright then goes to Hedgebrook (see Colonies and Residencies) for a week to work on any revisions that come out of reading. **Financial arrangement:** $1000 stipend, travel and lodging. **Guidelines:** woman playwright; unproduced play. **Application procedure:** professional nomination only; theatre panel selects finalists. **Deadline:** Nov 2001; exact date TBA. **Notification:** Jan 2002. **Dates:** May 2002.

ANNUAL BACKDOOR THEATRE NEW PLAY PROJECT

Wichita Falls Backdoor Players, Inc; Box 896; Wichita Falls, TX 76307;
    (940) 322-5000, FAX 322-8167; email backdoor@wf.net
Linda Bates, *Managing Director*

Open to: playwrights. **Description:** 1 play each Sep receives 5 weeks of rehearsal and workshop production with a minimum of 6 performances. **Financial arrangement:** $500 honorarium; travel and housing. **Guidelines:** special interest in playwrights from Texas and surrounding region; full-length plays which have not received professional production. **Application procedure:** script, brief synopsis, resume and SASP for acknowledgment of receipt. **Deadline:** 15 Mar 2002. **Notification:** Jul 2002. **Dates:** Sep 2002.

ASCAP MUSICAL THEATRE WORKSHOP

1 Lincoln Plaza; New York, NY 10023; (212) 621–6234
Michael A. Kerker, *Director of Musical Theatre*

Open to: composers, lyricists. **Description:** 10-session workshop under the direction of Stephen Schwartz; works presented to panels of musical theatre professionals. **Financial arrangement:** free. **Guidelines:** write for guidelines and dates. **Application procedure:** resume and cassette of 4 theatrical songs (no pop songs). **Deadline:** 15 Mar 2002. **Notification:** exact date TBA. **Dates:** exact dates TBA.

ASHLAND NEW PLAYS FESTIVAL

ArtWork Enterprises, Inc.; Box 453; Ashland, OR 97520;
    (541) 482–4357; website www.ashlandplays.org

Open to: playwrights. **Description:** 4 new works given 16-20 hours of rehearsal with actors and director, culminating in 2 public readings. **Financial arrangement:** $500 stipend and housing. **Guidelines:** U.S. resident; unproduced full-length play; cast limit of 8; 1 submission limit; author's name and contact information on script cover sheet only. **Application procedure:** script, 1-page synopsis and 2-paragraph bio. **Deadline:** 15 Mar 2002; no submission before 1 Jan 2002. **Notification:** Jul 2002. **Dates:** 16-20 Oct 2001.

ASIAN AMERICAN THEATER COMPANY
EMERGING ARTISTS PROJECT

1840 Sutter St, Suite 207; San Francisco, CA 94115; (415) 440–5545,
    FAX 440–5597; email info@asianamericantheater.org;
    website www.asianamericantheater.org
Pamela A. Wu, *Producing Director*

Open to: playwrights. **Description:** developmental workshop for 2-4 plays, leading to staged reading or production; plays not selected for workshop considered for inclusion in series of 8-10 readings presented each season. **Financial arrangement:** free; honorarium contingent on funding. **Guidelines:** playwright of Asian-Pacific descent writing in English; prefers plays depicting Asian-Pacific-American perspective. **Application procedure:** script, synopsis and character breakdown. **Deadline:** ongoing. **Notification:** 1-6 months. **Dates:** exact dates TBA.

A.S.K. THEATER PROJECTS

11845 West Olympic Blvd, Suite 1250 West; Los Angeles, CA 90064;
(310) 478-3200, FAX 478-5300; email info@askplay.org;
website www.askplay.org
Mead K. Hunter, *Director of Literary Programs*

Open to: playwrights. **Description:** approximately 15 playwrights receive public rehearsed reading of play or participate in private writer's retreat; plays considered for subsequent workshop production. **Financial arrangement:** $250 stipend for reading, $500 for retreat. **Guidelines:** unproduced full-length play-in-progress. **Application procedure:** script submissions accepted only from agents; playwrights may submit 5-10 page dialgue sample and resume. **Deadline:** 1 Dec for retreat; 1 Jun for readings. **Dates:** retreat: spring 2002; readings: fall 2002.

BALTIMORE PLAYWRIGHTS FESTIVAL

251 South Ann St; Baltimore, MD 21231; (410) 276-2153
Rodney Bonds, *President*

Open to: playwrights, composers, librettists, lyricists. **Description:** selected plays receive 3-5 developmental readings Sep-Mar; from these, participating theatres choose scripts for full production in summer festival. **Financial arrangement:** $100 honorarium for produced scripts. **Guidelines:** past or current resident of MD; unproduced play or musical; send SASE for guidelines. **Application procedure:** 3 copies of script and letter of inquiry with $5 fee. **Deadline:** 30 Sep 2001. **Notification:** 15 Apr 2002. **Dates:** summer 2002.

BAY AREA PLAYWRIGHTS FESTIVAL

The Playwrights Foundation; Box 460357; San Francisco, CA 94106;
(415) 263-3986; email bayplays@best.com;
website www.bayareaplaywrights.org
Arturo Catricala and Amy Mueller, *Co-Artistic Directors*

Open to: playwrights. **Description:** 6-9 scripts given dramaturgical attention and 2 rehearsed readings separated by 5-6 days for rewrites during 2-week festival; mandatory prefestival weekend retreat for initial brainstorming with directors and dramaturgs. **Financial arrangement:** small stipend, travel. **Guidelines:** unproduced full-length play only. **Application procedure:** script and resume. **Deadline:** 15 Feb 2002. **Notification:** Jun 2002. **Dates:** summer 2002.

BMI-LEHMAN ENGEL MUSICAL THEATRE WORKSHOP

Broadcast Music, Inc.; 320 West 57th St; New York, NY 10019;
(212) 830-2508, FAX 262-2824; email jbanks@bmi.com
Jean Banks, *Senior Director, Musical Theatre*

Open to: composers, librettists, lyricists. **Description:** 2-year program of weekly workshop meetings; ongoing advanced group for invited alums of Workshop; showcase presentations to invited members of entertainment industry; members eligible for annual Jerry Harrington Musical Theatre Awards, cash prizes for outstanding achievement in workshop. **Financial arrangement:** free. **Application procedure:** application and work samples. **Deadline:** 1 May 2002 for librettists; 1 Aug 2002 for composers and lyricists. **Notification:** Sep 2002.

BROADWAY TOMORROW

191 Claremont Ave, Suite 53; New York, NY 10027; (212) 531-2447,
FAX 531-2447
Elyse Curtis, *Artistic Director*

Open to: composers, librettists, lyricists. **Description:** new musicals presented in concert with writers' involvement. **Financial arrangement:** participant pays $50 annual membership fee. **Guidelines:** resident of NY metropolitan area. **Application procedure:** synopsis, resume, cassette of 3 songs with description of scenes in which they occur, reviews if available and SASE for response. **Deadline:** 31 Aug 2002. **Notification:** 3-6 months. **Dates:** year-round.

CAC PLAYWRIGHT'S UNIT

Contemporary Arts Center; 900 Camp St; New Orleans, LA 70130;
(504) 528-3805, FAX 528-3828; website www.cacno.org
Performance Support Coordinator

Open to: playwrights. **Description:** 9-month workshop for 8-15 writers; participants' works developed and given staged readings. **Financial arrangement:** write or call for information. **Guidelines:** writer living in New Orleans area. **Application procedure:** call for information. **Deadline:** ongoing. **Dates:** ongoing.

CHARLOTTE FESTIVAL/NEW PLAYS IN AMERICA

Charlotte Repertory Theatre; 129 West Trade St;
 Charlotte, NC 28244; (704) 333-8587
Claudia Carter Covington, *Literary Manager*
Carol Bellamy, *Literary Associate*

Open to: playrights, translators. **Description:** 4 plays each given 12-16 hours of rehearsal with Equity company, culminating in 2 public staged readings during week-long festival; some scripts subsequently receive full production as part of theatre's regular season. **Financial arrangement:** honorarium, travel and housing. **Guidelines:** only full-length plays and translations that have not received professional production. **Application procedure:** script only. **Deadline:** ongoing. **Dates:** 4-18 Feb 2002.

THE CHESTERFIELD FILM COMPANY/WRITER'S FILM PROJECT

1158 26th St, Box 544; Santa Monica, CA 90401; (213) 683-3977,
 FAX (310) 260-6116; website www.chesterfield-co.com

Open to: playwrights, screenwriters. **Description:** up to 5 writers annually chosen for year-long screenwriting workshop; writer creates 2 feature-length screenplays; company intends to produce best of year's work. **Financial arrangement:** $20,000 stipend. **Guidelines:** current and former writing-program students encouraged to apply; write or call for information. **Application procedure:** 2 copies of application, writing samples, SASE, SASP and $39.50 fee. **Deadline:** May 2002; exact date TBA. **Dates:** TBA.

CORNERSTONE DRAMATURGY AND DEVELOPMENT PROJECT

Penumbra Theatre Company; 270 North Kent St;
 St. Paul, MN 55102-1794; (651) 224-4601, FAX 224-7074
Lou Bellamy, *Artistic Director*

Open to: playwrights. **Description:** 1 playwright a year offered mainstage production with possible 3-4-week residency; 1 playwright offered 4-week workshop-residency culminating in staged reading. **Financial arrangement:** varies according to needs of project. **Guidelines:** full-length play dealing with the African-American and/or Pan-African experience which has not received professional full production; one-acts considered. **Application procedure:** script and resume; write for guidelines. **Deadline:** ongoing.

CSF STUDIO

Cincinnati Shakespeare Festival; 717–719 Race St;
  Cincinnati, OH 45202; (513) 381–2289, FAX 381–2298;
  email csfed@cincyshakes.com; website www.cincyshakes.com
Jasson Minadakis, *Artistic Director*

Open to: playwrights, translators. **Description:** 3 plays each given 1 week of development, culminating in public staged reading or workshop. **Financial arrangement:** $500 stipend, travel and housing. **Guidelines:** prefer language-focused works-in-progress. **Application procedure:** first 20 pages of script, synopsis and letter of inquiry including current projects and new project ideas. **Deadline:** ongoing. **Notification:** 6 months. **Dates:** ongoing. (See Cincinnati Shakespeare Festival in Production.)

DAVID HENRY HWANG WRITERS INSTITUTE

East West Players; 244 South San Pedro St, Suite 301;
  Los Angeles, CA 90012; (213) 625–7000, FAX 625–7111;
  email info@eastwestplayers.org;
  website www.eastwestplayers.org
Ken Narasaki, *Literary Manager*

Open to: playwrights, screenwriters. **Description:** 2 20-week workshops each year culminating in a public staged reading. **Financial arrangement:** $350 fee; 1 scholarship available. **Application procedure:** application form and work sample with $50 nonrefundable deposit. **Deadline:** visit website. (See East West Players in Production.)

DENVER CENTER THEATRE COMPANY THEATREFEST

1050 13th St; Denver, CO 80204; website www.denvercenter.org
Bruce K. Sevy, *Associate Artistic Director/New Play Development*

Open to: playwrights. **Description:** new plays receive workshops and rehearsed readings during spring festival; most plays given 15–30 hours of rehearsal, culminating in 1 public presentation. **Financial arrangement:** stipend, travel, housing. **Application procedure:** send SASE for guidelines or download from web. **Deadline:** 31 Dec 2002. **Dates:** late May–early Jun. (See Denver Center Theatre Company in Production.)

DRAMA LEAGUE NEW DIRECTORS–NEW WORKS SERIES

The Drama League of New York; 165 West 46th St, Suite 601;
New York, NY 10036; (212) 302-2100, FAX 302-2254;
email directorsproject@dramaleague.org;
website www.dramaleague.org

Open to: collaborative teams of playwrights, translators, composers, librettists, lyricists. **Description:** 3 projects each summer receive up to 4 weeks of rehearsal space in New York City; writer or composer applies in collaborative team with director; development ranges from exploratory rehearsals to workshop production according to needs of collaborative team. **Financial arrangement:** $1000 for each project. **Application procedure:** proposal describing project submitted by collaborative team; collaborators' bios; write, call or visit website for guidelines. **Deadline:** 15 Feb 2002. **Notification:** 1 May 2002.

DRAMA WEST PRODUCTIONS

Box 5022-127; Lake Forest, CA 92630
Catherine Stanley, *Artistic Director*

Open to: playwrights. **Description:** every 3 months 5-6 plays given staged reading with professional actors at Los Angeles venue. **Financial arrangement:** free. **Guidelines:** short one-acts appropriate for a general audience which have not received professional production. **Application procedure:** script only. **Deadline:** ongoing. **Notification:** 4 weeks, if script is accepted.

FIRST STAGE

Box 38280; Los Angeles, CA 90038; (323) 850-6271,
FAX 850-6295; email firststagela@aol.com;
website www.firststagela.org
Dennis Safren, *Literary Manager*

Open to: playwrights, solo performers, screenwriters. **Description:** organization providing year-round developmental services using professional actors, directors and dramaturgs; weekly staged readings of plays and screenplays followed by discussions; bimonthly playwriting and screenwriting workshops; periodic dramaturgy workshops; annual short-play marathon; annual One-Act Play Contest with $100 first prize, $50 second and third prizes and videotaped staged reading for all winners, *deadline:* 1 Jul 2001 (send SASE for guidelines), *notification:* 1 Nov 2001. **Financial arrangement:** subscription of $160 a year or $45 a quarter for resident of Los Angeles, Orange or Ventura counties; $60 annual subscription for nonresident; nonmember may submit script for reading. **Application procedure:** script only. **Deadline:** ongoing. **Notification:** 2-6 months. **Dates:** year-round.

FLORIDA PLAYWRIGHTS' PROCESS

PACT Institute for the Performing Arts at Ruth Eckerd Hall;
    111 McMullen-Booth Rd; Clearwater, FL 33759;
    (727) 791-7060, FAX 791-7449; email elizbrinck@hotmail.com;
    website www.rutheckerdhall.net
Elizabeth Brincklow, *Artistic and Program Director*

Open to: playwrights. **Description:** 3 plays (2 by playwright 19 or younger) receive 3-4 months of workshop, rehearsal and staged reading, culminating in workshop production with moderated audience discussion. **Financial arrangement:** $400 and maximum travel stipend of $250. **Guidelines:** FL playwright; unproduced and unpublished one-act or full-length play; cast limit of 6; maximum running time 2 hours; simple props and set. **Application procedure:** write or call for guidelines. **Deadline:** 8 Nov 2001. **Notification:** 31 Jan 2002. **Dates:** Feb-May 2002.

THE 42ND STREET WORKSHOP

432 West 42nd St, 5th Floor; New York, NY 10036; (212) 695-4173,
    FAX 695-3384
Sheila Walsh, *Literary Manager*

Open to: playwrights, screenwriters. **Description:** writers meet weekly to develop scripts through in-house readings and critiques; approximately 30 works a year receive staged readings; 3-4 works receive showcase productions. **Financial arrangement:** $25 monthly fee. **Application procedure:** script and letter of reference from company member. **Deadline:** ongoing. **Notification:** 2-3 months. **Dates:** year-round.

THE FRANK SILVERA WRITERS' WORKSHOP

Box 1791; Manhattanville Station; New York, NY 10027;
    (212) 281-8832, FAX 281-8839 (call first);
    email playrite@artswire.org; website www.artswire.org/~playrite
Garland Lee Thompson, *Founding Executive Director*

Open to: playwrights. **Description:** upper Manhattan- and Harlem-based program which includes Monday series of readings of new plays by new and established writers, followed by critiques; Saturday seminars conducted by master playwrights; staged readings; and 2-3 showcases and readers' theatre productions a year. **Financial arrangement:** $35 annual fee plus $10 per Saturday class; Monday-night readings free. **Guidelines:** interested in new plays by writers of all colors and backgrounds. **Application procedure:** attend Sep open house; submitting script and attending a Monday-night session encouraged; call for information.

FREDERICK DOUGLASS CREATIVE ARTS CENTER WRITING WORKSHOPS

270 West 96th St; New York, NY 10025; (212) 864-3375,
    FAX 864-3474 (call first); email fdcac@aol.com;
    website www.fdcac.org
Fred Hudson, *Artistic Director*

Open to: playwrights, screenwriters, television writers. **Description:** 4 cycles a year of 8-week beginning and advanced playwriting workshops; advanced workshops include readings and possible productions; also film and television writing workshops; weekly meetings. **Financial arrangement:** $200 fee per workshop; author of play given staged reading receives $50, author of produced play receives $500. **Application procedure:** contact FDCAC for information. **Deadline:** Sep 2001 for 1st cycle; Jan 2002 for 2nd cycle; May 2002 for 3rd cycle; Jul 2002 for 4th cycle; call for exact dates. **Dates:** Oct-Nov 2001; Jan-Mar 2002; Apr-Jun 2002; Jul-Sep 2002.

THE GENESIUS GUILD PROGRAMS FOR THE DEVELOPMENT OF NEW PLAYS & MUSICALS

Box 2213; New York, NY 10108-2213; (212) 946-5625;
    email literary@genesiusguild.org;
    website www.genesiusguild.org
Thomas Morrissey, *Artistic Director*

Open to: playwrights, translators, composers, librettists, lyricists, solo performers. **Description:** program offering range of developmental services including in-house readings, staged readings, and workshop and showcase productions; development process varies according to needs of script. **Financial arrangement:** free. **Guidelines:** emerging or established playwright. **Application procedure:** 1- or 2-page synopsis, scene breakdown, cast requirements, production needs, cassette for musical and bio or resume. **Deadline:** ongoing. **Dates:** Sep-Jun.

THE HARBOR THEATRE WORKSHOP

Harbor Theatre Company; 160 West 71st St, PHA;
New York, NY 10023; (212) 787–1945
Stuart Warmflash, *Artistic Director*

Open to: playwrights, composers, librettists. **Description:** developmental lab for 8 member writers and composers with a company of 30 actors; 3-hour meetings held every Thursday providing cold and/or rehearsed readings, followed by short, playwright-driven critiques; full productions, annual one-act festival and public readings of developed work are produced by the Harbor Theatre Company at least once during the season. **Financial arrangement:** TBA ($400 for 2000-2001 season). **Guidelines:** artists with full body of work committed to rewrites and interested in year-long workshop membership. **Application procedure:** no unsolicited scripts; synopsis and letter of inquiry. **Deadline:** ongoing. **Notification:** 2 weeks letter; 3 months script. **Dates:** year-round.

HAROLD PRINCE MUSICAL THEATRE PROGRAM

The Directors Company; 311 West 43rd St, Suite 307;
New York, NY 10036; (212) 246–5877, FAX 246–5882;
website www.thedirectorscompany.org
HPMTP Selection Committee

Open to: playwrights, composers, librettists, lyricists. **Description:** program supports creation, development and production of new musicals; writers and composers work collaboratively with director under guidance of program's artistic directors and Harold Prince; process includes monthly meetings, readings and presentation for invited audience in New York City. **Financial arrangement:** commissioning and optioning fees available. **Guidelines:** musicals in any stage of development; call for guidelines. **Application procedure:** full scripts accepted from agent or with professional recommendation; all others submit synopsis, 15-page dialogue sample and 6-song cassette or CD. **Deadline:** ongoing. **Notification:** 6-9 months.

HARVEST FESTIVAL OF NEW AMERICAN PLAYS

State Theater Company; Box 1566; Austin, TX 78767;
(512) 692–0509, FAX 472–7199;
email mpolgar@austintheatrealliance.org;
website www.austintheatrealliance.org
Michelle Polgar, *Artistic Associate*

Open to: playwrights, solo performers. **Description:** 3-6 plays receive 1 month of rehearsals culminating in staged readings; plays considered for future full production. **Financial arrangement:** stipend, travel and housing. **Guidelines:** full-length play or adaptation not produced professionally; 1 submission limit. **Application procedure:** 10-page dialogue sample, brief synopsis and resume with SASE. **Deadline:** 1 Mar 2002; no submission before 1 Dec 2002. **Notification:** 1 Sep 2002. **Dates:** Nov 2002.

HEDGEROW HORIZONS

146 West Rose Valley Rd; Wallingford, PA 19086; (610) 565–4211
Walt Vail, *Literary Manager*

Open to: playwrights. **Description:** 5 full-length plays and 2 one-acts each given 1 rehearsal and 1 public reading. **Financial arrangement:** free. **Guidelines:** playwright must be resident of DE, PA or NJ; play not produced professionally. **Application procedure:** send SASE for guidelines. **Deadline:** 28 Feb 2002. **Notification:** 30 Apr 2002. **Dates:** 30 May 2002.

HISPANIC PLAYWRIGHTS PROJECT

South Coast Repertory; Box 2197; Costa Mesa, CA 92628–2197;
(714) 708–5500, ext 5405
Juliette Carrillo, *Project Director*

Open to: playwrights. **Description:** up to 3 scripts given 1-3-week workshop with director, dramaturg and professional cast, culminating in public reading or workshop production and discussion; playwright meets with director and dramaturg prior to workshop. **Financial arrangement:** per diem, travel, housing. **Guidelines:** Hispanic-American playwright; unproduced play preferred but produced play which would benefit from further development will be considered; play must not be written entirely in Spanish; no musicals. **Application procedure:** script, synopsis and bio. **Deadline:** 15 Nov 2001. **Notification:** 1 Feb 2002. **Dates:** Apr 2002.

KEY WEST THEATRE FESTIVAL

Box 992; Key West, FL 33041–0992; (305) 295–9278,
   FAX 293–0845; email jmcgkw@earthlink.net;
   website www.keywesttheatrefestival.org
Joan McGillis, *Artistic Director*

Open to: playwrights, translators, solo performers. **Description:** 5-6 plays given staged readings and 3-4 plays given full productions during 10-day festival, which also includes workshops and seminars. **Financial arrangement:** travel and housing. **Guidelines:** unproduced full-length play, one-act, musical, work for young audiences. **Application procedure:** script, resume and 2 letters of recommendation. **Deadline:** 31 Dec 2001. **Notification:** Apr 2002. **Dates:** late Jun–early Jul 2002.

L. A. BLACK PLAYWRIGHTS

5926 5th Ave; Los Angeles, CA 90043; (323) 292–9438
James Graham Bronson, *President*

Open to: playwrights, librettists, lyricists. **Description:** group meets every second Sunday for guest speakers, private and public readings, and showcases. **Financial arrangement:** free. **Guidelines:** resident of Los Angeles area; members mainly but not exclusively African-American; prefers produced playwright. **Application procedure:** submit full-length play. **Deadline:** ongoing. **Dates:** year-round.

THE LARK THEATRE COMPANY

939 Eighth Ave, Suite 301; New York, NY 10019; (212) 246–2676,
   FAX 246–2609; email info@larktheatre.org;
   website www.larktheatre.org
John C. Eisner, *Producing Director*

Open to: playwrights, translators, composers, librettists, lyricists. **Description:** organization providing year-round developmental services. Playwrights Week: 8 plays receive 10 hours of rehearsal with actors, director and dramaturg, culminating in staged reading followed by audience discussion. Studio Retreat: some plays receive 20 hours of rehearsal with actors, director and dramaturg, culminating in staged reading followed by audience discussion. BareBones: 10 plays receive workshop production. **Financial arrangement:** some travel stipends and housing fellowships available, contingent on funding. **Guidelines:** write or visit website for guidelines. **Application procedure:** script and $15 fee. **Deadline:** ongoing. **Notification:** 6 months. **Dates:** year-round.

THE LEHMAN ENGEL MUSICAL THEATRE WORKSHOP

335 North Brand Blvd; Glendale, CA 91203; (818) 502-3309,
    FAX 502-3365; email jsparksco@aol.com
John Sparks, *Artistic Director*

Open to: composers, librettists, lyricists. **Description:** Sep-Jun workshop; in-house staged readings; skeletal productions (Equity contract). **Financial arrangement:** 1st-year workshop members pay dues of $600, which include nonrefundable application fee (see below); in subsequent years, members pay dues of $400. **Application procedure:** application; 1-page resume; cassette of 3 songs or equivalent for composer; 3 lyrics for lyricist; short scene for librettist; nonrefundable $50 fee. **Deadline:** 15 Aug 2002; late applications will be considered for following year. **Notification:** Sep 2002. **Dates:** Sep 2001-Jun 2002.

LORNA LITTLEWAY'S JUNETEENTH JAMBOREE OF NEW PLAYS

Box 3463; Louisville, KY 40201-3463; (502) 636-4200;
    email juneteenthlegacy@aol.com
Lorna Littleway, *Founder/Producing Director*

Open to: playwrights. **Description:** 12 plays given professional staged reading during 3-week festival in Jun. **Financial arrangement:** free. **Guidelines:** plays which address the African-American experience and explore any of 5 themes: 19th-century African-American experience; pre- and Harlem Renaissance era; Caribbean/Native American influence on African-Americans; African-American youth and contemporary issues; and new images of women; young writers encouraged to apply. **Application procedure:** 2 copies of script and $10 fee (1 script and fee to Louisville address and 1 script to: 605 Water St, #21B; New York, NY 10002). **Deadline:** 15 Apr 2002; no submission before 15 Dec 2001. **Notification:** 30 Apr 2002. **Dates:** Jun 2002.

MANHATTAN PLAYWRIGHTS UNIT

338 West 19th St, #6B; New York, NY 10011-3982; (212) 989-0948
Saul Zachary, *Artistic Director*

Open to: playwrights, screenwriters. **Description:** developmental workshop meeting weekly for in-house readings and discussions of members' works-in-progress; end-of-season series of staged readings of new plays. **Financial arrangement:** free. **Guidelines:** produced or published writer. **Application**

procedure: letter of inquiry, resume and SASE for response. **Deadline:** ongoing.

MARK TAPER FORUM DEVELOPMENTAL PROGRAMS

135 North Grand Ave; Los Angeles, CA 90012; (213) 972–8033
Pier Carlo Talenti, *Literary Manager*
  (Also see entry in Production)

ASIAN THEATRE WORKSHOP (ATW)

Open to: playwrights, solo performers. **Description:** ongoing developmental program including Asian Pacific American Friends of Center Theatre Group (APAF) Reading Series; discussions with outside theatre artists; workshop productions. **Financial arrangement:** honorarium. **Guidelines:** Asian-Pacific playwright. **Application procedure:** script and resume. **Deadline:** ongoing.

BLACKSMYTHS

Open to: playwrights, solo performers. **Description:** ongoing developmental program including writers' group, staged readings and workshops. **Financial arrangement:** honorarium. **Guidelines:** African-American playwright; resident of Los Angeles area. **Application procedure:** script and resume. **Deadline:** ongoing.

LATINO THEATRE INITIATIVE (LTI)

Open to: playwrights, solo performers. **Description:** ongoing developmental program including staged readings and workshops. **Financial arrangement:** remuneration varies. **Guidelines:** Latino playwright. **Application procedure:** script and resume. **Deadline:** ongoing.

NEW WORK FESTIVAL

Open to: playwrights, solo performers. **Description:** 16–18 plays given workshops (2 weeks of rehearsal, 2 public presentations) or rehearsed readings. **Financial arrangement:** remuneration varies. **Guidelines:** unproduced, unpublished play. **Application procedure:** brief synopsis, 5–10 sample pages and resume. **Deadline:** 1 Apr 2002.

OTHER VOICES PROJECT

Open to: playwrights, solo performers. **Description:** ongoing developmental program including community and professional development; staged readings; workshops; Summer Chautauqua: biennial week-long seminar.

Financial arrangement: remuneration varies. **Guidelines:** disabled playwright writing about disability; program designed to increase presence of disabled community in mainstream theatre. **Application procedure:** script and resume; call for guidelines for Summer Chautauqua. **Deadline:** call for information.

MUSICAL DEVELOPMENT WORKSHOP

Musical Writers' Playground, LLC; 215 West 75th St, Suite 3E;
New York, NY 10023; (212) 841–0143, FAX (425) 671–1722;
email musicalwriters@aol.com;
website www.musicalwritersplayground.com
Leslie Becker, *Executive Director*
DJ Salisbury, *Artistic Director*

Open to: composers, librettists, lyricists. **Description:** 20 writers meet bimonthly for 1 year to present and develop new projects in a structured environment; established Broadway directors, producers, composers and lyricists brought in as guest speakers; 4 shows given Oct staged reading with cast and director for audience of producers, professional developmental organizations and directors. **Financial arrangement:** $300 annual membership fee; some scholarships available. **Application procedure:** application and work samples; call or download application from web. **Deadline:** 1 Dec 2001. **Notification:** 15 Jan 2002. **Dates:** Jan–Nov 2002.

MUSICAL THEATRE WORKS' RESIDENT ARTIST PROGRAM

Musical Theatre Works; 440 Lafayette St; New York, NY 10003;
(212) 677–0040, FAX 598–0105; email mtw2000@akula.com
Randy Lutterman, *Producing Director*

Open to: composers, librettists, lyricists. **Description:** new composers, librettists and lyricists work with established musical theatre professionals to develop projects through labs, readings, workshop productions and a 6-week professional workshop culminating in public presentation; free rehearsal space and casting, technical, administrative, legal and dramaturgical support. **Financial arrangement:** free. **Guidelines:** completed unproduced work. **Application procedure:** send letter of inquiry and SASE for guidelines. **Deadline:** ongoing.

MUSIC THEATER CONFERENCE

O'Neill Theater Center; 305 Great Neck Rd; Waterford, CT 06385;
  (860) 443-5378
Paulette Haupt, *Artistic Director*
Michael E. Nassar, *Associate Director*

Open to: composers, librettists, lyricists. **Description:** development period of 2-4 weeks at O'Neill Theater Center, Waterford, CT for new music-theatre works of all genres, traditional and nontraditional; some works developed privately, others presented as staged readings. **Financial arrangement:** stipend, round-trip travel from NYC, room and board. **Guidelines:** unproduced work; adaptations acceptable if rights have been obtained. **Application procedure:** send SASE for guidelines and application form after 1 Sep 2001. **Deadline:** TBA (1 Mar in 2001). **Dates:** Aug 2002.

NEWGATE THEATRE NEW PLAY DEVELOPMENT

90 Armington St; Cranston, RI 02905;
  website www.newgatetheatre.org
New Works Coordinator

Open to: playwrights, solo performers. **Description:** organization providing year-round developmental services; 3-4 scripts each season receive staged reading, in some cases leading to workshop production. Test Tube Theatre Festival for playwrights interested in deeper rehearsal involvement: 3 full-length plays receive 4-5 weeks of rehearsal culminating in workshop production. **Financial arrangement:** small stipend and possible housing. **Guidelines:** playwright available for rehearsal process; full-length plays in need of development. **Application procedure:** script, resume and SASE for response. **Deadline:** 15 Oct 2001 for Test Tube Festival; 1 Feb 2002 for regular program. **Dates:** Test Tube Festival: Jan-Feb; regular program: year-round.

THE NEW HARMONY PROJECT

613 North East St; Indianapolis, IN 46202; (317) 464-1103,
  FAX 635-4201; website www.newharmonyproject.org
Anna D. Shapiro, *Artistic Director*

Open to: playwrights, composers, librettists, screenwriters, television writers. **Description:** 4-6 scripts given up to 2 weeks intensive development with professional community of directors, actors, producers, dramaturgs and musical directors. **Financial arrangement:** $400 stipend; travel, room and board. **Guidelines:** narrative works that "emphasize the dignity of the human spirit and the worth of the human experience." **Application procedure:** 10-page writing sample, project proposal and statement of artistic purpose. **Deadline:** mid-Nov 2001; exact date TBA. **Notification:** 15 Mar 2002. **Dates:** May–Jun 2002.

NEW PERSPECTIVES NEW PLAY DEVELOPMENT PROGRAM

750 Eighth Ave, #601; New York, NY 10036; (212) 730–2030,
    FAX 730–2030; email npertheat@aol.com;
    website www.newperspectivestheatre.org
Deirdre Hollman, *Literary Manager*

Open to: playwrights. **Description:** 5-10 plays chosen each year for range of developmental services from rehearsed staged readings with audience feedback to full workshop productions; development process varies according to needs of script; special interest in works by women and minority writers and/or works with a multicultural focus; annual staged reading series in May. **Financial arrangement:** free. **Guidelines:** full-length play. **Application procedure:** 15-page dialogue sample, synopsis and character breakdown. **Deadline:** ongoing. **Notification:** 2-6 months from submission date. **Dates:** year-round.

NEW VISIONS/NEW VOICES

The Kennedy Center–Youth and Family Programs; 2700 F Street NW;
    Washington, DC 20566; (202) 416–8880, FAX 416–8297;
    email yfp@kennedy–center.org
Kim Peter Kovac, *Senior Program Director*

Open to: playwrights. **Description:** biennial program; up to 8 plays given rehearsals and staged readings. **Guidelines:** unproduced plays for young and family audiences; playwright must be sponsored by theatre; call for information and application. **Financial arrangement:** small stipend. **Application procedure:** sponsoring theatre submits completed application and supporting materials. **Deadline:** 1 Oct 2001. **Notification:** 15 Jan 2002. **Dates:** May 2002.

NEW VOICES PLAY DEVELOPMENT PROGRAM

Plowshares Theatre Company; 2870 East Grand Blvd, Suite 600;
    Detroit, MI 48202–3146; (313) 872–0279, FAX 872–0067;
    email plowshares@earthlink.net; website www.plowshares.org
Gary Anderson, *Producing Artistic Director*

Open to: playwrights, solo performers. **Description:** up to 6 plays-in-progress given 2 weeks of rehearsal with professional company of actors, directors and dramaturgs, culminating in 2 staged readings followed by audience discussion; program provides marketing assistance following development; possible future full production. **Financial arrangement:** $1000 to play chosen best of festival; some travel stipends available. **Guidelines:** African-American playwright; unproduced play addressing the African-American experience. **Application procedure:** 3 copies of script, synopsis, resume and bio. **Deadline:** ongoing. **Dates:** summer 2002.

NEW YORK FOUNDATION FOR THE ARTS
FISCAL SPONSORSHIP PROGRAM

155 Avenue of the Americas, 14th Floor; New York, NY 10013-1507;
   (212) 366-6900, ext 223, FAX (646) 486-3285;
   email sponsor@nyfa.org
Mary Six Rupert, *Program Officer, Services and Technology*

Open to: playwrights, translators, composers, librettists, lyricists, solo performers, screenwriters, television and radio writers. **Description:** program provides fiscal sponsorship, financial services and technical assistance to individuals or organizations without not-for-profit status so that they can seek funds from foundations, corporations and individuals that require not-for-profit status in order to contribute funds. The program has two categories: Artists' Projects (individual artists or collaborating artists); and Emerging Organizations (emerging arts organizations in the process of obtaining not-for-profit status). Program does not offer grants or provide funding. **Financial arrangement:** as a service fee, NYFA retains a percentage of grants and contributions it receives on behalf of a project; $50-100 one-time processing fee. **Guidelines:** selection based on artistic excellence, uniqueness and fundability of project, and on artist's previous work and proven ability to complete proposed work. **Application procedure:** write for application form and guidelines. **Deadline:** Nov 2001; Mar 2002; Jul 2002; contact NYFA for exact dates. **Notification:** 6 weeks.

THE NEXT STAGE FESTIVAL OF NEW PLAYS

The Cleveland Play House; 8500 Euclid Ave;
   Cleveland, OH 44106-0189; (216) 795-7010, ext 207,
   FAX 795-7005
Seth Gordon, *Director of New Play Development*

Open to: playwrights. **Description:** annual mid-winter festival of 4-8 rehearsed readings over a 1-month period; plays receive 4-6 rehearsal days with director, dramaturg and professional cast and 2 public readings with audience discussion; at least 1 play will be fully produced in following theatre season. **Financial arrangement:** stipend, travel and housing. **Guidelines:** unproduced full-length play or musical; must give theatre 90-day option on future production. **Application procedure:** letter of inquiry, brief synopsis, 10-page dialogue sample, resume, reviews and SASP for acknowledgement of receipt; include cassestte for musicals. **Deadline:** 15 Jun 2002; no submission before 1 May 2002. **Notification:** 2-4 months. (See The Cleveland Play House in Production.)

NORTHWEST REGIONAL NEW PLAYS COMPETITION

Department of English; Montana State University;
   Bozeman, MT 59717-2300; (406) 994-3768, FAX 994-2110;
   email steen@english.montana.edu
Sara Jayne Steen, *Professor*

Open to: playwrights. **Description:** up to 3 plays given rehearsed reading followed by discussion. **Financial arrangement:** housing. **Guidelines:** unpublished play not previously produced. **Application procedure:** script, cast list, synopsis and resume. **Deadline:** Feb 2002; exact date TBA. **Notification:** Mar 2002. **Dates:** Apr 2002.

NYC PLAYWRIGHTS LAB

Box 171; Peck Slip Station; New York, NY 10272; (212) 732-1020
Dina von Zweck, *Director of New Plays*

Open to: playwrights. **Description:** 2 10-session developmental workshops each year; writers meet weekly for readings of work-in-progress and critiques. **Financial arrangement:** free. **Guidelines:** playwrights must attend all 10 workshops. **Application procedure:** send SASE for guidelines and application. **Deadline:** 1 Mar 2002. **Notification:** 1 Jun 2002. **Dates:** Mar-Jun; Sep-Dec.

OFF-OFF BROADWAY ORIGINAL SHORT PLAY FESTIVAL

45 West 25th St; New York, NY 10010-2751; (212) 206-8990,
   FAX 206-1429
Karen Keri, *Festival Coordinator*

Open to: playwrights. **Description:** festival production hosted by Love Creek Productions on Theatre Row in New York City; possible publication by Samuel French (see Publication). **Financial arrangement:** free. **Guidelines:** one-acts or segments of full-length plays less than 40 minutes long only; play must have been developed and produced by theatre, professional school or college that has playwriting program; send SASE for application after Jan 2002. **Application procedure:** no submission by playwright; completed application submitted by organization producing work. **Deadline:** Jun 2002; exact date TBA. **Notification:** within 2 weeks. **Dates:** Aug 2002.

OLD PUEBLO PLAYWRIGHTS

Box 64914; Tucson, AZ 85728; (520) 529-2937, FAX 529-2411;
    email mgoldfed@excite.com
Marc Goldfeder, *President*

Open to: playwrights, translators, screenwriters, television and radio writers. **Description:** members meet weekly to develop scripts; staged readings at annual New Play Festival in Jan. **Financial arrangement:** $36 annual dues. **Application procedure:** submit writing sample at weekly meeting. **Deadline:** ongoing. **Dates:** ongoing.

ONE ACTS IN PERFORMANCE

Polaris North, c/o Diane Martella; 1265 Broadway, Room 803;
    New York, NY 10001; (212) 684-1985
Diane Martella, *Treasurer/Co-Sponsor*

Open to: playwrights. **Description:** approximately every 2 months, 3-5 plays given brief rehearsal period, culminating in workshop production followed by informal audience discussion. **Guidelines:** unproduced one-act play not more than 30 minutes long; 4-character maximum; single set. **Financial arrangement:** free. **Application procedure:** script with SASE for response. **Deadline:** ongoing. **Notification:** 2-6 weeks. **Dates:** year-round.

O'NEILL PLAYWRIGHTS CONFERENCE

534 West 42nd St; New York, NY 10036; (212) 244-7008,
    FAX 967-2957
James Houghton, *Artistic Director*
Beth Whitaker, *Artistic Associate*

Open to: playwrights. **Description:** 4-week conference at O'Neill Theater Center, Waterford, CT; 12-15 plays developed and presented as staged readings. **Financial arrangement:** stipend, travel, room and board. **Application procedure:** send SASE for guidelines. **Deadline:** 1 Nov 2001. **Notification:** Apr 2002. **Dates:** Jun-Jul 2002.

ORANGE COUNTY PLAYWRIGHTS' ALLIANCE DEVELOPMENTAL WORKSHOP

Box 6927; Fullerton, CA 92834; (714) 850–1176, FAX 738–7833;
    website www.ocpaplaywrights.org
Eric Eberwein, *Director*

Open to: playwrights. **Description:** ongoing developmental workshop meeting every 2 weeks; up to 12 scripts each year receive staged reading or production. **Financial arrangement:** $80 annual membership fee. **Guidelines:** residents of Orange County and greater Los Angeles area only. **Application procedure:** work sample and resume. **Deadline:** ongoing. **Notification:** 2 months.

PITTSBURGH NEW WORKS FESTIVAL

Box 42419; Pittsburgh, PA 15203; (412) 881–6888;
    email info@pittsburghnewworks.org;
    website www.pittsburghnewworks.org
Tracey Taylor Perles, *President*

Open to: playwrights. **Description:** 12 plays for adult audiences and 2 for young audiences given full production and 6 given staged reading by 14 collaborating theatre companies during annual 4-week fall festival. **Financial arrangement:** $50 stipend. **Guidelines:** unproduced one-acts for young or adult audiences; no longer than 40 minutes; cast limit of 8; 1 submission limit in each category. **Application procedure:** 3 copies of script, $5 fee and SASE for response; call or visit website for guidelines. **Deadline:** 28 Apr 2002. **Notification:** mid-Jun 2002. **Dates:** Sep 2002.

PLAYFORMERS

20 Waterside Plaza, Apt 11G; New York, NY 10010; (212) 213–9835
John Fritz, *Executive Director*

Open to: playwrights. **Description:** playwrights' support group meets once a month for readings of works-in-progress and critiques. **Financial arrangement:** $15 initiation fee on acceptance; $75 annual dues. **Guidelines:** playwright invited to attend meetings as guest before applying for membership. **Application procedure:** script and resume. **Deadline:** ongoing. **Dates:** Sep-Jun.

PLAYLABS

The Playwrights' Center; 2301 Franklin Ave;
    Minneapolis, MN 55406-1099; (612) 332-7481;
    email info@pwcenter.org; website www.pwcenter.org
Megan Monaghan, *PlayLabs Artistic Director*

Open to: playwrights, solo performers. **Description:** 4-6 new works given 2 weeks of development with playwright's choice of professional director, dramaturg and Twin Cities actors, culminating in staged reading followed by audience discussion. **Financial arrangement:** honorarium, travel, housing and per diem. **Guidelines:** U.S. citizen or permanent resident; writer must be available to attend entire conference and preconference weekend; unproduced, unpublished play, solo performance piece or mixed-media piece; full-length works preferred. **Application procedure:** application and work sample; send SASE for application after 1 Oct 2001. **Deadline:** 1 Dec 2001. **Notification:** 1 May 2002. **Dates:** preconference weekend: May/Jun 2002; exact dates TBA; conference: 7-21 Jul 2002.

THE PLAY PEN

The Asylum; Box 13380; Las Vegas, NV 89112; (702) 433-6640
Chris Mann, *Artistic Director*

Open to: playwrights. **Description:** 3 times a year, 3 plays-in-progress given 1 week of rehearsal each with resident company culminating in 2 public staged readings followed by audience discussion. **Financial arrangement:** $50 stipend and housing. **Guidelines:** U.S. citizen or permanent resident; play not produced professionally. **Application procedure:** script only. **Deadline:** 31 Aug 2001. **Notification:** 31 Jan 2002. **Dates:** Dec 2001; Feb 2002; Mar 2002.

PLAYWRIGHTS' CENTER OF SAN FRANCISCO STAGED READINGS

Box 460466; San Francisco, CA 94146-0466; (415) 626-4603,
    FAX 863-0901; email playctrsf@aol.com;
    website www.playwrights.org
Sheppard B. Kominars, *Chairman of the Board*

Open to: playwrights. **Description:** developmental program meeting weekly for 1 staged reading, monthly for reading and discussion of works-in-progress. **Financial arrangement:** $55 annual membership fee; some scholarships available for students. **Application procedure:** completed application. **Deadline:** ongoing.

PLAYWRIGHTS FORUM

Box 5322; Rockville, MD 20848; (301) 816-0569;
 email pforum@erols.com;
 website www.erols.com/pforum/welcome.htm
Ernest Joselovitz, *President*

Open to: playwrights. **Description:** ongoing developmental program including 3-tier range of membership options: Forum 1, workshop program offering three 3-month sessions a year for apprentice playwrights; Forum 2, professional playwriting groups meeting biweekly; and Associate membership offering participation in many of Forum's auxiliary programs but not in workshops; depending on type of membership, members variously eligible for in-house and public readings, series of playwright-centered workshop productions, Musical Theatre Wing, mentorships, special classes, production observerships, free theatre tickets, internet activities, semiannual conference, organization's newsletter and handbook, published series of members' scripts, and a commissioning program for original plays for young audiences. **Financial arrangement:** for Forum 1, $90 per 15-week session; for Forum 2, $90 every 4 months; Associate membership $25 fee a year; financial aid available. **Guidelines:** resident of mid-Atlantic area only; for Forum 2, prefers produced playwright or former Forum 1 participant, willing to make long-term commitment; send SASE or visit website for further information. **Application procedure:** for Forum 1, send SASE or call for information; for Forum 2, script and bio; for Associate membership, send annual fee. **Deadline:** for Forum 1: 10 Sep 2001, 10 Jan 2002, 10 May 2002; for Forum 2: ongoing. **Notification:** 4 weeks.

PLAYWRIGHTS GALLERY

Abraham Goodman House: Theatre Wing; 2124 Broadway;
 Box 2700; New York, NY 10023; (212) 595-4597,
 FAX 595-6129; email savadge@juno.com
Deborah Savadge, *Coordinator*

Open to: playwrights, solo performers. **Description:** developmental workshop meeting bimonthly Sep-Jun; plays receive staged readings at 3-day festivals in fall and spring. **Financial arrangement:** playwrights share cost of space rental. **Application procedure:** 15-20 page work sample. **Deadline:** 1 Sep 2001. **Notification:** 1 Oct 2001.

PLAYWRIGHTS' KITCHEN ENSEMBLE

c/o Coronet Theatre; 368 North La Cienega; Los Angeles, CA 90048;
(310) 652-9602; FAX 652-6401
Dan Lauria, *Artistic Director*

Open to: playwrights. **Description:** 1 play per week given staged reading by celebrity actors and directors for audience including theatre, film and TV professionals. **Financial arrangement:** free. **Guidelines:** full-length play unproduced in Los Angeles. **Application procedure:** script only. **Deadline:** 31 Dec 2001; no submission before 1 Sep 2001.

PLAYWRIGHTS LAB

Pulse Ensemble Theatre; 432 West 42nd St; New York, NY 10036;
(212) 695-1596, FAX 736-1255
Brian Richardson, *Company Manager*

Open to: playwrights, solo performers, screenwriters. **Description:** 4-month workshop meeting weekly culminating in public staged reading or workshop production in either Open Pulse Arts Lab (OPAL) for one-acts or the Studio Series for full-length plays. **Guidelines:** experienced playwrights. **Financial arrangement:** $100 monthly fee. **Application procedure:** application, writing sample and professional recommendation. **Deadline:** ongoing. **Notification:** ongoing. **Dates:** year-round.

PLAYWRIGHTS' PLATFORM

164 Brayton Rd; Boston, MA 02135; (617) 630-9704;
website www.tiac.net/users/ghorton/playplat.html
Beverly Creasey, *President*

Open to: playwrights. **Description:** ongoing developmental program including weekly workshop held at Massachusetts College of Art, staged readings, summer festival of full productions, dramaturgical and referral services. **Financial arrangement:** playwright receives percentage of box office for festival productions; participants encouraged to become members of organization ($35 annual dues). **Guidelines:** MA resident available for regular meetings only; unpublished, unproduced play; write for membership information. **Application procedure:** letter of inquiry only. **Deadline:** ongoing.

PLAYWRIGHTS PROJECT

Henry Street Settlement/Abrons Arts Center; 466 Grand St;
New York, NY 10002-4804; (212) 598-0400, FAX 388-1418
Jonathon Ward, *Director of Drama Program*

Open to: playwrights. **Description:** 5-6 plays developed through staged readings, culminating in workshop production. **Financial arrangement:** $500 production budget. **Guidelines:** New York City playwrights only. **Application procedure:** first act or first 10 pages of script, synopsis, character breakdown, resume or brief bio; finalists will be interviewed. **Deadline:** ongoing. **Dates:** year-round.

PLAYWRIGHTS THEATRE OF NEW JERSEY
NEW PLAY DEVELOPMENT PROGRAM

33 Green Village Rd; Madison, NJ 07940; (973) 514-1787, ext 18
Peter Hays, *Literary Manager*

Open to: playwrights. **Description:** new plays developed through sit-down readings, staged readings and workshop productions; liaison with other producing theatres provided. **Financial arrangement:** playwright receives royalty. **Guidelines:** American playwright; unproduced play; send SASE for guidelines. **Application procedure:** 10-page dialogue sample, developmental history, if any, resume and SASP for acknowledgment of receipt. **Deadline:** 30 Apr 2002; no submission before 1 Sep 2001. **Notification:** 8 months. **Dates:** year-round.

PUERTO RICAN TRAVELING THEATRE PLAYWRIGHTS' UNIT

141 West 94th St; New York, NY 10025; (212) 354-1293,
FAX 307-6769
Allen Davis III, *Director*

Open to: playwrights, solo performers. **Description:** 7-9-month workshops comprised of 2 units, 1 for professional playwrights, 1 for beginners; weekly meetings; spring staged reading series; City "In Sight" showcase production series. **Financial arrangement:** $100 fee per workshop cycle. **Guidelines:** resident of New York City area; Latino or other minority playwright or playwright interested in multicultural theatre. **Application procedure:** for professional unit, submit full-length play; beginners contact director. **Deadline:** 30 Sep 2001. **Notification:** within 2 weeks. **Dates:** Oct 2001-Jul 2002.

REMEMBRANCE THROUGH THE PERFORMING ARTS NEW PLAY DEVELOPMENT

Box 162446; Austin, TX 78716; (512) 329-9118, FAX 329-9118;
    email RemPerArts@aol.com
Marla Dean Macdonald, *Director of New Play Development*

Open to: playwrights. **Description:** 8 playwrights chosen annually for developmental workshops, culminating in staged readings or work-in-progress productions; plays subsequently given referral to nationally recognized theatres for world premieres. **Financial arrangement:** free. **Guidelines:** resident of central TX; full-length play that has not received Equity production. **Application procedure:** script, synopsis, resume and SASE. **Deadline:** ongoing.

THE RICHARD RODGERS AWARDS

American Academy of Arts and Letters; 633 West 155th St;
    New York, NY 10032-7599; (212) 368-5900, FAX 491-4615
Richard Rodgers Awards

Open to: playwrights, composers, librettists, lyricists. **Description:** 1 or more works a year given full production, studio/lab production or staged reading by not-for-profit theatre in New York City; writer(s) participate in rehearsal process. **Financial arrangement:** free. **Guidelines:** U.S. citizen or permanent resident; new work by writer/composer not already established in musical theatre; innovative, experimental material encouraged; 1 submission limit; previous submissions ineligible. **Application procedure:** send SASE for application and information. **Deadline:** 1 Nov 2001. **Notification:** Mar 2002.

THE SCHOOLHOUSE

Owens Rd; Croton Falls, NY 10519; (914) 234-7232
Douglas Michael, *Literary Manager*

Open to: playwrights. **Description:** about 6 plays a year receive development with director and actors, culminating in public reading and possible full production; ongoing weekly writer's group. **Financial arrangement:** small fee to help offset costs. **Guidelines:** resident of Westchester or Putnam counties, NY or Fairfield County, CT, who can participate in program; prefers full-length plays. **Application procedure:** script or excerpt (at least 10 pages) and letter of inquiry. **Deadline:** ongoing. **Notification:** 1 month.

THE SCRIPTEASERS

3404 Hawk St; San Diego, CA 92103-3862; (619) 295-4040,
   FAX 299-2084
Jonathan Dunn-Rankin, *Corresponding Secretary*

Open to: playwrights, screenwriters, television writers. **Description:** writers, directors and actors meet every other Friday evening in private home for cold readings of new scripts, followed by period of constructive criticism; 1 or 2 rehearsed staged readings a year presented at local theatres as showcases. **Financial arrangement:** donations of $1 accepted at each reading. **Guidelines:** guest writer must attend at least 2 readings before submitting script; unproduced script by new or established writer who is resident of San Diego County. **Application procedure:** write or call for guidelines. **Deadline:** ongoing.

SHENANDOAH INTERNATIONAL PLAYWRIGHTS

ShenanArts; 717 Quick's Mill Rd; Staunton, VA 24401;
   (540) 248-1868, FAX 248-7728; email theatre@shenanarts.org;
   website www.shenanarts.org
Robert Graham Small, *Artistic Director*
Kathleen Tosco, *Managing Director*

Open to: playwrights, screenwriters. **Description:** 4-week retreat for 4-6 American writers and 4 international writers at Pennyroyal farm in Shenandoah Valley; program geared to facilitate major rewrite or new draft of existing script; personal writing balanced by workshops and staged readings with professional company of dramaturgs, directors and actors. **Financial arrangement:** travel, room and board. **Guidelines:** competitive admission based on submitted work. **Application procedure:** 2 copies of completed draft of script to be worked on at retreat; personal statement of applicant's background as a writer; SASP for acknowledgment of receipt; write or call for guidelines. **Deadline:** 1 Feb 2002. **Notification:** after 10 Jun 2002. **Dates:** Jul-Aug 2002.

SIRENS ONE ACT FESTIVAL

Muse of Fire Theatre Company; Box 20875; Columbus Circle Station;
   New York, NY 10023; (212) 397-2757, FAX 397-2757;
   musevfire@aol.com; website www.museoffiretheatreco.org
Glenn English, *Co-Artistic Director*

Open to: playwrights, solo performers. **Description:** 4-6 projects developed in 4-week rehearsal period with resident company of actors and directors; 2-

week workshop production for invited industry audience and general public; Festival judged by independent panel of jurors; writers may be invited to join Muse Writers Workshop. **Financial arrangement:** 1st place winner receives $100. **Guidelines:** American women playwrights only; unproduced one-acts no longer than 60 minutes with modest production elements and cast limit of 8. **Application Procedure:** script, resume, development history, letter of inquiry and $10 fee. **Deadline:** 1 Feb 2002. **Notification:** 1 Mar 2002. **Dates:** spring; exact date TBA. (See Muse of Fire in Membership and Service Organizations.)

SOUTHERN APPALACHIAN PLAYWRIGHTS' CONFERENCE

Southern Appalachian Repertory Theatre; Box 1720;
  Mars Hill, NC 28754; (828) 689–1384, FAX 689–1272;
  email sart@mhc.edu; website www.sartheatre.com
Bill Gregg, *Artistic Director*

Open to: playwrights, composers, librettists, lyricists. **Description:** up to 5 writers selected to participate in annual 3-day spring conference at which 1 work by each writer is given reading and critiqued by panel of theatre professionals; 1 work may be selected for production as part of summer 2002 season. **Financial arrangement:** room and board; writer of work selected for production receives $500 honorarium. **Guidelines:** unproduced, unpublished full-length play or musical; works that explore South Appalachian life, traditions and culture encouraged. **Application procedure:** script with synopsis, character breakdown and resume. **Deadline:** 31 Oct 2001. **Dates:** 22-24 2002.

SOUTHWEST FESTIVAL FOR NEW PLAYS

Stages Repertory Theatre; 3201 Allen Pkwy, #101;
  Houston, TX 77019–1897; (713) 527–0240, FAX 527–8669
Kent Davidson, *Festival Coordinator*
  (Also see entry in Production)

CHILDREN'S THEATRE PLAYWRIGHTS' DIVISION

Open to: playwrights. **Description:** 2 plays chosen for development with actors and director over period of 1 week, culminating in staged reading for 1st place and concert reading for 2nd. **Financial arrangement:** stipend, contingent on funding. **Guidelines:** play for 4-10-year-old audience to be performed by adult actors; maximum 50 minutes long; cast limit of 8; play not produced professionally. **Application procedure:** script only; author's name should not appear on script; include title page with author info.

Deadline: 14 Feb 2002; no submission before 1 Oct 2001. **Notification:** May 2002. **Dates:** Jun 2002.

LATINO PLAYWRIGHTS' DIVISION

Open to: playwrights. **Description:** 2 plays chosen for development with professional actors and director over period of 1 week, culminating in staged reading for 1st place and concert reading for 2nd. **Financial arrangement:** stipend, contingent on funding. **Guidelines:** Latino playwright; play written in Spanish must be sent with English translation; play not produced professionally. **Application procedure:** script only; author's name should not appear on script; include title page with author info. **Deadline:** 14 Feb 2002; no submission before 1 Oct 2001. **Notification:** May 2002. **Dates:** Jun 2002.

TEXAS PLAYWRIGHTS' DIVISION

Open to: playwrights. **Description:** 2 plays chosen for development with dramaturg, director and actors over period of 1 week, culminating in staged reading for 1st place and concert reading for 2nd. **Financial arrangement:** stipend, contingent on funding. **Guidelines:** TX native or resident or non-TX playwright writing on TX theme; play not produced professionally; prefers small cast. **Application procedure:** script only; author's name should not appear on script; include title page with author info. **Deadline:** 14 Feb 2002; no submission before 1 Oct 2001. **Notification:** May 2002. **Dates:** Jun 2002.

WOMEN'S PLAYWRIGHTS' DIVISION

Open to: playwrights. **Description:** 2 plays chosen for development with professional actors and director over period of 1 week, culminating in staged reading for 1st place and concert reading for 2nd. **Financial arrangement:** stipend, contingent on funding. **Guidelines:** woman playwright; play not produced professionally. **Application procedure:** script only; author's name should not appear on script; include title page with author info. **Deadline:** 14 Feb 2002; no submission before 1 Oct 2001. **Notification:** May 2002. **Dates:** Jun 2002.

STREISAND FESTIVAL OF NEW JEWISH PLAYS

c/o San Diego Center for Jewish Culture; The Lawrence Family JCC;
　4126 Executive Dr; La Jolla, CA 92037;
　(858) 457–3161, ext 1155, FAX 457–2422;
　email sdcjc@lfjcc.com
D. Candis Paule, *Artistic Director*

Open to: playwrights, composers, librettists, lyricists. **Description:** 4 plays receive 3 days of rehearsal, culminating in staged reading followed by audience discussion; possible future full production. **Financial arrangement:** travel and housing. **Guidelines:** play or musical with Jewish content or theme. **Application procedure:** 3 copies of script and resume. **Deadline:** 1 Dec 2001. **Notification:** Apr 2002. **Dates:** Jun 2002.

SummerNITE

School of Theatre, Stevens Bldg; Northern Illinois University;
　DeKalb, IL 60115–2854; (815) 753–8258, FAX 753–8415
Christopher Markle, *Artistic Director*

Open to: playwrights. **Description:** 2 plays chosen for full production; some plays chosen for periodic staged readings. **Financial arrangement:** royalties for plays chosen for production. **Guidelines:** special interest in large-cast full-length plays or translations not previously produced in Chicago area. **Application procedure:** agent submission. **Deadline:** ongoing. **Notification:** 2 months. **Dates:** May–Aug 2002.

THE SUNDANCE INSTITUTE FEATURE FILM PROGRAM

8857 West Olympic Blvd; Beverly Hills, CA 90211; (310) 360–1981,
　FAX 360–1969; website www.sundance.org

Open to: playwrights, screenwriters, filmmaking teams (e.g., writer/director). **Description:** program includes 5-day Screenwriters Labs each Jan and Jun offering participants one-on-one problem-solving sessions with professional screenwriters; 3-week Filmmakers Lab in Jun in which projects are explored through work with directors, writers, actors, cinematographers, producers, editors and other resource personnel; network/advisory service offers practical and creative assistance to selected projects. **Financial arrangement:** travel, room and board for at least 1 writer/filmmaker per project; possible room and board for additional members of team. **Guidelines:** "compelling, original, narrative feature film scripts (they can be based on a true story or be adaptations of plays, novels, short stories, etc.) which represent the unique vision of the writer and/or director"; special interest in supporting new talent and artists in transition (e.g., theatre artist who wants to work in film, writer who wants to direct); send SASE for guidelines. **Application procedure:** application, cover letter, first 5 pages of screenplay, synopsis, bios of project participants and $30 fee; applicants who pass 1st round of selection will be asked to send full screenplay. **Deadline**: 4 May 2002. **Notification:** Jul 2002.

THE SUNDANCE THEATRE LABORATORY

8857 West Olympic Blvd; Beverly Hills, CA 90211; (310) 360–1981, FAX 360–1975; email philip_himberg@sundance.org; website www.sundance.org
Philip Himberg, *Artistic Director, Sundance Theatre*
Robert Blacker, *Artistic Director, Sundance Theatre Lab*

Open to: playwrights, solo performers. **Description:** 8-10 scripts workshopped for 20 days. **Financial arrangement:** honorarium, travel, room and board. **Guidelines:** full-length play, new adaptation and/or translation of classic material, musical, play for young audiences, solo piece; playwright-director teams encouraged. **Application procedure:** send SASE for guidelines and application. **Deadline:** 15 Dec 2001. **Notification:** Apr 2002. **Dates:** Jul 2002.

THE TEN-MINUTE MUSICALS PROJECT

Box 461194; West Hollywood, CA 90046
Michael Koppy, *Producer*

Open to: composers, librettists, lyricists, solo performers. **Description:** up to 10 brief pieces selected during annual cycle for possible inclusion in full-length anthology-musicals to be produced at Equity theatres in U.S. and Canada; occasionally some pieces workshopped using professional actors and director. **Financial arrangement:** $250 royalty advance with equal share of licensing royalties when produced. **Guidelines:** complete work with a definite beginning, middle and end, 7-14 minutes long, in any musical style or genre; adaptations of strongly structured material in the public domain, or for which rights have been obtained, are encouraged; cast of 2-10, prefers 6-10; write for guidelines. **Application procedure:** script, lead sheets and cassette of sung material. **Deadline:** 31 Aug 2002. **Notification:** 30 Nov 2002.

THEATRE WEST WRITERS WORKSHOP

3333 Cahuenga Blvd W; Los Angeles, CA 90068; (323) 851-4839,
   FAX 851-5286; website www.theatrewest.org
Doug Haverty and Chris DiGiovanni, *Moderators*

Open to: playwrights, translators, librettists, lyricists. **Description:** weekly development workshop presenting 2 staged readings a year and limited run workshop productions. **Financial arrangement:** $40 monthly fee. **Guidelines:** full-length plays, translators, adaptations and plays for young audiences; large-cast works encouraged. **Application procedure:** script and resume with SASE for response. **Deadline:** ongoing. **Notification:** 4 months. **Dates:** ongoing.

THEATREWORKS/USA COMMISSIONING PROGRAM

Theatreworks/USA; 151 West 26th St, 7th Floor; New York, NY
   10001; (212) 647-1100, FAX 924-5377;
   email info@theatreworksusa.org;
   website www.theatreworksusa.org
Barbara Pasternack, *Artistic Director*

Open to: composers, librettists, lyricists. **Description:** step commissioning process, possibly leading to 2-week developmental workshop and production. **Financial arrangement:** free. **Guidelines:** works dealing with issues relevant to youth audiences K-12; special interest in historical/biographical subject matter and musical adaptations of fairy tales and traditional or contemporary classics; 1 hour long; cast of 5-6 actors, set suitable for touring. **Application procedure:** prefers treatment with sample scenes, lyric sheets and cassette or CD of music; will accept script only. **Deadline:** ongoing. **Notification:** 6 months.

THROUGH HER EYES: WOMEN OF COLOR ARTS FESTIVAL

Women of Color Productions; 545 8th Ave, Suite 402;
   New York, NY 10018; (212) 501-3842;
   email jackiewade10@hotmail.com
Jacqueline Wade, *Executive Producer*

Open to: playwrights, composers, librettists, lyricists, screenwriters, solo performers, performance artists. **Description:** annual 4-week festival held at various venues throughout New York City; 3 producing levels: Tier 1, 10 guest artists receive $300-600 honorarium, rehearsal space, minimal technical staff and marketing support; Tier 2, some artists receive rehearsal space, minimal technical staff and marketing support; Tier 3, 40 artists contribute to production cost, receive percentage of ticket sales, marketing support and 10-15 hours rehearsal time; additional reading series and special presentation of work by playwrights ages 11-18. **Financial arrangement:** $10 fee per submission for reading series; $35 fee per submission for Festival. **Guidelines:** prefers woman playwright of color or any writer whose work features female characters of color; special interest in one-acts, plays for young audiences. **Application procedure:** application, 2 copies of script, 1-page synopsis, professional recommendation, character breakdown, resume with SASE; write for application and guidelines. **Deadline:** ongoing for reading series; 1 Nov 2001 for Festival. **Notification:** ongoing for reading series; 15 Dec 2001 for Festival. **Dates:** Mar-Apr 2002.

THE TUESDAY GROUP

321 West 24th St, #16E; New York, NY 10011; (212) 645-3143
Larry Kunofsky, *Coordinator*

Open to: playwrights. **Description:** group meets every 2 weeks to read and discuss members' works; some plays workshopped with resident directors and ensemble. **Financial arrangement:** $60 fee per trimester. **Guidelines:** New York City playwright. **Application procedure:** writing sample and letter of inquiry with SASE for response. **Deadline:** ongoing. **Notification:** 2 months.

UNIVERSITY OF ALABAMA NEW PLAYWRIGHTS' PROGRAM

Department of Theatre and Dance; University of Alabama;
  Box 870239; Tuscaloosa, AL 35487-0239; (205) 348-9032,
  FAX 348-9048; email pcastagn@woodsquad.as.ua.edu;
  website www.as.ua.edu/theatre/npp.htm
Paul C. Castagno, *Director and Dramaturg*

Open to: playwrights, composers, librettists, lyricists, solo performers. **Description:** opportunity for writer to develop unproduced script or to pursue further development of produced work, culminating in full production; writer may visit campus several times during rehearsal process and is required to offer limited playwriting workshops during visit(s). **Financial arrangement:** substantial stipend, travel and expenses. **Guidelines:** writer with some previous experience and script that has had some development; special interest in works with Southern themes. **Application procedure:** script or synopsis and letter of inquiry. **Deadline:** submit Aug-Mar only. **Notification:** 6 months. **Dates:** fall-spring. **Special programs:** department will also consider one-acts for festival by its directing students and writers' proposals for workshops with its playwriting and acting students; submit by 1 Oct for Janusfest, a festival of new full-length plays.

THE WATERFRONT ENSEMBLE, INC.

Box 1486; Hoboken, NJ 07030; (201) 963-2235;
email info@waterfrontensemble.org;
website www.waterfrontensemble.org
Jason Grote, *Literary Manager*

Open to: playwrights, translators, solo performers. **Description:** playwright-driven company of actors, directors and playwrights that meets weekly to work on new plays in preparation for productions in New York and New Jersey; 25 one-acts and 3 full-length plays produced each year. **Financial arrangement:** $75 membership fee per year; $25 for 2 months (suggested donation). **Guidelines:** NY/NJ-area playwright. **Application procedure:** up to 30-page writing sample and resume. **Deadline:** ongoing. **Notification:** 4-12 months. **Dates:** year-round. **Special programs:** New Jersey All Ages Playwright Festival, *deadline:* 31 Mar 2002; *dates:* Jun 2002; call or write for more information.

WESTBETH NEW WORKS PROGRAM

Westbeth Theatre Center; 151 Bank St; New York, NY 10014;
(212) 691-2272, FAX 924-7185; email wbethzach@aol.com;
website www.westbeththeatre.com
Zachary Morris, *Program Curator*

Open to: playwrights, composers, solo performers, performance artists. **Description:** developmental program where artists develop ideas into fully realized pieces with feedback from Westbeth production team. **Financial arrangement:** free. **Guidelines:** resident of NY metropolitan area; urban, contemporary, nontraditional and interdisciplinary work preferred; send SASE for guidelines. **Application procedure:** no unsolicited scripts; 1-page synopsis, character breakdown, resume and SASE for response. **Deadline:** ongoing. **Notification:** 4 months. (See Westbeth Theatre Center in Production.)

WILLIAMSTOWN THEATRE FESTIVAL

229 West 42nd St, Suite 801; New York, NY 10036 (212) 395-9090,
FAX 395-9099; website www.wtfestival.org
Michael Ritchie, *Producer*

Open to: playwrights, composers, librettists, lyricists. **Description:** 4 plays each season given public reading. **Financial arrangement:** stipend, travel and housing. **Guidelines:** American playwright; play not professionally produced. **Application procedure:** agent submission only. **Deadline:** 15 Feb 2002; no submission before 1 Oct 2001.

WOMEN AT THE DOOR STAGED READING SERIES (9TH ANNUAL)

Famous Door Theatre; Box 57029; Chicago, IL 60657;
   (773) 404–8283, FAX 404–8292;
   email theatre@famousdoortheatre.org;
   website www.famousdoortheatre.org
Carson Becker, *Producer*

Open to: playwrights. **Description:** 4 plays receive 3-4 rehearsals culminating in professional staged readings; plays considered for subsequent workshop and/or mainstage production. **Guidelines:** woman playwright; unproduced full-length play; 1 submission limit; no musicals or adaptations. **Financial arrangement:** $750 stipend; travel and housing for out-of-town playwrights. **Application procedure:** 1-page synopsis, 10-15 page dialogue sample and resume. **Deadline:** 31 Oct 2000. **Notification:** finalists: 31 Dec 2001; winners: 28 Feb 2002. **Dates:** spring 2002.

WOMEN PLAYWRIGHTS PROJECT

Centenary Stage Company; 400 Jefferson St;
   Hackettstown, NJ 07840; (908) 979–0900, FAX 813–1984
Catherine Rust, *Project Director*

Open to: playwrights. **Description:** 1 play given 1 week of rehearsal with professional actors and director, followed by staged reading and possible mainstage production. **Financial arrangement:** $150-200 honorarium; travel, room and board. **Guidelines:** woman playwright; full-length play preferred. **Application procedure:** script only; script will not be returned. **Deadline:** 1 Nov 2001. **Notification:** 1 Jan 2002. **Dates:** Mar 2002.

WOMEN'S WORK PROJECT

New Perspectives Theatre Company; 750 Eighth Ave, Suite 601;
   New York, NY 10036; (212) 730–2030, FAX 730–2030;
   email npertheat@aol.com;
   website www.newperspectivestheatre.org
Miriam Eusebio, *Women's Work Director*

Open to: playwrights. **Description:** 2 playwrights chosen for 6-9 month residency to develop full-length play. **Financial arrangement:** free. **Guidelines:** woman playwright; special interest in works by writers of color; unproduced full-length play; call for application and guidelines. **Application procedure:** application and script. **Deadline:** 15 May 2002. **Notification:** 15 Aug 2002. **Dates:** year-round.

THE YOUNG PLAYWRIGHTS URBAN RETREAT

Young Playwrights Inc.; 321 West 44th St, Suite 906;
New York, NY 10036; (212) 307–1140, FAX 307–1454;
email writeaplay@aol.com; website youngplaywrights.org
Coordinator

Open to: playwrights. **Description:** 1-week New York City retreat for young playwrights; guest lectures by prominent American playwrights; one-on-one sessions with teaching artists; 3 intensive daily writing workshops; viewing of Broadway and Off-Broadway plays; development of new short play for public performance with professional actors and director. **Financial arrangement:** $1,250 tuition includes meals, transportation in NYC, supervised housing and theatre tickets; limited financial aid available. **Guidelines:** playwright aged 14–21. **Application procedure:** completed application, writing sample, recommendation from teacher or mentor and $100 fee (applied to tuition; refundable if applicant does not attend); call for application. **Deadline:** 1 Apr 2002. **Dates:** 14–22 Jul 2002.

PART 2

CAREER

OPPORTUNITIES

Agents

Fellowships and Grants

Emergency Funds

State Arts Agencies

Colonies and Residencies

Membership and Service Organizations

AGENTS

I'm wondering whether or not I should have an agent. Where can I get information to help me decide?

Send a check or money order for $7 and a 55¢ SASE to the Association of Authors' Representatives, Box 237201, Ansonia Station, New York, NY 10023, to receive their brochure which describes the role of the literary agent, the canon of ethics, and which contains their membership list. The list may be found at AAR's website: www.AAR-online.org. Also, see Useful Publications for books you may consult on the subject, ask your fellow playwrights, look at copies of scripts for the names of agents and make an intelligent guess as to whether they would be interested in representing your work.

How do I select the names of appropriate agents to contact?

All of the agents listed here represent playwrights. The Dramatists Guild also has a list of agents available to its members, and provides advice on relationships with agents (see Membership and Service Organizations). You may come across names that appear on none of these lists, but be wary, especially if someone tries to charge you a fee to read your script.

How do I approach an agent?

Do not telephone, do not drop in, do not send manuscripts. Write a brief letter describing your work and asking if the agent would like to see a script. Enclose your professional resume; it should show that you have had work produced or published, and make clear that you look at writing as an ongoing career, not an occasional hobby. If you're a beginning writer who's just finished your first play, you'd probably do better to work on getting a production rather than an agent.

ABRAMS ARTISTS AGENCY

275 7th Ave, 26th Floor; New York, NY 10001; (646) 486-4600
Charmaine Ferenczi, John B. Santoianni, Jack Tantleff, *Agents*

ALAN BRODIE REPRESENTATION LTD.

211 Piccadilly; London W1J 9HF; England; 44-207-917-2871
Alan Brodie, Sarah McNair, *Agents*

ANN ELMO AGENCY

60 East 42nd St; New York, NY 10165; (212) 661-2880
Mari Cronin, Letti Lee, *Agents*

THE BARBARA HOGENSON AGENCY, INC.

165 West End Ave, Suite 19C; New York, NY 10023; (212) 874-8084
Barbara Hogenson, *Agent*

BERMAN, BOALS, & FLYNN, INC.
A TALENT & LITERARY AGENCY

208 West 30th St, Suite 401; New York, NY 10001; (212) 868-1068
Judy Boals, Jim Flynn, *Agents*

THE BETHEL AGENCY

311 West 43rd St, Suite 602; New York, NY 10036; (212) 664-0455
Lewis Chambers, *Agent*

BRET ADAMS LTD.

448 West 44th St; New York, NY 10036; (212) 765-5630
Bret Adams, Melissa Hardey, Bruce Ostler, *Agents*

DON BUCHWALD & ASSOCIATES

10 East 44th St; New York, NY 10017; (212) 867-1200
John Ufland, *Agent*

DOUGLAS & KOPELMAN ARTISTS, INC.

(Formerly Flora Roberts)
393 West 49th St, Suite 5G; New York, NY 10019; (212) 445-0160
Sarah Douglas, Charles Kopelman, *Agents*

THE DRAMATIC PUBLISHING COMPANY

311 Washington St; Box 129; Woodstock, IL 60098; (815) 338-7170
Linda Habjan, *Agent*

DUVA-FLACK ASSOCIATES, INC.

200 West 57th St, Suite 1008; New York, NY 10019; (212) 957-9600
Robert Duva, *Agent*

FARBER LITERARY AGENCY

14 East 75th St, 2E; New York, NY 10021; (212) 861-7075
Ann Farber, Seth Farber, *Agents*

FIFI OSCARD ASSOCIATES

24 West 40th St, 17th Floor; New York, NY 10018; (212) 764-1100
Carolyn French, Carmen LaVia, Kevin McShane, Fifi Oscard,
Peter Sawyer, *Agents*

GAGE GROUP

9255 Sunset Blvd, Suite 515; Los Angeles, CA 90069; (310) 859-8777;
315 West 57th St, Suite 408; New York, NY 10019; (212) 541-5250
Martin Gage, *Agent*

THE GERSH AGENCY

130 West 42nd St, Suite 2400; New York, NY 10036; (212) 997-1818
John Buzzetti, Peter Hagan, Mike Lubin, Scott Yoselow, *Agents*

GRAHAM AGENCY

311 West 43rd St; New York, NY 10036; (212) 489-7730
Earl Graham, *Agent*

GSK AND ASSOCIATES

6399 Wilshire, Suite 414; Los Angeles, CA 90048; (323) 782-1854
Don Kopaloff, *Agent*

HARDEN-CURTIS ASSOCIATES

850 Seventh Ave, Suite 405; New York, NY 10019; (212) 977-8502
Mary Harden, *Agent*

HAROLD MATSON COMPANY, INC.

276 Fifth Ave; New York, NY 10001; (212) 679-4490
Ben Camardi, Jonathan Matson, *Agents*

HELEN MERRILL LTD.

295 Lafayette St, Suite 915; New York, NY 10012; (212) 226-5015
Beth Blickers, Patrick Herold, Morgan Jenness, *Agents*

INTERNATIONAL CREATIVE MANAGEMENT

40 West 57th St; New York, NY 10019; (212) 556-5600
Mitch Douglas, Sarah Jane Leigh, *Agents*

THE JOYCE KETAY AGENCY

1501 Broadway, Suite 1908; New York, NY 10036; (212) 354-6825
Joyce P. Ketay, Carl Mulert, Wendy Streeter, *Agents*

THE LANTZ OFFICE

200 West 57th St, Suite 503; New York, NY 10019; (212) 586-0200
Robert Lantz, *Agent*

THE MARTON AGENCY

1 Union Square, Room 612; New York, NY 10003-3303; (212) 255-1908
Tonda Marton, *Agent*

PARAMUSE ARTISTS ASSOCIATES, INC.

25 Central Park W; New York, NY 10023; (212) 758-5055
Mike Sbabo, *Agent*

PEREGRINE WHITTLESEY AGENCY

345 East 80th St, #31F; New York, NY 10021; (212) 737-0153
Peregrine Whittlesey, *Agent*

PINDER LANE & GARON-BROOKE ASSOCIATES

159 West 53rd St; New York, NY 10019; (212) 489-0880
Dick Duane, Robert Thixton, *Agents*

ROBERT A. FREEDMAN DRAMATIC AGENCY

1501 Broadway, Suite 2310; New York, NY 10036; (212) 840-5760
Robert A. Freedman, Selma Luttinger, Marta Praeger, *Agents*

ROSENSTONE/WENDER

3 East 48th St, 4th Floor; New York, NY 10017; (212) 832-8330
Ronald Gwiazda, Howard Rosenstone, Phyllis Wender, *Agents*

SAMUEL FRENCH

45 West 25th St; New York, NY 10010-2751; (212) 206-8990

SHUKAT COMPANY, LTD.

340 West 55th St, Suite 1A; New York, NY 10019; (212) 582-7614
Maribel Rivas, Scott Shukat, Lysna Scriven-Marzani, *Managers*

STEPHEN PEVNER, INC.

8 St. Marks Place, Suite 1A; New York, NY 10003; (212) 496-0474
Stephen Pevner, *Producer*

THE SUSAN GURMAN AGENCY

865 West End Ave, #15A; New York, NY 10025; (212) 749-4618
Gail Eisenberg, Susan Gurman, *Agents*

SUSAN SCHULMAN A LITERARY AGENCY

454 West 44th St; New York, NY 10036; (212) 713-1633

WILLIAM MORRIS AGENCY

1325 Ave of the Americas; New York, NY 10019; (212) 586-5100
Peter Franklin, David Kalodner, George Lane, Owen Laster, Biff Liff, Roland
Scahill, Mark Surjas, Susan Weaving, *Agents*

WRITERS & ARTISTS AGENCY

19 West 44th St, Suite 1000; New York, NY 10036; (212) 391-1112
William Craver, Nicole Graham, *Agents*

FELLOWSHIPS AND GRANTS

Can I apply directly to all the programs listed in this section?

No. A number of the grant programs we list must be applied to by a producing or presenting organization. However, you should be aware that these programs exist so that you can bring them to the attention of organizations with which you have a working relationship. All or most of the funds disbursed benefit the individual artist by covering commissioning fees, residencies and other expenses related to the creation of new works.

How can I enhance my chances of winning an award?

Apply for as many awards for which you qualify; once you have written the first grant proposal, you can often, with little additional work, adapt it to fit other guidelines. Start early. This is so important that we give full listings to the increasing number of awards offered in alternate years, even when the deadline falls outside the period this *Sourcebook* covers. Use the Submission Calendar in the back of this book to help you plan your campaign. In the case of all awards for which you can apply directly, write for guidelines and application forms months ahead. Study the guidelines carefully and follow them meticulously. Don't hesitate to ask for advice and assistance from the organization to which you are applying. Submit a well-thought-out, clearly written, neatly typed application—and make sure it arrives in the organization's office by the deadline. (Never assume, without checking, that the deadline is the postmark date.)

THE ALFRED HODDER FELLOWSHIP
The Council of the Humanities; Joseph Henry House;
    Princeton University; Princeton, NJ 08544-5264;
    (609) 258-4717, FAX 258-2783;
    website www.princeton.edu/~humcounc

Open to: playwrights, translators. **Frequency:** annual. **Remuneration:** $48,000 (approx) fellowship. **Guidelines:** emerging artist; writer spends academic year at Princeton pursuing independent project; prefers writer outside of academia. **Application procedure:** maximum 10-page work sample (materials will not be returned), 2-3 page project proposal and resume; send SASE for guidelines. **Deadline:** 1 Nov 2001.

THE AMERICAN-SCANDINAVIAN FOUNDATION
58 Park Ave; New York, NY 10016; (212) 879-9779, FAX 249-3444;
    email grants@amscan.org; website www.amscan.org
Fellowship Program

Open to: playwrights, translators, composers, librettists, lyricists. **Frequency:** annual. **Remuneration:** $3000-18,000. **Guidelines:** U.S. citizen or permanent resident with undergraduate degree; grants and fellowships for research and study in Scandinavian countries. **Application procedure:** application, supplementary materials and $10 fee. **Deadline:** 1 Nov 2001. **Notification:** Mar 2002.

ARIZONA COMMISSION ON THE ARTS
PERFORMING ARTS FELLOWSHIP
417 West Roosevelt St; Phoenix, AZ 85003; (602) 255-5882,
    FAX 256-0282; email general@arizonaarts.org;
    website www.arizonaarts.org
Claire West, *Performing Arts Director*

Open to: playwrights, composers. **Frequency:** award rotates triennially among disciplines. **Remuneration:** $5000 fellowship. **Guidelines:** AZ resident 18 years of age or older who is not enrolled for more than 3 credit hours at college or university; send SASE for guidelines and application. **Application procedure:** application and work sample. **Deadline:** 13 Sep 2001. **Notification:** Mar 2002.

ARTISTS-IN-BERLIN PROGRAMME

To obtain application only:
> German Academic Exchange Service (DAAD); 950 Third Ave,
> 19th Floor; New York, NY 10022; (212) 758-3223,
> FAX 755-5780; email daadny@daad.org; website www.daad.org

All applications and inquiries to:
> Deutscher Akademischer Austauschdienst (DAAD);
> Markgrafenstr 37/Taubenstr 30; D-10117 Berlin, Germany;
> 49-030-202-2080, FAX 49-030-204-1267;
> email bkp.berlin@daad.de;
> website www.daad.de/berlin/

Open to: playwrights, composers. **Frequency:** annual. **Remuneration:** monthly grant to cover living costs and rent during 1-year residency in Berlin (6 months in exceptional cases); workspace provided or paid for; travel for writer and any members of immediate family who will be staying in Berlin for period of residency; health and accident insurance; in some cases specific projects such as readings or publications can be subsidized. **Guidelines:** to enable 15-20 internationally known and qualified young artists to pursue own work while participating in city's cultural life and making contact with local artists; must reside in Berlin for period of grant; German nationals and foreign writers who are resident in Germany ineligible; write for guidelines or download from web. **Application procedure:** application, samples of published work (no manuscripts), preferably in German, otherwise in English or French, for playwrights; scores, records, tapes or published work for composers. **Deadline:** 31 Dec 2001. **Notification:** Spring 2002. **Dates:** residency begins between 1 Jan and 30 Jun 2003.

ARTIST TRUST

1402 Third Ave, Suite 404; Seattle, WA 98101-2118;
> (206) 467-8734, FAX 467-9633; email info@artisttrust.org;
> website www.artisttrust.org

Heather Dwyer, *Program Director*

FELLOWSHIPS

Open to: playwrights, composers, librettists, lyricists, screenwriters, radio and television writers. **Frequency:** award rotates among disciplines. **Remuneration:** $5500 award. **Guidelines:** WA resident only; practicing professional artist of exceptional talent and demonstrated ability; award based on creative excellence and continuing dedication to an artistic discipline; send SASE for guidelines (available mid-Apr). **Application procedure:** application and work sample. **Deadline:** mid-Jun, exact date TBA (16 Jun in 2001) for composers, librettists, lyricists, screenwriters, radio and television writers; mid-Jun 2002; exact date TBA, for playwrights.

GAP (GRANTS FOR ARTIST PROJECTS)

Open to: playwrights, composers, librettists, lyricists, screenwriters, radio and television writers. **Frequency:** annual. **Remuneration:** grant up to $1400. **Guidelines:** WA resident only; grant provides support for artist-generated projects which can include (but is not limited to) the development, presentation or completion of new work; award based on quality of work as represented by supporting material and on creativity and feasibility of proposed project; send SASE for guidelines (available Dec 2001). **Application procedure:** application and work sample. **Deadline:** 22 Feb 2002.

ARTS INTERNATIONAL/THE FUND FOR U.S. ARTISTS AT INTERNATIONAL FESTIVALS AND EXHIBITIONS

251 Park Ave S, 5th Floor; New York, NY 10010; (212) 674-9744, FAX 674-9092; email thefund@artsinternational.org; website www.artsinternational.org/programs/index.htm
Kay Takeda, *Program Manager*

Open to: performing artists and organizations. **Frequency:** triannual. **Remuneration:** grants of up to $25,000 (most grants $1000-10,000) to cover expenses related to festival participation including travel, lodging, artist's fees and per diem. **Guidelines:** U.S. citizen or permanent resident who has been invited to international festival. **Application procedure:** application, work sample, proposal, bio, copy of invitation from festival, full budget showing all costs of participation in festival and festival's contribution to these costs. **Deadline:** 5 Sep 2001; 16 Jan 2002; 2 May 2002. **Notification:** 2 months. (See National Endowment for the Arts International Partnerships in this section.)

ASIAN CULTURAL COUNCIL

437 Madison Ave, 37th Floor; New York, NY 10022-7001; (212) 812-4300, FAX 812-4299; email acc@accny.org; website www.asianculturalcouncil.org

ACC RESIDENCY PROGRAM IN ASIA

Open to: playwrights, composers, librettists, lyricists. **Frequency:** annual.

Remuneration: amount varies. **Guidelines:** to support American artists, scholars and specialists undertaking collaborative research, teaching or creative residencies at cultural and educational institutions in East and Southeast Asia. **Application procedure:** write for application, include project description. **Deadline:** 1 Feb 2002; Aug 2003 (if funds remain).

JAPAN-UNITED STATES ARTS PROGRAM

Open to: playwrights, composers, librettists, lyricists. **Frequency:** annual. **Remuneration:** amount varies. **Guidelines:** to support residencies in Japan for American artists for a variety of purposes, including creative activities (other than performances), research projects, professional observation tours and specialized training. **Application procedure:** write for application, include project description. **Deadline:** 1 Feb 2002.

ATLANTA BUREAU OF CULTURAL AFFAIRS ARTISTS PROJECT

675 Ponce de Leon Ave; Atlanta, GA 30308; (404) 817–6815,
     FAX 817–6827; email bcacas@mindspring.com;
     website www.bcaatlanta.org
Camille Russell Love, *Director*

Open to: playwrights, composers, librettists, lyricists. **Frequency:** annual. **Remuneration:** grant up to $4000. **Guidelines:** practicing professional artist; Atlanta resident for at least 1 year prior to deadline. **Application procedure:** write for guidelines and application. **Deadline:** 14 Dec 2001. **Notification:** Mar 2002.

AURAND HARRIS CHILDREN'S THEATRE GRANTS AND FELLOWSHIPS

The Children's Theatre Foundation of America; Box 8067;
     New Orleans, LA 70182; (504) 897–1839
Orlin Corey, *President*
(See listing for The Children's Theatre Foundation of America in Membership and Service Organizations)

FELLOWSHIPS

Open to: playwrights. **Frequency:** annual. **Remuneration:** $2500 maximum award. **Guidelines:** U.S. resident; funds to be used for specific projects or professional development of theatre artists who work in the area of children's theatre. **Application procedure:** write for guidelines. **Deadline:** 1 May 2002. **Notification:** 1 Sep 2002.

GRANTS

Open to: not-for-profit theatres. **Frequency:** annual. **Remuneration:** grant up to $3000. **Guidelines:** grant to assist in production costs of premiere of new play for children including expenses to enable playwright to participate in rehearsals and attend performances. **Application procedure:** write for guidelines. **Deadline:** 1 May 2002. **Notification:** 1 Sep 2002.

BUSH ARTIST FELLOWS PROGRAM

Bush Foundation; 332 Minnesota St, E–900; St. Paul, MN 55101;
(651) 227–5222; website www.bushfoundation.org
Julie Dalgleish, *Program Director*

Open to: playwrights, composers, screenwriters. **Frequency:** award rotates biennially among disciplines. **Remuneration:** $40,000 in equal monthly installments for 12-18 months. **Guidelines:** MN, ND, SD or western WI resident at least 25 years old who is not a student; playwright must have had at least 1 play given full production or workshop production for which admission was charged; screenwriter must have had 1 public staged reading or workshop production for which admission was charged, or screenplay sale or option. **Application procedure:** write for guidelines and application. **Deadline:** next deadline for playwrights, composers and screenwriters Oct 2002; exact date TBA. **Notification:** Apr 2003.

CINTAS FELLOWSHIPS

c/o Institute of International Education;
U.S. Student Programs Division; 809 United Nations Plaza;
New York, NY 10017–3580; (212) 984–5565, FAX 984–5325;
email cintas@iie.org; website www.iie.org/cintas
Scott Pentzer, *Program Officer*

Open to: playwrights. **Frequency:** annual; award rotates among artistic disciplines. **Remuneration:** $10,000 paid in quarterly stipends. **Guidelines:** artist of Cuban decent or citizenship living outside of Cuba. **Application procedure:** call or visit website after Dec 2001 for guidelines. **Deadline:** exact date TBA.

CITY OF LOS ANGELES (C.O.L.A.) PERFORMING ARTS FELLOWSHIPS

City of Los Angeles Cultural Affairs Department;
  433 South Spring St, 10th floor; Los Angeles, CA 90013;
  (213) 473-8590, FAX 473-8352; email cadgrants@earthlink.net;
  website www.culturela.org
Arleen Arikami, *Grants Manager*

Open to: composers, solo performers, performance artists. **Frequency:** annual. **Remuneration:** $10,000 grant. **Guidelines:** resident of L.A. County; minimum 15 years production/performance experience; not open to artists specializing in group presentations; funds to be used to create new solo work to be showcased by city in non-thematic presentation; write for guidelines or download from web. **Deadline:** 1 Sep 2001. **Notification:** Jun 2002.

DOBIE-PAISANO FELLOWSHIP

University of Texas at Austin; J. Frank Dobie House;
  702 East Dean Keeton St; Austin, TX 78705; (512) 471-8542,
  FAX 471-9997; email aslate@mail.utexas.edu;
  website www.utexas.edu/ogs/paisano
Audrey Slate, *Director*

Open to: playwrights. **Frequency:** annual. **Remuneration:** living allowance to cover 6-month residency at 265-acre ranch; free housing; families welcome. **Guidelines:** native Texan, or playwright who has lived in TX for at least 2 years or has published work about TX; ordinarily 2 writers selected each year. **Application procedure:** write for application or visit website after 1 Oct 2001. **Deadline:** 25 Jan 2002. **Notification:** May 2002.

THE DON AND GEE NICHOLL FELLOWSHIPS IN SCREENWRITING

Academy of Motion Picture Arts and Sciences; 8949 Wilshire Blvd;
  Beverly Hills, CA 90211-1972; (310) 247-3059;
  website www.oscars.org/nicholl
Greg Beal, *Program Coordinator*

Open to: playwrights, screenwriters. **Frequency:** annual. **Remuneration:** up to 5 fellowships of $30,000. **Guidelines:** playwright, screenwriter or fiction writer who has not worked as a professional screenwriter for theatrical films or television or sold screen or television rights to any original story, treatment, stage play, screenplay or teleplay; 1st-round selection based on submission of original screenplay or screen adaptation of writer's, or of two collaborators, own original work, 100–130 pages, written in standard screenplay format; send SASE for guidelines after 1 Jan 2002; application may be downloaded from web. **Application procedure:** application, screenplay and $30 application fee. **Deadline:** 1 May 2002. **Notification:** Aug 2002 for 1st-round selection; late Oct 2002 for winners.

ELECTRONIC ARTS GRANT PROGRAM

Experimental Television Center; 109 Lower Fairfield Rd;
    Newark Valley, NY 13811; (607) 687–4341, FAX 687–4341;
    email etc@experimentaltvcenter.org;
    website www.experimentaltvcenter.org
Sherry Miller Hocking, *Program Director*

FINISHING FUNDS

Open to: media artists, including writers and composers, involved in creation of film, audio, video or computer-generated time-based works. **Frequency:** annual. **Remuneration:** up to $1500. **Guidelines:** resident of NY State; funds to be used to assist completion of work which is time-based in conception and execution; work must be presented as installation performance, on video, as website production or must utilize new technologies; work must be completed before 30 Sep 2002; write for guidelines. **Application procedure:** 3 copies of application, project description, work samples and resume. **Deadline:** 15 Mar 2002. **Notification:** 6–8 weeks.

PRESENTATION FUNDS

Open to: not-for-profit organizations presenting audio, film, video or computer-generated time-based works. **Frequency:** ongoing. **Remuneration:** grant of up to $1000 to assist presentation of work and artist's involvement in activities related to presentation. **Guidelines:** NY State organization; event must be open to public; write for guidelines. **Application procedure:** individual may not apply; application and supporting materials submitted by organization well in advance of event. **Deadline:** ongoing. **Notification:** 15th of month following month of submission.

FULBRIGHT SENIOR SCHOLAR AWARDS FOR FACULTY AND PROFESSIONALS

Council for International Exchange of Scholars (CIES);
3007 Tilden St NW, Suite 5L; Washington, DC 20008-3009;
(202) 686-7877, FAX 362-3442; email apprequest@cies.iie.org;
website www.cies.org

Open to: scholars and professionals in all areas of theatre and the arts, including playwrights, translators, composers, librettists and lyricists. **Frequency:** annual. **Remuneration:** grant for university lecturing or research in one of more than 140 countries for 2-9 months; amount varies with country of award; travel; maintenance allowance for living costs of grantee and possibly family. **Guidelines:** U.S. citizen; Ph.D., MFA or comparable professional qualifications; university or college teaching experience for lecturing awards; application may be obtained from website. **Application procedure:** application. **Deadline:** 1 Aug 2002. **Notification:** up to 11 months, depending on country.

GEORGE BENNETT FELLOWSHIP

Phillips Exeter Academy; 20 Main St; Exeter, NH 03833-2460;
website www.exeter.edu
Charles Pratt, *Coordinator, Selection Committee*

Open to: playwrights. **Frequency:** annual. **Remuneration:** academic-year stipend of $6000; room and board for fellow and family. **Guidelines:** individual who is seriously contemplating or pursuing a career as a writer (in any genre) and who needs time and freedom from material considerations to complete a project in progress; committee favors playwrights who have not yet been produced commercially or at a major not-for-profit theatre; fellow expected to make self and talents available in informal and unofficial way to students interested in writing; send SASE for guidelines and application or visit website (no phone inquiries). **Application procedure:** application, work sample, statement concerning work-in-progress, names of 2 references and $5 fee. **Deadline:** 1 Dec 2001. **Notification:** 15 Mar 2002. **Dates:** Sep 2002-Jun 2003.

HARVARD UNIVERSITY RADCLIFFE INSTITUTE FOR ADVANCED STUDY FELLOWSHIPS

(Formerly Harvard University Bunting Fellowship Program)
The Radcliffe Institute for Advanced Study; Application Office;
    34 Concord Ave; Cambridge, MA 02138; (617) 495-8212,
    FAX 495-8136; website www.radcliffe.edu/bunting

Open to: playwrights, composers, librettists. **Frequency:** annual. **Remuneration:** up to $45,000 1-year fellowship. **Guidelines:** to provide opportunity and support for professionals of demonstrated accomplishment and exceptional promise to complete substantial project in their field; full-time appointment; fellow required to reside in Boston area and expected to present work-in-progress in public colloquia during year; office or studio space, auditing privileges and access to libraries and other resources at Harvard provided; call, write or visit website for guidelines and application. **Application procedure:** application. **Deadline:** 15 Oct 2001. **Notification:** Apr 2002. **Dates:** 10 Sep 2002-9 Aug 2003.

THE JAPAN FOUNDATION

152 West 57th St, 39th Floor; New York, NY 10019; (212) 489-0299,
    FAX 489-0409; website www.jfny.org/jfny/index.html
Artist Fellowship Program

Open to: specialists in the fields of fine arts, performing arts, music, journalism and creative writing, including playwrights, composers, librettists, lyricists and screenwriters. **Frequency:** annual. **Remuneration:** monthly stipend of ¥370,000 (about $2950) or ¥430,000 (about $3429), depending on grantee's professional career; travel; other allowances. **Guidelines:** U.S. citizen or permanent resident; fellowship of 2-6 months, not to be held concurrently with another major grant, to support project substantially related to Japan. **Application procedure:** write for guidelines and application, stating theme of project, present position and citizenship. **Deadline:** 1 Dec 2001. **Notification:** early-mid Apr 2002. **Dates:** residency begins between 1 Apr 2002 and 31 Mar 2003.

JOHN SIMON GUGGENHEIM MEMORIAL FOUNDATION

90 Park Ave; New York, NY 10016; (212) 687-4470, FAX 697-3248;
    email fellowships@gf.org; website www.gf.org

Open to: playwrights, composers. **Frequency:** annual. **Remuneration:** 1-year fellowship (in 2000, 182 fellowships with average grant of $34,863). **Guidelines:** citizen or permanent resident of U.S. or Canada; recipient must demonstrate exceptional creative ability; grant to support research in any field of knowledge or creation in any of the arts under the freest possible conditions. **Application procedure:** write for guidelines. **Deadline:** 1 Oct 2001. **Notification:** Apr 2002.

JONATHAN LARSON PERFORMING ARTS FOUNDATION

Box 672; Prince Street Station; New York, NY 10012;
   (212) 529-0814, FAX 253-7604; email jlpaf@aol.com;
   website www.jlpaf.org
Nancy Kassak Diekmann, *Executive Director*

Open to: composers, librettists, lyricists, producing organizations. **Frequency:** annual. **Remuneration:** grants of $2500-15,000 for general or project support. **Guidelines:** professional musical theatre artists who have completed formal training and are committed to a career in musical theatre. **Application procedure:** 2 copies of the following: application form, work sample, artist bio, production history and 2 letters of recommendation; project budget, proof of rights with SASP; lyricists include cassette with 3 lyrics/songs; composers include cassette with 3 songs and accompanying lyric sheet; librettists include 1 act of musical with 1 page synopsis and cassette with 3 selections of accompanying music. **Deadline:** 10 Sep 2001. **Notification:** Jan-Feb 2002.

THE KENNEDY CENTER FUND FOR NEW AMERICAN PLAYS

The John F. Kennedy Center for the Performing Arts; 2700 F St NW;
   Washington, DC 20566; (202) 416-8024, FAX 416-8205;
   email rsfoster@kennedy-center.org;
   website kennedy-center.org/fnap
Max Woodward, *Director*
Rebecca Foster, *Manager*

DEVELOPMENT GRANTS

Open to: not-for-profit professional theatres. **Frequency:** annual. **Remuneration:** $2500 playwright grant, additional support to theatre to underwrite expenses of both a reading and workshop production. **Guidelines:** awarded to not-for-profit professional theatre to support the development of new work. **Application procedure:** individual may not apply; producing organization submits application; application, production budgets for both reading and workshop production, 5 copies of script sample of at least one act in length, outline of play and synopsis, history of theatre, proof of not-for-profit status, copy of exclusive arrangement between playwright and theatre, development history, disclosure of encumbrances to the script or of any coproduction agreements, press materials. **Deadline:** TBA (4 May in 2001). **Notification:** TBA (Oct in 2001). **Dates:** production must occur between 1 Nov 2001 and 31 Dec 2003.

PRODUCTION GRANTS

Open to: not-for-profit professional theatres. **Frequency:** annual. **Remuneration:** $10,000 playwright grant; additional support to not-for-profit professional theatre based on production budget. Occasional Roger L. Stevens Award of $2500 awarded to playwright of extraordinary promise who did not receive a Production or Development Grant (5 awarded in 2002). **Guidelines:** awarded to not-for-profit professional theatre to produce world premieres of new plays; coproduction possible. **Application procedure:** individual may not apply; producing organization submits application; application, production budget, 5 nonreturnable copies of either full-length script or series of one-acts written by same playwright, history of the theatre, proof of not-for-profit status, copy of exclusive/arrangement between playwright and theatre, production history, disclosure of encumbrances or coproduction agreements, and press materials. **Deadline:** TBA (4 May in 2001). **Notification:** TBA (Oct in 2001). **Dates:** production must occur between 1 Jan 2002 and 31 Dec 2003.

THE KLEBAN AWARD

c/o New Dramatists; 424 West 44th St; New York, NY 10036;
(212) 757–6960; email newdramatists@newdramatists.org;
website www.newdramatists.org
Christie Brown, *Director of Playwright and Literary Services*

Open to: librettists and/or lyricists. **Frequency:** annual. **Remuneration:** TBA ($100,000 each to lyricist and librettist, paid in installments of $50,000 a year, in 2000–2001). **Guidelines:** applicant whose work has received a full or workshop production, or who has been a member or associate of a professional musical workshop or theatre group (e.g., ASCAP or BMI workshops; see Development); writer whose work has been performed on the Broadway stage for a cumulative period of 2 years ineligible; write for guidelines or download from web. **Application procedure:** application and work sample. **Deadline:** postmarked 15 Sep 2001. (See New Dramatists in Membership and Service Organizations.)

MANHATTAN THEATRE CLUB PLAYWRITING FELLOWSHIPS

311 West 43rd St, 8th Floor; New York, NY 10036; (212) 399-3000,
FAX 399-4329; email lit@mtc-nyc.org;
website www.manhattantheatreclub.com
Christian Parker, *Literary Manager*

MTC PLAYWRITING FELLOWSHIP

Open to: playwrights. **Frequency:** annual. **Remuneration:** $10,000
fellowship. **Guidelines:** New York-based playwright who has completed
formal education and can demonstrate financial need; writers from all
backgrounds encouraged to apply; fellowship includes commission for new
play, production assistantship, 1-year residency at MTC; send SASE for
guidelines or visit website. **Application procedure:** sample script, resume,
statement of purpose and letter of recommendation from theatre
professional or professor. **Deadline:** 31 Dec 2001.

MTC SLOAN FOUNDATION FELLOWSHIP

Open to: playwrights, solo performers. **Frequency:** annual. **Remuneration:**
$10,000 fellowship. **Guidelines:** fellowship supports commissioning and
development of new plays addressing contemporary issues of science and
technology. **Application procedure:** write for guidelines. **Deadline:** 15 Jun
2002.

MARIN ARTS COUNCIL INDIVIDUAL ARTIST GRANT

650 Las Gallinas Ave, Suite C; San Rafael, CA 94903;
(415) 499-8350, FAX 499-8537; email alison@marinarts.org;
website www.marinarts.org
Alison DeJung, *Grants Coordinator*

Open to: playwrights, composers. **Frequency:** biennial. **Remuneration:**
$2000-10,000 grant. **Guidelines:** Marin County artist only; award given
based on completion of original work. **Application procedure:** application
and work sample. **Deadline:** Jan 2003; exact date TBA. **Notification:** Jun
2003.

MARY FLAGLER CARY CHARITABLE TRUST COMMISSIONING PROGRAM

122 East 42nd St, Room 3505; New York, NY 10168;
(212) 953-7705, FAX 953-7720; email gmorgan@carytrust.org;
website www.carytrust.org
Gayle Morgan, *Music Program Director*

Open to: performance institutions including theatre and opera companies. **Frequency:** biennial. **Remuneration:** grant to help not-for-profit professional organization commission new musical work from established or emerging composer; amount varies (total of $400,000 available for 2001 grants). **Guidelines:** New York City organization only; funds to be used to compensate composer and librettist for creative work and to cover copying costs; guidelines available Apr 2003. **Application procedure:** individual may not apply; letter of application and representative audiotape of composer's music submitted by organization. **Deadline:** Jun 2003; exact date TBA (30 Jun in 2001).

MATURE WOMAN SCHOLARSHIP AWARD

The National League of American Pen Women; 1300 17th St NW;
Washington, DC 20036-1973
Mary Jane Hillery, *National Scholarship Chairman*
All inquiries in writing to: 66 Willow Rd; Sudbury, MA 01776-2663

Open to: playwrights, composers, librettists, lyricists. **Frequency:** biennial. **Remuneration:** $1000 grant. **Guidelines:** American woman age 35 and over; 3 awards (1 in art, 1 in music, 1 in letters) to further creative goals of women at an age when encouragement can lead to realization of long-term purposes; present and past NLAPW members ineligible; send SASE for guidelines. **Application procedure:** work sample; statement of purpose for which money will be used; proof that applicant is over age 35; statement that applicant is not a member of NLAPW; and $8 fee. **Deadline:** 1 Oct 2001. **Notification:** 1 Mar 2002.

THE MCKNIGHT INTERDISCIPLINARY FELLOWSHIP GRANT

Intermedia Arts; 2822 Lyndale Ave S; Minneapolis, MN 55408;
(612) 871-4444, FAX 871-6927; email info@intermediaarts.org;
website www.intermediaarts.org

Sandy Agustín, *Director of Community and Education Programs*

MINNESOTA FELLOWSHIP

Open to: interdisciplinary artists. **Frequency:** annual. **Remuneration:**
$25,000 fellowship; $2000 in travel expenses. **Guidelines:** resident of MN
for 1 year before application; mid-career interdisciplinary artist; fellowship
and technical support to pursue educational/presentational activity during
18-month fellowship period. **Application procedure:** application, 2-page
maximum artist statement, work sample, resume and optional SASP for
acknowledgment of receipt. **Deadline:** 25 Jan 2002. **Notification:** spring
2002.

NATIONAL MCKNIGHT INTERDISCIPLINARY FELLOW IN RESIDENCE

Open to: interdisciplinary artists. **Frequency:** biennial. **Remuneration:**
$10,000 artist's fee; up to $4000 in travel expenses. **Guidelines:** artists with
accomplished body of work; must have teaching and/or mentoring
experience; must be in Minneapolis for at least 4 weeks (not necessarily
consecutive) during 2004. **Application procedure:** letter of intent no more
than 2 pages in length describing artist's body of interdisciplinary work,
teaching and/or mentoring experience and previous residency experience.
Deadline: Jan 2003 intent to apply; Mar 2003 application; exact dates TBA.
Notification: spring 2003.

MEET THE COMPOSER GRANT PROGRAMS

2112 Broadway, Suite 505; New York, NY 10023; (212) 787-3601;
FAX 787-3745; email mtrevino@meetthecomposer.org;
website www.meetthecomposer.org

COMMISSIONING MUSIC/USA

Mark Treviño, *Director of Programs*

Open to: theatre, music-theatre, opera companies; orchestras; choruses; arts
presenters; festivals; public radio and television stations; internet providers;
soloists and chamber ensembles of all kinds (jazz, chamber, new music,
etc.). **Frequency:** annual. **Remuneration:** commissioning grant up to $30,000
to cover composer, librettist fees and copying costs. **Guidelines:**
organizations that have been producing or presenting for at least 3 years;

plans must involve full production of new work and a minimum of 4 performances for a single organization or a minimum of 6 for a consortium; write for complete guidelines or refer to MTC website. **Application procedure:** individuals may not apply; 1 host organization submits application and supporting materials; application may be from a single organization for grants up to $15,000 or from consortium of organizations for grants up to $30,000. **Deadline:** 15 Jan 2002.

MEET THE COMPOSER FUND
William Towns, *Program Manager*

Open to: theatre, music-theatre, opera companies; orchestras; choruses; arts presenters; festivals; music ensembles of all kinds (jazz, chamber, new music, etc.). **Frequency:** quarterly. **Remuneration:** up to $250 per individual composer. **Guidelines:** awards are based solely on the overall quality of the application, including: merit of composer participation, level of audience/community involvement, and general strength of compositions; administered by Meet The Composer in New York and by four regional offices that comprise the National Affiliate Network; write for complete guidelines or refer to MTC website. **Application procedure:** varies from region to region; individuals may not apply; performing organizations apply on behalf of composer. **Deadline:** 1 Oct 2001; 2 Jan 2002; 1 Apr 2002; 1 Jun 2002.

MUSIC ALIVE
MEET THE COMPOSER/AMERICAN SYMPHONY ORCHESTRA LEAGUE
Mark Treviño, *Director of Programs*

Open to: composers in association with League professional and youth member orchestras. **Frequency:** annual. **Remuneration:** grant for composer's fee ($2500 per residency week); composer's expenses (up to one roundtrip for every 2-week residency, and up to $175 per day for food and lodging); orchestra expenses (up to $1000 per residency week). **Guidelines:** supports composer residencies ranging from 2 to 8 weeks in duration scheduled in conjunction with performance(s) of the composer's work; the work(s) may be a world premiere or an existing work(s) by a living American composer; the performance of a world premiere or commissioned work is not a requirement of the program; residency weeks may be scheduled contiguously or divided into multiple visits and must take place between 1 Sep 2002 and 31 Aug 2003; the minimum duration for each residency visit is 7 days inclusive of travel; write for complete guidelines or refer to MTC website. **Application procedure:** individuals may not apply; performing organizations apply on behalf of composer. **Deadline:** 17 Aug 2002.

NEW RESIDENCIES

Mark Treviño, *Director of Programs*

Open to: theatre, music-theatre, opera companies; orchestras; choruses; music organizations; performing ensembles of all kinds (jazz, chamber, new music, etc.). **Frequency:** annual. **Remuneration:** grant for composer's salary ($40,000 per annum for 2 years; $20,000 towards 3rd year salary, must be matched 1-to-1 by host organizations); up to $25,000 toward production expenses (each expenditure must be matched 1-to-1 by host organizations); up to $15,000 toward institutional partnership building activities; possible $1500 for composer's relocation costs. **Guidelines:** up to 4 organizations, including at least 2 producing or presenting organizations and at least 1 community-based organization, form Residency Partnerships to sponsor 3-year composer residency; composer writes works for all host organizations and works a minimum of 60 hours per month "making music a positive force in community life" through organizing cultural events, teaching, recruiting other composers to community work, etc.; host organizations produce residency works, provide office space and logistical support, and offer health insurance for composer; write for complete guidelines or refer to MTC website. **Application procedure:** individuals may not apply; performing organizations apply on behalf of composer. **Deadline:** 17 Sep 2001.

NATIONAL ENDOWMENT FOR THE ARTS INTERNATIONAL PARTNERSHIPS

1100 Pennsylvania Ave NW, Room 704; Washington, DC 20506;
(202) 682–5429, FAX 682–5024; website www.arts.gov
Pennie Ojeda, *International Coordinator*

ARTSLINK PROJECTS

All applications and inquiries to: CEC International Partners;
12 West 31st St; New York, NY 10001–4415;
(212) 643–1985, ext 22, FAX 643–1996;
email artslink@cecip.org; website www.cecip.org

Open to: creative, interpretive and traditional artists, including playwrights, translators, composers, librettists, lyricists and solo performers; award rotates biennially among disciplines. **Frequency:** annual. **Remuneration:** grant up to $10,000 (average grant $4500). **Guidelines:** U.S. citizen or permanent resident; to enable individual artist or groups of artists and arts organizations to work with their counterparts in Central or Eastern Europe, the former Soviet Union or the Baltics; mutually beneficial collaborative project that will enrich artist's work and/or create new work that draws inspiration from knowledge and experience gained in country visited; write for guidelines. **Application procedure:** application and supporting materials. **Deadline:** next deadline for playwrights: 15 Jan 2002. **Notification:** Apr 2002.

THE FUND FOR U.S. ARTISTS AT INTERNATIONAL FESTIVALS AND EXHIBITIONS

All applications and inquiries to: Arts International;
251 Park Ave S, 5th Floor; New York, NY 10010; (212) 674-9744, FAX 674-9092; email thefund@artsinternational.org; website www.artsinternational.org/programs/index.htm
Kay Ta Keda, *Program Manager*

Open to: performing artists and organizations. **Frequency:** triannual. **Remuneration:** grants of up to $25,000 (most grants $1000-10,000) to cover expenses related to festival participation including travel, lodging, artists' fees and per diem. **Guidelines:** U.S. citizen or permanent resident who has been invited to international festival. **Application procedure:** application, work sample, proposal, bio, copy of invitation from festival, full budget showing all costs of participation in festival and festival's contribution to these costs. **Deadline:** 5 Sep 2001; 16 Jan 2002; 2 May 2002. **Notification:** 2 months. (See Arts International in this section.)

UNITED STATES/JAPAN CREATIVE ARTISTS' FELLOWSHIPS

All applications and inquiries to: Japan/U.S. Friendship Commission;
1120 Vermont Ave NW, Suite 925; Washington, DC 20005;
(202) 418-9800; email artist@jusfc.gov; website www.jusfc.gov

Open to: creative artists, including playwrights, translators, composers, librettists and lyricists. **Frequency:** annual. **Remuneration:** monthly stipend to cover housing, living expenses and modest professional support services; round-trip transportation for artist and family members; stipend to study Japanese language in U.S. if necessary. **Guidelines:** U.S. citizen or permanent resident; to enable established artist to pursue discipline in Japan for 6 consecutive months. **Application procedure:** write or call for guidelines and application materials or download from web. **Deadline:** 26 Jun 2002. **Notification:** Oct 2002.

NATIONAL ENDOWMENT FOR THE ARTS LITERATURE PROGRAM FELLOWSHIPS FOR TRANSLATORS

1100 Pennsylvania Ave NW, Room 720; Washington, DC 20506;
(202) 682-5428; website arts.endow.gov
Amy Stolls, *Literature Specialist*

Open to: translators of verse, drama and poetry. **Frequency:** annual. **Remuneration:** $20,000 fellowship. **Guidelines:** previously published translators of exceptional talent; guidelines available Jan 2001. **Application procedure:** write for guidelines and application. **Deadline:** Mar 2002; exact date TBA.

NATIONAL ENDOWMENT FOR THE HUMANITIES DIVISION OF PUBLIC PROGRAMS/HUMANITIES PROJECTS IN MEDIA

1100 Pennsylvania Ave NW; Washington, DC 20506;
(202) 606-8286, FAX 606-8557; website www.neh.gov
Jim Vore, *Assistant Deputy*

Open to: independent radio and television writers and producers of PBS-style documentaries. **Frequency:** annual. **Remuneration:** varies. **Guidelines:** support for planning, writing or production of, as well as collaboration on, television and radio projects focused on issues central to the humanities, and aimed at a national adult or broad regional audience; no adaptations of literary works. **Application procedure:** submit draft proposal before making formal application; write or visit website for guidelines. **Deadline:** 11 Sep 2001 and 16 Apr 2002 for consultation grants; 1 Nov 2001 for planning grants; 1 Feb 2002 for planning, scripting and production grants. **Notification:** Nov 2001 for Sep deadline; Mar 2002 for Nov deadline; Jul 2002 for Feb and Apr deadlines.

NATIONAL ENDOWMENT FOR THE HUMANITIES DIVISION OF RESEARCH PROGRAMS/COLLABORATIVE RESEARCH

1100 Pennsylvania Ave NW; Washington, DC 20506;
(202) 606-8209; email mbackas@neh.gov; website www.neh.gov
Margot Backas, *Senior Academic Advisor*

Open to: translators. **Frequency:** annual. **Remuneration:** amount varies according to project. **Guidelines:** U.S. citizen or resident for 3 years; money to support collaborative projects to translate into English works that provide insight into the history, literature, philosophy and artistic achievements of other cultures and that make available to scholars, students, teachers and the public the thought and learning of those civilizations. **Application procedure:** application and supporting materials; write for guidelines or download from web. **Deadline:** 1 Sep 2001. **Notification:** Apr 2002.

NATIVE ARTS RESEARCH AND ARTIST IN RESIDENCE FELLOWSHIPS

Native Arts Program; National Museum of the American Indian; Smithsonian Institution; George Gustave Heye Center; One Bowling Green; New York, NY 10004; (212) 514-3787, FAX 514-3800; email agardn@ic.si.edu; website www.si.edu/nmai
Nadema Agard, *Community Services Outreach Specialist*

Open to: playwrights, translators, composers, librettists, lyricists, solo performers, screenwriters. **Frequency:** annual. **Remuneration:** $3000, travel, housing, 14-21 day visits to New York City and Washington, D.C. **Guidelines:** Native American of the Western Hemisphere; professional artist; no students; download guidelines from web. **Application procedure:** application form, work sample, 2 letters of recommendation, resume, 1 page artist statement, budget proposal and tribal identification. **Deadline:** 25 Jun 2002. **Notification:** Aug-Sep 2002.

NEW PLAY COMMISSIONS IN JEWISH THEATRE

National Foundation for Jewish Culture; 330 Seventh Ave, 21st Floor; New York, NY 10001; (212) 629-0500, ext 205, FAX 629-0508; email nfjc@jewishculture.org; website www.jewishculture.org
Kim Bistrong, *Grants Administrator*

Open to: North American not-for-profit theatres. **Frequency:** annual. **Remuneration:** grant of $1000-5000. **Guidelines:** approximately 5 awards a year to theatres that have completed at least 2 seasons of public performances and are commissioning either new full-length play, adaptation, work for young audiences, musical or opera dealing substantively with issues of Jewish history, tradition, values or contemporary life; theatre must commit to presenting at least a public workshop production and/or staged reading of work, followed by discussion with audience; funds may be applied to commissioning fee, playwright's residency expenses or workshop costs; write, call or email for guidelines. **Application procedure:** completed proposal, cover sheet and supporting materials, submitted by theatre. **Deadline:** 10 Oct 2001. **Notification:** Dec 2001; exact date TBA. (See listing for The National Foundation for Jewish Culture in Membership and Service Organizations.)

NEW YORK FOUNDATION FOR THE ARTS (NYFA)

155 Avenue of the Americas, 14th Floor; New York, NY 10013-1507;
    (212) 366-6900, FAX 366-1778; email nyfaafp@nyfa.org;
    website nyfa.org
Penelope Dannenberg, *Director of Programs*

ARTISTS' FELLOWSHIPS

Open to: playwrights, composers, librettists, screenwriters. **Frequency:** award alternates biennially among disciplines. **Remuneration:** $7000 fellowship. **Guidelines:** NY State resident for 2 years prior to deadline; students ineligible. **Application procedure:** application and supporting materials; application seminars held each Sep. **Deadline:** next deadline for playwrights, composers, librettists and screenwriters postmarked 2 Oct 2001.

ARTISTS IN THE SCHOOL COMMUNITY

Open to: schools. **Frequency:** ongoing. **Description:** matching grant to assist schools that bring in artists, including playwrights, composers, librettists and lyricists, for residencies of 12 days-10 months; residency activities include artist-conducted student, teacher or parent workshops, lecture-demonstrations, readings and performances. **Remuneration:** artist is paid by school; recommended minimum fee of $250 a day. **Guidelines:** artist must be NY state resident. **Application procedure:** application from school; individual artist may not apply but is encouraged to write for guidelines and to collaborate with eligible sponsors to set up residencies; artist may also contact program for information and for help in finding sponsors. **Deadline:** Apr 2002; subsidiary deadlines for smaller grants in Oct, Nov, Feb, Jun each year. **Notification:** Jul 2002. **Dates:** Sep 2002-Jun 2003.

NEW YORK THEATRE WORKSHOP PLAYWRITING FELLOWSHIP

New York Theatre Workshop; 79 East 4th St; New York, NY 10003;
    (212) 780-9037, FAX 460-8996
Chiori Miyagawa, *Artistic Associate*

Open to: playwrights. **Frequency:** annual. **Remuneration:** commission; amount of award varies. **Guidelines:** writer of color under 30 years of age and resident of New York City; must be available to attend monthly group meetings and 1-week summer retreat. **Application procedure:** script, artistic statement, resume and cover letter. **Deadline:** TBA; contact theatre in Jan 2002 for exact date. (See New York Theatre Workshop in Production.)

PEW FELLOWSHIPS IN THE ARTS

230 South Broad St, Suite 1003; Philadelphia, PA 19102;
(215) 875-2285, FAX 875-2276; website www.pewarts.org
Melissa Franklin, *Director*

Open to: playwrights, composers, screenwriters. **Frequency:** annual; award rotates among various disciplines. **Remuneration:** up to 12 $50,000 fellowships. **Guidelines:** to give artists living in Southeastern PA the opportunity to dedicate themselves wholly to the development of their work for up to 2 years; artists under age 25 or students not eligible; call or write for application and guidelines or download from web after Sep 2001. **Application procedure:** application and work sample. **Deadline:** Dec 2001; exact date TBA.

PILGRIM PROJECT

156 Fifth Ave, Suite 400; New York, NY 10010; (212) 627-2288,
FAX 627-2184
Davida Goldman, *Secretary*

Open to: playwrights, solo performers, individual producers and theatre companies. **Frequency:** ongoing. **Remuneration:** grant of $1000-7000. **Guidelines:** grant toward cost of reading, workshop production or full production of play that deals with questions of moral significance. **Application procedure:** script only; write for further information. **Deadline:** ongoing.

THE PLAYWRIGHTS' CENTER GRANT PROGRAMS

2301 Franklin Ave E; Minneapolis, MN 55406-1099;
(612) 332-7481; email info@pwcenter.org;
website www.pwcenter.org
Carlo Cuesta, *Executive Director*

JEROME PLAYWRIGHT-IN-RESIDENCE FELLOWSHIPS

Open to: playwrights, solo performers. **Frequency:** annual. **Remuneration:** 5 1-year fellowships of $9000. **Guidelines:** U.S. citizen or permanent resident; emerging playwright whose work has not received more than 2 professional full productions; fellow must spend year in residence at Center, where fellow has access to developmental workshops, readings and other services; send SASE for guidelines. **Application procedure:** application and supporting materials. **Deadline:** 15 Sep 2001. **Notification:** 15 Jan 2002. **Dates:** 1 Jul 2002-30 Jun 2003.

MANY VOICES MULTICULTURAL COLLABORATION GRANTS

Open to: playwrights, translators, composers, librettists, solo performers, screenwriters. **Frequency:** annual, contingent on funding. **Remuneration:** $200-2000 grant each to 2-4 teams. **Guidelines:** team of 2 or more artists of differing cultural backgrounds with commitment from MN organization to produce proposed collaborative work; team's lead artist must be MN playwright of color. **Application procedure:** send SASE for guidelines. **Deadline:** 31 Jul 2002. **Notification:** 1 Oct 2002. **Dates:** 1 Oct 2002-30 Jun 2003.

MANY VOICES PLAYWRITING RESIDENCY AWARDS

Open to: playwrights, solo performers. **Frequency:** annual, contingent on funding. **Remuneration:** 8 awards: $1250 stipend; playwriting class scholarship; 1-year Playwrights' Center membership; opportunity to participate in playwriting roundtables; dramaturgical assistance; workshop and public reading. **Guidelines:** MN resident of color. **Application procedure:** send SASE for guidelines. **Deadline:** 31 Jul 2002. **Notification:** 1 Oct 2002. **Dates:** 1 Oct 2002-30 Jun 2003.

MCKNIGHT ADVANCEMENT GRANTS

Open to: playwrights, solo performers. **Frequency:** annual. **Remuneration:** 3 grants of $25,000; up to $1500 per fellow for workshops and staged readings using Center's developmental program or for allocation to partner organization for joint development and/or production. **Guidelines:** U.S. citizen or permanent resident and legal MN resident since 1 May 2000; playwright of exceptional merit and potential who has had at least 2 plays fully produced by professional theatres; funds intended to significantly advance fellow's art and/or career and may be used to cover a variety of expenses, including writing time, residency at theatre or other arts organization, travel/study, production or presentation; fellow must designate 2 months of grant year during which he or she plans to participate actively in Center's programs, including weekly attendance at and critical participation in readings and workshops of other members' work; send SASE for guidelines after 1 Dec 2001. **Application procedure:** application and supporting materials. **Deadline:** 1 Feb 2002. **Notification:** 1 May 2002. **Dates:** 1 Jul 2002-30 Jun 2003.

MCKNIGHT NATIONAL PLAYWRITING RESIDENCY AND COMMISSION

Open to: playwrights, solo performers in association with MN theatre. **Frequency:** annual. **Remuneration:** $20,000 commission; $2000 to support the creation of a new work during 3-month residency; housing; and round-trip travel to Minneapolis. **Guidelines:** U.S. citizen or permanent resident, not MN resident; playwright must have had at least 2 works fully produced by professional theatres; work must have made a significant impact on contemporary theatre; must spend 3 months in residency at the Center, where playwright has access to developmental readings, workshops and other services; send SASE for list of eligible MN theatres and guidelines. **Application procedure:** playwright may not apply; application submitted in collaboration with MN theatre with project description, writing sample and supporting materials. **Deadline:** 1 Feb 2002. **Notification:** 15 Apr 2002. **Dates:** 1 Jul 2002-30 Jun 2003.

PRINCESS GRACE AWARDS: PLAYWRIGHT FELLOWSHIP

Princess Grace Foundation–USA; 150 East 58th St, 21st Floor;
New York, NY 10155; (212) 317–1470, FAX 317–1473;
email pgfusa@pgfusa.com; website www.pgfusa.com
(Ms.) Toby Boshak, *Executive Director*

Open to: playwrights. **Frequency:** annual. **Remuneration:** $7500 grant; residency at New Dramatists (see listing in Membership and Service Organizations), with travel to New York City; inclusion of submitted script in New Dramatists' lending library and in its ScriptShare national script-distribution program for 1 year. **Guidelines:** U.S. citizen or permanent resident; award based primarily on artistic quality of submitted play and potential of fellowship to assist writer's growth; send SASE for guidelines and application. **Application procedure:** application; unproduced, unpublished play (no adaptations); letter of recommendation and resume. **Deadline:** 31 Mar 2002.

TCG ARTISTIC PROGRAMS

Theatre Communications Group; 355 Lexington Ave;
New York, NY 10017–6603; (212) 697–5230, FAX 983–4847;
email grants@tcg.org; website www.tcg.org
Emilya Cachapero, *Director of Artistic Programs*

AT&T:FIRSTSTAGE

Open to: playwrights, translators, composers, lyricists, librettists in association with TCG member theatres. **Frequency:** annual (contingent on funding). **Remuneration:** 6-8 grants of $10,000 for plays, translations, adaptations; $25,000 for musicals. **Guidelines:** funds to support the commission and development of new plays, translations, adaptations or musicals intended for inter-generational audience by a TCG member theatre in good standing; write for guidelines or download from web. **Application procedure:** artist may not apply; 2 copies of application and supporting materials submitted by artistic leader of TCG member theatre. **Deadline:** TBA.

EXTENDED COLLABORATION GRANTS

Open to: not-for-profit theatres, in collaboration with playwrights. **Frequency:** annual, contingent on funding. **Remuneration:** 12 grants of $5,500. **Guidelines:** augments normal development resources of TCG Constituent theatre by enabling playwright to develop work over an extended period of time in collaboration with director, designer, choreographer, composer and/or artist from another discipline; period of collaboration must exceed that which theatre would normally support; funds cover inter-city transportation within the U.S. and Canada and other expenses related to research and meetings among the collaborators; write or call for guidelines or download from web. **Application procedure:** playwright may not apply; application submitted by artistic leader of TCG Constituent theatre. **Deadline:** late fall 2001, spring 2002 (both contingent on funding; exact dates TBA).

NATIONAL THEATRE ARTIST RESIDENCY PROGRAM

CATEGORY I: RESIDENCY GRANTS

Open to: playwrights, translators, composers, librettists, lyricists and other theatre artists in association with not-for-profit professional theatres. **Frequency:** annual (contingent on funding). **Remuneration:** approximately 10-14 grants of $50,000 or $100,000. **Guidelines:** experienced theatre artists who have created significant body of work and theatres with high artistic standards and organizational capacity to provide substantial support services to artists; funds cover compensation and residency expenses of 1 or 2 resident artists, working singly or in collaboration, during discrete periods used exclusively for residency-related activities that total at least 6 full months over 2-year period; proposals must be developed jointly by artists and institutions; theatres applying for $100,000 grant must have minimum operating budget of $500,000 in most recently completed fiscal year; theatres applying for $50,000 grant must have minimum operating budget of $250,000 in most recently completed fiscal year; write or call for guidelines or download from web. **Application procedure:** 2 copies of application and supporting materials. **Deadline:** TBA.

CATEGORY II: MATCHING GRANTS

Open to: playwrights, translators, composers, librettists, lyricists and other theatre artists in association with not-for-profit professional theatres. **Frequency:** annual, contingent on funding. **Remuneration:** $25,000 or $50,000 in matching funds. **Guidelines:** matching funds to support the continuation of particularly fruitful partnerships; to be considered, applicant must meet Category I eligibility requirements; write or call for guidelines or download from web. **Application procedure:** 2 copies of application and supporting materials. **Deadline:** TBA.

NEA/TCG THEATRE RESIDENCY PROGRAM FOR PLAYWRIGHTS

Open to: playwrights in association with not-for-profit professional theatres. **Frequency:** annual (contingent on funding). **Remuneration:** grant of $25,000 to playwright and $5000 Vivendi Universal Residency Award to host theatre (12 awarded in 2000). **Guidelines:** playwright must be citizen or permanent resident of U.S. at the time of application and have had at least one play published or produced within the last 5 years; theatre must have history of developing new work, high artistic standards and a minimum operating budget of $150,000 in the most recently completed fiscal year; a total of 6 months (not necessarily consecutive) must be dedicated to the development of a new work with the host theatre; write or call for application and guidelines or download from web. **Application procedure:** intent to apply card, followed by application and supporting materials. **Deadline:** TBA.

TRAVEL AND STUDY GRANT PROGRAM

c/o Jerome Foundation; 125 Park Square Ct; 400 Sibley St;
    St. Paul, MN 55101; (651) 224-9431, FAX 224-3439;
    website www.jeromefdn.org
Cynthia Gehrig, *President*

Open to: MN theatre artists and not-for-profit theatre administrators, including playwrights, composers, librettists and lyricists. **Frequency:** annual. **Remuneration:** grant up to $5000 for foreign or domestic travel. **Guidelines:** resident of Minnesota; program funded by Target, General Mills and Jerome foundations to support period of significant professional development through travel and study for independent professional artist or staff member of not-for-profit organization; write for guidelines. **Application procedure:** application, work sample and resume. **Deadline:** 15 Mar 2002.

U.S. DEPARTMENT OF STATE FULBRIGHT STUDENT PROGRAM AT THE INSTITUTE OF INTERNATIONAL EDUCATION

809 United Nations Plaza; New York, NY 10017–3580;
(212) 984–5330; website www.iie.org/fulbright

Open to: playwrights, translators, composers, librettists, lyricists. **Frequency:** annual. **Remuneration:** fellowship or grant; amount varies with country of award. **Guidelines:** specific opportunities for study abroad in the arts; write for brochure. **Application procedure:** application and supporting materials. **Deadline:** 25 Oct 2001. **Notification:** Jan 2002.

U.S.-MEXICO FUND FOR CULTURE

Londres 16, 3rd Floor; Col. Juarez México; 06600 Mexico D.F.;
52–5–592–5386, FAX 52–5–566–8071;
email usmexcult@fidemexusa.org.mx;
website www.fidemexusa.org.mx
Beatriz Nava, *Program Officer*

Open to: playwrights, translators, librettists, lyricists, screenwriters, TV and radio writers, and producing organizations. **Frequency:** annual. **Remuneration:** grants of $2000–25,000. **Guidelines:** Mexican and North American artists and cultural institutions; program sponsored by Bancomer Cultural Foundation, the Rockefeller Foundation and Mexico's National Fund for Culture and the Arts to fund performing arts projects of excellence that reflect artistic and cultural diversity of Mexico and U.S. and encourage mutual collaboration between artists of both countries; media arts, script translation and adaptation of fiction, drama and poetry also considered; for brochure and application materials, send $1.01 postage 8½" x 11" SASE to U.S. Mexico Fund for Culture, c/o Benjamin Franklin Library, Laredo, TX 78044-3087. **Application procedure:** write or email for guidelines and application or download from web. **Deadline:** postmarked 16 Apr 2002. **Notification:** Aug 2002.

THE WALT DISNEY STUDIOS AND ABC ENTERTAINMENT WRITING FELLOWSHIP PROGRAM

500 South Buena Vista St; Burbank, CA 91521–4389;
  (818) 560–6894; email abc.fellowships@abc.com;
  website www.abcnewtalent.disney.com

Open to: playwrights, screenwriters, television writers. **Frequency:** annual. **Remuneration:** 1-year salary of $34,000 for up to 8 writers; travel and 1 month's housing for fellows from outside Los Angeles area. **Guidelines:** to enable writers to work full-time at developing their craft in Disney Studios features or television division; no previous film or TV writing experience necessary; writer with Writers Guild of America credits eligible but should apply through the Guild's Employment Access at (213) 782-4648; call for guidelines and application or download from web. **Application procedure:** application and notarized standard letter agreement with resume and writing sample (for feature division: screenplay approximately 120 pages long or full-length play; for TV division: 30-minute TV script approximately 45 pages long, full-length play or one-act more than 24 pages long). **Deadline:** 22 Jun 2002; no submission before 1 Jun 2002. **Notification:** finalists notified winter 2002. **Dates:** fellowship year begins Jan 2003; exact date TBA.

WISCONSIN ARTS BOARD ARTIST FELLOWSHIP AWARDS

101 East Wilson St, 1st Floor; Madison, WI 53702; (608) 264–8191,
  FAX 267–0380; email mark.fraire@arts.state.wi.us;
  website arts.state.wi.us
Mark Fraire, *Grant Programs and Services Specialist*

Open to: playwrights, composers. **Frequency:** biennial. **Remuneration:** $8000 fellowship. **Guidelines:** WI resident for at least 1 year at time of application; artist must produce 1 public presentation of work as part of fellowship; send SASE for guidelines and application. **Application procedure:** application and work sample. **Deadline:** 15 Sep 2002. **Notification:** Jan 2003.

EMERGENCY FUNDS

How do emergency funds differ from other sources of financial aid?

Emergency funds aid writers in severe temporary financial difficulties. Some funds give outright grants, others make interest-free loans. For support for anything other than a genuine emergency, turn to Fellowships and Grants.

THE AUTHOR'S LEAGUE FUND

1501 Broadway, Suite 701; New York, NY 10036; (212) 391-8384,
    FAX 944-0420
Susan Drury, *Administrator*

Open to: playwrights. **Type of assistance:** interest-free loan; request should be limited to immmediate needs. **Guidelines:** published or produced working professional; must demonstrate real need. **Application procedure:** application and supporting materials. **Notification:** 2-4 weeks.

CARNEGIE FUND FOR AUTHORS

1 Old Country Rd, Suite 113; Carle Place, NY 11514

Open to: playwrights. **Type of assistance:** emergency grant. **Guidelines:** playwright who has had at least 1 play or collection of plays published commercially in book form (anthologies excluded); emergency which has placed applicant in substantial verifiable financial need. **Application procedure:** write for application form.

THE DRAMATISTS GUILD FUND

1501 Broadway, Suite 701; New York, NY 10036; (212) 391-8384,
    FAX 944-0420
Susan Drury, *Administrator*

Open to: playwrights, composers, librettists, lyricists. **Type of assistance:** interest-free loan; request should be limited to immediate needs. **Guidelines:** published or produced working professional; must demonstrate real need. **Application procedure:** application and supporting materials. **Notification:** 2-4 weeks.

MARY MASON MEMORIAL LEMONADE FUND

Theatre Bay Area, 870 Market St, Suite 375;
    San Francisco, CA 94102; (415) 430-1140, FAX 430-1145;
    email richard@theatrebayarea.org;
    website www.theatrebayarea.org/lemonade.html
Richard Ryan, *Office Administrator*

Open to: playwrights, translators, lyricists, librettists, composers. **Type of assistance:** grants of up to $1000. **Guidelines:** resident of San Francisco Bay Area who has worked professionally or vocationally in theatre with minimum 2 years experience within the last 5; persons diagnosed with terminal or life-threatening illness; monies cannot be used for hospital expenses. **Application procedure:** call or email for application. **Notification:** 2-4 weeks. (See Theatre Bay Area in Membership and Service Organizations.)

PEN FUND FOR WRITERS & EDITORS WITH AIDS

PEN American Center; 568 Broadway; New York, NY 10012;
(212) 334-1660, FAX 334-2181; email pen@pen.org
Pamela Pearce, *Program Coordinator*

Open to: playwrights, translators, librettists, lyricists, screenwriters, television writers, radio writers. **Type of assistance:** grant or interest-free loan of up to $1000. **Guidelines:** emergency assistance for published and/or produced writer who is HIV-positive and having financial difficulties. **Application procedure:** application, work sample, documentation of financial emergency and resume. **Notification:** 6-8 weeks.

PEN WRITERS FUND

PEN American Center; 568 Broadway; New York, NY 10012;
(212) 334-1660, FAX 334-2181; email pen@pen.org
Pamela Pearce, *Program Coordinator*

Open to: playwrights, translators, librettists, lyricists, screenwriters, televisionwriters, radio writers. **Type of assistance:** grant or interest-free loan of up to $500. **Guidelines:** emergency assistance for published and/or produced writer having financial difficulties. **Application procedure:** application, work sample, documentation of financial emergency and resume. **Notification:** 6-8 weeks.

STATE ARTS AGENCIES

What can my state arts agency do for me?

Possibly quite a bit—ask your agency for guidelines and study them carefully. State programs vary greatly and change frequently. Most have some sort of residency requirement, but eligibility is not always restricted to current residents, and may include people who were born in, raised in, attended school in or had some other association with the state in question.

What if my state doesn't give grants to individual artists?

A number of state arts agencies are restricted in this way. However, those with such restrictions, by and large, are eager to help artists locate not-for-profit organizations that channel funds to individuals. The New York State Council on the Arts, for example, is prohibited from funding individuals directly, and must contract with a sponsoring not-for-profit organization when it awards grants to individual artists. Yet NYSCA has a number of ways of supporting the work of theatre writers. The Literature Program funds translations and writers' residencies in communities. The Individual Artists Program assists not-for-profit organizations in commissioning new theatre works. NYSCA also subgrants funds to the New York Foundation for the Arts (see Fellowships and Grants, and Development), which provides funds and project development assistance for individual artists.

At the least, every state has some kind of Artist-in-Education program; if you are able and willing to function in an educational setting you should certainly investigate this possibility.

ALABAMA STATE COUNCIL ON THE ARTS

201 Monroe St; Montgomery, AL 36130-1800; (334) 242-4076,
FAX 240-3269; email staff@arts.state.al.us;
website www.arts.state.al.us
Al Head, *Executive Director*

ALASKA STATE COUNCIL ON THE ARTS

411 West 4th Ave, Suite 1E; Anchorage, AK 99501-2343;
(907) 269-6610, (888) 278-7424, FAX (907) 269-6601;
email info@aksca.org; website www.aksca.org
Helen Howarth, *Executive Director*

AMERICAN SAMOA COUNCIL ON CULTURE, ARTS AND HUMANITIES

Box 1540; Office of the Governor; Pago Pago, AS 96799;
011-684-633-4347, FAX 011-684-633-2059;
website www.nasaa-arts.org/new/nasaa/gateway/AS
(Ms.) Le'ala E. Pili, *Executive Director*

ARIZONA COMMISSION ON THE ARTS

417 West Roosevelt St; Phoenix, AZ 85003-1326; (602) 255-5882,
FAX 256-0282; email general@ArizonaArts.org;
website az.arts.asu.edu/artscomm
Shelley Cohn, *Executive Director*

ARKANSAS ARTS COUNCIL

1500 Tower Bldg; 323 Center St; Little Rock, AR 72201;
(501) 324-9766, 324-9150 (TDD), FAX 324-9207;
email info@arkansasarts.com; website www.arkansasarts.com
Joy Pennington, *Executive Director*

CALIFORNIA ARTS COUNCIL

1300 I St, Suite 930; Sacramento, CA 95814; (916) 322-6555,
FAX 322-6575; email cac@cwo.com; website www.cac.ca.gov
Barry Hessenius, *Executive Director*

COLORADO COUNCIL ON THE ARTS

750 Pennsylvania St; Denver, CO 80203; (303) 894-2617,
FAX 894-2615; email coloarts@state.co.us;
website www.coloarts.state.co.us
Fran Holden, *Executive Director*

CONNECTICUT COMMISSION ON THE ARTS

755 Main St; 1 Financial Plaza; Hartford, CT 06103;
(860) 566-4770, FAX 566-6462; email kdemeo@ctarts.org;
website www.ctarts.org
John Ostrout, *Executive Director*

DELAWARE DIVISION OF THE ARTS

Carvel State Office Bldg; 820 North French St, 4th Floor;
Wilmington, DE 19801; (302) 577-8278, FAX 577-6561;
email delarts@artswire.org; website www.artsdel.org
Paul Weagraff, *Acting Director*

DISTRICT OF COLUMBIA (DC) COMMISSION ON THE ARTS AND HUMANITIES

410 8th St NW, 5th Floor; Washington, DC 20004;
(202) 724-5613, 727-3148 (TDD), FAX 727-4135;
email dcart@dcgov.org; website dcarts.dc.gov
Anthony Gittens, *Executive Director*

FLORIDA DIVISION OF CULTURAL AFFAIRS

Department of State, The Capitol; Tallahassee, FL 32399-0250;
(850) 487-2980, FAX 922-5259; website www.dos.state.fl.us/dca
Peg Richardson, *Director*

GEORGIA COUNCIL FOR THE ARTS

260 14th St NW, Suite 401; Atlanta, GA 30318;
(404) 685-ARTS (2787), FAX 685-2788; email info@arts-ga.com;
website www.ganet.org/georgia-arts
Betsy C. Baker, *Executive Director*

GUAM COUNCIL ON THE ARTS & HUMANITIES AGENCY

Box 2950; Agana, GU 96910; (671) 475-2242,
FAX 472-2781; website www.guam.net/gov/kaha
Deborah J. Bordallo, *Executive Director*

STATE FOUNDATION ON CULTURE AND THE ARTS (HAWAII)

44 Merchant St; Honolulu, HI 96813; (808) 586-0300,
586-0740 (TDD), FAX 586-0308; email sfca@sfca.state.hi.us;
website www.state.hi.us/sfca
David C. Farmer, *Executive Director*

IDAHO COMMISSION ON THE ARTS

Box 83720; Boise, ID 83720-0008; (208) 334-2119,
(800) 278-3863, FAX (208) 334-2488; email cconley@ica.state.id.us;
website www2.state.id.us/arts
Dan Harpole, *Executive Director*

ILLINOIS ARTS COUNCIL

James R. Thompson Center; 100 West Randolph St, Suite 10-500;
Chicago, IL 60601; (312) 814-6750, FAX 814-1471;
email info@arts.state.il.us; website www.state.il.us/agency/iac
Rhoda A. Pierce, *Executive Director*

INDIANA ARTS COMMISSION

402 West Washington St, Room W072; Indianapolis, IN 46204-2741;
(317) 232-1268, FAX 232-5595; email arts@state.in.us;
website www.state.in.us/iac
Dorothy L. Ilgen, *Executive Director*

IOWA ARTS COUNCIL

Capitol Complex; 600 East Locust; Des Moines, IA 50319-0290;
(515) 281-4451, 242-5147 (TDD), FAX 242-6498;
website www.culturalaffairs.org/iac
Anita Walker, *Executive Director*

KANSAS ARTS COMMISSION

700 Southwest Jackson, Suite 1004; Topeka, KS 66603-3761;
(785) 296-3335, FAX 296-4989; email KAC@arts.state.ks.us;
website arts.state.ks.us
David Wilson, *Executive Director*

KENTUCKY ARTS COUNCIL

Old Capitol Annex; 300 West Broadway; Frankfort, KY 40601–1950;
(502) 564–3757, (888) 833–2787, FAX (502) 564–2839;
email kyarts@mail.state.ky.us; website www.kyarts.org
Gerri Combs, *Executive Director*

LOUISIANA DIVISION OF THE ARTS

Box 44247; Baton Rouge, LA 70804; (225) 342–8180,
FAX 342–8173; email arts@crt.state.la.us;
website www.crt.state.la.us/arts
Maida Owens, *Interim Executive Director*

MAINE ARTS COMMISSION

55 Capitol St; 25 State House Station; Augusta, ME 04333–0025;
(207) 287–2724, 287–2360 (TTY), FAX 287–2335;
email jan.poulin@state.me.us; website www.mainearts.com
Alden C. Wilson, *Executive Director*

MARYLAND STATE ARTS COUNCIL

175 West Ostend St, Suite E; Baltimore, MD 21230; (410) 767–6555,
333–4519 (TTY), FAX 333–1062; email
moliver@mdbusiness.state.md.us;
website www.msac.org
James Backas, *Executive Director*

MASSACHUSETTS CULTURAL COUNCIL

10 St. James Ave, 3rd Floor; Boston, MA 02116–3803;
(617) 727–3668, FAX 727–0044; email web@art.state.ma.us;
website www.massculturalcouncil.org
Mary Kelley, *Executive Director*

MICHIGAN COUNCIL FOR THE ARTS & CULTURAL AFFAIRS

525 West Ottawa; Box 30705; Lansing, MI 48909–8205;
(517) 241–4011, FAX 241–3979; email artsinfo@cis.state.mi.us;
website www.commerce.state.mi.us/arts
Betty Boone, *Director*

Minnesota State Arts Board

Park Square Court; 400 Sibley St, Suite 200;
St. Paul, MN 55101-1928; (651) 215-1600, 215-6235 (TTY),
(800) 866-2787, FAX (651) 215-1602;
email msab@arts.state.mn.us; website www.arts.state.mn.us
Robert C. Booker, *Executive Director*

Mississippi Arts Commission

239 North Lamar St, Suite 207; Jackson, MS 39201;
(601) 359-6030, (800) 735-2966 (TDD), FAX (601) 359-6008;
email msartcom@artswire.org; website www.arts.state.ms.us
Betsy Bradley, *Executive Director*

Missouri Arts Council

111 North 7th St, Suite 105; St. Louis, MO 63101-2188;
(314) 340-6845, (800) 735-2966 (TDD), FAX (314) 340-7215;
email moarts@mail.state.mo.us;
website www.missouriartscouncil.org
Norree Boyd, *Executive Director*

Montana Arts Council

Box 202201; Helena, MT 59620-2201; (406) 444-6430,
FAX 444-6548; email mac@state.mt.us; website www.art.state.mt.us
Arlynn Fishbaugh, *Executive Director*

Nebraska Arts Council

Joslyn Carriage House; 3838 Davenport St;
Omaha, NE 68131-2329; (402) 595-2122, FAX 595-2334;
email cmalloy@nebraskaartscouncil.org;
website www.nebraskaartscouncil.org
Jennifer A. Severin, *Executive Director*

Nevada Arts Council

716 North Carson St, Suite A; Carson City, NV 89701;
(775) 687-6680, FAX 687-6688;
website dmla.clan.lib.nv.us/docs/arts
Susan Boskoff, *Executive Director*

New Hampshire State Council on the Arts

40 North Main St; Concord, NH 03301-4974; (603) 271-2789,
(800) 735-2964 (TTY), FAX (603) 271-3584;
website www.state.nh.us/nharts
Rebecca Lawrence, *Director*

New Jersey State Council on the Arts

Box 306; 225 West State St; Trenton, NJ 08625-0306;
(609) 292-6130,
633-1186 (TDD), FAX 989-1440; email njsca@arts.sos.state.nj.us;
website www.njartscouncil.org
Barbara F. Russo, *Executive Director*

New Mexico Arts

Box 1450; Santa Fe, NM 87504-1450; (505) 827-6490,
(800) 879-4278, FAX (505) 827-6043; website www.nmarts.org
Margaret Brommelsiek, *Executive Director*

New York State Council on the Arts

915 Broadway, 8th Floor; New York, NY 10010; (212) 387-7000,
(800) 895-9838, FAX (212) 387-7164; website www.nysca.org
Nicolette B. Clarke, *Executive Director*

North Carolina Arts Council

Department of Cultural Resources; Raleigh, NC 27699-4632;
(919) 733-2111, FAX 733-4834; email ncarts@ncmail.net;
website www.ncarts.org
Mary B. Regan, *Executive Director*

North Dakota Council on the Arts

418 East Broadway, Suite 70; Bismarck, ND 58501-4086;
(701) 328-3954, (800) 366-6888 (TDD), FAX (701) 328-3963;
email comserv@state.nd.us; website www.state.nd.us/arts
Jan Webb, *Executive Director*

COMMONWEALTH COUNCIL FOR ARTS AND CULTURE (NORTHERN MARIANA ISLANDS)

Box 5553, CHRB; Saipan, MP 96950; (670) 322-9982, 322-9983,
FAX 322-9028; email galaidi@gtepacifica.net;
website www.nasaa-arts.org/new/nasaa/gateway/NorthernM.html
Robert Hunter, *Executive Director*

OHIO ARTS COUNCIL

727 East Main St; Columbus, OH 43205-1796; (614) 466-2613,
FAX 466-4494; website www.oac.state.oh.us
Wayne P. Lawson, *Executive Director*

OKLAHOMA ARTS COUNCIL

Box 52001-2001; Oklahoma City, OK 73152-2001; (405) 521-2931,
FAX 521-6418; email okarts@arts.state.ok.us;
website www.oklaosf.state.ok.us/~arts
Betty Price, *Executive Director*

OREGON ARTS COMMISSION

775 Summer St, NE, Suite 350; Salem, OR 97301-1284;
(503) 986-0082, 986-0123 (TDD), (800) 233-3306,
FAX (503) 986-0260; email oregon.artscomm@state.or.us;
website art.econ.state.or.us
Christine T. D'Arcy, *Executive Director*

PENNSYLVANIA COUNCIL ON THE ARTS

Finance Bldg, Room 216; Harrisburg, PA 17120; (717) 787-6883,
(800) 654-5984 (TDD), FAX (717) 783-2538;
website artsnet.org/pca
Philip Horn, *Executive Director*

INSTITUTE OF PUERTO RICAN CULTURE

Box 9024184; San Juan, PR 00902-4184;
(787) 725-5137, FAX 724-8393; website icp.prstar.net
Lcdo. Robert L. Bounds Davila, *Interim Director*

RHODE ISLAND STATE COUNCIL ON THE ARTS

83 Park St, 6th Floor; Providence, RI 02903-1062;
(401) 222-3880, 222-7808 (TTY), FAX 422-3018;
email info@risca.state.ri.us; website www.risca.state.ri.us
Randall Rosenbaum, *Executive Director*

SOUTH CAROLINA ARTS COMMISSION

1800 Gervais St; Columbia, SC 29201; (803) 734-8696,
734-8983 (TDD), FAX 734-8526; website www.state.sc.us/arts
Suzette M. Surkamer, *Executive Director*

SOUTH DAKOTA ARTS COUNCIL

Office of the Arts; 800 Governors Dr; Pierre, SD 57501-2294;
(605) 773-3131, (800) 423-6665, FAX (605) 773-6962;
email sdac@stlib.state.sd.us; website www.state.sd.us/deca/sdarts
Dennis Holub, *Executive Director*

TENNESSEE ARTS COMMISSION

401 Charlotte Ave; Nashville, TN 37243-0780;
(615) 741-1701, FAX 741-8559; email dadkins@mail.state.tn.us;
website www.arts.state.tn.us
Rich Boyd, *Executive Director*

TEXAS COMMISSION ON THE ARTS

Box 13406; Austin, TX 78711-3406; (512) 463-5535,
475-3327 (TTY), (800) 252-9415, FAX (512) 475-2699;
email front.desk@arts.state.tx.us; website www.arts.state.tx.us
John Paul Batiste, *Executive Director*

UTAH ARTS COUNCIL

617 East South Temple; Salt Lake City, UT 84102-1177;
(801) 236-7555, FAX 236-7556; website www.arts.utah.org
Bonnie H. Stephens, *Director*

VERMONT ARTS COUNCIL

136 State St, Drawer 33; Montpelier, VT 05633-6001;
(802) 828-3291, (800) 253-0191 (TTY), FAX (802) 828-3363;
email info@arts.vca.state.vt.us; website www.vermontartscouncil.org
Alexander L. Aldrich, *Executive Director*

VIRGINIA COMMISSION FOR THE ARTS

Lewis House, 2nd Floor; 223 Governor St;
Richmond, VA 23219-2010; (804) 225-3132,
FAX 225-4327; email vacomm@artswire.org;
website www.arts.wire.org/~vacomm
Peggy J. Baggett, *Executive Director*

VIRGIN ISLANDS COUNCIL ON THE ARTS

Box 103; St. Thomas, VI 00802; (340) 774-5984,
FAX 774-6206; email vicouncil@islands.vi;
website www.nasaa-arts.org/new/nasaa/gateway/VI
John Jowers, *Executive Director*

WASHINGTON STATE ARTS COMMISSION

234 East 8th Ave; Box 42675; Olympia, WA 98504-2675;
(360) 753-3860, FAX 586-5351; email pamm@wsac.wa.gov;
website www.arts.wa.gov
Kristen Tucker, *Executive Director*

WEST VIRGINIA COMMISSION ON THE ARTS

1900 Kanawha Blvd E; Charleston, WV 25305-0300;
(304) 558-0220, 558-3562 (TDD), FAX 558-2779;
email ressmeyr@wvlc.wvnet.edu;
website www.wvculture.org
Richard Ressmeyer, *Director of Arts*

WISCONSIN ARTS BOARD

101 East Wilson St, 1st Floor; Madison, WI 53702; (608) 266-0190,
267-9629 (TDD), FAX 267-0380; email artsboard@arts.state.wi.us;
website arts.state.wi.us/static
George Tzougros, *Executive Director*

WYOMING ARTS COUNCIL

2320 Capitol Ave; Cheyenne, WY 82002; (307) 777-7742,
FAX 777-5499; website www.wyoarts.com,
website commerce.state.wy.us/cr/arts/
John G. Coe, *Executive Director*

COLONIES AND RESIDENCIES

What entries make up this section?

Though artist colonies that admit theatre writers constitute the majority of the listings, there are other kinds of residencies, such as artist-in-residence positions at universities, listed here as well. You can also find listings in Development and the Fellowships and Grants sections that could be considered residencies. We have also included some "writers' rooms" where playwrights in need of a quiet place for uninterrupted work are welcome. Of course there are hotels and inns throughout the country that would be desirable for an artist seeking a quiet place to work, but we have chosen to limit our listings to those places set up as retreats for writers or that, in addition to reasonable lodging, provide services to benefit writers.

Note: you should assume that each deadline listed in this section is the date application materials must be *received*, unless stated otherwise.

ALDEN B. DOW CREATIVITY CENTER

Northwood University; 4000 Whiting Dr; Midland, MI 48640;
   (517) 837–4478, FAX 837–4468;
   email creativity@northwood.edu;
   website www.northwood.edu/abd
Director

Open to: playwrights, translators, composers, librettists, lyricists, screenwriters. **Description:** 4 "Creativity Fellowships" each year for individuals working in any field, including the arts; 10-week summer residency at Northwood University, which provides environment for intense independent study; program includes interaction among fellows and formal presentation of work at end of program. **Financial arrangement:** travel, room, board, $750 stipend for project costs. **Guidelines:** projects that are creative, innovative and unique; prefers 1 applicant per project; no accommodation for spouses, children or pets; write for brochure or visit website for more information. **Application procedure:** project description, work sample, resume and $10 application fee. **Deadline:** 31 Dec 2001. **Notification:** 1 Apr 2002. **Dates:** Jun–Aug 2002.

ALTOS DE CHAVON

c/o Parsons School of Design; 2 West 13th St, Room 707;
   New York, NY 10011; (212) 229–5370, FAX 229–8988;
   email altos@spacelab.net
Stephen D. Kaplan, *Arts/Education Director*

Open to: playwrights, composers, screenwriters. **Description:** residencies of 3½ months for 15 artists a year, 1-2 of whom may be writers or composers, at not-for-profit arts center located in tropical Caribbean surroundings 8 miles from town of La Romana in the Dominican Republic; efficiency studios or apartments with kitchenettes; small individual studios nearby; small visual-arts-oriented library. **Financial arrangement:** $100 nonreturnable reservation fee; resident pays rent of $400 per month and provides own meals (estimated cost $20 a day). **Guidelines:** prefers Spanish-speaking artists who can use talents to benefit community, and whose work relates to Dominican or Latin American context; residents may teach workshops and are expected to contribute to group exhibition/performance at end of stay; write for further information. **Application procedure:** letter explaining applicant's interest in program, work sample and resume. **Deadline:** 15 Jul 2002. **Notification:** 1 Aug 2002. **Dates:** residencies start 1 Feb 2003, 1 Jun 2003, 1 Sep 2003.

ATLANTIC CENTER FOR THE ARTS

1414 Art Center Ave; New Smyrna Beach, FL 32168; (386) 427-6975,
(800) 393-6975, FAX (386) 427-5669;
email program@atlanticcenterforthearts.org;
website www.atlanticcenterforthearts.org
Paul Markunas, *CEO*
Nicholas Conroy, *Program Director*

Open to: playwrights, composers. **Description:** 7 3-week workshops each year offering writers, choreographers, media, visual and performing artists opportunity of concentrated study with internationally known Master Artists-in-Residence. **Financial arrangement:** free housing which includes private room and bath and access to communal studio; weekday meals provided for selected artists. **Application procedure:** Master Artist specifies submission materials and selects participants; write or call for brochure. **Deadline:** 3 months before residency. **Notification:** 2 months before residency. **Dates:** exact dates TBA; see website.

BLUE MOUNTAIN CENTER

Box 109; Blue Mountain Lake, NY 12812; (518) 352-7391
Harriet Barlow, *Director*

Open to: playwrights, composers, librettists, lyricists, solo performers. **Description:** 4-week residencies for 14 writers, composers and visual artists at center in Adirondack Mountains. **Financial arrangement:** free room and board. **Guidelines:** artist whose work is aimed at a general audience and reflects social concerns. **Application procedure:** send SASE for information. **Deadline:** 1 Feb 2002. **Notification:** early Apr 2002. **Dates:** mid-Jun–Oct.

BYRDCLIFFE ART COLONY

The Woodstock Guild; 34 Tinker St; Woodstock, NY 12498-1233;
(845) 679-2079, FAX 679-4529; email wguild@ulster.net;
website www.woodstockguild.org
Artists Residency Program

Open to: playwrights, translators, librettists, lyricists, solo performers, screenwriters. **Description:** 4-week residencies for writers, composers and visual artists at historic 300-acre colony in the Catskill Mountains, 1½ miles from Woodstock village center, 90 miles north of New York City; private room and separate individual studio space in Villetta Inn, spacious turn-of-the-century mountain lodge; common dining room and living room;

residents provide own meals, using community kitchen. **Financial arrangement:** resident pays fee of $500 per session. **Guidelines:** proof of serious commitment to field of endeavor is major criterion for acceptance; professional recognition helpful but not essential; send SASE for further information. **Application procedure:** application, work sample, project description, resume, reviews and articles if available, contact information for 2 references and $5 fee. **Deadline:** 1 Apr 2002 (applications received after deadline considered for space still available). **Notification:** 15 May 2002. **Dates:** Jun-Sep.

CAMARGO FOUNDATION

125 Park Square Ct; 400 Sibley St; St. Paul, MN 55101–1928
William Reichard, *U.S. Secretariat*

Open to: playwrights, translators, composers. **Description:** 11 concurrent residencies, most for scholars and teachers pursuing projects relative to Francophone culture, but also including 1 for writer, 1 for composer and 1 for visual artist, at estate in ancient Mediterranean fishing port 30 minutes from Marseilles; furnished apartments; music studio available for composer. **Financial arrangement:** $3500 stipend; free housing; residents provide own meals. **Guidelines:** resident outlines project to fellow colony members during stay and writes final report; families welcome when space available; write for guidelines and application. **Deadline:** 1 Feb 2002. **Notification:** 30 Apr 2002. **Dates:** Sep-Dec; Jan-May.

CENTRUM CREATIVE RESIDENCIES PROGRAM

Fort Worden State Park; Box 1158; Port Townsend, WA 98368;
    (360) 385–3102, FAX 385–2470; website www.centrum.org
Ted Senecal, *Residency Program Facilitator*

Open to: playwrights, translators, composers, librettists, lyricists, solo performers, screenwriters, television writers. **Description:** creative residencies for writers, composers, poets, visual artists and choreographers at center near Victorian seaport in 440-acre Fort Worden State Park; self-contained cabins near beach and hiking trails; separate studio space. **Financial arrangement:** free; some stipends available. **Guidelines:** artist who has clear direction and some accomplishment in field; artist who wants to explore new style, medium or genre. **Application procedure:** application, project description, work sample and resume; download guidelines from web. **Deadline:** 21 Aug 2002. **Notification:** 31 Nov 2002. **Dates:** Jan–May 2003; Sep–Dec 2003.

DJERASSI RESIDENT ARTISTS PROGRAM

2325 Bear Gulch Rd; Woodside, CA 94062–4405; (650) 747–1250,
    FAX 747–0105; email drap@djerassi.org;
    website www.djerassi.org
Dennis O'Leary, *Executive Director*
Judy Freeland, *Residency Coordinator*

Open to: playwrights, translators, composers, librettists, lyricists, solo performers, screenwriters. **Description:** 1-month residencies for writers, choreographers, composers, media, visual and interdisciplinary artists and performers concurrently at 600-acre ranch in Santa Cruz mountains 1 hour south of San Francisco; interdisciplinary projects encouraged; collaborative projects considered. **Financial arrangement:** free room and board. **Guidelines:** emerging or established artist whose work has clear direction; send SASE for application or download from web. **Application procedure:** application, sample of published work or work-in-progress, resume and $25 fee. **Deadline:** 15 Feb 2002 for 2003 residencies. **Notification:** 15 Aug 2002. **Dates:** Apr–Nov.

DORLAND MOUNTAIN ARTS COLONY

Box 6; Temecula, CA 92593; (909) 302–3837;
    email dorland@ez2.net; website www.ez2.net/dorland/

Open to: playwrights, composers, lyricists. **Description:** 1-month residencies for 6 writers, composers and visual artists concurrently in individual studios on 300-acre nature preserve 50 miles northeast of San Diego; no electricity. **Financial arrangement:** $50 nonrefundable processing fee upon scheduling, if accepted; resident pays cabin donation of $300 per month. **Guidelines:** artist must demonstrate clear direction and accomplishment in field. **Application procedure:** send SASE for application and information or download from web. **Deadline:** 1 Sep 2001; 1 Mar 2002. **Notification:** 2 months. **Dates:** year-round.

DORSET COLONY FOR WRITERS

Box 519; Dorset, VT 05251–0510; (802) 867–2223, FAX 867–0144;
   email theatre@sover.net; website www.theatredirectories.com
John Nassivera, *Executive Director*

Open to: playwrights, composers, librettists, lyricists. **Description:** residencies of 1 week–1 month at house located in historic village in southern VT. **Financial arrangement:** resident pays fee for housing according to means (suggested fee $120 a week); meals not provided; large, fully equipped kitchen. **Guidelines:** artist must demonstrate seriousness of purpose and have record of professional achievement (readings or productions of works); collaborative teams may apply; work sample may be requested from less established artist. **Application procedure:** letter of inquiry with description of proposed project and desired length and dates of stay; resume. **Deadline:** open. **Notification:** 2–3 weeks. **Dates:** 20 Sep–30 Nov; 15 Mar–20 May; winter residencies available in ancillary space.

THE GELL WRITERS CENTER

c/o Writers & Books; 740 University Ave; Rochester, NY 14607;
   (716) 473–2590, FAX 442–9333; website www.wab.org
Joseph Flaherty, *Executive Director*

Open to: playwrights, translators, librettists, lyricists, solo performers, screenwriters, television writers. **Description:** 2 private bedrooms available in house surrounded by 23 acres of woodlands; workshops on creative writing sometimes available at extra cost; residents provide own meals. **Financial arrangement:** resident pays $35 a day. **Application procedure:** write or call for application and brochure. **Deadline:** open. **Notification:** 1 week. **Dates:** year-round.

THE HAMBIDGE CENTER FOR CREATIVE ARTS AND SCIENCES

Box 339; Rabun Gap, GA 30568; (706) 746–5718, FAX 746–9933;
   email hambidge@rabun.net; website www.rabun.net/~hambidge

Open to: playwrights, translators, composers, librettists, lyricists. **Description:** residencies of 2 weeks–2 months for professionals in all areas of arts and humanities on 600 acres in northeast GA mountains; 8 private cottages with bedroom, kitchen, bathroom and studio/work area; evening meal provided Mon-Fri, Apr-Nov only; send SASE for guidelines. **Financial arrangement:** resident pays minimum of $125 a week toward total cost. **Application procedure:** application, work sample, resume, reviews, 3 letters of recommendation from professionals in applicant's field and $20 fee (applications received after deadline considered for space still available). **Deadline:** 1 Nov for spring and summer residencies; 1 May for fall and winter residencies. **Notification:** 2–3 months. **Dates:** year-round.

HAWTHORNDEN CASTLE INTERNATIONAL RETREAT FOR WRITERS

Lasswade, Midlothian; Scotland EH18 1EG; 44-131-440-2180
Administrator

Open to: playwrights. **Description:** residencies of 4 weeks for playwrights, poets and novelists at medieval castle on secluded crag overlooking valley of the River Esk 8 miles south of Edinburgh; 5 writers in residence at any one time; fully furnished study-bedroom; communal breakfast and dinner, lunch brought to writer's room; typewriter rental and use of excellent libraries in Edinburgh can be arranged. **Financial arrangement:** free room and board. **Guidelines:** author of at least 1 published work. **Application procedure:** write for application and further information. **Deadline:** 30 Sep 2001. **Notification:** mid-Jan 2002. **Dates:** Feb–Dec 2002.

HEADLANDS CENTER FOR THE ARTS

944 Fort Barry; Sausalito, CA 94965; (415) 331-2787,
    FAX 331-3857
Kathryn Reasoner, *Executive Director*

Open to: playwrights, composers, librettists, lyricists, screenwriters, television writers. **Description:** residencies of 1–3 months for artists in all disciplines at center in national park on 13,000 acres of coastal wilderness across the bay from San Francisco; accommodation in 4-bedroom house with communal kitchen; evening meal provided in mess hall Sun–Thur; 11-month "live-out" residencies available for Bay Area artists only, providing studio space, 2 meals a week and access to center's facilities but no housing; all residents encouraged to interact with fellow artists in other media and with the environment. **Financial arrangement:** stipend of $500 a month, travel and free housing for artist from outside Bay Area; $2500 stipend and studio space for Bay Area artist. **Guidelines:** CA, NC, NJ or OH residents only; students ineligible. **Application procedure:** call or write for information (applications available Apr 2002). **Deadline:** 7 Jun 2002. **Dates:** Feb–Dec 2003.

HEDGEBROOK

2197 East Millman Rd; Langley, WA 98260; (360) 321–4786;
    website www.hedgebrook.org
Denise Lee, *Operations Manager*

Open to: playwrights, librettists. **Description:** residencies of 1 week–2 months for women writers of diverse cultural backgrounds working in all literary genres; 6 individual cottages on 30 wooded acres on Whidbey Island, near Seattle; writer furnishes own computer. **Financial arrangement:** free room and board. **Guidelines:** woman writer of any age, published or unpublished; women of color encouraged to apply. **Application procedure:** application, project description, work sample and $15 fee; send SASE for application. **Deadline:** 1 Oct 2001 for winter–spring 2002; 15 Mar 2002 for summer–fall 2002. **Notification:** 2 months. **Dates:** year-round.

HELENE WURLITZER FOUNDATION OF NEW MEXICO

Box 1891; Taos, NM 87571; (505) 758–2413, FAX 758–2559
Michael Knight, *Director*

Open to: playwrights, composers, screenwriters. **Description:** 11 studio/apartments available to writers, composers and poets; length of residency flexible, usually 3 months; residencies currently booked through 2002. **Financial arrangement:** free housing and utilities; resident provides own meals; no financial aid. **Application procedure:** application, project description, work sample and resume; write or fax for application. **Deadline:** 18 Jan 2002. **Dates:** residencies available on limited basis 1 Oct–31 Mar.

ISLE ROYALE NATIONAL PARK ARTIST-IN-RESIDENCE

800 East Lakeshore Dr; Houghton, MI 49931;
    (906) 482–0984 (general information), 487–7152 (Greg Blust),
    FAX 482–8753; email greg_blust@nps.gov;
    website www.nps.gov/isro/

Open to: playwrights, composers, lyricists, solo performers. **Description:** 1 artist at a time housed for 2–3 weeks in cabin on remote island near Lake Superior; no electricity; resident must bring 2-3-week supply of food. **Financial arrangement:** free housing. **Guidelines:** writer with artistic integrity, ability to live in wilderness environment and to relate to park through their work; must donate 1 work to park and communicate experience of residency through programs for public. **Application**

procedure: application, project description, work sample and resume. **Deadline:** 16 Feb 2002. **Notification:** 15 Apr 2002. **Dates:** Jun-Sep.

THE JAMES THURBER WRITER-IN-RESIDENCE

The Thurber House; 77 Jefferson Ave; Columbus, OH 43215;
(614) 464-1032, FAX 228-7445;
email ThHouse@thurberhouse.org;
website www.thurberhouse.org
Michael J. Rosen, *Literary Director*

Open to: playwrights. **Description:** 4 residencies a year, each for 1 academic quarter (2 for journalists, 1 for playwright, 1 for poet or fiction writer); writer teaches course at Ohio State University. **Financial arrangement:** $6000 stipend; furnished apartment provided. **Guidelines:** playwright who has had at least 1 play produced by a major theatre; teaching experience helpful. **Application procedure:** letter of interest and curriculum vitae. **Deadline:** 15 Dec 2001. **Notification:** 3 months. **Dates:** winter or spring 2003.

THE JOHN STEINBECK WRITER'S ROOM

Long Island University-Southampton Campus Library;
Southampton, NY 11968; (631) 287-8382, FAX 287-4049;
email library@southampton.liu.edu
Robert Gerbereux, *Library Director*

Open to: playwrights. **Description:** small room, space for 4 writers; carrel, storage space, access to reference material in room and to library. **Financial arrangement:** free. **Guidelines:** writer working under contract or with specific commitment. **Application procedure:** application. **Notification:** 1 week. **Dates:** year-round.

KALANI OCEANSIDE ECO-RESORT INSTITUTE FOR CULTURE AND WELLNESS

RR2 Box 4500; Pahoa-Beach Road, HI 96778-9724; (808) 965-7828,
FAX 965-0527; email kalani@kalani.com;
website www.kalani.com
Richard Koob, *Director*

Open to: playwrights, translators, composers, librettists, lyricists, solo performers screenwriters, television writers. **Description:** up to 20 artists share four 500-1000-square-foot studio spaces for 2-week to 2-month residencies at 113-acre coastal resort spa with private rooms, resturaunt and shared or private baths. **Financial arrangement:** artist eligible for 50% discount on regular daily room rates of $110-240; meals available at resort restaurant, artist pays per meal or $29 per day. **Guidelines:** any artist with demonstrated ability to complete projects. **Application procedure:** application, project description, work sample and resume with $10 fee. **Deadline:** open. **Notification:** within 1 week of receipt of application. **Dates:** ongoing, but discounted rates more likely available May–Nov.

LANESBORO RESIDENCY PROGRAM FELLOWSHIPS

Cornicopia Arts Center; Box 152; Lanesboro, MN 55949;
  (507) 467-2446, FAX 467-4446; email cac2446@acegroup.cc
John Davis, *Executive Director*

Open to: playwrights, composer, librettists, lyricists, screenwriters, television writers, visual artists. **Description:** 4-6 residencies of 1-, 2- and 4-weeks in small Minnesota town with historic Main Street, 200-foot bluffs, trout river and bike trail; active arts and cultural community; artist spends minimum 6-8 hours working in community as part of their proposed project. **Financial arrangement:** $500-2000 stipend depending on duration of residency; housing and studio space. **Guidelines:** innovative and creative projects which further artists' work and promote meaningful community experience; write for application and guidelines. **Application procedure:** application form, work sample, 1 page community project description, resume, artist statement and 2 letters of reference. **Deadline:** 15 June for residencies Sep-Jan; 15 Oct for residencies Feb-Jul. **Notification:** 1-2 months. **Dates:** Sep-Jan; Feb-Jul.

LEDIG HOUSE INTERNATIONAL WRITERS' COLONY

55 Fifth Ave; 15th Floor; New York, NY 10003; (518) 392-7656,
  FAX 392-7656; email artomi55@aol.com;
  website www.artomi.org
David Knowles, *Executive Director*

Open to: playwrights, translators, screenwriters, television writers. **Description:** residencies of 1 week-2 months for up to 10 writers of all genres at 150-acre farm in upstate NY with library and computer access; private sleeping and work space; communal living and dining rooms; all meals provided. **Financial arrangement:** free room and board. **Guidelines:** published and unpublished writers proficient in English. **Application procedure:** project description, work sample, resume and letter of recommendation with SASE for notification; call or fax for guidelines.

Deadline: 30 Nov 2001. **Notification:** 31 Dec 2001. **Dates:** spring session 2 Apr-26 Jun; fall session 20 Aug-29 Oct.

LEIGHTON STUDIOS FOR INDEPENDENT RESIDENCIES

The Banff Centre for the Arts; Box 1020, Station 28;
107 Tunnel Mountain Dr; Banff, Alberta; Canada T0L 0C0;
(403) 762-6180, (800) 565-9989, FAX (403) 762-6345;
email arts_info@banffcentre.ab.ca;
website www.banffcentre.ab.ca/leighton_studios/
Office of the Registrar

Open to: playwrights, composers, performance artists, screenwriters, television writers. **Description:** residencies of 1 week-3 months for writers and composers at studios situated in mountains of Banff National Park; 8 furnished studios, each with washroom, kitchenette, Macintosh G3 laptop or G4 desktop with printing capabilities, CD/cassette player and internet and email access; living accommodations (single room with bath) on Centre's main campus; nearby access to all amenities of Centre, including dining room, library and recreation complex. **Financial arrangement:** resident pays approximate daily cost of $110 Canadian (about $71 U.S.) for studio, room and meals; discount on studio cost available for those who demonstrate need. **Guidelines:** established or emerging artist who demonstrates sustained contribution to own field and shows evidence of significant achievement. **Application procedure:** write or email for application and further information or download from web. **Deadline:** open; apply at least 6 months before desired residency. **Dates:** year-round.

THE MACDOWELL COLONY

100 High St; Peterborough, NH 03458-2485; (603) 924-3886,
(212) 535-9690, FAX (603) 924-9142;
email info@macdowellcolony.org;
website www.macdowellcolony.org
Cheryl Young, *Executive Director*

Open to: playwrights, composers, screenwriters, video writers. **Description:** residencies of up to 2 months for writers, composers, visual artists, video/filmmakers, architects and interdisciplinary artists at 450-acre estate; free room, board and exclusive use of studio; studios and common areas accessible for those with mobility impairments. **Financial arrangement:** voluntary contributions accepted; travel grants available; writers in need of financial assistance are eligible for grants of up to $1000 to relieve financial burdens related to their stay at the Colony. **Guidelines:** admission based on talent. **Application procedure:** application, work samples, project description, names of 2 professional references and $20 fee; collaborating artists must apply separately; send SASE, call or visit website for application. **Deadline:** 15 Sep 2001 for 1 Jan-30 Apr 2002; 15 Jan 2002 for 1 May-31 Aug 2002; 15 Apr 2002 for 1 Sep-31 Dec 2002. **Notification:** 2 months. **Dates:** year-round.

MARY ANDERSON CENTER FOR THE ARTS

101 St. Francis Dr; Mount St. Francis, IN 47146; (812) 923–8602,
   FAX 923–0294; email maca@iglou.com;
   website www.maryandersoncenter.org
Debra Carmody, *Executive Director*

Open to: playwrights, translators, composers, librettists, lyricists. **Description:** residencies of 1 week-3 months for 7 writers and visual artists concurrently at center on beautiful 400-acre wooded site with lake, 15 minutes from Louisville, KY; private studio/bedroom, communal kitchen and dining room. **Financial arrangement:** resident pays suggested minimum fee of $150 a week for room and board; possibility of funded residencies; write for information. **Guidelines:** formal education and production credits are not requirements but will be taken into consideration when applications are reviewed. **Application procedure:** application, project description, work sample, resume and 2 references. **Deadline:** open. **Notification:** 2-4 weeks. **Dates:** year-round.

THE MILLAY COLONY FOR THE ARTS

444 East Hill Rd; Box 3; Austerlitz, NY 12017–0003;
   (518) 392–3103; email giles@millaycolony.org;
   website www.millaycolony.org
Gail Giles, *Director of Admissions*

Open to: playwrights, composers, screenwriters. **Description:** 1-month residencies for up to 6 writers, composers and visual artists concurrently at 600-acre estate in upstate NY; studio space and separate bedroom; colony accommodates artists with disabilities. **Financial arrangement:** free room, board and studio space. **Application procedure:** application and supporting materials; send SASE or email (application@millaycolony.org) for application. **Deadline:** 1 Sep for Feb-May; 1 Feb for Jun-Sep; 1 May for Oct-Jan. **Notification:** 12-15 weeks after deadline. **Dates:** year-round.

MONTANA ARTISTS REFUGE

Box 8; Basin, MT 59631; (406) 225-3500;
  email mtrefuge@earthlink.net; website montanaartistsrefuge.org
Jennifer Pryor, *Administrative Coordinator*

Open to: playwrights, translators, composers, librettists, lyricists, solo performers, television writers, screenwriters. **Description:** 1-month-1-year residencies for 4-5 artists of all disciplines, located in a former gold camp in the midst of the Rocky Mountains, approximately 12 miles from the Continental Divide; Basin has 250 residents, two restaurant/bars, post office and town park; artists housed in 3 fully equipped apartments and one studio apartment, all with kitchens and private phones. **Financial arrangement:** resident pays $395-550 per month; meals not provided; financial aid available for up to full rent. **Guidelines:** open to all artists; send SASE for guidelines or download from web. **Application procedure:** application, work sample, project description and resume. **Deadline:** 15 Aug for Jan-Apr; 15 Jan for May-Sep; 15 May for Sep-Dec.

NEW YORK MILLS ARTS RETREAT

24 North Main Ave, Box 246; New York Mills, MN 56567;
  (218) 385-3339, FAX 385-3366; email nymills@uslink.net
Kent Scheer, *Coordinator*

Open to: playwrights, composers, librettists, lyricists, solo performers, screenwriters. **Description:** 1 artist at a time housed for 2-4 weeks in small farming community in north central Minnesota; housing in small one-bedroom home; resident provides own meals. **Financial arrangement:** Minnesota and New York City residents eligible to apply for 1 of 6 $1500 Jerome Foundation Fellowships. **Guidelines:** emerging artist of demonstrated ability; must donate 8 hours per week during residency to community outreach. **Application procedure:** application, project description, work sample, resume and 2 letters of recommendation. **Deadline:** 1 Oct 2001; 1 Apr 2002. **Notification:** 8 weeks after deadline. **Dates:** Sep-May.

NORCROFT

Box 218; Lutsen, MN 55612; (800) 770-0058;
  website www.norcroft.org
Kay Grindland, *Managing Director*

Open to: playwrights, translators, librettists, screenwriters, television writers. **Description:** 4 concurrent residencies of 1-4 weeks for women writers in all genres at remote lodge on shores of Lake Superior; private bedroom and separate individual "writing shed." **Financial arrangement:** free housing; groceries provided, resident does own cooking. **Guidelines:** women only; artist whose work demonstrates an understanding of and commitment to feminist change; download application from web. **Application procedure:** application, 5-page writing sample and one essay each on feminism and commitment to writing. **Deadline:** 1 Oct 2001. **Notification:** 1 Apr 2002. **Dates:** May–Oct.

RAGDALE FOUNDATION

1260 North Green Bay Rd; Lake Forest, IL 60045;
    (847) 234–1063, ext 206, FAX 234–1075;
    email ragdaleadmission@aol.com
Melissa Mosher, *Director of Admissions*

Open to: playwrights, composers, librettists, lyricists. **Description:** residencies of 2 weeks–2 months for writers, composers and visual artists from the U.S. and abroad on property situated on edge of 55-acre prairie, 1 mile from town center. **Financial arrangement:** resident pays $105 a week for room and board; partial or full fee waivers awarded on basis of financial need. **Guidelines:** admission based on quality of work submitted. **Application procedure:** application, description of work-in-progress, work sample, resume, 3 references and $20 fee; send 55¢ SASE for application. **Deadline:** 15 Jan for Jun–Dec; 1 Jun for Jan–Apr. **Notification:** 15 Apr for Jan deadline; 1 Sep for Jun deadline. **Dates:** year-round except for May, 1st week in Oct and last 2 weeks in Dec.

ROCKY MOUNTAIN NATIONAL PARK
ARTIST-IN-RESIDENCE PROGRAM

1000 Highway 36; Estes Park, CO 80517; (970) 586–1206;
    website www.nps.gov/romo
Information Office

Open to: playwrights, composers, lyricists, solo performers, visual artists. **Description:** 2-week residencies for 1 artist at a time in renovated historic furnished cabin overlooking meadow and stream with Rocky Mountains in distance; 1 bedroom, kitchen, living/dining room, bathroom and porch; artist gives 2 45-minute public presentations. **Financial arrangement:** free housing; resident provides own meals; must donate 1 appropriate work within 1 year of residency. **Guidelines:** professional artist. **Application procedure:** 6 copies of application, work sample, 6 copies of list of professional works, 6 copies of resume. **Deadline:** Jan 2002; exact date TBA. **Notification:** Mar 2002, exact date TBA. **Dates:** Jun–Sep.

SNUG HARBOR CULTURAL CENTER

1000 Richmond Terrace; Staten Island, NY 10301–9926;
    (718) 448–2500, FAX 442–8534
Rental Coordinator

Open to: playwrights, composers. **Description:** studio workspace in performing and visual arts center with theatre, art galleries, shops, museum, meeting rooms and banquet hall, located in 80-acre historic park. **Financial arrangement:** current monthly rental approximately $15-18 per sq. ft.; renewable 1-year lease; tenant must carry own insurance. **Guidelines:** professional artist. **Application procedure:** work sample with resume. **Dates:** year-round.

STUDIO FOR CREATIVE INQUIRY

Carnegie Mellon University; College of Fine Arts;
    Pittsburgh, PA 15213–3890; (412) 268–3454, FAX 268–2829;
    email mmbm@andrew.cmu.edu; website www.cmu.edu/studio/
Marge Myers, *Associate Director*

Open to: playwrights, translators, composers, librettists, lyricists, solo performers, screenwriters, television writers. **Description:** residencies of 6 months-3 years concurrently for artists in all disciplines; residency provides studio facility located in Carnegie Mellon's College of Fine Arts building, including office and meeting space, work area, computers, sound and video editing equipment; fellows may also use resources of university, including library. **Financial arrangement:** stipend; assistance in finding housing in community. **Guidelines:** writer able to use science and technology in work, interested in taking leadership role in collaborative projects and able to relate work to larger community. **Application procedure:** concept proposal, work sample and resume; admission based on quality of work, clear statement of intention, experience with collaboration and project feasibility. **Deadline:** open. **Notification:** 2 months. **Dates:** year-round.

THE TYRONE GUTHRIE CENTRE

Annaghmakerrig; Newbliss; County Monaghan;
    Ireland; 353-47-54003, FAX 353-47-54380;
    email thetgc@indigo.ie;
    website www.tyroneguthrie.ie
Resident Director

Open to: playwrights, composers, librettists, lyricists, screenwriters, television writers. **Description:** residencies of 1 week-6 months for artists in all disciplines at former country home of Tyrone Guthrie, set amid 450 acres of forested estate overlooking large lake; private apartments; music room, rehearsal/performance space and extensive library. **Financial arrangement:** non-Irish artists pay about Irish £2000 (about $2150) a month for housing and meals; self-catering houses also available at reasonable rents; fees may be negotiable depending on factors such as length of stay, nature of project, involvement with Irish artists or institutions, etc. **Guidelines:** artist must show evidence of sustained dedication and a significant level of achievement; prefers artist with clearly defined project; artist teams (e.g., writer/director, composer/librettist) welcome. **Application procedure:** write for application and further information. **Deadline:** open. **Dates:** year-round.

UCROSS FOUNDATION RESIDENCY PROGRAM

30 Big Red Ln; Clearmont, WY 82835; (307) 737-2291,
    FAX 737-2322; email ucross@wyoming.com
Sharon Dynak, *Executive Director*

Open to: playwrights, translators, composers, librettists, lyricists. **Description:** residency of 2 weeks-2 months at "Big Red," restored historic site in the foothills of the Big Horn Mountains; 8 concurrent residencies for writers, composers and visual artists; opportunity to concentrate on own work without distraction and to present work to local communities, if desired. **Financial arrangement:** free room, board and studio space. **Guidelines:** criteria are quality of work and commitment; send SASE for application and further information. **Application procedure:** application, project description and work sample. **Deadline:** 1 Oct for Feb-Jun; 1 Mar for Aug-Dec. **Notification:** 8 weeks. **Dates:** year-round except Jan and Jul.

THE U.S./JAPAN CREATIVE ARTISTS' PROGRAM

Japan–U.S. Friendship Commission; 1120 Vermont Ave NW,
   Suite 925; Washington, DC 20005; (202) 418–9800,
   FAX 418–9802; email jusfc@jusfc.gov; website www.jusfc.gov
Eric J. Gangloff, *Executive Director*

Open to: playwrights, composers, librettists, lyricists, solo performers, screenwriters, television writers. **Description:** residencies of 6 continuous months for 3-5 artists each year; residents find own housing in location of their choice in Japan. **Financial arrangement:** monthly stipend of ¥400,000 (about $3350) plus ¥100,000 (about $840) for housing and ¥100,000 (about $840) for professional expenses; free travel and pre-departure Japanese language instruction. **Guidelines:** U.S. citizen or permanent resident; mid-career professional artist with compelling reason to work in Japan and whose work "exemplifies the best in U.S. art"; visit website for application and further information. **Application procedure:** application, work sample and resume. **Deadline:** Jun 2002; exact dates TBA.

VIRGINIA CENTER FOR THE CREATIVE ARTS

Box VCCA, Mt. San Angelo; Sweet Briar, VA 24595; (804) 946–7236,
   FAX 946–7239; email vcca@vcca.com; website www.vcca.com
Director

Open to: playwrights, translators, composers, librettists, lyricists, screenwriters. **Description:** residencies of 2 weeks–2 months for writers, composers and visual and performance artists at 450-acre estate in Blue Ridge Mountains; separate studios and bedrooms; all meals provided. **Financial arrangement:** resident pays suggested minimum of $30 a day for room and board or as means allow; financial status not a factor in selection process. **Guidelines:** admission based on achievement or promise of achievement. **Application procedure:** application, work sample, resume and 2 recommendations. **Deadline:** 15 Sep for Feb–May; 15 Jan for Jun–Sep; 15 May for Oct–Jan. **Notification:** 3 months. **Dates:** year-round.

WALDEN RESIDENCY PROGRAM

Extended Campus Programs; Southern Oregon University;
1250 Siskiyou Blvd; Ashland, OR 97520–5038; (541) 552–6901,
FAX 552–6047; email friendly@sou.edu;
website www.sou.edu/ecp/arts/walden.html
Brooke Friendly, *Arts Coordinator*

Open to: playwrights. **Description:** 3 6-week residencies for writers of drama, fiction, poetry and creative nonfiction at farm near Ashland, OR; 1 writer at a time housed in cabin with kitchen facilities, which opens onto meadow surrounded by forest. **Financial arrangement:** free; no meals provided. **Guidelines:** OR resident only; send SASE for full application or download from web. **Application procedure:** application, project description, work sample and list of publications or productions. **Deadline:** 30 Nov 2001. **Notification:** mid-Dec 2001. **Dates:** Mar-Jul 2002.

WILLIAM FLANAGAN MEMORIAL CREATIVE PERSONS CENTER

Edward F. Albee Foundation; 14 Harrison St;
New York, NY 10013; (212) 226–2020;
website www.pipeline.com/~jtnyc/albeefdtn.html

Open to: playwrights, translators, composers, librettists, screenwriters. **Description:** 1-month residencies for up to 5 writers, composers and visual artists concurrently at "The Barn" in Montauk, Long Island. **Financial arrangement:** free housing. **Guidelines:** admission based on talent and need; write for further information. **Application procedure:** application, script (recording for composers) and supporting materials. **Deadline:** 1 Apr 2002; no submission before 1 Jan 2002. **Notification:** May 2002. **Dates:** 1 Jun-1 Oct 2002.

THE WRITERS ROOM

10 Astor Pl, 6th Floor; New York, NY 10003; FAX (212) 533–6059;
website www.writersroom.org
Donna Brodie, *Executive Director*

Open to: playwrights, translators, composers, librettists, lyricists. **Description:** large room with 35 desks separated by partitions, space for 300 writers each quarter; open 24 hours a day year-round; kitchen, lounge and bathrooms, storage for files and laptops, small reference library; monthly readings. **Financial arrangement:** $50 application fee; $60 key desposit; $110-185 quarterly fee (3-month period). **Guidelines:** writer, emerging or established, must show seriousness of intent. **Application procedure:** application and references; all inquiries by mail or through website (no visits without appointment).

THE WRITERS' STUDIO

The Mercantile Library Association; 17 East 47th St;
    New York, NY 10017; (212) 755-6710, FAX 758-1387;
    email mercantile_library@msn.com;
    website www.fictionlibrary.org
Harold Augenbraum, *Director*

Open to: playwrights, composers. **Description:** carrel space for 17 writers (3 reserved for writers of children's literature) in not-for-profit, private lending library of 175,000 volumes; storage for personal computers or typewriters, library membership, access to special reference collection and rare collection of 19th-century American and British literature. **Financial arrangement:** $200 fee for 3 months, renewal possible for up to 1 year. **Guidelines:** open to all writers; unpublished writer must submit evidence of serious intent. **Application procedure:** application and work sample or project outline.

YADDO

Box 395; Saratoga Springs, NY 12866-0395; (518) 584-0746,
    FAX 584-1312; email yaddo@yaddo.org; website www.yaddo.org
Admissions Committee

Open to: playwrights, composers, performance artists, screenwriters. **Description:** residencies of 2 weeks-2 months for artists in all genres, working individually or as collaborative teams of up to 3 persons, at 19th-century estate on 400 acres; approximate total of 200 residents a year (15 concurrently Sep-May, 35 concurrently May-Labor Day). **Financial arrangement:** free room, board and studio space. **Guidelines:** admission based on review by panels composed of artists in each genre; quality of work submitted is major criterion; send 55¢ SASE for application and further information. **Application procedure:** application, work sample, resume, 2 letters of support, $20 fee and SASP for acknowledgment of receipt. **Deadline:** 15 Jan 2002 for mid-May 2002-Feb 2003; 1 Aug 2002 for 1 Nov 2002-mid-May 2003. **Notification:** 1 Apr 2002 for Jan deadline; 15 Oct 2002 for Aug deadline. **Dates:** year-round except early Sep.

MEMBERSHIP AND SERVICE ORGANIZATIONS

What's included here?

A number of organizations that exist to serve either the American playwright or a wider constituency of writers, composers and arts professionals. Some have a particular regional or special-interest orientation; some provide links to theatres in other countries. Taken together, these organizations represent an enormous range of services available to those who write for the theatre, and it is worth getting to know them.

THE ALLIANCE OF LOS ANGELES PLAYWRIGHTS

7510 Sunset Blvd, #1050; Los Angeles, CA 90046-3418;
  (323) 957-4752
Dan Berkowitz and Dick Dotterer, *Co-Chairs*

Founded in 1993, ALAP is a support and service organization dedicated to addressing the professional needs of the Los Angeles playwriting community. ALAP's programs and activities include the Playwrights Expo, which brings together L.A. playwrights and dozens of representatives of local and national theatres; the series In Our Own Voices, in which members read from and share their work; the annual Playreading Festival in which local theatres present rehearsed readings of members' plays; the C. Bernard Jackson Award, given in recognition of individuals and organizations that nurture, develop and support L.A. playwrights; symposia and panel discussions; networking and social events; and a hotline listing upcoming events. ALAP's publications include the bimonthly *NewsFlash*, which keeps members posted on upcoming events; the journal *InterPlay*; and an annual *Membership Directory*. Annual dues are $35.

THE ALLIANCE OF RESIDENT THEATRES/NEW YORK

575 Eighth Ave, Suite 17S; New York, NY 10018; (212) 244-6667,
  FAX 714-1918; email questions@art-newyork.org
  website www.offbroadwayonline.com
Virginia P. Louloudes, *Executive Director*
Mary Harpster, *Deputy Director*

The Alliance of Resident Theates (A.R.T./New York) is the trade and service organization for the not-for-profit professional theatre, serving more than 300 New York-based theatre companies and professional affiliates (theatres outside NY, colleges and universities, and organizations providing services to the theatre field). Publications of interest include the *Member Directory*, *Rehearsal and Performance Space Guide*; *Internship Directory*; and *Where to Send Unsolicited Resumes, Manuscripts and Headshots*.

ALTERNATE ROOTS

1083 Austin Ave; Atlanta, GA 30307; (404) 577-1079,
  FAX 577-7991; email altroots1@earthlink.net;
  website www.alternateroots.org
Alice Lovelace, *Managing Director*

Founded in 1976, Alternate ROOTS is a service organization run by and for southeastern artists. Its mission is to support the creation and presentation of original performing art that is rooted in a particular community of place, tradition or spirit. It is committed to social and economic justice and the protection of the natural world, and addresses these concerns through its programs and services. ROOTS now has more than 260 individual members across the country, including playwrights, directors, choreographers, musicians, storytellers, clowns and new vaudevillians—both solo artists and representatives of 65 performing and presenting organizations. ROOTS aims to make artistic resources available to its members through workshops; to create appropriate distribution networks for the new work being generated in the region via touring, publications and liaison activity; and to provide opportunities for enhanced visibility and financial stability via publications and periodic performance festivals. Opportunities for member playwrights include readings and peer critiques of works-in-progress at the organization's annual meeting. Membership is open to all artists whose work is consistent with the goals of ROOTS; members are accepted throughout the year. The organization's meetings and workshops are open to the public and its newsletter is available to the public for a small fee. Annual membership dues are $50 for members, $75 for Board Members.

THE AMERICAN ALLIANCE FOR THEATRE & EDUCATION (AATE)

c/o Department of Theatre; Arizona State University; Box 872002;
    Tempe, AZ 85287–2002; (480) 965–6064, FAX 965–5351;
    email aateinfo@asu.edu; website www.aate.com
Joseph Juliano, Jr., *President*
Christy M. Taylor, *Administrative Director*

AATE is a membership organization created in 1987 with the merger of the American Association of Theatre for Youth and the American Association for Theatre in Secondary Education. AATE provides a variety of services to support the work of theatre artists and educators who work with young people and to promote theatre and drama/theatre education in elementary and secondary schools. To encourage the development and production of plays for young audiences, the AATE Unpublished Play Reading Project annually selects and publicizes promising new plays in this field. AATE also sponsors annual awards for the best play for young people and the outstanding book relating to any aspect of the field published in the past calendar year; only the play or book's publisher may nominate a candidate for these awards. AATE's publications, which are free to members, include a quarterly online newsletter with a Playwright's Page; the yearly *Youth Theatre Journal*; and the quarterly *STAGE of the Art*. Membership is open to all and costs $60 for students, $71 for retirees, $98 for individuals and $131 for organizations; please add $20 (U.S. funds) for foreign members (outside the U.S. and Canada).

AMERICAN INDIAN COMMUNITY HOUSE

708 Broadway, 8th Floor; New York, NY 10003; (212) 598-0100,
    FAX 598-4909; website www.aich.org
Rosemary Richmond, *Executive Director*
Jim Cyrus, *Director of Performing Arts*

American Indian Community House was founded in 1969 to encourage the interest of all U.S. ethnic groups in the cultural contributions of the American Indian, and to foster intercultural exchanges. The organization now serves the Native American population of the New York City region through a variety of social, economic and educational programs, and through cultural programs which include theatre events, an art gallery and a newsletter. Native Americans in the Arts, the performing arts component of the Community House, is committed to the development and production of works by Indian authors, and presents staged readings, workshops and full productions in The Circle, their in-house performance space. The Community House also sponsors several other performing groups, including Spiderwoman Theatre, Coatlicue Theatre Company, the actors' group Off the Beaten Path, the Thunderbird American Indian Dancers, the Silver Cloud Singers and the jazz-fusion and traditional singing group Ulali. A showcase for Native American artists is presented to agents and casting directors once a year.

AMERICAN MUSIC CENTER (AMC)

30 West 26th St, Suite 1001; New York, NY 10010-2011;
    (212) 366-5260, FAX 366-5265; email center@amc.net;
    websites www.amc.net and www.newmusicbox.org
Richard Kessler, *Executive Director*
Lyn Liston, *New Music Information Specialist*

Founded in 1939, the American Music Center provides numerous programs and services for composers, performers and others interested in contemporary American jazz and classical music. The Jory Copying Assistance Program helps composers pay for copying music and extracting performance materials. The center's library contains more than 60,000 scores and recordings, including a large collection of opera and music-theatre works, available for perusal by interested performers. The AMC provides information on competitions, publishers, performing ensembles, composers and other areas of interest in new music, and its publication Opportunities in New Music is updated annually. Members receive the monthly "Opportunity Update"; can access AMC's free monthly online magazine, (www.newmusicbox.org) which features interviews, news and samples of new recordings; and are eligible for discounts on AMC publications; new members receive a free packet of information and articles of interest to the American composer. All members may vote in the annual board elections and attend the annual meeting. Membership is open to any person or organization wishing to support the center's promotion of the creation, performance and appreciation of American music. Annual dues are $55 for individuals ($35 for students under 25 and senior citizens).

AMERICAN TRANSLATORS ASSOCIATION (ATA)

225 Reinekers Ln, Suite 590; Alexandria, VA 22314-2840;
(703) 683-6100, FAX 683-6122; email ata@atanet.org;
website www.atanet.org
Walter W. Bacak, Jr., *Executive Director*

Founded in 1959, the ATA is a national not-for-profit association which seeks to promote recognition of the translation profession; disseminate information for the benefit of translators and those who use their services; define and maintain professional standards; foster and support the training of translators and interpreters; and provide a medium of cooperation with persons in allied professions. Members receive the monthly *ATA Chronicle* and a membership directory. Other publications include a *Translation Services Directory* containing professional profiles of individual members. ATA holds an annual conference and sponsors several honors and awards (see American Translators Association Awards in Prizes). Active membership is open to U.S. citizens and permanent residents who have professionally engaged in translating or closely related work and have passed an ATA accreditation examination or demonstrated professional attainment by other prescribed means. Those who meet these professional standards but are not U.S. citizens or residents may hold Corresponding membership; other interested persons may be Associate members. Interested persons should contact ATA for a membership application, or visit the ATA website. Annual dues are $50 for Associate-Students; $95 for Active, Corresponding and Associate members; $120 for institutions; and $175 for corporations.

ASCAP (American Society of Composers, Authors and Publishers)

1 Lincoln Plaza; New York, NY 10023; (212) 621-6234,
FAX 621-6558; website www.ascap.net
Michael A. Kerker, *Director of Musical Theatre*

ASCAP is a not-for-profit organization whose members are writers and publishers of musical works. It operates as a clearinghouse for performing rights, offering licenses that authorize the public performance of all the music of its composer, lyricist and music publishing members, and collecting license fees for these members. ASCAP also sponsors workshops for member and nonmember theatre writers (see ASCAP Musical Theatre Workshop in Development). Membership in ASCAP is open to any composer or lyricist who has been commercially recorded or regularly published. Annual dues are $10 for individuals.

Asian American Arts Alliance

74 Varick St, Suite 302; New York, NY 10013-1914; (212) 941-9208,
FAX 941-7978; email info@aaartsalliance.org;
website www.aaartsalliance.org
Lillian Cho, *Executive Director*

Asian American Arts Alliance is a not-for-profit arts service organization founded in 1983 to increase the support, recognition and appreciation of Asian-American arts. The Arts Alliance strives to assist Asian-American artists and arts groups and works to raise the awareness of the diversity of Asian-American arts and cultures. The organization provides information resources, networking and advocacy services, and professional assistance through technical aid, public forums and roundtables, and a resource library. Public programs and special projects include Artist Series forums, Nuts & Bolts technical assistance workshops and the Chase SMARTS Regrant Program for New York City Asian American arts groups. Publications include the *Directory of Asian American Arts Organizations and Touring Artists*, a bimonthly *Asian American Arts Calendar/Resources and Opportunities* and a semiannual art magazine, *Dialogue*. There are 7 membership levels: Starving Artist, $20; Mover & Shaker, $45; Arts Organization, $60; Project Leader, $100; Arts Patron, $250; Philanthropist, $500; and Leadership Council, $1000. Members receive discounts on advertising, special publications and events; additional benefits are provided to major donors.

A.S.K. THEATER PROJECTS

11845 West Olympic Blvd, Suite 1250 W; Los Angeles, CA 90064;
   (310) 478-3200, FAX 478-5300; email info@askplay.org;
   website www.askplay.org

Since 1989, A.S.K. Theater Projects has been a local and national resource for the theatre and its artists. A.S.K. facilitates the creation of new work through a broad range of artistic and educational programs, including readings and workshop productions; symposia, festivals, caucuses and labs which explore issues vital to the theatre; a playwrights-in-the-schools program; online services; and publications. (See A.S.K. Theater Projects in Development.)

ASSITEJ/USA (INTERNATIONAL ASSOCIATION OF THEATRE FOR CHILDREN AND YOUNG PEOPLE)

724 Second Ave S; Nashville, TN 37210; (615) 254-5719,
   FAX 254-3255; email usassitej@aol.com;
   website www.assitej-usa.org
Steve Bianchi, *Membership Director*

Founded in 1965, ASSITEJ/USA is a not-for-profit theatre agency which advocates the development of professional theatre for young audiences in the USA and facilitates interchange among theatre artists and scholars of the 60 member countries of ASSITEJ. ASSITEJ/USA sponsors festivals and seminars, operates an international playscript exchange and, with ASSITEJ/Japan, is founder of the Pacific-Asia Exchange Program. Members are theatres, institutions and individuals concerned about the theatre, young audiences and international goodwill. Members receive *Theatre for Young Audiences Today*, published 2-3 times annually, and priority consideration for participation in national and international events. Membership costs $30 a year for students, $35 for retirees, $50 for libraries, $65 for individuals, $125-375 for organizations (depending on size of budget). Write or call for membership application.

THE ASSOCIATED WRITING PROGRAMS (AWP)

Tallwood House, Mail Stop 1E3; George Mason University;
   Fairfax, VA 22030; (703) 993-4301, FAX 993-4302;
   email awp@gmu.edu; website www.awpwriter.org
David Fenza, *Executive Director*

Founded in 1967, AWP is a not-for-profit organization serving the needs of writers, college and university writing programs, and students of writing by providing information services, job placement assistance, publishing opportunities, literary arts advocacy and forums on all aspects of writing and its instruction. Writers' Conferences & Centers (WC&C), an association of 88 nonacademic conferences for writers, is now a division of AWP. Writers not affiliated with colleges and universities but who support collective efforts to improve opportunities are also represented by AWP. The *Writer's Chronicle,* published 6 times annually and available for $20 a year, includes listings of publishing opportunities, grants, awards and fellowships; interviews with writers; and essays on writing technique. The *AWP Official Guide to Writing Programs* (9th edition, $25.95 including shipping) offers a comprehensive listing of writing programs and an expanded section on writing conferences, colonies and centers. Write or call AWP for information on membership requirements.

ASSOCIATION FOR JEWISH THEATRE

c/o Winnipeg Jewish Theatre; C402-123 Doncaster;
   Winnipeg, MB R3N2B2; (204) 477-7518, FAX 477-7516;
   email Kayla@wjt.ca; website www.wjt.ca/ajt.htm
Kayla Gordon, *President*

Founded in 1987, the Association for Jewish Theatre is dedicated to promoting the development and production of plays relevant to Jewish life and values. AJT acts to promote the visibility and viability of those theatres dedicated to a Jewish mission. Membership is open to theatres, as well as individual artists, who have shown a commitment to Jewish theatre. Services include annual conference (reduced fee for members), new play showcases at conferences, free tickets to member theatre productions, publication of semiannual newsletter, networking opportunities and assistance in coordinating cooperatively developed projects. Annual dues range from $35-100 depending on theatre budget and individual financial situation; dues are reevaluated by Board each year.

ASSOCIATION FOR THEATRE IN HIGHER EDUCATION (ATHE)

Box 4537; Boulder, CO 80306-4537; (888) 284-3737,
   FAX (303) 440-0852; email nericksn@aol.com;
   website www.hawaii.edu/athe
Nancy Erickson, *Administrative Director*

Founded in 1986, ATHE is an organization composed of individuals and institutions that provides vision and leadership for the profession and promotes excellence in theatre education. Membership services include insurance benefits, scholarships, annual professional awards including the

Jane Chambers Playwriting Award (see Prizes) and assistance with issues such as tenure and alternate employment opportunities. The annual conference convenes theatre scholars, educators and professionals from all over the world to participate in workshops, performances, plenary sessions and group meetings. ATHE publishes several periodicals of interest to the theatre professional, including *ATHENEWS*, a quarterly newsletter that includes a list of teaching positions available at member organizations; *Theatre Topics*, a semiannual journal; *Theatre Journal,* a quarterly journal; a membership directory and pamphlets on various topics such as assessment guidelines for higher education theatre programs and tenure. There are 5 annual membership levels: Students, $50; Retirees, $80; Individuals, $105; 2-Person Households, $155; Organizations, $195. Members receive all publications.

THE ASSOCIATION OF HISPANIC ARTS (AHA)

250 West 26th St, 4th Floor; New York, NY 10001; (212) 727-7227,
    FAX 727-0549; email ahanews@mindspring.com
Sandra Perez, *Executive Director*

A not-for-profit organization founded in 1975, AHA promotes the Latin American arts as an integral part of this country's cultural life. It acts as a clearinghouse for information on all the arts, including theatre, and publishes a quarterly newsletter, *AHA! Hispanic Arts News*, that provides information on playwriting contests, workshops, forums and other items of interest to Latin American artists. AHA also provides technical assistance to Latin American artists seeking funding.

ASSOCIATION OF INDEPENDENT VIDEO AND FILMMAKERS (AIVF)

304 Hudson St, 6th Floor; New York, NY 10013; (212) 807-1400,
    FAX 463-8519; email info@aivf.org; website www.aivf.org
Elizabeth Peters, *Executive Director*

Founded in 1975, the Association of Independent Video & Filmmakers (AIVF) is the membership organization of the Foundation for Independent Video and Film (FIVF). Its mission is to increase the creative and professional opportunities for independent video and filmmakers and to enhance the growth of independent media by providing services and information such as health and production insurance, networking seminars and events, a resource library and publication of books and directories, as well as *The Independent Film & Video Monthly.* As one of the largest organizations serving and representing independent film and video makers, as well as public television and cable access producers, AIVF's membership consists of media artists working in all genres, including documentary, animation, experimental, narrative, interactive and multimedia.

AUSTIN SCRIPT WORKS (ASW)

Box 9787; Austin, TX 78766; (512) 454-9727;
email info@scriptworks.org; website www.scriptworks.org
John Walch, *Artistic Director*

Founded in 1997, Austin Script Works is a playwright-driven organization which provides support for playwrights at all stages in the writing process. ASW's programs include salon readings, staged readings, workshops, one-act commissions, writing retreats, online services and full productions. ASW also coproduces, with the State Theater Company, the Harvest Festival of New American Plays (see Prizes). Associate Membership ($35 annually) is open to anyone. Benefits of Associate membership include participation in salon readings and the 10-minute playwriting retreat; the opportunity to apply for staged readings, 10-minute play showcase productions and the Harvest Festival; and discounts to all ASW events. Core membership ($50 annually) is open only to playwrights living in the central Texas region. Playwrights are selected based on script submission for a 4-year period. Core members receive all benefits of Associate members and are also eligible to apply for small stipends, commissions and full productions.

BLACK THEATRE NETWORK (BTN)

c/o Kuntu Repertory Theatre; 3T01 Wesley W. Posvar Hall;
230 South Bouquet St; Pittsburgh, PA 15260;
email rroebuck@pitt.edu; website www.btnet.org
Eileen Morris, *President*
Rachel Roebuck, *Office Manager*

Black Theatre Network (BTN) is a national network of professional artists, scholars and community groups founded in 1986 to provide an opportunity for the interchange of ideas; to publish information regarding black theatre activity; to provide an annual national forum to view and discuss black theatre; and to encourage and promote black dramatists and the production of plays about the black experience. BTN members are eligible to attend national conferences and workshops and receive complimentary copies of all BTN publications, which include the quarterly *Black Theatre Network News*, listing conferences, contests, BTN business matters and national items of interest; *Black Theatre Directory*, which contains over 800 listings of black theatre artists, scholars, companies, higher education programs and service organizations; *Dissertations Concerning Black Theatre: 1900–1994*, a listing of Ph.D. theses; and *Black Theatre Connections*, a quarterly listing of jobs in educational and professional theatre, and other career development opportunities. *Black Voices*, a catalog of works by black playwrights, is available from BTN for $20. Annual dues are $35 for retirees and students, $75 for individuals, $110 for organizations.

BMI (BROADCAST MUSIC INCORPORATED)

320 West 57th St; New York, NY 10019–3790; (212) 586–2000,
    FAX 262–2824
Jean Banks, *Senior Director, Musical Theater and Jazz*

BMI, founded in 1940, is a performing rights organization which acts as a steward for the public performance of the music of its writers and publishers, offering licenses to music users. BMI monitors music performances and distributes royalties to those whose music has been used. Any writer whose songs have been published and are likely to be performed can join BMI at no cost. BMI also sponsors a musical theatre workshop (see BMI-Lehman Engel Musical Theatre Workshop in Development).

The BMI Foundation (President, Theodora Zavin) was established in 1984 to provide support for individuals in furthering their musical education and to assist organizations involved in the performance of music and music training.

BROADWAY ON SUNSET

10800 Hesby St; North Hollywood, CA 91601; (818) 508–9270,
    FAX 508–1806; email BroadwayonSunset@cs.com;
    website www. BroadwayonSunset.org
Kevin Kaufman, *Executive Director*
Libbe HaLevy, *Literary Director*

Broadway on Sunset, a not-for-profit organization established in 1993, sponsors the First Look Competition of new unproduced musicals; the winner receives a concert reading at their Annual West Coast Musical Theatre Conference. Since its inception, Broadway on Sunset has presented more than 100 original musicals as well as interviews and symposia.

CENTRE FOR CREATIVE COMMUNITIES

118 Commercial St; London E1 6NF; England; 44-20-7247-5385,
    FAX 44-20-7247-5256; email info@creativecommunities.org.uk;
    website www.creativecommunities.org.uk
Jennifer Williams, *Executive Director*

Founded in 1978, the Centre for Creative Communities is a not-for-profit
organization dedicated to promoting community development through arts
and education. CCC conducts research, organizes conferences, produces a
quarterly newsletter and is part of an international network of arts and
education organizations. CCC's specialized arts and education library
houses information on opportunities for artists and performers both in the
U.K. and abroad. CCC is not a grant-giving organization.

THE CENTRE FOR INDIGENOUS THEATRE

401 Richmond St W; Box 75; Suite 260; Toronto, Ontario M5V 1X3;
    (416) 506-9436; FAX 506-9430; email cit@interlog.com;
    website www.interlog.com/~cit/cit.html
Bruce Chown, *Managing Director*

Founded in 1974, The Centre for Indigenous Theatre is primarily a training
program for Aboriginal writers, directors and actors. The Centre serves as a
reference source for the native Aboriginal theatre community in Canada,
offering listings of events; catalogs of scripts; information about actors and
writers; cold and staged readings of new plays with students; and the
quarterly publication *Onsookad*, which describes school and student
activities. There are no membership dues, but all members must self-
identify as Aboriginal.

CHICAGO ALLIANCE FOR PLAYWRIGHTS (CAP)

Theatre Building; 1225 West Belmont; Chicago, IL 60657-3205;
    (773) 929-7367, ext 60, FAX 327-1404
Joanne Koch, *President*

The Chicago Alliance for Playwrights is a service organization founded in
1990 to establish a network for Chicago-area playwrights and others
committed to the development of new work for the stage. Members of the
coalition include Chicago Dramatists (see listing below), Columbia College
New Musicals Project, New Tuners Theatre/Workshop (see Production),
Studio Z and Writers Bloc. The alliance sponsors forums of interest to
writers and publishes an annual directory of Chicago-area playwrights and

their principal works. Write or call for membership details; annual dues are $25 for individuals and $100 for groups.

CHICAGO DRAMATISTS

1105 West Chicago Ave; Chicago, IL 60622–5702; (312) 633–0630,
FAX 633–0610; email newplays@aol.com
Russ Tutterow, *Artistic Director*

Founded in 1979, Chicago Dramatists is dedicated to the development of playwrights and new plays. It employs a variety of year-round programs to nurture the artistic and career development of both established and emerging playwrights, including play readings, productions, classes, workshops, symposia, discussions, panels, festivals, talent coordination, marketing services, collaborative projects with other theatres, national playwright exchanges and referrals to producers.

The Resident Playwright program seeks to nurture the work and careers of Chicago-area dramatists who will potentially make significant contributions to the national theatre repertory. At no charge, Resident Playwrights benefit from Chicago Dramatists' fullest and longest-term support (a 3-year, renewable term), with complete access to all programs and services. Admittance to the program is selective, with emphasis on artistic and professional accomplishment or potential. Interested playwrights should contact Chicago Dramatists for full information and details of the application procedure, which includes the submission of 2 plays, a resume and letters of recommendation and intent. *Deadline:* 1 Apr each year (no submission before 1 Mar).

The Playwrights' Network provides any U.S. playwright the opportunity to form an association with Chicago Dramatists. For an annual fee of $95, Network playwrights receive written script critiques, consideration for all programs and productions, class discounts, free admittance to events and other benefits.

Classes and the quarterly 10-Minute Workshop are open to all playwrights. Quarterly flyers announce events and programs, and include application procedures.

THE CHILDREN'S THEATRE FOUNDATION OF AMERICA (CTFA)

Box 8067; New Orleans, LA 70182; (504) 897–1839,
(FAX) 866–0502
Orlin Corey, *President*

Founded in 1958, The Children's Theatre Foundation of America (CTFA) is a not-for-profit organization which seeks to advance the artistic and professional interests of theatre and theatre education for children and youth by funding proposals of artists and scholars working in those fields. In the past CTFA has funded playwriting grants, scholarships, research, performances and lectures, theatre festivals, conferences, symposia, publications and crisis-management assistance. CTFA also administers the annual Aurand Harris Children's Theatre Grants and Fellowships (see Fellowships and Grants), as well as awarding a Medallion for significant achievement in the field of children's theatre.

COLORADO DRAMATISTS

Box 40516; Denver, CO 80204; (303) 675-6500;
    email mgraves@ecentral.com
Marina Graves, *President*

Founded in 1981, Colorado Dramatists, with chapters in Denver and Boulder, is a service organization for playwrights at all levels of development. In addition to bimonthly public readings, the organization sponsors small, private developmental groups; readings; workshops; seminars; a program that enters playwrights in regional 10-minute play festivals; and a mentoring program. Members receive a bimonthly newsletter, *Colorado Dramatists Newsletter*, and access to rehearsal space. Members are also eligible to enter the one-act playwriting contest from which 2 winners will receive professional production. Membership dues for first-time members are $25, thereafter annual dues are $10 for actors and students, $30 for all other individuals.

CORPORATION FOR PUBLIC BROADCASTING

401 9th St NW; Washington, DC 20004-2037; (202) 879-9600,
    FAX 783-1019; website www.cpb.org
Vice President, Program Strategies

Founded in 1967, the Corporation for Public Broadcasting, a private not-for-profit organization funded by Congress, promotes and helps finance public television and radio. CPB provides grants to local public television and radio stations; conducts research in audience development, new broadcasting technologies and other areas. The corporation helped establish the Public Broadcasting Service and National Public Radio (see entries in this section). It supports public radio programming through programming grants to stations and other producers, and television programming by funding proposals made by stations and independent producers.

THE DRAMATISTS GUILD OF AMERICA, INC.

1501 Broadway, Suite 701; New York, NY 10036; (212) 398-9366,
FAX 944-0420; email tstratton@dramaguild.com
John Weidman, *President*
Christopher Wilson, *Executive Director*

The Dramatists Guild of America, founded over 75 years ago, is the only professional association governed by and established to advance the rights of playwrights, composers and lyricists. The Guild has more than 6000 members worldwide, from beginning writers to Broadway veterans. Membership benefits include a business affairs toll-free hotline, which offers advice on all theatre-related topics, including options, commissions, copyright procedures and contract reviews; model production contracts, which provide the best protection for the writer at all levels of production; collaboration, commission and licensing agreements; seminars led by experienced professionals concerning pressing topics for today's dramatist; access to a national health insurance program and a group term life insurance plan; free/discounted tickets to Off-Broadway/Broadway performances; and a meeting room that can accommodate more than 50 people for readings and backers auditions, available for a nominal rental fee. The Guild has 4 levels of membership: 1. Active ($125 a year): writers who have been produced on Broadway, Off-Broadway or on the mainstage of a LORT theatre; 2. Associate ($75 a year): theatrical writers who have been produced in other venues or who have completed a full script; 3. Student ($35 a year): full-time students enrolled in an accredited writing degree program; 4. Estate ($125 a year): representatives of the estates of deceased authors.

Members receive *The Dramatists Guild Newsletter*, issued 6 times a year with up-to-date business affairs articles and script opportunities; *The Dramatist*, a magazine that contains interviews as well as articles on all aspects of theatre; *The Dramatists Guild Resource Directory*, a biannual collection of contact information on producers, agents, contests, workshops and production companies. The periodicals are available to nonwriters on a subscription basis: Individual Subscribers ($25 a year): individuals receive *The Dramatist* only; Institutional Subscribers ($135 a year): educational institutions, libraries and educational theatres receive all 3 periodicals and have access to audiotapes of Guild seminars; Professional Subscribers ($200 a year): producers and agents receive all 3 periodicals.

EDUCATIONAL THEATRE ASSOCIATION

2343 Auburn Ave; Cincinnati, OH 45219; (513) 421-3900;
FAX 421-7077; website www.etassoc.org
Michael Peitz, *Executive Director*

The Educational Theatre Association is an international not-for-profit professional association for theatre educators and an honorary society for their students. Its mission is to promote and strengthen theatre in education. The Association focuses efforts on student development, teacher training and advocacy. It operates the International Thespian Soceity, an honorary organization for high school students, and sponsors the International Thespian Festival for students, an annual convention for teachers, Professional Development Institutes, a middle school theatre forum and various awards and scholarship programs. The Association publishes *Dramatics* (see Publications), a monthly magazine, and *Teaching Theatre*, a quarterly journal. Membership is available to individuals and for active participants in chartered middle school or high school troupes of the International Thespian Society.

THE FIELD

161 Sixth Ave; New York, NY 10013; (212) 691-6969,
FAX 255-2053; email info@thefield.org;
website www.thefield.org
Katherine Longstreth, *Director of Art-Based Programs*
Steve Gross, *Director of Career-Based Programs*

The Field, founded in 1986, is a not-for-profit organization dedicated to helping independent performing artists develop artistically and professionally through a variety of performance opportunities, workshops, services and publications. The Field does not engage in curatorial activity; all artists are eligible to participate in its programs. Of special interest to New York metropolitan area playwrights wishing to produce their own work are programs such as Fielday, a showcase of 12-minute work and Fieldwork, 10-week workshops for works-in-progress, guided by trained facilitators, culminating in performances. Writers should also note Artward Bound, free 10-day summer residencies at various rural locations on the East Coast for multidisciplinary groups of 6-10 artists with at least 3 years professional experience; transportation, room and board, rehearsal space, workshops and career guidance seminars all provided; send resume and application. The Field assists artists with many aspects of producing their work, including grant writing, fundraising, project management, securing performance and rehearsal space, and cooperative promotional efforts.

Publications include a monthly member newsletter; the *Self-Production Guide*; *Funding Guide for Independent Artists*; *Space Chase Guide to New and Lesser Known Performance Opportunities*, a listing of local performance spaces throughout New York City as well as out-of-town festivals, residencies and artist colonies; and *Gone with the Field Guide*, a listing of performing possibilities for independent artists in 40 cities across the United States. All programs are available to members and nonmembers; members receive all publications, discounts on programs and may use the Field as an umbrella organization, falling under its not-for-profit status. Annual membership costs $75; individual programs range in cost from $15–75. Field programs are also offered in Atlanta, Chicago, Dallas, Houston, Miami, Philadelphia, Salt Lake City, San Francisco, Seattle, Tokyo, Toronto and Washington, DC.

FIRST STAGE

Box 38280; Los Angeles, CA 90038; (323) 850–6271,
    FAX 850–6295; email firststagela@aol.com;
    website www.firststagela.org
Dennis Safren, *Literary Manager*

Founded in 1983, First Stage is a service organization for playwrights that holds staged readings, which are videotaped for the author's archival purposes; conducts workshops; provides referral services for playwrights; and publishes *First Stage Newsletter*. Services are free to nonmembers, except for workshops, which are available to members only. Membership dues are $45 per quarter or $160 per year; $60 per year for nonlocal members.

THE FOUNDATION CENTER

National Libraries:
1627 K St NW; Washington, DC 20006; (202) 331–1400;
79 Fifth Ave; New York, NY 10003; (212) 620–4230, FAX 807–3677;
    website www.fdncenter.org
Judith Margolin, *Vice President, Public Services, New York Library*
Field Offices:
312 Sutter St; San Francisco, CA 94108; (415) 397–0902;
Hurt Bldg, Suite 150, Grand Lobby; 50 Hurt Plaza;
    Atlanta, GA 30303; (404) 880–0094;
1422 Euclid, Suite 1356; Cleveland, OH 44115; (216) 861–1934

The Foundation Center is a nationwide service organization established and supported by foundations to provide a single authoritative source of information on foundation giving. It disseminates information on foundations through a public service program and through such publications as *The Foundation Directory* and *The Foundation Grants Index.* Of special interest is *Foundation Grants to Individuals,* which lists scholarships, fellowships, residencies, internships, grants, loans, awards, prizes and other forms of assistance available to individuals from approximately 4200 grantmakers (2001 edition $65). The center maintains 5 libraries and a national network of more than 213 cooperating collections. For the name of the collection nearest you or for more information about the center's programs, call toll free (800) 424-9836 or visit the website.

GREENSBORO PLAYWRIGHTS' FORUM

c/o City Arts; 200 North Davie St, Box #2; Greensboro, NC 27401;
(336) 335-6426, FAX 373-2659;
email stephen.hyers@ci.greensboro.nc.us;
website www.ci.greensboro.nc.us/leisure/drama
Stephen D. Hyers, *Director*

GPF was founded in 1993 to facilitate a monthly gathering for playwrights to discuss works in progress, share knowledge and encourage each other's artistic growth. Programs include cold and staged readings of member's plays and the annual North Carolina New Play Project open to NC playwrights; winner receives $100 and workshop production; *deadline:* 10 Oct 2001. GPF also provides members with studio space for play development and publishes *New Play Catalog*, which lists plays written by members. Membership is open to anyone. Annual dues are $25.

HATCH-BILLOPS COLLECTION

491 Broadway, 7th Floor; New York, NY 10012-4412;
(212) 966-3231, FAX 966-3231 (call first);
email hatchbillops@worldnet.att.net
James V. Hatch, *Executive Secretary*

Founded in 1975, the Hatch-Billops Collection is a not-for-profit research library specializing in black American art and theatre history. It collects and preserves primary and secondary resource materials in the black cultural arts; provides tools and access to these materials for artists and scholars, as well as the general public; and develops programs in the arts which use the collection's resources. The library's holdings include 1800 oral-history tapes; theatre programs; approximately 300 unpublished plays by black American writers from 1858 to the present; files of clippings, letters, announcements and brochures on theatre, art and film; slides, photographs and posters; and more than 4000 books and 400 periodicals. The collection also presents a number of salon interviews and films, which are open to the public; and publishes transcriptions of its annual "Artist and Influence" series of salon interviews, many of which feature playwrights. The collection is open to artists, scholars and the public by appointment only at a rate of $5 per hour.

HISPANIC ORGANIZATION OF LATIN ACTORS (HOLA)

Clemente Soto Vélez Cultural Center; 107 Suffolk St, 3rd Floor;
New York, NY 10002; (212) 253-1015, FAX 253-9651;
email holagram@aol.com; website www.hellohola.org
Manuel Alfaro, *Executive Director*

Founded in 1975, HOLA is a not-for-profit arts service organization for Hispanic performers and related artists. HOLA provides information, a 24-hour hotline, casting referral services, professional seminars and workshops. The organization publishes a biennial *Directory of Hispanic Talent: HOLA Pages* (including an online version) and a newsletter, *La Nueva Ola*, which lists job opportunities, grants and contests of interest to Hispanic artists. Members pay annual dues of $49.

INDEPENDENT FEATURE PROJECT (IFP)

104 West 29th St, 12th Floor; New York, NY 10001-5310;
(212) 465-8200, FAX 465-8525; email ifpny@ifp.org;
website www.ifp.org
Michelle Byrd, *Executive Director*

The Independent Feature Project (IFP), a not-for-profit membership-supported organization, was founded in 1979 to encourage creativity and diversity in films produced outside the established studio system. The IFP produces the IFP Market, which features 300 American independent features, shorts, works-in-progress, documentaries and feature scripts. The IFP and IFP/West publish *Filmmaker*, a quarterly magazine. IFP also sponsors a series of screenings, professional seminars and industry showcases, including a conference on screenplay development. Group health insurance, production insurance, discounts, a Resource Program, publications and a series of transcripts of previous seminars and workshops are available to members. Membership dues start at $100 a year ($65 for students).

INSTITUTE OF OUTDOOR DRAMA

CB #3240; University of North Carolina; Chapel Hill, NC 27599-3240;
(919) 962-1328, FAX 962-4212; email outdoor@unc.edu;
website www.unc.edu/depts/outdoor/
Scott J. Parker, *Director*

The Institute of Outdoor Drama, founded in 1963, is a research and advisory agency of the University of North Carolina. It serves as a communications link between producers of existing outdoor dramas and is a resource for groups, agencies or individuals who wish to create new outdoor dramas or who are seeking information on the field. The institute provides professional consultation and conducts feasibility studies; holds annual auditions for summer employment in outdoor drama; sponsors conferences, lectures and symposia; and publishes a quarterly newsletter, as well as information bulletins. Writers should note that the institute maintains a roster of available artists and production personnel, including playwrights and composers. It seeks to interest established playwrights and composers in participating in the creation of new outdoor dramas, and to encourage and advise new playwrights who wish to write for this specialized form of theatre.

INTERNATIONAL THEATRE INSTITUTE—U.S. CENTER (ITI/US)

Theatre Communications Group; 355 Lexington Ave;
New York, NY 10017-6603; (212) 697-5230, FAX 983-4847;
email iti@tcg.org; website www.tcg.org
Martha W. Coigney, *Director*

Now operating centers in 92 countries, ITI was founded in 1948 by UNESCO "to promote the exchange of knowledge and practice in the theatre arts." The U.S. Center of ITI became part of Theatre Communications Group in November 1999. ITI assists foreign theatre visitors in the U.S. and American theatre representatives traveling abroad. The ITI International Theatre Collection is a reference library which documents theatrical activity in 146 countries and houses over 12,700 plays from 97 countries. American playwrights, as well as other theatre professionals, frequently use the collection to make international connections; to consult foreign theatre directories for names of producers, directors or companies with a view to submitting plays abroad; and to research the programs and policies of theatres or managements. ITI answers numerous requests from abroad about American plays and also provides information on rights to foreign plays to American producers, directors and literary managers. TCG/ITI Travel Grants, funded by the Trust for Mutual Understanding, offer modest support ($1000–$2500) for travel and exchange between U.S. theatres and theatre artists and their colleagues in Russia and Central/Eastern Europe. (See TCG Artistic Programs in Fellowships and Grants. Program guidelines are also available on TCG's website.)

THE INTERNATIONAL WOMEN'S WRITING GUILD

Box 810, Gracie Station; New York, NY 10028–0082;
　　(212) 737–7536, FAX 737–9469; email iwwg@iwwg.com;
　　website www.iwwg.com
Hannelore Hahn, *Executive Director*

The International Women's Writing Guild, founded in 1976, is a network of international women writers. Playwrights, television and film writers, songwriters, producers and other women involved in the performing arts are included in its membership. Workshops are offered throughout the U.S. and annually at a week-long writing conference/retreat at Skidmore College in Saratoga Springs, NY. Members may also submit playscripts to theatres who have offered to read, critique and possibly produce IWWG members' works. *Network*, a 32-page newsletter published 6 times a year, provides a forum for members to share views and to learn about playwriting contests and awards, and theatre- and TV-related opportunities. The guild offers contacts with literary agents, as well as other services to its members. Annual dues are $45.

LEAGUE OF CHICAGO THEATRES/LEAGUE OF CHICAGO THEATRES FOUNDATION

228 South Wabash, Suite 300; Chicago, IL 60604; (312) 554–9800,
　　FAX 922–7202; email theleague@aol.com;
　　website www.chicagoplays.com

Founded in 1979, the League of Chicago Theatres/League of Chicago Theatres Foundation is a member organization which advocates for the business and artistic needs of the Chicago theatre community. It operates as an information clearinghouse; offers vendor discounts, including a cooperative advertising program; conducts the Annual Theatre CommUNITY Conference; markets "Play Money" Theater Gift Certificates; coordinates the non-Equity general auditions; implements marketing initiatives such as the award-winning Sears Theater Fever; and sells half-price theatre tickets through its seven Hot Tix locations. Publications include the bimonthly *Theater Guide* in partnership with *Stagebill* magazine. Theatre companies, producers and presenters incorporated for at least one year and located within 50 miles of Chicago may be eligible to join.

LEAGUE OF PROFESSIONAL THEATRE WOMEN/NEW YORK

c/o Isobel Robins; 248 East 68th St; New York, NY 10021;
    (212) 744-6003, FAX 744-6838;
    website www.theatrewomen.org
Isobel Robins and Harriet Slaughter, *Co-Presidents*

Founded in 1979, the league is a not-for-profit organization of theatre professionals providing programs and services which promote women in all areas of professional theatre; create industry-related opportunities for women; and highlight contributions of theatre women, past and present. Through its salons, seminars, educational programs, social events, awards and festivals, the league links professional theatres with theatre women nationally and internationally and provides an ongoing forum for ideas, methods and issues of concern to the theatrical community and its audiences. Programs include the Lee Reynolds Award, given annually to a woman or women whose work for, in, about or through the medium of theatre has helped to illuminate the possibilities for social, cultural or political change; the Oral History Project, which seeks to chronicle and document the contribution of significant theatre women; a membership directory; and panels discussing topics of interest to women theatre professionals with well-known experts in the field. Regular monthly meetings enable members to network, initiate programs and serve on committees. To be eligible for membership in the league, playwrights, composers, librettists and lyricists must have had a work presented in a First Class production in the U.S. or Canada; or in a New York City theatre under Equity's Basic Minimum Contract, excluding showcases; or at least 2 productions presented in a resident theatre, as defined under Equity's Minimum Basic Contract for Resident Theatres. All other theatre professionals must meet criteria listed in brochure. Annual dues are $100. For further details of membership eligibility and application procedure, write or call for membership information brochure.

LITERARY MANAGERS AND DRAMATURGS OF THE AMERICAS (LMDA)

Box 728, Village Station; New York, NY 10014; (718) 437-5462;
    email lmda2000@aol.com
DD Kugler, *President*

LMDA is the professional service organization for American and Canadian literary managers and dramaturgs, founded in 1985 to affirm, examine and develop these professions. Among the programs and services it offers to members are a toll-free telephone job line; discussion and announcement listservs; Early Career Dramaturgs, which identifies and encourages new members of the profession and works to establish them in productive professional affiliations, as well as publishing a guide to internships; the University Caucus, which acts as a liaison between training and liberal arts programs and the profession, in addition to publishing a guide to training programs, sourcebooks for teachers of dramaturgy and an annual bibliography; and the Advocacy Caucus, which examines and reports on current working conditions of dramaturgs and literary managers. Publications include the quarterly *LMDA Review*; the *LMDA Script Exchange*; and the *Production Notebooks Project* that documents the conception, research, planning and realization of oustanding theatre productions. Each June, LMDA holds an annual conference. Voting membership is open to dramaturgs and literary managers only. Associate membership is open to playwrights, artistic directors, literary agents, educators and other theatre professionals interested in dramaturgy. Dues are $25 for students, $45 for associate members, $60 for voting members and $130 for institutional memberships.

LUMINOUS VISIONS

267 West 89th St; New York, NY 10024; (212) 581-7455, 724-7059, FAX 581-3964
Carla Pinza, *Co-Founder and Artistic Director*

Founded in 1976, Luminous Visions is a multicultural, not-for-profit organization dedicated to developing the creative skills of film and television writers, directors and actors seeking employment within the English-speaking film and television mainstream. Luminous Visions offers year-round youth workshops to develop acting, writing and musical talent in students ages 6-17. The organization sponsors a weekly workshop for writers, an annual Writers Forum and a spring Staged Reading Festival.

MARY ANDERSON CENTER FOR THE ARTS

101 St. Francis Dr; Mount Saint Francis, IN 47146; (812) 923-8602, FAX 923-0294; email maca@iglou.com;
website www.maryandersoncenter.org
Debra Carmody, *Executive Director*

The Mary Anderson Center, founded in 1989, is a not-for-profit organization dedicated to providing artists with a quiet place where they can concentrate and work on their craft. Named after the 19th-century actress from Louisville who rose to become an international celebrity, the center is located on 400 acres in southern Indiana. The center's goal is to provide retreats and residencies for artists in many disciplines (see the organization's entry in Colonies and Residencies). As part of its outreach effort to the Midwest and the nation, the center sponsors symposia, conferences and other gatherings which explore, in a multidisciplinary mode, topics of major interest to society and to artists. Contributors to the center receive a quarterly newsletter featuring center activities and news of area artists.

MEET THE COMPOSER

2112 Broadway, Suite 505; New York, NY 10023; (212) 787-3601, FAX 787-3745
Heather Hitchens, *President*

Founded in 1974, Meet The Composer is a national service organization whose mission is to increase opportunities for composers by fostering the creation, performance, dissemination and appreciation of their music. With support from foundations, corporations, individual patrons and government sources, Meet The Composer designs programs that support composers writing in all styles of music–classical, jazz, folk, electronic, symphonic, opera, dance, experimental, etc. Through a variety of programs, Meet The Composer provides composer fees to not-for-profit organizations that perform, present and commission original works. Applications to all Meet The Composer programs are submitted by sponsoring organizations, not individual composers. Its programs include: Commissioning Music/USA, Music Alive, New Residencies, the Fund for Small Ensembles and the Meet The Composer Fund (see Meet The Composer Grant in Fellowships and Grants).

MISSOURI ASSOCIATION OF PLAYWRIGHTS

830 North Spoede Rd; St. Louis, MO 63141-7748; (314) 567-6341, FAX 647-0945
Jo Lovins, *President*

Missouri Association of Playwrights (MAP) was founded in 1976 to assist playwrights in developing their skills. The association's activities include monthly meetings which are open to the public (Sep-Jun) at which members' scripts are presented as fully staged readings or workshops; guest speakers and seminars on playwriting are offered. Periodically the Association presents a full production of one-act plays. Script submission for full productions and staged readings are limited to works of MAP members only. Membership is open to all playwrights, but most members live in the greater St. Louis area (including southwest IL and out-state MO). Annual dues are $20.

MUSE OF FIRE THEATRE COMPANY

Box 20875; Columbus Circle Station; New York, NY 10023;
   (212) 397-2757, FAX 397-2757; musevfire@aol.com;
   website www.museoffiretheatreco.org
Glenn English and Vivian Paxton, *Co-Artistic Directors*

Founded in 1999, Muse of Fire Theatre Company is a not-for-profit organization dedicated to developing and producing original plays by American playwrights. With a resident company of actors, directors and playwrights, Muse of Fire seeks to promote new playwriting and develop new audiences, particularly young audiences. Its programs include the ongoing Readers Workshop which offers regular staged readings of new plays, the Muse Writers Workshop open to members only and the Sirens One Act Festival (see listing in Development), dedicated to promoting work by women writers. The organization publishes the quarterly *Muse of Fire Newsletter*. Writers interested in becoming a part of Muse of Fire should submit writing samples, bio and letter of inquiry.

NATIONAL ALLIANCE FOR MUSICAL THEATRE

330 West 45th St, Lobby B; New York, NY 10036-3854;
   (212) 265-5376, FAX 582-8730; email namtheatre@aol.com;
   website www.namt.net
Trudi Biggs, *Executive Director*

The National Alliance for Musical Theatre, founded in 1985, is the national service organization for musical theatre. The Alliance's goal is to serve as a champion of the musical and to foster its continued growth, both by providing national networking and collaboration opportunities, and by nurturing the creation, development, production and recognition of new musicals. It has 120 member organizations in 32 states, Canada, the United Kingdom, Spain and Finland, including theatres and performing arts centers that produce or present musicals. As part of its services, the Alliance organizes two annual conferences, maintains a website and publishes newletters and a membership directory. The Alliance also produces an annual Festival of New Musicals in New York City.

THE NATIONAL AUDIO THEATRE FESTIVALS (NATF)

115 Dikeman St; Hempstead, NY 11550; (516) 483-8321;
    FAX 538-7583; website www.natf.org
Sue Zizza, *Executive Director*

Founded in 1979, The National Audio Theatre Festivals is a national
resource center for audio theatre. NAFT hosts the annual Audio Theatre
Workshop, a week-long hands-on intensive at William Woods University in
Fulton, Missouri. NATF is a membership-based professional and educational
not-for-profit arts organization, whose services include providing
information and referral services and technical assistance to interested
individuals and groups; distributing educational materials; and publishing a
newsletter and an online *Audio Dramatists Directory*, a guide to current
audio artists, producers, programmers and profesional resources. NATF
also holds an annual script contest to identify and promote emerging and
established audio script writers (see NATF Script Competition in Prizes).
Winning scripts may be produced during one of a series of audio theatre
workshops held each year. Membership fees vary; check website for more
information.

THE NATIONAL FOUNDATION FOR JEWISH CULTURE

330 Seventh Ave, 21st Floor; New York, NY 10001; (212) 629-0500,
    FAX 629-0508; email nfjc@jewishculture.org;
    website www.jewishculture.org
Richard A. Siegel, *Executive Director*

Founded in 1960, The National Foundation for Jewish Culture (NFJC) is the
central cultural agency of the American Jewish community. The NFJC,
dedicated to the enhancement of Jewish life in America through the support
and promotion of the arts and humanities, provides programs and services
to cultural institutions, local communities and individual artists and
scholars in every region of the country. The NFJC serves as advocate and
coordinator for the fields of Jewish culture through its Council of American
Jewish Museums and Council of Archives and Research Libraries in Jewish
Studies; sponsors grants and awards to artists, scholars and major cultural
institutions such as YIVO, Leo Baeck Institute, American Jewish Historical
Society, Histadrut Ivrit and the Jewish Publication Society of America;
promotes an understanding and appreciation of contemporary Jewish life
and culture through conferences, symposia, publications, media
productions, traveling exhibitions, residencies and performances; and
presents the annual Jewish Cultural Achievement Awards recognizing
outstanding contributions to Jewish life in America through the arts and

scholarship. (See listing for New Play Commissions in Jewish Theatre in Fellowships and Grants.)

THE NATIONAL LEAGUE OF AMERICAN PEN WOMEN, INC.

1300 17th St NW; Washington, DC 20036–1973; (202) 785–1997, FAX 452–6868; email nlapw1@juno.com; website members.aol.com/penwomen/pen.htm
Wanda A. Rider, *National President*

Founded in 1897, NLAPW is a national membership organization for professional women writers, composers and visual artists. It holds local monthly meetings, annual State Association meetings, Mid-Administration Congress, National Biennial Convention and a National Art Show, and will sponsor the Mature Woman Scholarship Award in 2002 (see Fellowships and Grants). Members, who receive a bimonthly magazine, *The Pen Woman*, and a national roster, pay national dues of $30 a year; dues for individual branches are separate and vary.

NATIONAL PUBLIC RADIO

635 Massachusetts Ave NW; Washington, DC 20001–3753; (202) 414–2399, FAX 414–3032; email atrudeau@npr.org; website www.npr.org
Andy Trudeau, *Director, Program Acquisition and Production*

Founded in 1970, National Public Radio is a private not-for-profit membership organization which provides a national program service to its more than 500 member noncommercial radio stations. It is funded by its member stations, the Corporation for Public Broadcasting and corporate grants. Among the programs available to member stations is NPR Playhouse, which presents 29-minute dramatic programs, series and serials. Writers should note that NPR does not itself read or produce plays. It acquires broadcast rights to produced packages and will consider fully produced programs or works-in-progress on tape only.

THE NATIONAL THEATRE WORKSHOP OF THE HANDICAPPED

354 Broome St, Loft 5-F; New York, NY 10013; (212) 941–9511, FAX 941–9486; email ntwh@aol.com; website ntwh.org
Rick Curry S.J., *Founder and Artistic Director*

Founded in 1977, the National Theatre Workshop of the Handicapped (NTWH) is a not-for-profit organization founded to provide persons with disabilities the opportunity to learn the communication skills necessary to pursue a life in professional theatre and to enhance their opportunities in the workplace. NTWH advocates for persons with physical disabilities in the theatre and offers a forum for dramatic literature on themes of disability. NTWH runs the Playwrights Workshop, a 2-week program held each spring for 4 playwrights to develop new works in residence at NTWH-Crosby, a fully accessible residential facility in Belfast, ME; selected works are fully produced later. NTWH also offers professional instruction in acting, singing, voice, movement, playwriting and fine arts at the NTWH studio in New York City. Persons with disabilities who are interested in participating in these training programs should contact NTWH for more information.

NEW DRAMATISTS

424 West 44th St; New York, NY 10036; (212) 757-6960,
    FAX 265-4738; email newdramatists@newdramatists.org;
    website www.newdramatists.org
Joel Ruark, *Executive Director*
Todd London, *Artistic Director*

Founded in 1949, New Dramatists is the nation's oldest playwright development center, designed to provide member playwrights with the resources they need to create plays for the American theatre. Rather than producing plays, New Dramatists aids playwrights in the development of their craft through play readings and workshops; dramaturgy; a resident director program; musical theatre development and training; ScriptShare (a national script distribution program); fellowships, awards and prizes; a free ticket program for Broadway and Off-Broadway productions; writing spaces and accommodations; and photocopying. All services are provided free of charge to members.

In addition, New Dramatists hosts several playwright exchanges, including the Brooks Atkinson Exchange/Max Weitzenhoffer Fellowship to the Royal National Theatre, England; the Sumner Locke Elliott Exchange to the Australian National Playwrights Centre; the Danish American National Cultural Exchange; and a bicoastal exchange with A.S.K. Theater Projects, Los Angeles.

Membership is open to emerging playwrights living in the greater New York area, and to those living outside the area who demonstrate a willingness to regularly travel to New York and actively participate in this community of artists. Playwrights interested in applying for membership should write for guidelines.

NEW ENGLAND THEATRE CONFERENCE (NETC)

Northeastern University; 360 Huntington Ave; Boston, MA 02115;
(617) 424-9275, FAX 424-1057; email info@NETConline.org;
website www.NETConline.org
Clinton D. Campbell, *Managing Director*

Founded in 1952, New England Theatre Conference is a membership organization primarily but not exclusively for the New England theatre community, including playwrights, teachers, students and theatre professionals. Services include an annual conference, publication of a member directory and annual summer theatre auditions. NETC also administers both the John Gassner Memorial Playwriting Award and Aurand Harris Memorial Playwriting Award (see Prizes). The organization publishes New England Theatre Journal and NETC News. Membership dues are $30 for students, $45 for individuals and $95 for groups.

NEW PLAYWRIGHTS FOUNDATION

c/o 608 San Vicente Blvd, #18; Santa Monica, CA 90402;
(310) 393-3682; website www.newplaywrights.org
Jeffrey Lee Bergquist, *Artistic Director*

Founded in 1968, New Playwrights Foundation is a service organization for writers working in theatre, film, television and video. The foundation runs developmental workshops, holds readings, produces video and film projects and assists members in furthering their careers. Membership in NPF is limited to a maximum of 15 writers who must be able to attend meetings in Santa Monica every other Thursday night. Candidates for membership attend 3 meetings before submitting materials to be reviewed by the group. Annual membership dues are $25.

THE NEW YORK PUBLIC LIBRARY FOR THE PERFORMING ARTS

Library Annex; 521 West 43rd St; New York, NY 10036;
(212) 870-1639, FAX 870-1868; email rtaylor@nypl.org;
website www.nypl.org
Bob Taylor, *Curator, The Billy Rose Theatre Collection*

Founded in 1931, The Billy Rose Theatre Collection, a division of the Library for the Performing Arts, is open to the public (aged 18 and over) and contains material on all aspects of theatrical art and the entertainment world, including stage, film, radio, television, circus, vaudeville, burlesque and numerous other genres. The Theatre on Film and Tape Project (TOFT) is a special collection of films and videotapes of theatrical productions recorded during performance, as well as informal dialogues with important theatrical personalities. Tapes are available for viewing by appointment (call 212-870-1641) to students, theatre professionals and researchers.

Non-Traditional Casting Project

1560 Broadway, Suite 1600; New York, NY 10036;
(212) 730–4750 (voice), –4913 (TDD), FAX 730–4820;
email info@ntcp.org; website www.ntcp.org
Sharon Jensen, *Executive Director*

Founded in 1986, the Non-Traditional Casting Project is a not-for-profit organization which exists to address and seek solutions to the problems of racism and exclusion in the theatre and related media, particularly those which involve creative personnel: including, but not limited to, actors, directors, writers, designers and producers. The project works to advance the creative participation of artists of color and artists with disabilities through both advocacy and specific projects. Key NTCP programs include Artist Files/Artist Files Online, a national talent bank; roundtable discussions with industry leaders; forums; and a national Consulting and Information Program. Writers of color and/or with disabilities, who are citizens or residents of the U.S. or Canada and have had at least one play given a professional production or staged reading should send a resume for inclusion in Artist Files/Artist Files Online, indicating their cultural identification and, in the case of disabled artists, any accommodation they may use; those interested in contacting listed artists will call them or their agents directly.

North Carolina Writers' Network

Box 954; Carrboro, NC 27510; (919) 967–9540, FAX 929–0535;
email mail@ncwriters.org; website www.ncwriters.org
Linda Hobson, *Executive Director*

Founded in 1985, North Carolina Writers' Network (NCWN) is an independent literary arts service organization serving writers at all stages of development. NCWN provides workshops, critiques, readings, an annual conference held every November and the Paul Green Playwrights Prize. NCWN also publishes *Writers' Network News*, a 24-page bimonthly newsletter. Membership is available to anyone interested in writing and reading; annual membership dues are $55.

NORTHWEST PLAYWRIGHTS GUILD

Box 1728; Portland, OR 97207; (503) 452-4778;
   email bjscript@teleport.com; website www.nwpg.org
Bill Johnson, *Office Manager*

Founded in 1982, Northwest Playwrights Guild is an information clearinghouse and support group for playwrights. The guild sponsors public readings, holds workshops and produces regional conferences on theatre that include the full production of original scripts. The guild publishes a quarterly, *Script*, that contains articles on theatre in the Northwest, as well as update newsletters that provide information on current script opportunities. Membership dues are $25 a year.

OLLANTAY CENTER FOR THE ARTS

Box 720636; Jackson Heights, NY 11372-0636; (718) 565-6499,
   FAX 446-7806
Pedro R. Monge-Rafuls, *Executive and Artistic Director*

Founded as a multidisciplinary Hispanic arts center in 1977, OLLANTAY has developed a Hispanic Heritage Center for the Arts in America which provides the resources needed to pursue research and develop new programs and initiatives in the field. The center maintains a resource bank of video and audio tapes, slides, books, plays and articles, which may be viewed by writing for an appointment. Its unique Playwriting Workshop, an annual intensive course of 2-4 weeks, provides an opportunity for playwrights wishing to write in Spanish to work under the direction of major Latin-American playwrights who reside outside the U.S. *OLLANTAY Theater Magazine* is a biannual journal in English and Spanish which gives local playwrights, critics and scholars the opportunity to share their knowledge and experience of Hispanic theatre within the framework of American and world drama. The magazine, which publishes at least one play in each issue, is available to subscribers. Annual subscription is $20 for individuals, $35 for organizations.

OPERA AMERICA

1156 15th St NW, Suite 810; Washington, DC 20005-3287;
   (202) 293-4466, FAX 393-0735; email frontdesk@operaam.org;
   website www.operaamerica.org
Jamie Driver, *Managing Director*

Founded in 1970, OPERA America is the not-for-profit service organization for the professional opera field in North America and allied international members. OPERA America provides a variety of informational, technical and financial services to its membership and serves as a resource to the media, funders, government agencies and the general public.

PEN AMERICAN CENTER

568 Broadway; New York, NY 10012; (212) 334-1660,
    FAX 334-2181; email pen@pen.org; website www.pen.org
Michael Roberts, *Executive Director*

Founded in 1921, PEN is an international association of writers; the American Center is the largest of the 130 centers that comprise International PEN. The 2700 members of PEN American Center are established North American writers and translators, and literary editors. PEN activities include the Freedom-to-Write program; monthly symposia, readings and other public events; a prison writing program; and a translator-publisher clearinghouse. Among PEN's annual prizes and awards are The Gregory Kolovakos Award, PEN-Book-of-the-Month Club Translation Prize and the PEN/Laura Pels Foundation Award for Drama (see Prizes); and Writing Awards for Prisoners, awarded to the authors of the best fiction, nonfiction, drama and poetry received from prisoner-writers in the U.S. The PEN Writers Fund and the PEN Fund for Writers & Editors with AIDS assist writers (see Emergency Funds). PEN's publications include *Grants and Awards Available to American Writers*, a biennially updated directory of prizes, grants, fellowships and awards (2000-2001 edition $18 postpaid); *The PEN Prison Writing Information Bulletin*; and *A Handbook for Literary Translators*, available for free on the website.

PHILADELPHIA DRAMATISTS CENTER (PDC)

1516 South St; Philadelphia, PA 19146; (215) 735-1441;
    email pdc@libertynet.org; website www.libertynet.org/pdc
Ed Shockley, *Artistic Director*
Jon Dorf, *Managing Director*

Philadelphia Dramatists Center, founded in 1994, is a service organization for professional playwrights, screenwriters and musical theatre writers. Programs and services include developmental readings, writers' circles, chats with area artistic directors and literary managers, craft development workshops, access to actor/director files, discounted tickets to participating theatres, rehearsal space, a telephone hotline listing upcoming events and publication of the quarterly newsletter *First Draft*. Annual membership dues are $15 for students and $25 for individuals, which includes a subscription to *First Draft*.

PLAYMARKET

Box 9767; Wellington; New Zealand; 64-4-382-8462,
   FAX 64-4-382-8461; email info@playmarket.org.nz;
   website www.playmarket.org.nz
Dilys Grant, *Director*
Emily Roberts, *Administrator*

Playmarket is a service organization for New Zealand playwrights, established in 1973 as a result of a growing interest in plays by New Zealand writers and a need to find new writers. The organization runs a script advisory and critiquing service, arranges workshop productions of promising scripts, and serves as the country's principal playwrights' agency, preparing and distributing copies of scripts and negotiating and collecting royalties. Playmarket publishes the magazine *Playmarket News* 3 times a year.

THE PLAYWRIGHTS' CENTER

2301 Franklin Ave East; Minneapolis, MN 55406-1099;
   (612) 332-7481; email info@pwcenter.org;
   website www.pwcenter.org
Carlo Cuesta, *Executive Director*

The Playwrights' Center, founded in 1971, is a service organization for playwrights. Its programs include developmental services (cold readings and workshops using an Equity acting company); fellowships; exchanges with theatres and other developmental programs; a biannual journal; the Jones commissioning program; PlayLabs (see Development); playwriting classes; year-round programs for young writers; and the Many Voices program, designed to provide awards, education and lab services to new and emerging playwrights of color. The Center annually awards 5 Jerome Playwright-in-Residence Fellowships, for which competition is open nationally; 1 McKnight National Residency and Commission, for which competition is open to playwrights in partnership with eligible Minnesota professional theatre companies; 3 McKnight Advancement Grants open to Minnesota playwrights; 8 Many Voices Artist in Residency opportunities for Minnesota playwrights of color; and 3 Many Voices Multicultural Collaboration Grants (see The Playwrights' Center Grant Programs in Fellowships and Grants). A broad-based Center membership is available to any playwright or interested person. Benefits of general membership for playwrights include discounts on classes, applications for all Center programs, eligibility to apply for the Jones commission and scriptdevelopment readings, and the center's journal. Core (must be Minnesota resident) and Associate Member Playwrights are selected by a review panel each spring, based on script submission. They have primary access to all Center programs and services, including developmental workshops and public readings. Write for membership information.

THE PLAYWRIGHTS FOUNDATION

Box 460357; San Francisco, CA 94146; (415) 263–3986;
     email bayplays@best.com
Belinda Taylor, *President*
Arturo Catricala and Amy Mueller, *Co-Artistic Directors*

Founded in 1976, the Playwrights Foundation provides developmental support to playwrights throughout the U.S. It produces the annual Bay Area Playwrights Festival (see Development) and is developing a new year-round playwright services program, New Play Resources.

PLAYWRIGHTS THEATRE OF NEW JERSEY

33 Green Village Rd; Madison, NJ 07940; (973) 514–1787,
     FAX 514–2060
John Pietrowski, *Artistic Director*

Founded in 1986, the Playwrights Theatre of New Jersey is both a service organization for playwrights of all ages and a professional developmental theatre. In addition to its New Play Development Program (see Playwrights Theatre of New Jersey in Development), PTNJ co-sponsors, with the New Jersey Council on the Arts, the New Jersey Writers Project, a statewide program which teaches prose, poetry and dramatic writing in schools. Specialized programs include a playwriting-for-teachers project; adult playwriting classes; children's creative dramatics classes; acting classes; and "special needs" playwriting projects which include work in housing projects and with senior citizens, teenage substance abusers, persons with physical disabilities and court-appointed youth, as well as a playwriting-in-prisons initiative; and a program that teaches Spanish-language prose, poetry and dramatic writing. Young playwrights festivals are held in Madison and Newark, in addition to a statewide festival which is part of the New Jersey Young Playwrights Program. Gifted and talented playwriting symposia, hosted by well-known playwrights, provide intensive 2-day experiences for up to 60 students from various school districts.

PLAZA DE LA RAZA

3540 North Mission Rd; Los Angeles, CA 90031; (323) 223-2475,
    FAX 223-1804; email admin@plazaraza.org;
    website www.plazaraza.org
Rose Cano, *Executive Director*

Founded in 1970, Plaza de la Raza is a cultural center for the arts and education, primarily serving the surrounding community of East Los Angeles. Of special interest to playwrights is the center's Nuevo L.A. Chicano TheatreWorks project, designed to discover, develop and present the work of Chicano playwrights. Initiated in 1989 and recurring approximately every 4 years, depending on funding, as part of the Nuevo L.A. Chicano Art Series cycle (Visual Arts, Music, Dance and Theatre), the project develops new one-acts through a 2-week workshop with director and actors, culminating in public readings; some plays are selected for subsequent full production. Latino playwrights who are California residents should contact the center for information on when and how to apply for the next round of the program. Plaza de la Raza also conducts classes in drama, dance, music and the visual arts; provides resources for teachers in the community; and sponsors special events, exhibits and performances.

PROFESSIONAL ASSOCIATION OF CANADIAN THEATRES/ PACT COMMUNICATIONS CENTRE

30 St. Patrick St, 2nd Floor; Toronto, Ontario; Canada; M5T 3A3;
    (416) 595-6455, FAX 595-6450; email pactcomm@idirect.com;
    website www.pact.ca
Pat Bradley, *Executive Director*

PACT is the national service and trade association representing professional English-language theatres in Canada. PACT was incorporated in 1976 to work on behalf of its member theatres in the areas of advocacy, labor relations, professional development and communications. The members' newsletter *Impact!* is published quarterly. PACT Communications Centre (PCC) was established in 1985 as the charitable wing of PACT in order to improve and expand communications and information services. PCC publishes *The Theatre Listing*, an annual directory of English-language Canadian theatres, rehearsal and performance spaces, government agencies and arts service organizations; and *Artsboard*, the monthly bulletin of employment opportunities in the arts in Canada.

PUBLIC BROADCASTING SERVICE

1320 Braddock Pl; Alexandria, VA 22314-1698; (703) 739-5000,
FAX 739-0775; email www@pbs.org; website www.pbs.org

Founded in 1969, the Public Broadcasting Service is a private not-for-profit media enterprise owned and operated by the nation's 347 public television stations. Information for writers interested in submitting projects to PBS can be found under "Producing for PBS" on their website.

THE PURPLE CIRCUIT

921 North Naomi St; Burbank, CA 91505; (818) 953-5096, -5072;
email purplecir@aol.com;
website www.buddybuddy.com/pc.html/
Bill Kaiser, *Coordinator*

The Purple Circuit, founded in 1991, is a network of gay, lesbian, queer, bisexual and transsexual theatres, producers, performers and "Kindred Spirits" (theatres which are not exclusively gay or lesbian in orientation but are interested in producing gay or lesbian material on a regular basis). The Purple Circuit Hotline (818-953-5072) provides information on gay and lesbian shows currently playing in California and advises travelers on shows around the U.S. and abroad, as well as providing information for playwrights, journalists and others interested in promoting gay/lesbian/bisexual/transgender theatre and performance. The Purple Circuit publishes news, information and articles of interest to its constituency in its quarterly newsletter, On the Purple Circuit. The Purple Circuit Directory lists theatres and producers around the world that are interested in presenting gay, lesbian, bisexual and transsexual works.

THE SCRIPTWRITERS NETWORK

11684 Ventura Blvd, #508; Studio City, CA 91604; (323) 848-9477;
website scriptwritersnetwork.com
Bill Lundy, *Chair*

Though the Scriptwriters Network, founded in 1986, is predominantly an affiliation of film, television and corporate/industrial writers, playwrights are welcome. Meetings feature guest speakers; developmental feedback on scripts is available; and staged readings may be arranged in conjunction with other groups. The network sponsors members-only contests and publishes a newsletter. Prospective members submit a professionally formatted script and an application; membership is not based on the quality of the script. There is a $15 initiation fee, and dues are $65 a year for nonlocal U.S. members, $75 for Southern California residents and $100 for non-U.S. residents.

THE SONGWRITERS GUILD OF AMERICA

1560 Broadway, Room 1306; New York, NY 10036; (212) 768-7902,
    FAX 768-9048; email songnews@aol.com;
    website www.songwriters.org
George Wurzbach, *National Projects Director*
Head Office:
1500 Harbor Blvd; Weehawken, NJ 07087-6732; (201) 867-7603
Los Angeles Office:
6430 Sunset Blvd; Hollywood, CA 90028; (323) 462-1108
Nashville Office:
1222 16th Ave; Nashville, TN 37212; (615) 329-1782

Founded in 1931, the Songwriters Guild is a voluntary national association run by and for songwriters; all officers and directors are unpaid. Among its many services to composers and lyricists, the guild provides a standard songwriter's contract and reviews this and other contracts on request; collects writers' royalties from music publishers; maintains a copyright renewal service; conducts songwriting workshops and critique sessions with special rates for members; issues news bulletins with essential information for writers; and offers a group medical and life insurance plan. Full members of the guild must be published songwriters and pay dues on a graduated scale from $70-400. Unpublished songwriters may become associate members and pay dues of $70 per year. Write for membership application.

S.T.A.G.E. (SOCIETY FOR THEATRICAL ARTISTS' GUIDANCE AND ENHANCEMENT)

Box 214820; Dallas, TX 75221; (214) 630-7722, FAX 630-4468;
    email stage_tx@swbell.net; website www.stage-online.org
Julia Park, *Operations Manager*

Founded in 1981, S.T.A.G.E. is a not-for-profit membership organization based in Dallas/Fort Worth, which serves as an information clearinghouse and provides training and education for the theatre, broadcast and film industries in north central Texas. The society maintains a library of plays, theatre texts and resource information; offers counseling on agents, unions, personal marketing and other career-related matters; posts job opportunities; maintains a callboard for regional auditions in theatre and film; and sponsors an actor's showcase, Noon Preview. Members of

S.T.A.G.E. receive audition postings via email and a monthly publication, CENTERSTAGE. Annual dues are $65; $45 for volunteers.

STAGESOURCE

88 Tremont St, Suite 714; Boston, MA 02108; (617) 720-6066,
    FAX 720-4275; email info@stagesource.org;
    website www.stagesource.org
Jeffrey Poulos, *Executive Director*

Founded in 1985, StageSource, the Alliance for Theatre Artists and Producers, is a not-for-profit arts service organization committed to providing leadership and resources for the advancement of theatre in the Greater Boston/New England area. Its membership includes over 160 producing organizations and 1500 individual theatre artists. StageSource hosts annual Equity and non-Equity auditions, an annual theatre town meeting and a community social event, The Party. Its other programs include: Professional Development Series, offering career development and master classes on art and business; Playwrights Alliance, focusing on needs of area playwrights; Talent Bank, a library of resumes and headshots; and a 2-for-1 ticket discount program to more than 60 Greater Boston area theatres. The website posts job, audition and workshop opportunities; news; and a calendar of events. StageSource publishes a bimonthly newsletter *Marquee* and a biannual regional theatre guide, *The Source: The Greater Boston Theatre Resource Guide*. Membership is open to individuals, theatres and producing organizations. Annual dues for individuals are $45 for students and renewing members, $85 for new members; $75-397 for theatres and producing organizations based on operating budget.

THEATRE BAY AREA (TBA)

870 Market St, Suite 375; San Francisco, CA 94102;
    (415) 430-1140, FAX 430-1145; email tba@theatrebayarea.org;
    website www.theatrebayarea.org

Founded in 1976, TBA is a resource organization for San Francisco Bay Area theatre workers. Its membership includes 3200 individuals and more than 370 theatre and dance companies. Its programs include TIX Bay Area, San Francisco's half-price ticket booth; TIX By Mail, a half-price ticket catalog; professional workshops; and communications and networking services. Membership includes a subscription to *Callboard*, a monthly magazine featuring articles, interviews and essays on the Northern California theatre scene, as well as information on play contests and festivals, and listings of production activity, workshops, classes, auditions, jobs and services. TBA also publishes *Theatre Directory of the Bay Area*, which includes entries of local theatre companies; the *Performance and Rehearsal Rental Directory of the Bay Area* with listings of rehearsal and performance spaces; *Sources of Publicity*, and *Management Memo*, a monthly newsletter for theatre administrators and artistic directors. The website includes a playbill calendar, ticket information and sample *Callboard* articles. Annual dues are $40 (add $15 to receive *Callboard* 1st-class).

THEATRE COMMUNICATIONS GROUP
355 Lexington Ave; New York, NY 10017-6603; (212) 697-5230,
   FAX 983-4847; email tcg@tcg.org; website www.tcg.org
Ben Cameron, *Executive Director*

Founded in 1961 as the national service organization for the not-for-profit professional theatre, Theatre Communications Group (TCG) offers a wide array of services in line with its mission: to strengthen, nurture and promote the not-for-profit American theatre. TCG's programs and services encompass 5 primary areas of activity: artistic programs, including grants to artists and theatres; management programs, including conferences and forums, research and management training; international programs, including the U.S. Center of the International Theatre Institute; advocacy, serving as the primary national advocate for the field, in conjunction with the American Arts Alliance; and publications. Each of TCG's programs is designed to address at least one of its central strategies: increasing the organizational efficiency of TCG's member theatres, cultivating and celebrating the artistic talent and achievements of the field and broadening public understanding of and appreciation for the theatre field.

During 2000-2001, TCG claimed 17,000 individual members, including theatre professionals, educators, students, theatre enthusiasts and a network of more than 400 member theatres in 46 states and the District of Columbia, representing a wide range of institutional sizes, structures and aesthetics. In the belief that the diversity of the theatre field is its greatest strength, TCG's membership criteria embrace a broad sprectrum of theatres and practices.

TCG's artistic programs available to playwrights include the National Theatre Artist Residency Program, funded by The Pew Charitable Trusts, which supports extended relationships between theatres and individual artists; the NEA/TCG Theatre Residency Program for Playwrights, which provides $25,000 grants to help playwrights create new works and strengthen relationships with theatres, which also receive a $5000 Vivendi/Universal Residency Award when they host a resident playwright;

Extended Collaboration Grants, funded by Metropolitan Life Foundation, which help theatres hire playwrights for extended developmental work with other collaborators; the New Generations Program, funded by the Doris Duke Charitable Foundation and The Andrew W. Mellon Foundation, which offers full-time mentorships in resident professional theatres; and TCG/ITI Travel Grants, funded by the Trust for Mutual Understanding, which support travel to Russia and Central/Eastern Europe. (See TCG Artistic Programs in Fellowships and Grants. Program guidelines are also available on TCG's website.) TCG also administers the invitation-only AT&T:*OnStage* program, which supports productions of new plays and musicals, and the AT&T:*FirstStage* program, which provides commissioning grants of $10,000 for new plays, translations and adaptations and $25,000 for new musicals.

In addition to *American Theatre* magazine, which provides an up-to-date perspective on theatre throughout the country and includes the full texts of five new plays annually, other TCG publications of interest to theatre writers include *Theatre Directory*, which provides complete contact information for more than 400 U.S. not-for-profit professional theatres and related organizations; *Stage Writers Handbook: A Complete Business Guide for Playwrights, Composers, Lyricists and Librettists*, by Dana Singer; *The Production Notebooks: Theatre in Process*, Volumes I and II, edited by Mark Bly; *Stage Directors Handbook: Opportunities for Directors and Choreographers*, edited by the SDC Foundation; and *ArtSEARCH*, a biweekly bulletin of job opportunities in the arts which is available online or in print. TCG also publishes plays and musicals, theatre-related books, and resource books on the not-for-profit professional theatre. (For further information, see the Publications and Useful Publications chapters of this book. A complete publications catalog is available from TCG and on TCG's website.)

Individual members receive a free subscription to *American Theatre* magazine, discounted tickets to performances at more than 230 theatres nationwide and discounts on all TCG books, including TCG distribution titles. Other benefits include a no-fee affinity credit card and discounts on car rentals, hotel accommodations and express delivery service. Individual memberships are available for $35 a year, $20 for students. (See the TCG membership application in the back of this book.)

THEATRE LEAGUE ALLIANCE

644 South Figueroa St; Los Angeles, CA 90017; (213) 614-0556, FAX 614-0561; email info@theatrela.org; website www.theatrela.org

A not-for-profit association of more than 160 theatres and producers,

Theatre LA was founded in 1975 to unite, represent and promote theatre in Southern California. Theatre LA administers the annual Ovation Awards; produces the *Theatre Times Directory* (a cooperative advertising opportunity in the *Los Angeles Times*), operates WebTix (online half-price ticketing), and provides information and referral services for members. Asssociate membership opportunities are also available to individuals, professionals and businesses interested in supporting theatre.

THE THEATRE MUSEUM

1E Tavistock St; London WC2E 7PA; England; 44-207-943-4700, FAX 44-207-943-4777; website www.theatremuseum.org

Founded in 1987, the Theatre Museum, a branch of the Victoria & Albert Museum, is Britain's national museum of the performing arts. In addition to its regular displays, which feature 400 years of the history, technology, art and craft of theatre, and its special exhibitions, the museum houses the United Kingdom's largest archive of performing arts materials, including play texts, photographic and biographical files, theatre programs and reviews, and books about the theatre. The archive and study room is available by appointment (call during office hours) Wednesday to Friday, 10:30-1:00 P.M. and 2:00-4:30 P.M. The museum's education department runs workshops and study days on theatre practice for children, students and teachers. The museum also runs a program of celebrity play readings, seminars and events to give visitors insight into current theatre productions.

THEATRE PROJECT

45 West Preston St; Baltimore, MD 21201; (410) 539-3091, FAX 539-2137; email director@theatreproject.org; website www.theatreproject.org
Bobby Mrozek, *Artistic Director*

Founded in 1971, the Theatre Project, also known as Baltimore Theatre Project, is committed to offering established and emerging performing artists a supportive environment to develop and present their work. Theatre Project productions provide Baltimore with a professional international center for diverse and exceptional artistic voices. Artists receive visitor housing; technical, promotional and front-of-house support; and opportunities to meet with other artists. Additional services include workshops, roundtables, seminars, open auditions and a shared database of Baltimore-area affiliated artists.

VOLUNTEER LAWYERS FOR THE ARTS

1 East 53rd St, 6th Floor; New York, NY 10022–4201;
(212) 319–2787 (administrative office and Art Law Hotline),
FAX 752–6575; email vlany@vlany.org; website www.vlany.org
Elena Paul, *Executive Director*

Founded in 1969, Volunteer Lawyers for the Arts arranges free legal representation and legal education for the arts community. Individual artists and not-for-profit arts organizations unable to afford private counsel are eligible for VLA's services; VLA can be especially useful to playwrights with copyright or contract problems. There is an administrative fee per referral of $50-150 for individuals, $150-500 for not-for-profit organizations and $250 for not-for-profit incorporation and tax exemption. VLA's education program offers biweekly seminars on not-for-profit incorporation and evening seminars held regularly to educate attorneys and artists in specific areas of art law. Publications include *Model Contracts for Independent Contractors: Sample Provisions and Job Descriptions* ($15 plus $2.50 postage and handling); and the *VLA Guide to Copyright for Visual Artists* ($5.95 plus $2.50 postage and handling). For more information about VLA's publications and the 40 VLA affiliates across the country, contact Tina Cheung (ext 12) of the New York office; referrals can be made to volunteer lawyer organizations nationwide.

WOMEN'S THEATRE ALLIANCE (WTA)

2936 North Southport, Suite 210; Chicago, IL 60657–4120;
(312) 408–9910; email wtachicago@aol.com;
website www.wtachicago.org
Janel Winter, *President*

Founded in 1992, the Women's Theatre Alliance (WTA) is dedicated to the development of dramatic works by, for and/or about women and to the promotion of women's leadership within the Chicago theatre community. Programs of special interest to playwrights include the Play Development Workshop and New Plays Festival which unites women writers with a director and actors for a development process culminating in a 2-week festival of staged readings; Solo Voices, which facilitates the creation of one-woman shows and performance pieces; and the Salon Series, an informal presentation of new work offering social networking opportunities. WTA also publishes a monthly newsletter. Membership is open to all women and men. Annual dues are $40.

W.O.W. CAFÉ, ETP

59-61 East 4th St, 4th Floor; New York, NY 10003; (212) 777-4280;
email sil_1210@hotmail.com;
website www.geocities.com/probe_wowgrl

Founded in 1980, W.O.W. (Women's One World) Café is a women's theatre collective whose membership is primarily but not exclusively lesbian. W.O.W. produces the work of women playwrights and performers. It has no permanent staff and its members are encouraged to participate in all aspects of the group's operations. In lieu of dues, members volunteer their services backstage on fellow members' productions in exchange for the opportunity to present their own work. W.O.W. often hosts cabarets at 10:30 on Friday nights in which members and non-members can perform; the first Friday of every month is the Rivers of Honey cabaret for women performers of color. W.O.W. Café also hosts a biennial spring Latina Playwrights Festival (*deadline:* 1 Dec 2001) and an annual July 4th retreat during which they collect proposals for the following season; call, email or visit website for more information. W.O.W. also offers a mentor program for students from Satellite High School in the Bronx during the April spring break in which the students create and perform their own shows with the help of W.O.W. members. Women interested in becoming members of W.O.W. Café are encouraged to attend the July 4th retreat or one of the collective's regular meetings, which are scheduled every Tuesday at 6:30 P.M.

WRITERS GUILD OF AMERICA, EAST (WGAE), AFL-CIO

555 West 57th St; New York, NY 10019-2967; (212) 767-7800,
FAX 582-1909
Mona Mangan, *Executive Director*

WGAE is the union for freelance writers in the fields of motion pictures, television and radio who reside east of the Mississippi River (regardless of where they work). The union negotiates collective bargaining agreements for its members and represents them in grievances and arbitrations under those agreements. The guild gives annual awards, and sponsors a foundation which currently teaches film writing to disadvantaged high school students. WGAE participates in reciprocal arrangements with the International Affiliation of Writers Guilds and with its sister union, Writers Guild of America, west. The guild publishes a monthly newsletter, which is available to nonmembers by subscription; and a quarterly journal, *On Writing.* Write for information on WGAE's service for registering literary material, or call (212) 757-4360.

WRITERS GUILD OF AMERICA, WEST (WGAW)

7000 West 3rd St; Los Angeles, CA 90048-4329; (323) 951-4000,
    FAX 782-4800; website www.wga.org
John McLean, *Executive Director*

WGAw is the union for writers in the fields of motion pictures, television, radio and new media who write both entertainment and news programming. It represents its members in collective bargaining and other labor matters. It publishes a monthly magazine, *Written By.* The Guild registers material, including screen- and teleplays, books, plays, poetry and songs (call 323-782-4500). The library is open to the public Mon–Fri (call 323-782-4544).

YOUNG PLAYWRIGHTS INC.

321 West 44th St, #906; New York, NY 10036; (212) 307-1140,
    FAX 307-1454; email writeaplay@aol.com;
    website youngplaywrights.org
Sheri M. Goldhirsch, *Artistic Director*

Young Playwrights Inc. (YPI), founded in 1981 by Stephen Sondheim, introduces young people to the theatre and encourages their self-expression through the art of playwriting. YPI strives to identify, develop and encourage playwrights aged 18 years and younger to develop new works for the theatre and to aid in the creation of the next generation of professional playwrights through the Young Playwrights Festival National Playwriting Contest (see Prizes), the Young Playwrights Spring Conference, and the Urban Retreat; to expose young people to theatre and playwriting through WRITING ON YOUR FEET! in-school playwriting workshops; to train teachers to integrate playwriting into basic curriculum through the TEACHING ON YOUR FEET! Teacher Training Institute; to develop and serve audiences that reflect the complex makeup of our society and to create the next generation of theatregoers through the TAKE A GROWNUP TO THE THEATER! ticket subsidy program, student matinees and a discount voucher program; to bring the vital experience of professional theatre free of charge to neglected inner-city public schools, community organizations and youth centers through the Young Playwrights School Tour; and to serve as an advocate for young writers regardless of ethnicity, physical ability, sexual orientation or economic status, and to ensure that their voices are heard and acknowledged by a diverse community of artists and theatregoers.

PART 3

RESOURCES

Useful Publications

Online Resources

Submission Calendar

Special Interests Index

Book Index

USEFUL PUBLICATIONS

This is a selective listing of the publications that we think most usefully supplement the information given in the *Sourcebook*. Note that publications of interest to theatre writers are also described throughout this book, particularly in the chapter introductions, in the Membership and Service Organizations listings, and in the Online Resources chapter. We have purposely left out any "how to" books on the art of playwriting because we do not want to promote the concept of "writing-by-recipe." Pricing and ordering information may change after this book goes to press, so it would be wise to confirm details before ordering a publication.

AMERICAN THEATRE

Theatre Communications Group; 355 Lexington Ave;
New York, NY 10017-6603; (212) 697-5230, FAX 557-5817;
email custserv@tcg.org; website www.tcg.org

1-year subscription/TCG membership $35; single issue $4.95. This magazine, published 10 times per year, provides comprehensive coverage of all aspects of theatre. *American Theatre* regularly features articles and interviews dealing with theatre writers and their works, and publishes the complete texts of 5 new plays a year. A special Season Preview issue each October lists schedules for more than 400 theatres nationwide, and monthly schedules for more than 300 theatres are published in each issue. Selected feature articles and season schedules are posted on the website monthly.

BACK STAGE

770 Broadway, 6th Floor; New York, NY 10003;
email backstage@backstage.com; website www.backstage.com

1-year subscription $89, 2 years $139; single issue $2.75, $5 by mail. This performing arts weekly includes industry news; reports from cities across the country; reviews; and columns, including "Playwrights' Corner." The primary focus is on casting, theatres; other producers sometimes run ads soliciting scripts; workshops and classes for playwrights are also likely to be advertised here.

HOLLYWOOD SCRIPTWRITER

Box 10277; Burbank, CA 91510; (818) 845-5525;
email editor@hollywoodscriptwriter.com;
website hollywoodscriptwriter.com

1-year subscription (12 issues) $36 US, $39 Canada, $55 all other international. This 20-page trade paper contains interviews and articles giving advice to playwrights and screenwriters, and a "Markets for Your Work" section. A list of back issues with a summary of the contents of each issue is available; call for information.

INSIGHT FOR PLAYWRIGHTS

(Formerly Market Insight...for Playwrights)
Box 127778; San Diego, CA 92112-7778; (619) 388-2045;
email info@writersinsight.com; website www.writersinsight.com

1-year subscription (12 issues) $45, email subscription $35. This monthly newsletter for playwrights provides submission guidelines for theatres, residencies, publishers and contests, as well as updates on personnel changes at theatres, special programs for women writers, and more; contest application forms come with each issue; updates are provided via email; visit website for sample issue.

LITERARY MARKET PLACE 2001

R. R. Bowker; 121 Chanlon Rd; New Providence, NJ 07974;
(908) 464–6800, (888) BOWKER–2, FAX (908) 771–7704;
email info@bowker.com; website www.bowker.com

2000. 2203 pp, $199.95 (plus 7% postage and handling and sales tax where applicable) paper. Also available on the web at www.literarymarketplace.com (various fee options and subscription rates are given). This directory of the American book publishing industry gives contact information for book publishers and those in related fields, and includes 2 "Names & Numbers" indexes totaling over 600 pages. The 2002 LMP is due out in October 2001.

MUSIC, DANCE & THEATER SCHOLARSHIPS

Conway Greene Publishing Company; 1414 South Green Rd,
Suite 206; South Euclid, OH 44121; (800) 977–2665;
website www.conwaygreene.com

2nd edition, 1998. 490 pp, $24.95 (plus $4 postage and handling and sales tax where applicable) paper. This guide provides information on more than 1800 theatre, music and dance conservatory and undergraduate programs, as well as more than 5000 professional and educational scholarship opportunities. It also includes detailed information on audition requirements, decision processes at individual schools, special scholarship stipulations and student profiles.

POETS & WRITERS MAGAZINE

Poets & Writers, Inc; 72 Spring St; New York, NY 10012;
(212) 226–3586
Subscription office: Box 543; Mount Morris, IL 61054;
(815) 743–1123

1-year subscription (6 issues) $19.95, 2 years $38; single issue $4.95. A bi-monthly magazine delivering profiles of noted authors and publishing professionals, practical how-to articles, a comprehensive listing of grants and awards for writers and special sections on subjects ranging from small presses to writers conferences.

Professional Playscript Format Guidelines and Sample

Feedback Theatrebooks; 305 Madison Ave, Suite 1146;
New York, NY 10165; (800) 800-8671, FAX (207) 359-5532;
Order Department: Box 220; Brooklin, ME 04616; (207) 359-2781;
email feedback@hypernet.com

1991. 28 pp, $4.95 (plus $1.75 postage and handling and sales tax where applicable) paper. This booklet provides detailed instructions for laying out a script in a professional manner, includes a "Margin and Tab Setting Guide" and sample pages of script.

Songwriter's Market, Ian C. Bessler, ed

Writer's Digest Books; 1507 Dana Ave; Cincinnati, OH 45207;
(513) 531-2690, ext 423, FAX 531-2686;
email songmarket@fwpubs.com; website www.writersdigest.com

2001. 502 pp, $23.99 (plus $3 shipping and handling and sales tax where applicable) paper. This annually updated directory, which lists contact information for more than 2000 song markets, includes a section on musical theatre. It also lists associations, contests and workshops of interest to songwriters. The 2002 edition is due out in summer 2001.

Stage Directions Magazine

250 West 57th St, Suite 420; New York, NY 10107;
(212) 265-8890, ext 47, FAX 581-6217;
email cnorwood@lifestyleventures.com;
website www.stage-directions.com

1-year subscription (10 issues) $26, 2 years $48; single issue $4.95. This magazine provides information on royalty issues, play publishing, new play festivals and workshops/seminars for playwrights. A special Season Planner issue each November contains a directory of royalty houses.

Stage Writers Handbook:
A Complete Business Guide for Playwrights,
Composers, Lyricists and Librettists by Dana Singer

Theatre Communications Group; 355 Lexington Ave;
New York, NY 10017-6603; (212) 697-5230, FAX 983-4847;
email custserv@tcg.org; website www.tcg.org

1997. 320 pp, $18.95 (plus $3 postage and handling for 1 book, $1 for each additional book) paper. This comprehensive guide, written by the former Executive Director of The Dramatists Guild, covers such topics as copyright, collaboration, underlying rights, marketing and self-promotion, production contracts, representation (agents and lawyers), publishers, authors' relationships with directors, and videotaping and electronic rights.

THEATRE DIRECTORY 2001–02

Theatre Communications Group; 355 Lexington Ave;
New York, NY 10017–6603; (212) 697–5230, FAX 983–4847;
email custserv@tcg.org; website www.tcg.org

2001. 200 pp, $11.95 (plus $3 postage and handling for 1 book, $1 for each additional book) paper. TCG's annually updated directory provides complete contact information for more than 400 not-for-profit professional theatres, including new TCG theatres that join after this *Sourcebook* is published, and more than 60 arts resource organizations. Includes special interest, personnel and state-by-state indexes for all theatres.

THEATRE PROFILES 12

Theatre Communications Group; 355 Lexington Ave;
New York, NY 10017–6603; (212) 697–5230, FAX 983–4847;
email custserv@tcg.org; website www.tcg.org

1996. 240 pp, $22.95 (plus $3 postage and handling for 1 book, $1 for each additional book) paper. The 12th volume of this biennial series contains artistic profiles, production photographs, financial information and repertoire information for the 1993–95 seasons of 257 theatres.

U.S. COPYRIGHT OFFICE PUBLICATIONS

Library of Congress; Copyright Office; Publications Section, LM–455;
101 Independence Ave SE; Washington, DC 20559;
(202) 707–3000; website www.loc.gov/copyright

There are many ways to receive free informational circulars and registration forms: via website; call (202) 707-9100 and key in your fax number to receive them by fax; you may also call or write, but these methods take longer. Copyright information specialists can answer questions Monday–Friday 8:30 A.M. to 5:00 P.M. at (207) 707-3000.

THE WRITER

c/o Kalmbach Publishing Co; 21027 Crossroads Circle; Box 1612;
Waukesha, WI 53187-1612; (262) 796-8776, FAX 798-6468;
email editor@writermag.com; website www.writermag.com

1-year subscription (12 issues) $29, 2 years $55, 3 years $78. This monthly magazine announces contests in a "Prize Offers" column and publishes a special "Writers Wanted" section, which includes lists of play publishers.

WRITER'S MARKET, Kirsten Holm, ed

Writer's Digest Books; 1507 Dana Ave; Cincinnati, OH 45207;
(513) 531-2690, ext 287, FAX 531-2686;
email writersmarket@fwpubs.com;
website www.writersmarket.com

2001. 1120 pp, $29.99 (plus $3 postage and handling and sales tax where applicable) paper; it is also available in a book/CD-ROM/online package for $49.99. This annually updated directory lists more than 4000 places where writers may sell their manuscripts. It includes many opportunities for playwrights and screenwriters. The 2002 edition is due out in September 2001.

ONLINE RESOURCES

What's here and what's not.

Now that nearly every organization, theatre and otherwise, has established an internet presence, our goal in presenting Online Resources in Dramatists Sourcebook is to spotlight sites that offer useful information distinct from opportunities already included elsewhere in the book. Many URLs from local playwrights' home pages, community playwrights' forums and college playwriting courses appear in the far reaches of search engine results. In the interest of accuracy and longevity, we have opted to include a select menu of sites that are mainstays of the internet playwriting community—sites with free content and broad professional appeal.

As you well know, empires are destroyed in a day in the online world. The site you landed on this morning might not exist by the time you check back tomorrow. Or worse yet, it might exist but not have been updated or maintained for the last five years. Take the time to assess the editorial merit and accuracy of the site.

What we present here is a guide to the best that's currently available, which you can also use to measure the quality of new ventures. We urge you to take advantage of this powerful medium. Use it as a research tool, a reference desk, a host of networking opportunities and a creative space.

Note: Help us improve our listings for future editions. On your travels through cyberspace, if you happen upon some "must see" sites for playwrights that we've missed, please let us know: ksova@tcg.org.

For beginners.

If the internet is new to you, it can be an overwhelming experience, particularly when looking over the shoulder of a ten-year-old whiz kid. In fact, experienced users, of any age, may not be the best teachers. Consider picking up a copy of *The Internet: The Rough Guide 2002,* which will be released in Oct 2001 (Angus J. Kennedy, Rough Guides Ltd, London). It explains in jargon-free English what the internet is and how to use it. It also offers a topical index of worthwhile websites. Another place to start is *Yahoo! Internet Life's* "100 Best Web Sites for 2001" at: www.zdnet.com/techlife. Both publications will help you transition from page to screen.

Search Engines.

For experienced users, the better you can define your searches the more exacting the results will be. One of the often-overlooked tools for uprooting difficult or obscure information is your choice of search engine. There are over a hundred options available to you, the most popular of which are Alta Vista, Ask Jeeves, Excite, Go/Infoseek, Google, Hotbot, Looksmart, Lycos, MSN Search, Netscape Search, Snap, Web Crawler and Yahoo. So what's the difference? You have likely had the experience of typing "playwriting" in a search engine only to discover through related links on someone else's Web page that your original search results were incomplete. The reason for this is that each search engine indexes its websites in slightly different ways. Some do it by the amount of times a particular word appears on the site's homepage, others rank sites by the number of links on the web that point to them, and still others rely on humans to compile the listings. For detailed information about search engines, including capsule summaries of the 23 most popular sites, visit: searchenginewatch.com.

Once you get a handle on the functionality of search engines, Search Engines Worldwide: www.twics.com/~takakuwa/search/search.html offers a directory of links to international search engines organized by country (includes U.S.).

AFRICAN AMERICAN ONLINE WRITERS GUILD

www.blackwriters.org

Description: not-for-profit literary arts organization which uses technology to encourage community, provide content and celebrate the culture of African-American writers. **Site includes:** current issue of their newsletter *Cultured Writer*; information and application for AAOWG Mentor Program; bulletin boards and chat; conference information; links to writers' resources; and membership information.

AISLE SAY

www.aislesay.com/index.html

Description: no-frills compilation of reviews of professional and community theatre productions from around the country written by local theatre critics. The writing style and quality of the reviews varies significantly, but the coverage is thorough and fair. **Site includes:** reviews; links to critics' biographies; and an index of additional sources for reviews.

AMERICANTHEATER WEB

www.americantheaterweb.com

Description: interactive database where theatres around the country can post their production schedules. The listings are not comprehensive but the collection of theatres is diverse. **Site includes:** theatre headlines; current production listings by region; a small bookstore; and free email access and chat.

ARTS JOURNAL

www.artsjournal.com

Description: chronicle of feature articles on arts and culture from more than 180 English-language newspapers, magazines and publications. Direct links to the most interesting or important stories are posted every weekday beginning at 5 a.m. PST on the Arts Journal news pages. Stories from sites that charge for access are excluded, as are sites that require visitors to register, with the exception of the *New York Times*. **Site includes:** articles sorted by discipline and date; newsletter; and related links.

ARTSWIRE

www.artswire.org

Description: multi-service website designed to help artists and arts organizations take advantage of internet technologies through training, planning and technical support. **Site includes:** *ArtsWire CURRENT*, a weekly chronicle of arts and technology related articles; the *Nonprofit Toolkit*, a monthly magazine exploring technology and its relationship to the arts; Spiderschool, online tutorials and workshops; Web Base, a database of cultural resources that includes indices for playwriting and theatre; and job listings.

ASIAN AMERICAN THEATRE REVIEW

www.abcflash.com/a&e/r_tang/AATR.html

Description: hub site for Asian-American theatre. **Site includes:** news; calendar; list of Asian-American playwrights and their plays; directory of Asian-American theatre companies; reviews; library of anthologies, individual authors and critical perspectives; bulletin boards; and related links.

BARTLEBY.COM

www.bartleby.com

Description: online version of Bartleby's bookstore, which provides searchable databases of reference materials free of charge. **Site includes:** unlimited access to *Columbia Encyclopedia, Sixth Edition; American Heritage Dictionary, Fourth Edition; Roget's II: The New Thesaurus; American Heritage Book of English Usage; Simpson's Contemporary Quotations; Bartlett's Familiar Quotations; King James Bible; Oxford Shakespeare; Gray's Anatomy; Strunk's Elements of Style;* and *World Fact Book.*

BROADWAY ONLINE

(Formerly Theatre.com)
www.broadwayonline.com/pages/newsiteframesn.htm

Description: Broadway portal site. **Site includes:** theatre news; listings and ticket information; theatre merchandise; links to official Broadway show websites and general theatre links; membership information, including eligibility for discount tickets; and the "theatre district" composed of bulletin boards and chat.

CAMBRIDGE DICTIONARIES ONLINE

dictionary.cambridge.org

Description: *Cambridge Dictionary* online. **Site includes:** Full access to

Cambridge International Dictionary of English; American English; international dictionary of idiom; international dictionary of phrasal verbs; and learner's dictionary of English.

CITYSEARCH

www.citysearch.com

Description: nationwide, city-specific entertainment guide for arts, events, restaurants, etc. by city, date or subject. **Site includes:** database of cities by neighborhood and zip code; and links to local services.

CULTUREFINDER.COM

www.culturefinder.com

Description: database to search for and purchase tickets to arts events nationwide. Listings are searchable by event name, performer or composer, organization date and location. **Site includes:** season schedules for over 3000 arts organizations and listings for over 350,000 events in more than 1500 cities.

THE ENCYCLOPEDIA MYTHICA

www.pantheon.org/mythica.html

Description: capsule definitions and explanations from world mythology, folklore and legend. **Site includes:** lists of over 5700 articles, 300 illustrations, maps and genealogy tables from over 25 cultures.

INKSPOT

www.inkspot.com

Description: now defunct community resource center for writers. No new content will be added but valuable links remain. **Site includes:** market and networking information; online workshops; well-maintained classified ads, including contests; tips for young writers and teachers; and feature articles and columns.

INTERNATIONAL CENTRE FOR WOMEN PLAYWRIGHTS INC.

www.cadvision.com/sdempsey/icwphmpg.htm

Description: support site for international women playwrights. **Site includes:** membership list; member play list by genre; list of members' recent awards and productions; newsletter called *Seasons*; related links; membership and conference information; and articles on craft.

INTERNET MOVIE DATABASE
www.imdb.com

Description: comprehensive searchable database containing information about film, video and made-for-TV movies. **Site includes:** current selections; movie and TV news; U.S. movie show times searchable by date, city, state and zip code; photo galleries; IMDB staff recommendations; independent film index; new releases; box office hits; and user favorites.

KMC A BRIEF GUIDE TO INTERNET RESOURCES IN THEATRE AND PERFORMANCE STUDIES
www.stetson.edu/departments/csata/thr_guid.html

Description: selected list of theatre resources compiled by Ken McCoy, Assistant Professor of Communication Studies and Theatre Arts at Stetson College. **Site includes:** description of selection criteria; list of McCoy's most used sites; resources by theatre subject; primary source materials; listservs and newsgroups; and other guides.

NATIVE AMERICAN AUTHORS
www.ipl.org/ref/native

Description: provides information on contemporary Native North American authors including playwrights. **Site includes:** searchable database of writers with bibliographies of their published works and biographical information; links to interviews, online texts and tribal websites.

NATIVE AMERICAN WOMEN PLAYWRIGHT'S ARCHIVE
staff.lib.muohio.edu/nawpa/

Description: catalog of the writing by Native American Women Playwrights. **Site includes:** playwright's directory; online exhibit of Spiderwoman Theater; bibliography of Native American Women's Theater; author's roundtable; archive of *NAWPA* newsletters; listings of recent programs and productions; and related links.

NEW YORK THEATRE WIRE

www.nytheatre-wire.com

Description: source for what's playing on New York City stages. **Site includes:** articles; publication information; Broadway and Off-Broadway listings; reviews; a museum directory; and classifieds.

THE OFF-OFF BROADWAY REVIEW

www.oobr.com

Description: no-frills publication detailing the Off-Off-Broadway scene. **Site includes:** reviews; listings; archives; and information about the Midtown International Theatre Festival.

PLAYBILL ONLINE

www.playbill.com

Description: expanded version of *Playbill*'s print publication, including information about both Broadway and Off-Broadway theatre. **Site includes:** news from the U.S., Canada and international theatre communities; Broadway and Off-Broadway listings; online ticket sales; feature articles; jobs bank; and links to the Drama Bookshop and Theatre Central, among others.

PLAYS AND PLAYWRIGHTS

groups.yahoo.com/group/playsandplaywrights

Description: 265-member discussion group for those interested in the craft of playwriting, production information, submission and grant information and opportunities, teaching and professional development. **Site includes:** discussion comprised of 45–300 messages per month on plays and playwriting; discussion can be viewed online or emailed directly to participants.

PLAYSCRIPTS.COM

www.playscripts.com

Description: online publisher which licenses performances, distributes acting editions, and uses protected software to connect theatres more directly with scripts of interest. **Site includes:** searchable database of their full catalog; a protected environment to read but not reproduce full text of plays; information on ordering bound scripts and securing performance rights; submission information; author bios; and a searchable database of scripts published by all major American play publishers.

THE PLAYWRIGHTING SEMINARS

www.vcu.edu/artweb/playwriting/seminar.html

Description: online textbook by playwright Richard Toscan which covers both the craft and the business of playwriting. **Site includes:** seminar topics such as content, film, structure, writing life, script format and business; quotes from established playwrights; and a reading list.

PLAYWRIGHTS ON THE WEB

www.stageplays.com/writers.htm

Description: international database of playwrights and their websites. **Site includes:** plays listed alphabetically by author and genre; playwrights' discussion forum; callboard; and a link to The Internet Theatre Bookshop.

THEATRE CENTRAL

www.playbill.com/cgi–bin/plb/central?cmd=start

Description: one of the first theatre portal sites; maintained less vigorously than it used to be. **Site includes:** related links; and links to theatre professionals' websites.

THEATRE-LINK.COM

www.theatre–link.com

Description: well-organized and -maintained index of theatre-related websites. **Site includes:** database searchable by academic programs; Broadway and West End shows; casting and contact services; goods and services; news and information; Shakespeare; shows and performances; theatres and venues; theatre-related resources; groups and organizations; and other indices. Discussion boards are soon to come.

THEATREMANIA

theatermania.com

Description: theatre portal site featuring theatre news and information from major cities around the country including select international locations. **Site includes:** theatre tickets and listings organized by city;

feature and news articles; links to theatre festivals and awards; theatre store; and membership information.

THE U.S. COPYRIGHT OFFICE

lcweb.loc.gov/copyright

Description: branch of the Library of Congress. **Site includes:** what's new section; office information; general copyright information; copyright records; announcements; publications, including forms in downloadable format; legislation, international and copyright links.

WOMEN OF COLOR WOMEN OF WORDS

www.scils.rutgers.edu/~cybers/home.html

Description: features accomplished women playwrights of color with a focus on African-Americans. **Site includes:** writers' bios; list of completed works; links to Amazon.com; directory of libraries and research centers with an African-American focus; list of critical/biographical resources; links to wired theatres that produce multicultural work; directory of dissertations on featured playwrights; recommended books on African-American theatre history; and related links.

WRITEEXPRESS ONLINE RHYMING DICTIONARY

www.writeexpress.com/online2.html

Description: online rhyming dictionary. **Site includes:** searchable database by end, last, double, beginning and first syllable rhymes.

WRITERSDIGEST.COM
THE 101 BEST WEB SITES FOR WRITERS

www.writersdigest.com/101sites_2000

Description: well-indexed list of web resources for writers. **Site includes:** links to search engines; general reference; specialized reference; media, news and reference; job sites; the writing life; genre; poetry; screenwriting; zines; writers' organizations; and more.

WWW VIRTUAL LIBRARY THEATRE AND DRAMA

www.vl–theatre.com

Description: library of international theatre resources updated daily. **Site includes:** links to academic/training institutions; book dealers; conferences for theatre scholars; electronic text archives and plays online; general resources; online journals; monologues in print; plays in print; scholarly books; theatre books in print; theatre companies; theatre image bank; and theatre syllabus bank, among others.

WWW.YOURDICTIONARY.COM

www.yourdictionary.com

Description: index of online dictionaries. **Site includes:** dictionaries (of varying completion and quality) in 221 languages; multilingual dictionaries; specialty English dictionaries; thesauri and other vocabulary aids; language identifiers and guessers; index of dictionary indices; web of online grammar; and web of linguistic fun.

YAHOO THEATRE INDEX

dir.yahoo.com/Arts/Performing_Arts/Theater

Description: index of theatre-related sites. **Site includes:** thirty-eight different subjects, including playwrights and plays.

Submission Calendar

September 2001–August 2002

Included here are all *specified* deadlines contained in Production, Prizes, Publication, Development, Fellowships and Grants, Colonies and Residencies, and Membership and Service Organizations. Please note that suggested submission dates for theatres listed in Production are not included. There are always important deadlines that are not available at press time and so cannot be included here.

SEPTEMBER 2001

1 Anna Zornio Children's Playwriting Award, 145
1 City of Los Angeles Performing Arts Fellowships, 256
1 Dorland Mountain Arts Colony (1st deadline), 295
1 Francesca Primus Prize, 153
1 Great Plains Play Contest, 155
1 Millay Colony for the Arts (1st deadline), 302
1 NEH Division of Research Programs/Collaborative Research, 268
1 Playwrights Gallery, 228
5 Fund at Int'l Festivals and Exhibitions (1st deadline), 253, 267
10 Jonathan Larson Performing Arts Foundation, 260
10 Playwrights Forum (1st deadline), 228
11 NEH Projects in Media (consultation grants, 1st deadline), 268
13 Arizona Commission on the Arts Fellowships (playwrights only), 251
15 Jerome Playwright-in-Residence Fellowships, 271
15 Kleban Award, 261

15 MacDowell Colony (1st deadline), 301
15 Virginia Center for the Creative Arts (1st deadline), 307
17 New Residencies, 266
20 Susan Smith Blackburn Prize, 180
30 Attic Theatre Ensemble's One-Act Marathon, 146
30 Baltimore Playwrights Festival, 208
30 Hawthornden Castle International Retreat for Writers, 297
30 Puerto Rican Traveling Theatre Playwrights' Unit, 230
30 Theatre Three Annual Festival of One-Act Plays, 126
Contact for exact deadline during this month:
Frederick Douglass Writing Workshops (1st deadline), 214

OCTOBER 2001

1 Hedgebrook (1st deadline), 298
1 Janusfest, 239
1 John Simon Guggenheim Memorial Foundation, 259
1 Mature Woman Scholarship Award, 263
1 Meet The Composer Fund (1st deadline), 265
1 New Visions/New Voices, 222
1 New York Mills Arts Retreat (1st deadline), 303
1 Norcroft, 303
1 Stanley Drama Award, 179
1 Ucross Foundation Residency Program (1st deadline), 306
2 NYFA Artists' Fellowships, 270
10 New Play Commissions in Jewish Theatre, 269
10 North Carolina New Play Project, 327
15 Harvard University Radcliffe Institute Fellowships, 259
15 Lanesboro Residency Program Fellowships (2nd deadline), 300
15 Playwrights First Award, 175
15 Test Tube Festival, 221
19 Ensemble Studio Theatre First Light, 46
25 U.S. Department of State Fulbright Student Program, 276
30 Dayton Playhouse FutureFest, 150
31 Premiere Performances, 175
31 Southern Appalachian Playwrights' Conference, 233

31 Women at the Door Staged Reading Series (9th Annual), 240
Contact for exact deadline during this month:
Bush Artist Fellows Program, 255

NOVEMBER 2001

1 Alfred Hodder Fellowships, 251
1 American-Scandinavian Foundation, 251
1 Civic Theatre Holiday Competition, 149
1 Hambidge Center for Creative Arts and Sciences (1st deadline), 296
1 Julie Harris Playwriting Award, 148
1 Long Beach Playhouse New Works Festival, 73
1 NEH Projects in Media (planning grants), 268
1 O'Neill Playwrights Conference, 225
1 Richard Rodgers Awards, The, 231
1 Through Her Eyes: Women of Color Arts Festival, 237
1 Women Playwrights Project, 240
8 Florida Playwrights' Process, 213
15 American Renegade Playwriting Contest, 144
15 Hispanic Playwrights Project, 216
15 NATF Script Competition, 168
22 Mildred and Albert Panowski Playwriting Award, 167
30 Ledig House International Writers' Colony, 300
30 National Latino Playwriting Award, 169
30 New American Comedy (NAC) Workshop, 171
30 Walden Residency Program, 308
31 Theatre Conspiracy Annual New Play Contest, 181
Contact for exact deadline during this month:
ACT/Hedgebrook Women Playwrights Festival, 206
Kennedy Center ACTF Ten-Minute Play Festival, 161
New Harmony Project, 221
NYFA Sponsorship Program (1st deadline), 223

DECEMBER 2001

1 Anchorage Press Theater for Youth Playwriting Award, 160
1 A.S.K. Theater Projects Retreat, 208

31 Lois and Richard Rosenthal New Play Prize, 164

31 MTC Playwriting Fellowship, 262

31 Playwrights' Kitchen Ensemble, 229

31 Robert J. Pickering Award for Playwriting Excellence, 176

31 West Coast Ensemble Full-Length Play Competition, 185

Contact for exact deadline during this month:

New American Theater New Voices in the Heartland, 84

Pew Fellowships in the Arts, 271

JANUARY 2002

1 Mill Mountain Theatre New Play Competition, 167

1 Nantucket Short Play Festival and Competition, 168

1 TheaterFest Regional Playwriting Contest, 181

2 Meet The Composer Fund (2nd deadline), 265

3 PEN/Laura Pels Foundation Award for Drama, 173

4 Hawai'i Prize, 163

4 Pacific Rim Prize, 163

4 Resident Prize, 163

10 Playwrights Forum (2nd deadline), 228

15 ArtsLink Projects, 266

15 Commissioning Music/USA, 264

15 Jewel Box Playwrighting Award, 158

15 MacDowell Colony (2nd deadline), 301

15 Montana Artists Refuge (2nd deadline), 303

15 Poems & Plays Tennessee Chapbook Prize, 200

15 Ragdale Foundation (1st deadline), 304

15 Reva Shiner Contest, 175

15 Source Theatre Literary Prize (must be postmarked before), 178

15 Summerfield G. Roberts Award, 180

15 Virginia Center for the Creative Arts (2nd deadline), 307

15 Yaddo (1st deadline), 309

16 Fund at Int'l Festivals and Exhibitions (2nd deadline), 253, 267

18 Helene Wurlitzer Foundation of New Mexico, 298

25 Dobie-Paisano Fellowship, 256

25 McKnight Minnesota Fellowship, 264

FEBRUARY 2002

MARCH 2002

Contact for exact deadline during this month:

APRIL 2002

MAY 2002

Contact for exact deadline during this month:
Alternation One-Act Play Festival, 31
Chesterfield Film Company/Writer's Film Project, The, 210
Frederick Douglass Writing Workshops (3rd deadline), 214

JUNE 2002

1 ASF Translation Prize, 146
1 A.S.K. Theater Projects Readings, 208
1 Chicano/Literary Prize, 149
1 Coe College New Works for the Stage Competition, 150
1 George R. Kernodle Playwriting Contest, 154
1 Jackie White Children's Playwriting Contest, 157
1 Meet The Composer Fund (4th deadline), 265
1 New Professional Theatre Writers Festival, 171
1 Ragdale Foundation (2nd deadline), 304
1 Southeastern Theatre Conference New Play Project, 179
7 Headlands Center for the Arts, 297
15 Lanesboro Residency Program Fellowships (1st deadline), 300
15 MTC Sloan Foundation Fellowship, 262
15 Next Stage Festival of New Plays, 223
15 Towson University Prize for Literature, 182
22 The Walt Disney and ABC Writing Fellowship, 277
25 Native Arts Research and Artist in Residence Fellowships, 269
26 United States/Japan Creative Artists' Fellowships, 267
30 Main Street Arts Flying Blind Festival, 76
30 Siena College International Playwrights Competition, 178
30 West Coast Ensemble Musical Stairs, 185
Contact for exact deadline during this month:
Artist Trust Fellowships, 252
Off-Off Broadway Original Short Play Festival, 224
U.S./Japan Creative Artists' Program, 307

JULY 2002

1 First Stage One-Act Play Contest, 212
1 Henrico Theatre Company One-Act Playwriting Competition, 156

1 Maxim Maxumdar New Play Competition, 165
1 Theodore Ward Prize for African-American Playwrights, 182
15 Altos de Chavon, 292
31 Many Voices Multicultural Collaboration Grants, 272
31 Many Voices Playwriting Residency Awards, 272
Contact for exact deadline during this month:
Frederick Douglass Writing Workshops (4th deadline), 214
NYFA Sponsorship Program (3rd deadline), 223

AUGUST 2002

1 BMI Musical Theatre Workshop (composers, lyricists), 209
1 Cleveland Public Theatre New Plays Festival, 35
1 Fulbright Senior Scholar Awards for Faculty and Professionals, 258
1 Yaddo (2nd deadline), 309
15 Lehman Engel Musical Theatre Workshop, 218
15 Montana Artists Refuge (1st deadline), 303
17 Music Alive Meet The Composer/American Symphony League, 265
21 Centrum Creative Residencies Program, 294
31 Broadway Tomorrow, 209
31 Festival of Firsts Playwriting Competition, 153
31 National Children's Theatre Festival, 169
31 Play Pen, The, 227
31 Ten-Minute Musicals Project, 236
Contact for exact deadline during this month:
ACC Residency Program in Asia (2nd deadline), 253

SPECIAL INTERESTS INDEX

Here is a guide to entries which indicate a particular or exclusive interest in certain types of material, or which contain an element of special interest to writers in certain categories. Under Young Audiences, Media, Multimedia, Performance Art and Solo Performance, we list every entry of interest to writers in these fields. In the cases of Adaptations, Musicals, One-acts and Translations, there are numerous theatres willing to consider these types of material; we list here only those theatres and other organizations that give major focus to them. The Multicultural category is for those organizations expressing general interest in muticultural works. Under African-American, Asian-American, Hispanic/Latin-American and Native American Theatre, we have included only those organizations specifically seeking work by or about people from these ethnic groups. The Student/College Submission category refers to college writing students or students in an affiliated writing program. Young Playwrights is a special interest category only for playwrights 18 or under.

ADAPTATIONS

A Noise Within, 16
Arden Theatre Company, 16
Asolo Theatre Company, 20
Bailiwick Repertory, 22
California Shakespeare Festival, 28
California Theatre Center, 28

Children's Theatre Company, The, 32
Classic Stage Company, 35
Cornerstone Theater Company, 38
Coterie Theatre, The, 39
Court Theatre, 39
Dallas Children's Theater, 40
Dell'Arte Company, The, 41

AFRICAN -AMERICAN THEATRE

ASIAN-AMERICAN THEATRE

COMEDY

DISABILITIES: Theatre for and by People with Disabilities

EXPERIMENTAL THEATRE

GAY AND LESBIAN THEATRE

HISPANIC/LATIN-AMERICAN THEATRE

MULTICULTURAL THEATRE

MULTIMEDIA

MUSICAL THEATRE

NATIVE AMERICAN THEATRE

Award, 184
Waterfront Ensemble, Inc., The, 239

PERFORMANCE ART
(also see Experimental Theatre)

About Face Theatre, 5
American Writing: a Magazine, 189
Audrey Skirball-Kenis Play
  Collection, 190
Carmel Performing Arts Festival, 29
Childsplay, 32
City of Los Angeles Performing Arts
  Fellowships, 256
Double Edge Theatre, 43
Field, The, 325
Free Street Programs, 53
Jane Chambers Playwriting Award,
  158
La MaMa Experimental Theater Club,
  71
Lamia Ink!, 197
Leighton Studios for Independent
  Residencies, 301
Live Bait Theatrical Company, 73
Mark Taper Forum, 77
New York Theatre Workshop, 89
Northeast Theatre (TNT), The, 90
Theatre Outlet, The, 125
Theatre Project, 350
3 Legged Race: New Theatre &
  Performance, 129
Through Her Eyes: Women of Color
  Arts Festival, 237
Voice & Vision, 135
Westbeth New Works Program, 239
Women's Theatre Alliance (WTA),
  351
Yaddo, 309

RELIGIOUS/SPIRITUAL THEATRE

A. D. Players, 9
Baker's Plays, 191

Cunningham Prize for Playwriting,
  150
Eldridge Publishing Company, 194
Encore Performance Publishing, 194
Lillenas Drama Resources, 197
Love Creek Annual Short Play
  Festival, 165
Pioneer Drama Service, 198

SENIOR CITIZENS

Centre Stage-South Carolina!, 30
Cleveland Public Theatre, 35
Dudley Riggs Instant Theatre
  Company, 43
Horizon Theatre Company, 62
Open Eye Theater, The, 93
TOVA, Inc., 130
Worcester Foothills Theatre
  Company, 140

SOCIAL-POLITICAL THEATRE

A Contemporary Theatre, 5
Actors & Playwrights' Initiative, 6
Actor's Express, 7
Actors' Gang Theater, 7
Allied Theatre Group/Stage West, 12
Alternate ROOTS, 311
American Theater Company, 15
American Theatre of Actors, Inc., 16
Bailiwick Repertory, 22
Barter Theatre, 23
Bay Street Theatre, 24
Blue Mountain Center, 293
BoarsHead Theater, 26
Cleveland Public Theatre, 35
Colony Theatre Company, The, 36
Coterie Theatre, The, 39
Dallas Children's Theater, 40
Detroit Repertory Theatre, 42
Eye of the Storm Theatre, 49
Florida Stage, 50

SOLO PERFORMANCE

STUDENT/COLLEGE SUBMISSIONS

TRANSLATIONS

YOUNG PLAYWRIGHTS PROGRAMS

BOOK INDEX

Remember the two alphabetizing principles used throughout the book: First, entries beginning with a person's name are alphabetized by the first name rather than the surname. However, you can find these entries indexed by both names. Hence you will find the Robert J. Pickering Award for Excellence under R and P. Regardless of which way "theatre" is spelled in an organization's title, it is alphabetized as if it were spelled "re," not "er." This edition of the *Sourebook* is alphabetized differently than past editions. Please see Preface for details.

S

ABOUT THEATRE COMMUNICATIONS GROUP

Theatre Communications Group (TCG), the national organization for the American theatre, offers a wide array of services in line with our mission: to strengthen, nurture and promote the not-for-profit American theatre. Artistic programs support theatres and theatre artists by awarding grants ($4.4 million in 2001-2002), and offer career development programs for artists. Management programs provide professional development opportunities for theatre leaders through workshops, conferences, forums (including teleconferences and online) and publications, as well as industry research on the finances and practices of the American not-for-profit theatre. Advocacy, conducted in conjunction with the museum director, dance, presenting and opera fields, includes guiding lobbying efforts and providing theatres with timely alerts about legislative developments. The country's leading independent press specializing in dramatic literature, TCG's publications include *American Theatre* magazine, the *ArtSEARCH* employment bulletin, plays, translations and theatre reference books. As the U.S. Center of the International Theatre Institute, a worldwide network, TCG supports cross-cultural exchange through travel grants, assistance to traveling theatre professionals and maintenance of an international theatre research library. Through these programs, TCG seeks to increase the organizational efficiency of our member theatres, cultivate and celebrate the artistic talent and achievements of the field and promote a larger public understanding of and appreciation for the theatre field. TCG serves more than 420 member theatres and 17,000 individual members.

TCG is proud to publish the following authors:

Jon Robin Baitz
Eric Bogosian
Peter Brook
Caryl Churchill
Pearl Cleage
Constance Congdon
Culture Clash
The Five Lesbian
   Brothers
Dario Fo
Richard Foreman
Athol Fugard
Peter Hall

Karen Hartman
Tina Howe
David Henry Hwang
Adrienne Kennedy
Harry Kondoleon
Lisa Kron
Tony Kushner
Craig Lucas
Charles Ludlam
Eduardo Machado
Emily Mann
Donald Margulies
Conor McPherson

Lynn Nottage
Robert O'Hara
Suzan-Lori Parks
José Rivera
Nicky Silver
Stephen Sondheim
Alfred Uhry
Paula Vogel
Naomi Wallace
Thornton Wilder
August Wilson
George C. Wolfe

To order books, visit our website: www.tcg.org
Catalog available upon request

TCG INDIVIDUAL MEMBERSHIP

As a *Sourcebook* user, you're invited to become an Individual Member of **Theatre Communications Group** — the national organization for the American Theatre and the publisher of *American Theatre* magazine.

As an Individual Member of TCG, you'll get inside information about theatre performances around the country, as well as substantial discounts on tickets to performances and publications about the theatre. Plus, as the primary advocate for not-for-profit professional theatre in America, TCG will ensure that your voice is heard in Washington. We invite you to join us today and receive all of TCG's benefits!

MEMBERS RECEIVE A FREE SUBSCRIPTION TO
AMERICAN THEATRE AND THESE SPECIAL BENEFITS

- A FREE subscription to *American Theatre*—10 issues…5 complete playscripts… artist profiles…in-depth coverage of contemporary, classical and avant-garde performances…2 special issues—including *Season Preview* (October) and Theatre Training (January).
- Discounts on tickets to performances at participating theatres nationwide.
- 15% discount on resource materials including *Theatre Directory, ArtSEARCH, Stage Writers Handbook* and *Dramatists Sourcebook*—all musts for the theatre professional or the serious theatregoer.
- A FREE catalog of TCG publications.
- 10% discount on all books from TCG and other select theatre publishers.
- Your personalized Individual Membership card.
- Access to members-only areas of the TCG website.
- Opportunity to apply for a no fee TCG Credit Card.
- Special discounts for Hertz Rent-A-Car, Airborne Express and Hotel Reservations Network.

Take Advantage NOW and SAVE!
Become a TCG INDIVIDUAL MEMBER and
Receive Extraordinary Benefits

☐ **YES**, I would like a one-year Individual Membership to TCG, which includes a subscription to *American Theatre*.

    ☐ Individual Membership $35.00 $28.00

    ☐ Student Membership (enclose copy of ID) $20.00

☐ I prefer a two-year membership.

    ☐ Individual Membership $70.00 $50.00

**Not only would I like to become a member,
but I would like to take advantage of my discounts right now!**
(Discount prices are only good if you are a member. If you are not a member,
please use the full price for your order.)

☐ Please begin my one-year subscription to *ArtSEARCH*.

    Individual ☐ $54.00 $45.90

    Institutional ☐ $75.00 $63.75

☐ **TOTAL ORDER** _____

To order, send this form to: TCG Order Dept., 355 Lexington Ave., NY, NY 10017-6603 or Call (212) 697-5230; Fax (212) 983-4847; or send Email to: custserv@tcg.org; or visit our website at www.tcg.org. Credit card orders: please include your billing address if it is different than your mailing address.

☐ Check is enclosed. ☐ Please charge my credit card: ☐ VISA ☐ MC ☐ AMEX

NAME _____

OCCUPATION/DATE _____

ADDRESS _____

CITY _____ STATE _____ ZIP _____

*PHONE/FAX/EMAIL _____

CARD# _____ EXP. DATE _____

SIGNATURE _____

* All orders must have telephone number

For Individual Membership outside the U.S., please add $12 per year (U.S. currency only, drawn from a U.S. bank).
Allow 6-8 weeks from receipt of order.

[Mkt. code: DSB02]